The dying sun had turned the world to red.

Canyon de Chelly swept above Gray Eyes, its sandstone walls a mass of towering burgundy shadows and orange light. Despite the sun skittering in and out between impossibly high clouds, a soft rain began to fall.

Gray Eyes felt a swell of relief and understanding. The Holy People in charge of all female things were greeting her. She tilted her face upward, accepting the welcome. There, in the massive stretch of sky, a hawk hovered, his wings motionless; then, with a cry, he soared off toward the horizon. Confident now, she waited for another sign.

She saw the thin wisp of smoke almost immediately. She had found her Hawk.

Hawk had no time to question her presence; one moment she was distant, then she was close, her gray eyes gleaming like silver in the firelight. He had to send her away while he still possessed the sanity to do so, yet he knew in his soul that he couldn't do it. . . .

COMES THE RAIN

BEVERLY BIRD

AVON BOOKS ◆ NEW YORK

COMES THE RAIN is an original publication of Avon Books. This work has never before appeared in book form. This work is a novel. Any similarity to actual persons or events is purely coincidental.

AVON BOOKS
A division of
The Hearst Corporation
105 Madison Avenue
New York, New York 10016

Copyright © 1990 by Beverly Bird
Published by arrangement with the author
Library of Congress Catalog Card Number: 90-93005
ISBN: 0-380-75525-4

First Avon Books Printing: October 1990

AVON TRADEMARK REG. U.S. PAT. OFF. AND IN OTHER COUNTRIES, MARCA REGISTRADA, HECHO EN U.S.A.

Printed in the U.S.A.

RA 10 9 8 7 6 5 4 3 2 1

For my mother, Carol Bird,
who started it all.
Thanks!

Part One

Chapter 1

"Stop."

The command, spoken in Navajo, was neither hushed nor loud, but like the wind that buffeted the rugged grasslands, it demanded response. The forty riders stopped as one.

The warrior who had given the order rode to the front of the group. They called him Hawk, and his face possessed the arrogant and dangerous beauty of his namesake.

"They are here," he said. "On the far side of the arroyo."

A boy of fifteen summers shifted on his saddle blanket to scowl into the consuming darkness. "Where? I see no settlement," he complained. There was only buffalo grass as far as he could see, tall and undulating as the wind hit it, dotted here and there by short, stunted mesquite and rabbitbrush. It was little different from the immense country they had traveled across to get there, and he could barely contain his disappointment.

Hawk nearly smiled at the boy's chagrin. His name was *Na'acoci*, He Lives Dangerously, and he had done exactly that since the day last autumn when a hundred Mexicans had raided his family's camp, stealing his youngest sister. Finally, in an attempt to channel the boy's fury, his grandfather had asked Long Earrings, Hawk's maternal greatuncle, to allow Na'acoci to raid with his fierce and skilled Bitter Water clan. The *Naakaiidine'e'*, the Mexicans, had

seen to it that Na'acoci's own Lone Tree clan was short
of experienced men this season.

But it didn't appear as though Na'acoci would be able
to vent much of his anger on this, his first raid. "Not a
settlement," Hawk explained, pausing to time his voice
with the gusts. They were downwind of their intended victims and as long as the wind blew no one would hear him
and be forewarned. "Just their herds and a few *nelkaad*,
herders. We are still in *Dinetah*, in our homeland—and so
are they."

His words ignited the other warriors, just as he had
intended. They stiffened to a man, leaning forward aggressively as they gripped bows, spears, and an occasional
firearm. None of them felt that they would be stealing the
sheep whose pale wool was barely discernible in the distance. Instead they were exacting revenge against these
men who were trespassing on their land, the old Mexicans
and the paler ones from the east who had conquered their
Spanish-speaking brothers. They had named the land
they'd wrested "New" Mexico. But to Hawk and his men,
it was no different from the old Mexico, only more
crowded. The new pale-eyes and the old Spaniards lived
together, united in their enmity and greed against the tribe.
Now, they would share the People's wrath, a wrath that
was growing daily.

"Treaties." Hawk spat the word that was on everyone's
minds. "They give us a treaty so they can take away our
land. But even that is not enough for them. Now they send
their stock onto the land that they have left to us and say
it is their right. I say let them trespass if they will. They
make very convenient targets."

Heedless of the wind this time, he gave a shrill cry that
curdled with outrage. The group erupted into motion, dividing with an orderliness that mocked the ensuing chaos.
Nine men swung back the way they had come, galloping
to a point midway between the arroyo and a shallow canyon. The others charged after their leader. Na'acoci was

among them, even though Hawk had appointed him to stay behind.

He wasn't surprised at the boy's disobedience, nor was he particularly angry. He had assigned him to herd the stampede into the canyon, but he had known that Na'acoci's anger at these interlopers made him too aggressive to accept such a passive role. As Hawk watched, the boy swept gamely down the dusty slope of the arroyo, then charged up the other side, his eyes narrowed, his body tense and ready. Hawk let him go without a reprimand and turned his attention to the camp.

He counted only four herders. These Mexicans were not only brazen and greedy, they were stupid. One of the men left to defend their flocks was no older than Na'acoci. His blue eyes widened as the warriors swept into camp. So paralyzed by fear that it was impossible for him to regain his feet, he skittered backward on his bottom as the raiders bore down on him.

Hawk circled him as he crawled his way to a nearby horse. He waited calmly until the herder had managed to mount, then nudged his own pony in their direction. Holding out his shield as he swept by, he banged the boy's horse solidly on the rump. It leaped, then bolted, leaving the blue-eyed Mexican on the grass and much less likely to escape to bring help.

Hawk could easily have killed the boy, sprawled there as he was. But he had come for horses, for sheep, and for honor, and at least a thousand of the sheep were scattering away from the arroyo and out to unobstructed land. The boy's sleek and well-muscled mount was doing the same thing, and Hawk did not intend to let it get away. The boy was incidental, and so he left him.

Adrenaline coursed through his veins as he plunged through the center of the melee, by now a boiling cloud of dust. The warriors' raiding cry of *"Ahu! Ahu!"* rose up around him. It was a shrill, howling sound designed to terrify man and beast alike, and it split the night. Then, from somewhere in the choking dust, came the deadlier report of a rifle.

Hawk cleared the scuffle immediately, his pony lurching out on the other side of the camp. He found Na'acoci there, unharmed. He'd whipped his saddle blanket out from beneath himself and was waving it at the panicked sheep. He'd managed to turn a good portion of the flock back toward the arroyo. The remainder surged around him.

The boy was not doing badly for his first raid, Hawk thought. But then, hatred was an excellent incentive.

"You!" he shouted and aimed his spear toward the sheep and the horse escaping out to the open grasslands. Na'acoci's eyes flashed in that direction, then he whipped his pony around and galloped after them. He intercepted the sheep within a few hundred yards and waited while Hawk caught up with the tall bay stallion.

Together they turned the animals neatly toward the camp again. When they reached it, Hawk reined in and allowed Na'acoci to drive the herd into the hands of the men waiting on the other side of the wash. The dust was clearing quickly now. It revealed a ewe with a gaping hole torn in her side and a trampled lamb, but the rest of the livestock had been neatly removed.

The pale-eyes herders had vanished as well, having determined that the sheep were not worth their lives. Only one remained sprawled in the dirt, an arrow buried deep in his chest. Scowling at the foolish greed that had made the man fight rather than flee, Hawk touched his moccasins to his pony's sides and rode on.

He had passed the herders' shack and was almost to the arroyo again when twin spots of movement alerted him that the raid was not yet over. One came from the shack, a shadow moving under a shadow in the cavernous dark of the cloudy night. The other came from the wash itself and was more easily identifiable: Na'acoci on his splotchy paint. Hawk held up one hand, cautioning the boy to stop. But the young warrior ignored him and nudged his pony into a gallop.

Hawk froze, torn between admiration and anger. The boy had seen the shadow at the edge of the shack as well. He careened into the murkier darkness, armed with only an ancient, rusted carbine. There he leaped from his horse and into the arms of whatever awaited him.

A howl of rage rent the air. More dust billowed upward to be caught by the wind and dashed against the side of the shack. Hawk sat quietly, waiting, watching. The boy would have to find his vengeance alone. It was something no other man could share, something no one could give him.

Several more minutes passed before Na'acoci scrambled from the shadows, hauling a shrieking, hissing bundle behind him. But his grip wasn't enough to contain the child. Suddenly, she lunged forward rather than pulling back. Na'acoci disappeared beneath a flailing mass of arms, legs, and fingers hooked like talons.

Hawk took pity on him. The search for vengeance could last a lifetime, but once pride was gone it was often irretrievable. He dismounted quickly and hefted his spear, although he had no intention of killing this child either. This one had the spunk to make a useful captive.

He plucked the writhing bundle free of the boy and held her aloft by the back of her dress. Na'acoci scrambled to his feet, then clubbed her with the end of his carbine.

Hawk shoved the limp girl into his arms. "Maybe next time you will listen to reason," he said quietly. He mounted his horse. "All the warriors in my uncle's band obey their leader."

Shame infused Na'acoci's face with color. He ducked his head, staring down at the girl.

She wasn't the *Naakaiidine'e'* he had thought she was. Her face was round, not chiseled like a Spaniard's. Her skin was dark, ruddy, not pasty like the pale-eyes'. Her cheekbones were high; her eyes were small. She was an Indian. He dropped her so suddenly that a pained, subconscious grunt escaped her.

"Is vengeance sweet?" Hawk asked quietly. A small

smile played on his lips as he, too, looked down on the girl. "Always go slowly, my friend. Move carefully, wisely, and listen. You will make far fewer mistakes that way."

Na'acoci barely heard the admonition. "She is *Moqui!*" he cried. "A Hopi! One of the Dead Ones!"

Hawk shrugged. "True. But the *Moqui* make fine slaves and good wives. You did well. You simply did not do what you thought you had done."

"But I do not want a wife! I want justice!"

"Perhaps you will change your mind when winter comes again."

"She was in a Mexican camp!"

"She has been a captive for a long time. You will not have to train her."

"What was she doing in a camp with three old herders and a boy?"

Hawk chuckled softly. "As I said, you will not have to train her."

Na'acoci colored. Hawk turned his pony and rode to join the others.

They had made short work of separating the herd. A hundred or so ewes—either pregnant or nursing—grazed on the coarse grass near the wash. They would be left to the pale-eyes to ensure another flock to be stolen next year. The pale-eyes might be frightened out of *Dinetah* for a while, but no one doubted that they would return.

The men fell silent as Hawk rode among them. The gusts caught the silver bangles on his pony's headdress and stirred up a muted, triumphant jangle.

"The boy stole a girl," he commented. He was careful not to mention Na'acoci by name, knowing that he was close behind him. It was considered rude and insulting to speak even a man's nickname in his presence, since the nickname was so often derogatory.

Neither did he mention that the girl had almost gotten Na'acoci. Hawk both liked and respected the boy's boldness. As before, he decided to spare him his pride.

But Na'acoci's thin, arrogant face was still flushed with embarrassment as he rode up to join the others. He knew that he had broken one of the major rules of raiding. The survival of the group depended on cooperation, and instead he had acted as though he had no relatives. To the People, that was the worst sort of offense.

Then he glanced behind him at the still form tied on his pony and he knew that he couldn't have done anything else. And Hawk seemed to have known it. Long Earrings had recently renamed his nephew *Nat'aholel,* He Will Be Chief, and Na'acoci now understood why in an abstract way far beyond his years.

Hawk was a mighty warrior. But he was also a wise and compassionate man.

Chapter 2

▼▼▼▼▼▼▼▼▼▼

The sound of hoofbeats was distant, but Gray Eyes heard it. She'd been listening for it all night.

She fidgeted beneath her bedding as excitement skipped through her. Na'acoci's raiding party was finally returning. They would bring horses and trinkets, and, most importantly, sheep. The dry summer of 1857 had precipitated an unusually hungry winter. But now spring had touched the parched, rough land and the war bands could raid again. There would be feasting this day, and dancing and singing. And maybe, just maybe, there would be word of her sister, the one the *Naakaiidine'e'* had taken away.

Careful not to step over the sleeping figures of her parents—to do so was *ba'ha'dzid*, forbidden—she tossed her sheepskin aside and crept out of the shelter. The pale pink light of dawn was just beginning to touch the mountains. She needed no more encouragement than that. Wolf-men were never a problem in the daylight. It was in the darkness that they transformed themselves from ordinary people into witches. But the night was ending now, and she was sure she would be safe.

She cocked her head. The approaching hoofbeats were coming from the south. She veered in that direction, but when she reached the sweat lodge, the last shelter on that side of camp, she hesitated again. Despite the light in the eastern sky, it was still dark in the shadows of the mountain. She didn't have the nerve to venture much further on her own.

She hopped impatiently from foot to foot, waiting.

Then, just when she was sure she couldn't stand it any longer, she saw the riders. She started to run toward them, then, suddenly, she skidded to a stop.

The leader rode well ahead of the band. He presented a chilling image as he cut across the high desert at a full gallop. His tunic and buckskin breeches, even his moccasins, were dyed the color of night. His mount, too, was dark, and he rode bareback, without the customary saddle blanket slashed and crisscrossed with white and indigo and red.

Too late, it occurred to her that perhaps Na'acoci wasn't returning after all. Perhaps this was the trick of a witch, meant to draw her out into the last of the darkness alone. Who but a witch would dress so completely in black?

Gray Eyes began to back up instinctively, her heart hammering. But terror had held her still for too long. The wolf-man—for surely that was what he was—saw her. With a wild whoop, he beat his pony into an even harder gallop. She spun on her heel and ran, but before she could dart into the shadows, he whisked her off her feet.

Gray Eyes' shriek brought her clan tumbling out of their shelters. They rushed outside and watched, mouths agape, as she was carried through camp. The war pony was moving at a terrifying clip. Gray Eyes didn't care. She twisted around to face the demon and clawed desperately at his face, wriggling madly in an effort to free herself.

Then they reached her grandmother's lodge. With a jerk of the reins so sudden that it threw her into his arms, the demon brought his horse to a stop.

Stunned, she looked up into his proud, dark eyes. Her blood roared in her ears until she could barely hear his laughter. But she saw his smile. Furious, she scrambled free of him and dropped to the ground.

"I see you had a good raid, my friend's nephew." Vittorio chuckled. "You brought us a captive." Her grandfather and the clan's headman, he was a mountain of a man with a face the shape of a gourd. His huge girth rumbled with laughter as he stood in front of his first wife's lodge.

"A wolf-man, I think," the demon answered him. "I spotted her lurking in the darkness at the edge of your village."

Quite Enough had followed her husband out of their shelter. "For the last time, I think," she murmured. "The night holds many surprises."

There was more laughter as the clan gathered to see what the excitement was about. But Gray Eyes scarcely heard it. She glared up at the demon. He had eyes like glassy volcanic rock, but a faint light twinkled in the depths of them. She met them defiantly for a moment before she realized what she was doing. It was rude to look anyone right in the eye, much less the leader of a war band—no matter what he had done to her. She flushed and dragged her gaze away.

"I wanted to greet the raiders," she mumbled. "I wanted to know if they had found my sister or heard word of her." She was careful not to mention Little Dove by name. There were those in the camp who said that she was as lost to them as if she had died, and the only thing worse than speaking a person's name to his face was uttering the name of someone who was dead. It was sure to bring their ghost back.

More embarrassed than angry now, she began to stalk off. Then the demon spoke again. His voice was still amused, but surprisingly kind. "No, *Baa' Ya'zhi'*," he answered. "Not this time."

A murmur rose from the crowd. Her heart lurched as suddenly as it had when she'd first spotted him. She whirled around to face him again.

"What?" she breathed. "What did you say?"

"We went only as far as their herding camp," he explained, scowling at the general reaction. "They were grazing in *Dinetah*. We did not go into their 'new' Mexico. Perhaps next time, if we raid their settlements, we will find her."

But Gray Eyes shook her head frantically. She no longer cared where they had gone or who they'd raided. She wanted to know why he had used her name.

She knew that everyone called her *Binalbai*, Gray Eyes, after a Mexican woman who had been captured by their band long ago. She'd fought for the People, as fiercely and loyally as if she'd been one of their own. Gray Eyes had her beauty, her fine, delicate features, and her long-legged grace. She had her eyes as well. It seemed only fitting that she be given her name.

But Gray Eyes was only her nickname, and as such it had no great power. It was her war name, Baa' Ya'zhi', Little Warrior-girl, that gave her her strength. She had earned it by fighting the Mexican raiders, and it was special and sacred.

But how had this stranger, this demon, known that? And why had he spoken it aloud? Had he meant to wear her name out, to make her weak? *Was* he a wolf-man? Then another, more disturbing thought came to her. Had the Holy People, those mighty gods who watched over and censured all the People, sent him to her for some reason?

Panicked, she turned away again, wanting nothing more than to get away from him. She didn't care if the Holy People had sent him, she hated him. He'd scared her out of her wits and then he'd laughed at her.

She had nearly reached her mother's shelter when she heard Na'acoci call her. He trotted up beside her on his little paint.

"You are very popular this morning." He glared at her.

Gray Eyes flushed. "I was coming to meet you."

Na'acoci slumped on his pony. "I rode in second. No one even noticed. They were all watching Hawk tease you."

"Teasing?" Was that what he had been doing? Fresh anger rose up inside her, then vanished as whatever was wrapped in Na'acoci's blanket began to thump around on the back of his pony like a demented jackrabbit. Suddenly, she understood his anger. She'd stolen his thunder on his very first raid.

"Brother! You brought us a captive! A *Naakai-idine'e'*?"

His scowl only deepened. "No. She is *Moqui.*"

Gray Eyes shrugged. "That is good too. She can help with the work. Maybe we will even adopt her."

"No!" Na'acoci's response was immediate and vehement. "She is crazy. And *hahoo'a*, noisy." He hesitated. "I named her *Na'shdo'i'lbai'*, Wildcat."

Gray Eyes blinked in surprise. "You named her?"

He looked embarrassed. "I had to call her something. And I was the one who caught her."

She inspected the writhing bundle thoughtfully. "I thought the Dead Ones were dull. That's what Grandfather always says."

"Not this one. Perhaps the *Naakaiidine'e*'s craziness has rubbed off on her." He untied the twitching bundle. It slid to the ground with a hard *thunk,* and the blanket dropped to the girl's shoulders. Gray Eyes looked suddenly, speculatively, at her brother. With her delicate Hopi features, the *Moqui* was quite beautiful.

"Brother, she is about as old as you," she teased. "Perhaps that is why you do not want *'Ama'* to adopt her? You do not want her for a sister?"

Na'acoci colored slightly. "I do not want her at all," he muttered. "Keep her hands tied. If you forget, you will be sorry." And with that, he spun his pony around and began to trot away.

But Gray Eyes was no longer interested in the captive. As she watched Na'acoci go, she caught sight of the demon wolf-man again in the distance. "Brother!" she called out.

"What is it?" Na'acoci answered impatiently. The other warriors were already at his grandmother's lodge, eating and celebrating with Vittorio. He wanted to be among them.

"This man you call a *dzi'li'*, a hawk," she asked, then hesitated. "He is powerful?"

Something close to awe touched Na'acoci's features. "His medicine is very strong."

"I see."

She turned back to her mother's shelter, even more disturbed than before. But she remembered to keep a wary hand on the captive girl's elbow.

Wildcat seemed docile, if sullen and tense. Gray Eyes didn't believe the mood could last. How could the girl remain gloomy beneath such an immense sky of perfect, unbroken blue? Vittorio's band had left their winter hogans and moved closer to the mountain grazing areas only a moon ago. Now piñon and chaparral stood majestically on the slopes above them. Not far from the camp, a thin, icy stream trickled through a red-rock gorge. Bluetailed lizards skittered in and out among the rocks. A red-tailed hawk coasted lazily overhead. It was *Dinetah*, beloved *Dinetah*, and it was beautiful. Wildcat simply couldn't remain immune to it. Could she?

Gray Eyes glanced back at the girl speculatively, then pulled her through the narrow tunnel of the door that led into Quiet Woman's shelter. " *'Ama',*" she interrupted with typical enthusiasm. "Look what Na'acoci has brought."

Quiet Woman looked up at them from the cook fire she had been tending. She was a small woman whose face had worn a defeated look ever since Little Dove had been taken from her. Her expression didn't change as she regarded Wildcat.

Gray Eyes' heart sank. But she tried again. "And on his first raid, too," she boasted.

"Yes, he did very well," Quiet Woman agreed. "She is lovely. And she looks strong. She will be able to work hard." Then, briefly, she smiled.

Gray Eyes' spirits leaped. She knew that no one could fill the gap left by Little Dove. Even if Na'acoci had managed to bring back a Mexican, it wouldn't have eased Quiet

Woman's pain, only some of her anger. But Wildcat was not meant as a replacement for the other. She was an addition, another cherished young voice to keep their hogan warm on cold winter nights. And already, she had made Quiet Woman smile. For Gray Eyes, that was enough. In that moment, she accepted the other girl into her heart.

"Come," she said, turning back to her. "Na'acoci will be too excited to drive the sheep up the mountain this morning. We will do it for him, then we can make him do one of our chores later on—" She broke off. Wildcat was staring at her blankly.

Gray Eyes scowled for a moment, then dropped to her hands and knees. *"Dibe',* sheep," she tried. "Baaahh!" Wildcat only shook her head. Gray Eyes sighed and got up. "Come along, then. I will just have to show you." Throwing her brother's caution to the wind, she untied the girl's hands and pointed her at the door.

The camp was fully awake now and bustling with activity. Juniper branches creaked under the strain as women started the looms strung between them. Sheep bawled from the confines of the nearby corrals. Talks Often, Quiet Woman's sister, carried bedding out of her shelter to air, chattering all the while at the dogs who nipped at her heels.

The cacophony of happy, comforting sound faded out for Gray Eyes in an instant as they passed the sweat lodge. She froze, staring rudely.

The warriors were there, cleansing themselves after their contact with the *Naakaiidine'e'*. The demon leader, the Hawk, was among them, reclining against a swell of packed red earth. He was naked, and the sweat on his strong, bronzed body caught the sunlight like a haze of gold. Even relaxed, there was an inherent strength in his face that frightened her. Even at a distance, she could feel the power that coiled within him.

As she watched, he glanced up at her. At first his gaze was indifferent, almost as though he didn't recognize her.

Then, slowly, he began to grin and the teasing light came back into his eyes.

Gray Eyes turned and fled, leaving an astounded Wildcat free and unbound behind her. The sheep could wait. She wasn't going to venture out of her shelter again until he was gone.

Chapter 3

As Hawk's blood-bay pony carried him across the wind-swept ranges of the Chuska Valley, he scowled yet again at the incomprehensible gaffe he had committed. Gray Eyes, they called her. But he had called her Baa' Ya'zhi'. Even now, three weeks later, he grimaced at the affront.

He'd thought he'd been giving her a nickname—a fitting one. Absently, he traced a finger along the scratch she had left on his throat and remembered the ferocity with which she'd fought him. More than once on that short ride, she'd made him regret that he had ever started the game. Her reaction had evoked in him a puzzling kind of respect. He was a warrior, fierce and proud. She was a girl-child, young and soft. But something within her was as different as those silvery eyes promised. She had fought him even knowing that to fall off his horse was to die. And yet he still hadn't guessed that she had a war name and that he was using it until his uncle had told him.

In the laws set down by the Holy People long ago, the situation demanded an eye for an eye. In speaking her name, he had stolen some of her power. Now he would have to replace it.

He drew abreast of the Chuska Mountains and stopped. The scrubby meadow at the base of the mountain was deserted now, but further up on the ridges of red rock and velvet green Hawk saw wisps of smoke. The Lone Trees had moved again to the lusher pastures of the higher elevations.

Hawk nudged his pony and started up the slope. The

mountain terrain was rough and matted with dry, tangled growth. The pony's hooves gained purchase only to have the ground beneath them crumble away. Yet he scrambled determinedly until they reached the first plateau.

It was there that the pony finally balked, his ears pricking, his nostrils flaring. Hawk smelled it too. Water, too scarce to be ignored. He relaxed his hold on the reins and let the pony follow his nose.

They passed through more scrub and would have plowed right on through to the hidden ravine had Hawk not suddenly gripped the reins again, his tension communicating itself easily to his mount. They both went rigid as Hawk stared.

The gray-eyed one sat comfortably against the gnarled tentacles of a cottonwood tree uprooted by the first rushes of melted mountain snow. The *Moqui* her brother had stolen sat cross-legged at the edge of the stream. Another, younger girl with a devilish face splashed in the middle. But Hawk's gaze flickered over the other two only briefly. His eyes came back to lock on Gray Eyes.

She was rubbing the coarse, damp sand languidly over her body. She frowned a bit, as though the task of bathing required a great deal of concentration. Her fingers were long and slender as they worked over her strong thighs. Her breasts were small, just budding, but firm and high. As he watched, she pushed away from the roots and stood to wade into the water. Naked, she possessed a graceful, wild beauty that was debilitating. Hawk felt an unseen weight slam into his stomach. She was far too young to look so mature, so ripe.

He had every reason, every right, to ride out and meet her. It would have been natural for him to dispose of his business with her now while he had the chance. The fact that she wasn't clothed shouldn't have mattered, not if she were only a woman he wanted, not if she were only a child. But she was neither, and she was both. Instead of moving forward, he jerked on his reins and melted back

into the brush, toward the Lone Tree camp and the other
mission that had brought him back to the Chuskas.

Gray Eyes danced ahead of Wildcat and K'aalo'gii as
they left the wash and headed back to camp. The other
girls were content to dawdle. As they reached the outskirts
of the camp, she started to call out to them to hurry. But
the words died in her throat when she saw the war pony
that was tethered in front of her grandmother's lodge.

The demon Hawk was back.

Despite the fluttering in the pit of her stomach, she
wasn't surprised. It didn't seem at all odd to her that in
thirteen summers she had never seen this man before and
now, in less than a moon, he had turned up twice. It just
seemed obvious that the Holy People had sent him to her
after all.

Moving slowly now, she sidled up to her mother's shelter. She dropped down next to Quiet Woman, then hiked
her buckskin shift up to her thighs and rested her chin on
her knees.

"Is something wrong, daughter?" Quiet Woman asked
after a few moments, looking up from the wool she was
carding.

Gray Eyes glanced almost guiltily at her. "No, *'Ama'*.
I am fine. Why do you ask?"

"Because the one who spoke your name is here again."

Gray Eyes flinched. "Yes. I noticed."

"I wondered if that was why you are so unusually
quiet."

She scrambled to her feet again. "I feel lazy," she lied.
"Where are Na'acoci and *Ataa'*, Father? Should I bring
something from the garden? It is almost time for our evening meal."

Quiet Woman put down her wool. "Na'acoci and One
Whisker are at my mother's lodge. The one who knows
your name has brought a message from the Bitter Waters'
headman. We will eat later, when the council is through."
She stood and started into their shelter before pausing.

"Those fine, fat sheep your brother got from the raid are still grazing."

Gray Eyes nodded absently. "Wildcat and I will go get them."

But although the Hopi girl trotted off up the mountain, Gray Eyes wandered aimlessly through the camp to the big fire pit near her grandmother's lodge. Working absently, she began to gather the charred remnants of last night's fire.

Soon the men began to filter out of Quite Enough's lodge to congregate at the pit. Carrying the ashes, she moved over to the ash dump and hovered there.

The demon Hawk came out of the lodge last. Without his unusually dark war clothing, he looked younger than she remembered. She decided that he had probably seen no more than nineteen summers. He was young to have so much power but she didn't doubt its existence for a minute. Just as before, she felt it. He carried himself with a commanding air of authority. The skin pulled taut over the elegant ridge of his cheekbones gave him a profile that was strong and beautiful and proud.

She shivered even though the evening was still warm and noticed that he was the only one who didn't glance her way.

As Vittorio passed her, he quirked an eyebrow at her and smiled. Women were the backbone of *Dine'* society; they owned the hogans, the sheep, and the children. But very few of them ever chose to involve themselves in the men's affairs. Only Gray Eyes seemed to find Vittorio's councils interesting. But as she watched now, her attention strayed from her grandfather and moved to the warrior with the lava-rock eyes.

He rose just as the men were seated and the flames began to dance as though they were trying to touch the sky. Other men had joined them now; not one of them wavered in the rapt attention they gave Long Earrings' nephew.

Hawk's voice was quiet yet commanding. "I bring a

message from my uncle. It is about the fort these new Mexicans have built in *Dinetah*. The one they call Defiance. It is becoming a thorn in our leader's side." No one questioned what leader he meant. Although Long Earrings was a very powerful medicine man, he was old now, and he was a peace leader. In matters of strife and pale-eyes, Manuelito governed the band.

"Manuelito gave up his grazing rights to *Tsehotsohih*, the Meadow Between the Rocks, when it was demanded of him in the last treaty," Hawk continued. "The new pale-eyed Mexicans have put their *hual-te,* their fort, there. While our flocks starve from the drought and we go hungry, their animals flourish on the rich grass there and grow fat. When this treaty was signed, the blue-coats had no other way to feed their stock. Now they have wagons and their supply trains come often. Manuelito says they can now bring hay and seeds to feed their horses. He wants his land back so that he might graze his sheep and horses at *Tsehotsohih* again." He paused. "My grandmother's brother, Long Earrings, believes that if we go to their *hual-te* in great number and ask for the soldiers' understanding, they will give it. There is strength and much medicine when we gather."

"And Manuelito?" asked Vittorio.

"He is willing to share if he can use but a portion of the meadow to keep his stock alive. He has begun sending his sheep and horses in there already. But the pale-eyes chase his stock off again. Trouble is brewing."

"And what do you think, my friend's nephew?"

His black eyes smoldered now and his deep voice simmered with barely checked passion. He would never have volunteered his own opinion had he not been asked. But Vittorio had asked him.

"These new Mexicans never give back what they have taken," he declared. "In this last treaty, we also gave them our lands to the east. They drew an invisible line on Mother Earth and told us to stay behind it. They promised on their paper that they would leave us alone if we did this. Instead, they graze their sheep in *Dinetah*. When we take them, they cry out that *we* have broken *our* word by raiding them.'' He paused. ''There can be no reasoning with this. We should not waste the precious breath of the People asking them to give *Tsehotsohih* back. If Manuelito wants his family's land, we must simply take it.'' He sat abruptly to await a decision from Vittorio's band.

After a brief time, the headman rose laboriously to his feet. He was no longer young, and in any event he had never been slender. Now he felt as though he had the weight of the world on his shoulders as well.

''My friend's nephew,'' he began. ''I agree that the land should be taken. The People have never asked for what they want. But I am beginning to fear that neither that approach nor your uncle's method will make any difference with these pale-eyes.'' The warriors stirred uncomfortably. ''We will do as Long Earrings wishes,'' Vittorio announced abruptly. ''But the men I send will be warriors, in the event the land must be taken by force. I will give you my son, Yellow Horse, and my wife's nephew, *Gahtsoh*, Jackrabbit. He is young but very quick. *Achi'i'h*, The Nose, the husband of my granddaughter Sleepiness, can go. I am sure you have heard of his expertise—'' Barks of laughter interrupted him. Achi'i'h was renowned for his talents in a woman's bedding. Vittorio scowled at the chuckling men and went on, ''—with a bow. It would also please me greatly if you would take my grandson, Na'acoci.''

Hawk nodded. ''My uncle and I thank you. You are a fine warrior and a friend. We will leave tomorrow.''

The business dispensed with, Vittorio eased himself heavily to the ground again. The men's voices grew louder, and even the fire seemed to jump more wildly. Gray Eyes noticed that her brother seemed about to burst from excitement at being included with the band's bravest warriors. Gray Eyes smiled to herself. There'd be no living with him now.

Then her smile vanished. The demon, the Hawk, disengaged himself from the group and headed back to Quite Enough's lodge. Gray Eyes stared after him, recognizing her first opportunity to catch him alone.

Her heart began to pound hard. Did she dare confront him? She had to. She had to know how he had known her name. Skipping out from behind the ash dump, she hurried after him.

She found him near his pony. He had taken something from the gall bag tied inside his loincloth and was staring at it thoughtfully. She knew it had to be powerful medicine. A person's gall bag contained emetics to ward off the evils of wolf-men and witches—or, in the case of a witch, it contained those evils. She remained silent, not daring to interrupt.

Hawk noticed her with a start. Something inside him, something beyond his control, responded to her presence instantly.

Gray Eyes got right to the point. "You knew my war name," she said when he looked up at her.

He shrugged stiffly. "It was an accident."

She looked unconvinced. "It would only have been an accident if you had spoken a name you knew. But you could not have known mine."

He glanced up at her, surprised. Such wisdom from such a child disturbed him. It made her seem almost old enough to touch.

But he knew better, and regret made him arrogant. "You think I am lying then?"

Her heart didn't miss a beat although she trembled at the imperious glint in his eyes. "I think you are wrong in your opinion of me. I am not so stupid I can be lied to." Her chin lifted a notch, giving her a haughty elegance that matched incongruously with her youth.

A hot, hard knot of desire settled low in his groin. He forced himself to ignore her delicate, innocent face and the hair that fell like strands of gleaming onyx to her waist. He refused to think about the way she had looked by the wash.

"I have neither the time nor the inclination to argue with you, little one," he replied harshly. "I am willing to replace the power I stole from you, but I will not stand here chatting about it all night."

He glanced again at the heavy gold coin he'd taken from his gall bag. He'd stolen it from a Mexican on his very first raid. It was his strength; his talisman. He tossed it to her as he turned away. "May you be healthy," he finished abruptly. "May you be strong."

Startled, Gray Eyes caught the coin instinctively. As soon as it touched her palms, she flinched. It could be covered with corpse-poison; it could be evil. She waited for it to burn her hands, to scorch her flesh. But nothing happened. Finally, she turned the strange coin slowly in her hands.

She still had no idea why the Holy People had sent this man to her. But even her grandfather had been swayed by his judgment, which meant that his medicine was very powerful indeed. And now he had given her some of it. She knew she should be pleased.

Yet as she watched Hawk walk away, all she felt was a nervous distress she'd never known before.

Chapter 4

Hawk frowned as he rode ahead of the other warriors. His gall bag felt too light. Why had he felt compelled to give the girl the coin, of all things? She was only a child. She would have been satisfied with any small trinket he might have given her. But he'd volunteered the coin, because on some instinctual level it had seemed necessary. Then. Now he felt only an eerie vulnerability. As he rode toward *Tsehotsohih,* he prayed to the holy ones that his medicine would be strong enough to suffice on its own if the confrontation should escalate into violence.

Off in the distance, the Meadow Between the Rocks spread out between cliffs that were red and tall and proud. Tension thickened the dry air as the warriors approached it. They had reached a gaping hole in the rocks and many of the warriors had branched off to enter the valley before Manuelito held up a hand to stop them.

"No. We will go up onto the cliffs first."

Someone dared to question his judgment. "The pale-eyes will be able to see us there."

"Yes," Manuelito answered. "And we will be able to see them."

He spun away from the group and galloped toward the cliffs at the north of the valley. As the warriors followed and congregated behind him, a single horn sounded an alarm below. Soldiers spilled out of the unsightly buildings they called their Fort Defiance. Shielding their eyes against the glare of the desert sun, they looked up at the Indians.

"Something-Sticking-Out-of-the-Foreheads." The warrior beside Hawk spoke the Navajo name for the soldiers, given for the visors they wore on their caps.

Hawk moved up beside Manuelito. "They are not armed," he observed.

"No," Manuelito mused. "Not yet. We will go down."

They began moving down the bluff in groups of three and four. As the first of them reached the stream at its base and still more appeared behind them, a black man broke off from the crowd of soldiers and disappeared into a long, stout building that fronted the parade ground.

Hawk watched him go as he and Manuelito reached the valley floor. "I would prefer that they all stayed where we could see them," he muttered. "I do not trust them."

As he spoke, the Negro emerged from the building again, accompanied by another man in the uniform of an officer. "Gentlemen," the new man greeted them.

Snickers and guffaws sounded from the crowd of soldiers. Hawk stiffened. He didn't understand what the pale-eyes soldier had said, but he knew the sound of disdain.

"State your business," the officer went on. "I am Major Thomas Brooks. I am post commander of this fort."

Manuelito nodded. "That is good. We come to speak of this fort."

"What's your problem with it?"

"It is on my land."

Suddenly, the major grinned. "Precisely. We'd be hard-pressed to maintain law and order among you if we were in Richmond."

Manuelito's eyes narrowed. "It was my father's land," he stated, "and his father's before him."

"That may well be. But now it's the property of the United States government," Brooks pointed out mildly.

"This government is not my government."

"Indeed it is. Have you forgotten your treaty?"

"I have not forgotten it. I have come to take my name off it."

Brooks' smile faded. "That's not possible."

"I come to serve notice that I will no longer observe this agreement. You must change it."

"That's preposterous!" There was incredulity in the major's voice now. "You expect to ride in here and with a word negate an entire treaty?"

Manuelito hesitated, then attempted to explain what to him was painfully simple. "My horses, my wives' sheep, they starve. There is little grass in *Dinetah* this year, only here. We should share *Tsehotsohih* so that they might survive."

Brooks looked thunderstruck as something apparently dawned on him. "Have you been grazing your stock here? Every morning we find them in our hay fields. Every afternoon we drive them out again. Every night they return. Are these animals yours?"

Manuelito nodded. "They are mine. They will share the grass with yours."

But Brooks shook his head. "No."

"You refuse?" Manuelito asked.

"You're damned right I refuse. Take your horses back to your mountain hidey-holes. I won't tolerate them any longer."

The simmering quiet that fell over the warriors made Manuelito's answer seem unnaturally loud.

"No. You refuse, so I refuse."

Brooks looked as stunned as if he had been slapped. Dust rose and commotion erupted as over a hundred war ponies broke into movement and headed back for the cliffs. Yet the major's strident, angry voice was easily audible above it.

"Wait just one damn minute! I'm ordering you to get your stock out of here!"

Manuelito ignored him. As far as he was concerned, there was nothing left to discuss.

"I warn you, you stubborn red-skinned asses!" Brooks went on. "I will not let a bunch of savages encroach upon this land!" When he still got no response, he turned back to his soldiers. "Danzig!" he called. Then his eyes narrowed until he found the shock of red hair he was looking for. "And you, Sergeant!" he finished, pointing to Rush Michaels. "Get over to the hay fields. Arm yourselves. If they don't take their stock with them, shoot them all."

Michaels' eyes widened. "The Indians, sir?"

Brooks showed only a moment's hesitation. "If they offer resistance, yes. But start with that chief's horses."

He turned away, a nerve twitching visibly at his throat. He made his way back to his office and poured himself a hearty shot of whiskey. He nearly had it to his lips when Michaels stuck his head hesitantly through the door.

"Is something wrong, Sergeant?"

"They're headed to the south, sir. Away from the hay fields."

Brooks stared at the man, then looked down at the untouched amber liquid in his glass. He placed it on his desk with an exaggerated show of patience. "You have your orders, Sergeant."

"But there are over a hundred of them, sir."

"Are you a coward, Michaels?"

The man looked uncomfortable. "No, sir."

"Then go kill the goddamned horses before the Indians are too far away to know we've retaliated!"

"Retaliated, sir?" Michaels seemed uncertain.

Brooks' eyes glittered as they met his. He answered with one word. "Go."

Hawk had cleared the cliffs when he heard the first shot ring out. He spun his horse around, going still.

"The hay fields," he said to Manuelito. "Your stock. They are slaughtering your horses."

Manuelito's voice remained calm, but his eyes began to shine with a chilling, feral glint. "Yes," he said quietly. "And someday they will pay."

"They must pay now!" Hawk charged. "We can not allow them to slaughter that by which men live."

"We can not stop them. You forget that your uncle insisted we come in peace."

Hawk looked down at his hands. He held his reins,

nothing more, no lance, no bow. It occurred to him then that the pale-eyes were destroying more than their horses. They were destroying his people's dignity; they were playing them for stupid, trusting fools.

Two more shots rang out. He turned slowly to the men surrounding him.

"Shall we cower here like lambs while they spit in the face of our leader?" he demanded of the warriors. "Shall we bemoan this injustice as though we were women? Or shall we simply cut off that which makes us men?" He didn't wait for a response. With a curdling war cry, he made his own choice. Spurring his pony into a gallop, he charged the fort.

Behind him, men hesitated, then Na'acoci charged free of the crowd and galloped after him. As they descended upon the hay fields, the others broke their frozen tableau and followed. Their voices raised together in war cries of outrage. Beneath it sounded the staccato affront of gunfire.

Hawk heard only the heavy beating of his own heart. He dived into the surviving horses, herding them ahead of his own. When they had scattered out of the range of the pale-eyes' bullets, he circled back to the source of the gunfire.

Michaels saw him coming. He spun away from the slaughtered animals, his rifle coming up as he moved. The motion was purely reflexive; he felt almost numb with fear and regret. The Indians were enraged by the unwarranted slaughter of their animals, and their fury was aimed at him and Danzig. But it hadn't been his error in judgment, and it wasn't one for which Michaels was willing to die. He found the trigger and began pumping on it spasmodically.

The bullets chewed up the earth at Hawk's pony's hooves. The animal gave a maddened cry, then lunged boldly forward to charge the soldier.

In some distant part of his brain, Hawk registered the near-empty gall bag bouncing at his hip. He saw gray eyes, too wise to be so innocent. And in the instant before Michaels began to gain some control over his aim, he had the odd but certain feeling that he wasn't as unprotected as he'd thought. Then the barrel of Michaels' weapon lifted and Hawk saw fire flare from the gun just as his pony reared.

He felt the animal lurch and stumble beneath him. He felt himself falling, down and down until the rocky earth pounded the breath from his lungs. His sleek mount groaned and began to topple above him. Hawk jerked his leg out from beneath him and rolled.

He came to his feet again in one fluid motion. The world was a chaos of red dust and screams, both human and animal. But through it all he spotted a splotchy paint pony, his rider beating him frenziedly as they raced toward him.

Hawk threw himself up behind Na'acoci. It wasn't until they had raced back out into the desert that he accepted that his war pony was dead—and wondered why he was still alive.

Chapter 5

There was a quiet tension in the Lone Tree camp as the sun reached its zenith. Occasionally someone would stop in their work long enough to gaze speculatively toward the south, where Fort Defiance hid behind the distant buttes. But no one mentioned the warriors' mission. It was not their way to discuss that which only the holy ones could influence.

Instead, the women worked doggedly, doing the men's chores in addition to their own. If tempers were shorter, they took it in stride—all except K'aalo'gii.

She was working in the garden with Wildcat and Gray Eyes when one of the camp dogs began to inch stealthily toward her basket. She plucked a rock from the dusty soil and tossed it at him angrily.

The rock fell short, but the dog growled anyway and turned on her, his teeth bared, his belly low to the ground. Gray Eyes straightened away from a stalk of corn and shielded her eyes to glare at him.

"Off with you," she scolded. "You are not so fearsome."

He stopped and gave a halfhearted little whine, then he tucked his tail between his legs and slunk off. K'aalo'gii stared after him in amazement.

"How did you do that? He is a mean one. You must have strong medicine, sister," she teased. "It is said that dogs and coyotes will never bite a shaman."

Gray Eyes gave a little snort of derision. Most likely,

she thought, it was not medicine that had scared him off, but rather the evil that the Hawk had branded her with.

The coin he had given her must have been covered with corpse-poison. There was no other explanation for the way she had felt lately. Her back ached terribly, and there was a dull, methodical pain just below her navel. But no matter how badly she felt, she wouldn't let it show.

To believe that Hawk's honorable retribution of her power was nothing more than a curse was too hard for her to accept. That, and the thought of what would happen to him if she told anyone. Because she knew who had cursed her, the men of her village would have to make him confess. They would tie him down, denying him food or water until he spoke. They would hold hot coals to his feet. And if he still refused to confess, they would kill him. It was the only way to cure her.

Gray Eyes's stomach turned at the thought. She knew she would have to be very, very sure before she made an accusation.

"Get back to work," she snapped, looking up to find the others staring at her. "If you do not stop playing games, we will never finish."

"Something is wrong?" Wildcat asked cautiously, struggling with the newly learned Navajo words.

Gray Eyes wrenched an ear of corn free from its stalk. "No."

"Then you are not my cousin," K'aalo'gii countered. "She is fun even when we have to do dull chores." She grabbed her basket of beans and headed back toward the shelters with a grunt of disgust. "I am going to the wash. It is too hot to work, especially with someone who is grumpy."

Wildcat shot an apologetic glance at Gray Eyes. "I go too."

Gray Eyes stared after them miserably, but she let them

go. She dropped down on her haunches again and began searching among the stunted stalks of corn for another ear. Her gall bag thumped heavily against her thigh as she moved, and the pain clamored again in her belly. She closed her eyes and scrubbed her hand over it, willing it to go away. Instead, an unusually sharp pain stabbed through her.

She doubled over briefly, then, horrified, she scrambled to her feet. The corn forgotten, she dug the coin out of its pouch and ran as fast as she could up the mountain.

Only when she had put a safe distance between herself and the camp did she stop. She dropped to her knees and began digging furiously. She would bury it; she would hide the coin so that it could no longer hurt her or anyone in her clan. Centering the piece of gold above the hole in the ground, she opened her fingers and let it fall.

Then the pain gripped her again. It was worse, much worse, than before.

Baffled and badly frightened, she looked down. There was blood on the ground between her heels now. When she pulled up her shift, a smear of red blemished the tawny skin of her inner thigh. A soft cry escaped her. Then, slowly, realization dawned on her. Her power. Her power had come. Hawk hadn't witched her at all.

She drew her finger through the ruby drops in wonder. Then she held it up to the sun and laughed aloud. Slipping and sliding on the dry earth, she started back down the bluff toward camp.

That was when she noticed the hawk.

He appeared out of nowhere. Suddenly he was above her, his magnificent wings spread wide. Startled, she met the intelligent gleam in his small, shiny eyes. He gave a single cry.

She began running again, back the way she had come. The hawk followed her until she once again held the coin in her hand. Then he cried once more, drove his wings against his body, and was gone.

Gray Eyes fidgeted restlessly as her mother combed her hair. Finally, Quiet Woman placed a hand on her head to still her.

"For once in your life, be patient, daughter," she chided her. "Sit still. We must finish."

Gray Eyes went stoically rigid. Her mother was right. She didn't dare do anything to interfere with the ritual of her *Kinaalda'*.

A woman's power could be dangerous. Precautions were necessary if she were to control it. Since this first bleeding and her next would not be particularly heavy, it gave her family a chance to ceremonially counteract any future danger. For three days, they would feast and dance and sing despite the tension caused by the delay of news from the fort. Gray Eyes would observe the taboos that would keep her menses from harming anyone.

"You must appeal to the Holy People during these first two times," Quiet Woman explained. "There are many things you must remember so that you do not offend them. While you are bleeding, you must never enter a ceremonial hogan or shelter. You must not eat any meat. To do so will make you lazy and ugly. Do not scratch yourself, or you will be scarred where your nails touch. Will you remember this?"

Gray Eyes nodded carefully as her mother gathered her hair at the back of her neck and secured it with a special thong made from the skin of a mountain lion.

"Good," Quiet Woman finished. "Now off with you. The girls will be waiting for you. The holy ones say that you must run with them to the east to ensure that you will always be supple and strong." She stood, then offered a ghost of a smile. "Besides, you are underfoot. I have much to do before the other clans arrive."

Gray Eyes moved obediently for the door.

* * *

The old *hataali* went immediately to Quite Enough's shelter when he arrived. As he settled himself comfortably by the cook fire, Quite Enough brought him a large bowl of mutton stew.

"I am curious about this granddaughter of yours," he announced.

"She is just another girl-child," Vittorio answered humbly. It wouldn't have been seemly for him to boast about her.

Long Earrings' eyes smiled inside the wrinkled folds of his skin. "I am sure she is homely and fat. This is why my nephew thought to mention her to me."

"No. She is scrawny and is always getting in the way. *That* is why he mentioned her."

Long Earrings chuckled and put his bowl aside. "Perhaps. But Hawk thinks her medicine is strong. He tells me that she has very unique eyes and great wisdom for a child. Ah, but then, she is no longer a child, is she?"

"Perhaps you would like to meet her and see for yourself."

It was, of course, the reason Long Earrings had come to the *Kinaalda'*. Vittorio knew that the old medicine man was searching for an apprentice now that he was growing so old. Since it was common knowledge that he would prefer to have his power die with him rather than pass it on to someone unworthy, Vittorio was both pleased and surprised that he was considering his granddaughter.

"She brings much happiness to this old heart," he admitted. "But tell me, my friend. Why is it that you do not apprentice your own young nephew? He has very strong medicine."

Long Earrings' smile was vaguely sad. "His power is great, but it cannot heal. Hawk will be chief, not *hataali*. He will lead men, but I have dreamed of a woman to heal them." He gave his old friend a long look. "The Holy People have told me that she will have special eyes."

Before Vittorio could answer, the *hataali* nodded.

"Yes," he finished, "it would please me if you would bring this one to me. Let me see this girl-child of yours. Let me meet the one with the silver eyes and the coin of gold."

Chapter 6

Quiet Woman's shelter was crowded with all the women of the clan. Gray Eyes was at the center of the commotion as they worked to dress her for the evening ahead. She was growing decidedly restless under their ministrations, but she brightened when Quite Enough appeared at the door.

"Grandmother! Do you need me for some chore?"

Quite Enough smiled at her eagerness. "Not exactly. There is someone who wishes to see you, but it can wait until after you are dressed."

Gray Eyes' heart moved crazily. Perhaps the men had returned. Was the demon Hawk among them? "Who?" she demanded.

"If you do not stand still, daughter, you will never find out," Quiet Woman admonished. She adjusted Gray Eyes' best woolen leggings and buckskin moccasins while Little Left Hand, a woman whose beauty was marred only by the deformed arm that had relegated her to the position of Vittorio's second wife, cinched her dress at the waist with a wide, woven belt.

As soon as it was in place, Gray Eyes pulled away from her. "Who?" she prodded her grandmother again.

"The Bitter Waters' *hataali.*"

Gray Eyes stopped dead in her tracks. Her voice was incredulous. "Long Earrings is here? He wishes to see *me?*"

"You ask unnecessary questions, granddaughter. Would you keep him waiting while I repeat the answers?"

38

Gray Eyes shook her head. Of course she couldn't do that. It would be unspeakably rude. She hurried to follow her grandmother back to her shelter.

The *hataali* was seated on the south side, the place traditionally reserved for the men. Gray Eyes' glance darted between him and her grandfather. He was much smaller than Vittorio, and older. His long black hair was streaked generously with gray. She was fascinated by the profusion of silk and silver he wore—it could only have come from conquered *Naakaiidine'e'*. Then she realized that she was staring at him and quickly averted her eyes.

"I thought I would save you the trouble of spying on us, granddaughter," Vittorio teased. "Come. Sit and join us."

Gray Eyes blushed as she moved behind the men to the north side of the shelter, careful not to disgrace herself by stepping between them and the fire. Quite Enough brought her a bowl of stew, and she listened to the men murmuring among themselves as she popped mutton into her mouth. But she was ravenous and soon focused her full attention on the food.

She was tilting the bowl to her lips for the last bit of broth when Long Earrings spoke a name capable of garnering her attention again. "I did not hear this from Hawk," he said, and Gray Eyes slowly lowered the bowl to peer over the rim at him.

"The scoundrel Sandoval came and summoned me to the fort," the *hataali* went on. "He and the pale-eyes headman explained what happened there."

"And what did they say?" Vittorio's voice carried the same edge of distrust that Gray Eyes felt. Sandoval led the *Dine'' Ana'i*, the Enemy Navajo. They were of the People, but they were not welcomed among them. They were friends with the pale-eyes and the *Naakaiidine'e'*. They stole women and children from other clans and traded them to enemies, and there were even those who said that they were wolf-men.

But this did not seem to disturb Long Earrings. "They

say that my nephew killed a slave boy belonging to Major Brooks,'' he answered. ''I tend to believe them. I am told that Brooks is responsible for the debacle of the council. The men believe he is to blame for the slaughter of Manuelito's stock and Hawk's war pony as well. It would be the way of the People for my nephew to take an eye for an eye—the slave for the horses.'' Long Earrings paused. ''After the commotion of the meeting died down, Hawk returned to the fort. When no one was looking, he shot the dark one with an arrow.''

''Did he escape?''

''They say yes. I believe this too, although I have not seen him. The last horse he stole from the *Naakaiidine'e'* is big and very fast.''

Vittorio nodded thoughtfully. ''But we still have no proof that he is alive. The pale-eyes lie. So does Sandoval.''

''I have no proof, no. But I know that Hawk would fear retaliation against our band. If the pale-eyes major brought his men to our camp and found him there, we might all be in trouble. I think that is why we have not seen him— he has gone into hiding.''

Vittorio scowled. ''If this is true, then your nephew is safe and so are our people. Where is the problem that you have come to ask my help with?''

''Major Brooks has demanded I arrange restitution for his slave.''

Vittorio looked dumbfounded. ''Restitution? But this cannot be.''

''I have tried to tell him this. I have explained many times that the killing of his dark one *was* restitution for the slaughter of our horses. It was taken when the pale-eyes made no effort to volunteer it for themselves.''

''Surely he can understand that,'' Vittorio muttered. Gray Eyes nodded unconsciously.

But Long Earrings shook his head. ''No,'' he answered. ''He cannot. He wishes to punish the killer. He has given me the time of twenty suns to produce him.''

"You will not do this," Vittorio answered.

"No. I *cannot* do this, as you well know, my friend. Who am I to say if what my nephew has done is right or wrong? I am but a humble old *hataali*. I have no authority to punish anyone. That is a job for the holy ones." Then he gave a troubled sigh. "Unfortunately, the pale-eyes do not understand this. The man Brooks claims that he has sent word to another pale-eyes headman, one even more important than him. If I do not produce the murderer of his dark one, he will go to war against the People. He has the big headman's permission." He hesitated, then spoke the words that distressed him most of all. "The pale-eyes are foolish. We can easily elude them in their efforts at war. But he says that he will enlist the help of our enemies, the Utes. And they are not so easily hidden from."

Gray Eyes blanched. It was true then, what the adults had always said. These pale-eyes, these new Mexicans, were different from the old ones. They had no laws, no honor. They had killed their horses, and now they would kill Hawk as well, and all in the name of a vengeance that wasn't called for.

With her thoughts tangled and her head pounding, she barely heard Vittorio address her.

"Granddaughter, our *hataali* wishes a service from you."

She looked at him uncomprehendingly. "I do not understand. This has nothing to do with me."

"Indeed it does," Long Earrings answered. "We need your help."

"Mine?" she squeaked, and he chuckled.

"My body is old," he went on. "Because of that, I have need of your medicine."

Startled, she glanced from one adult to the other.

"We must find Hawk," he went on. "Only he and Manuelito can say what is to be done now. This is between them and the pale-eyes major. You must go to my nephew and instruct him to seek out Manuelito so that they can decide if we should acquiesce or go to war. It may take days of traveling. I am too old to stay on my pony that long.''

Gray Eyes shook her head frantically. "I do not know where he is! My medicine, my power—''

"If it is strong enough, it will lead you to him.''

She risked a quick glance at him. His face, long and thin and crisscrossed with wrinkles, was implacable.

Her mouth went dry. He truly meant for her to do this. But she didn't want to. Finding Hawk meant seeing him, speaking with him. He frightened her, confused her. She shook her head again stubbornly.

"He could be anywhere in *Dinetah*,'' she protested.

The *hataali* nodded. "Yes.''

"The four sacred mountains that mark the edges of our country reach far. I could never find him in all that land.''

"Perhaps. Perhaps not. We shall see.'' His face was solemn as he studied her.

Her heart skipped a beat. Then it seemed to flutter so furiously that she could scarcely catch her breath. Could she do it? She wasn't sure, but suddenly, she knew one thing as certainly as she knew her own war name, as certainly as she was learning to hate these pale-eyes. If she didn't try, terrible things would happen to her people.

Something driven, something righteous, rose up inside her and toppled her reluctance. She took an unsteady breath.

"I will try,'' she answered grimly. And she thought, Even if it means facing the Hawk.

Chapter 7

▼ ▼ ▼ ▼ ▼ ▼ ▼ ▼ ▼ ▼

She wondered if she would get lost.

It was nearly her worst fear, just behind the possibility of running into a band of *Naakaiidine'e'*. Gray Eyes scanned the horizon ceaselessly as she rode, expecting to see them cresting the buttes. But all through the first day, she saw no one.

She went south, not because she expected to find the Hawk there, but because she didn't want to leave the mountains. They rose tall and proud above her, their sandstone walls the color of blood where she rode in their shadows. She felt safe among them; they were home. But by midday they were little more than hills as the range ran down, and she still wasn't sure where to go.

Another more realistic fear than phantom *Naakaiidine'e'* began to haunt her then. Not once since she had left the Lone Tree camp had she seen water.

The sky had become a perfect, unbroken bowl of blue. Even the desert, a land long-accustomed to living on itself, looked parched and dying. The juniper and the mesquite bent beneath the assault of the sun like tired old men. She began to hoard her provisions but, despite her efforts, her water ran out on the second day.

She rode on because she knew that to stop was to die. No medicine came to her, no sense of certainty about where she ought to go, until she came upon rolling, sandstone cliffs. The paths leading upward were well-worn and traveled. But they fell away suddenly, and then, beneath her, was *Tsehotsohih,* the Meadow Between the Rocks.

She knew instinctively what she was looking at although she had never seen it before. A cold, clear stream trickled along a bed of stone there. Her eyes fixed on it and her hand went to the empty bladder bag at her hip. Then her eyes darted to the row of square, ugly barracks that lined the parade ground and her heart pounded.

She could make it. She knew she could. It would take only moments to refill the bag, and while she did the pony could drink. Then they could gallop right out through the mouth at the other side of the valley. Her legs trembled with the urge to dig into the pony's sides, to send him down to the water.

Then she saw the soldier. He came from the row of buildings she'd noticed against the cliffs to her left, and as he moved closer to the creek, her body stiffened in shock. She had known these men had eyes like hers, but she had never expected that their skin would be pale, too. The soldier looked ghostly and wan. Was he truly a man? He looked more like a *chindi* spirit, she thought, like the ghost of one who had died.

Then, suddenly, her pony nickered softly and moved, sending a shower of debris down the bluff. The pale-eyes' head snapped up and his gaze moved up the cliff toward her.

Her throat closed tightly. He would kill her; she was certain of it. He would know that she wanted to take his water and he would kill her for it, just as he had killed the horses for grazing, just as he wanted to kill Hawk.

Instead he shouted an unintelligible word. "Squaw!"

Gray Eyes recognized the reprieve. She groped for her reins and spun away from the bluff. Her heart galloped in time with the pony's hooves as she swerved west, not daring to slow down to listen for sounds of pursuit.

Finally, when she had gone a safe distance, she began to sob out her frustration. She had been close enough to smell, almost taste the water. Just who were these white, sickly men? What kind of man would lay claim to water so that no other could drink? Who would presume to own land so that no horse could eat, then slaughter those that did?

A cold shiver took her. But she was decisive now. Wherever Hawk was, she knew he wouldn't be near these strangers. Wherever he was, she had to find him.

She heard the water this time, running softly, chuckling to itself. Her pony stopped, his neck high and alert, his ears pricked forward.

She urged him on and suddenly, no more than ten horse lengths ahead, the desert disappeared and there was mesquite again and cottonwood, tangled together, clinging to the banks of the creek. The pony pushed his way through it and they trotted straight on into the wash. She slid from his back weakly and sat, the water curling around her hips. Then, finally, she drank, cupping her hands and guzzling insatiably.

Drained and exhausted, she crawled from the water, lay back, and slept instantly. When she woke with a start it was already morning. Panicked, she sat up and looked around for her mount. In the early light of dawn she saw why he hadn't left her. Pale green grass blanketed the banks, tufting up even from between the rocks. It was the first real grass they had seen in days, and the pony was not about to ignore it.

She, too, intended to take advantage of their find. She stripped off her shift and leggings and waded into the water. Grinning, she scrubbed the red-brown sand over her skin, pausing now and again to cup some of the water in her hand and swallow. She was relaxed, splashing happily, when she heard the cry. It was her hawk.

She looked up quickly and searched the massive stretch of sky. He hovered beneath the sun, his wings motionless, then he flapped hard and soared toward her. When he was directly above her, he cried again, then flew off toward the northern horizon.

Gray Eyes remained still, shaken, as she watched him go. Suddenly, she knew Long Earrings had been right. She did have medicine, and it was strong.

Exhilaration made her weak. Comprehension left her reeling. But she understood now. Her menses and her hawk had both come to her at the same time, when the holy ones had sent her her power through a gold coin carried by the warrior who bore her talisman's name.

She pushed to her feet and dressed again hurriedly. Moments later, she rode north, following the trail of the hawk.

Late on the seventh day, she realized that she was headed for the sacred place at the heart of *Dinetah*. The desert changed, its scant vegetation becoming even thinner. The earth lost its dusty veil. There was deep red sandstone and sparkling white quartz, occasionally broken by a tenacious yucca or rabbitbrush. Then, abruptly, the yawning, fertile chasm of Canyon de Chelly loomed before her.

Gray Eyes stopped just in time to keep her pony from tumbling over the edge. Despite the sun skittering in and out between impossibly high clouds, a soft rain began to fall.

It was her medicine again, but she wasn't surprised this time. She felt a swell of relief, a quiet understanding. In the world of the People where everything had two interlocking parts, this was a female rain. The Holy People who were in charge of all female things were greeting her.

She tilted her face upward, accepting the welcome. Then she turned the pony to retrace her steps. There were only a few entrances to the canyon, and all were perilous. She cut into one of the smooth, steep gorges and descended carefully to the canyon floor.

The dying sun had turned the world to red. Canyon de Chelly swept above her, its sandstone walls a mass of towering burgundy shadows and orange light. Gray Eyes rode to the wash that meandered through it all, a wash that never went dry. Confident now, she stopped and waited for another sign.

She saw the thin wisp of smoke almost immediately. Someone was camping in the canyon, and she knew it was Hawk.

Hawk knew it was her as well. The slim figure atop the horse moved with a dignity that was innocent and proud and uniquely hers. He rose from the fire abruptly.

He had no time to question her presence. One moment she was distant, then she was close and a traitorous desire began to clamor within him. Her gray eyes gleamed like silver in the firelight. Her face was both delicate and haughty, offering and denying. When she moved to slide down off her pony, her dress caught and tightened, accentuating slender curves.

She turned to face him and he realized abruptly that something about her had changed.

"You?" he demanded in a voice made coarse by wanting and confusion.

Gray Eyes managed to nod. She wouldn't let him frighten her. "I carry a message," she answered. "From your uncle."

"They found him? The pale-eyes went to my camp?"

She shook her head quickly. "No. Not yet. I do not think they know that you are of his clan. I think they summoned him with their threats because he is a peace chief."

"Threats?" he growled.

She wanted to retreat from the barely checked anger in his black eyes. Instead, she held her ground and his gaze. "They will wage war against us unless your uncle turns you over to them for punishment."

For a long time Hawk only stared stonily at the canyon walls. "I will have to go to them then."

"No!" she yelled, both pained and furious. She ducked her head, embarrassed at the outburst.

He chuckled. "You disagree, little one? What else can I do? I cannot have them ravaging our camps in search of me." He paused, watching her carefully. "They will do it, you know."

She shuddered, then eyed him haughtily. "Yes, I know. I have seen them."

His look of surprise was almost comical. "You? How could you meet up with pale-eyes?"

Her hand went unconsciously to her gall bag. "It was many days before I trusted my medicine. At first I went the wrong way because I was afraid. I stumbled upon their fort."

"You travel by yourself?" Anger hit him then, anger unlike any he had ever known. For the first time it dawned on him how much danger they had sent her off to face alone.

But she had found him nonetheless, and suddenly, he understood why. The change he'd detected was her medicine. It had been unleashed somehow, and it was strong.

"It was the only way," she answered indignantly. "Your uncle is too old to travel this far. And no one knew where to find you. Only medicine would lead us to you." Then her eyes flashed angrily. "Mine is not perfect yet. I have only just had my *Kinaalda'*. But it is strong enough and I am here. They sent me to tell you that you must find Manuelito and decide what is to be done now. It is your hide they want. Go to them if you will! But know that they will kill you. I have seen them. They are like *chindi* spirits and they are evil."

She turned away from him abruptly and hurried back to her pony. "Why should I care if they shoot their fireballs through you?" she muttered. "You are stupid and mean."

He was too stunned to smile at her outburst. She was leaving. He stopped her before he thought about it.

"Your *Kinaalda'*? You surprise me, little one. I had thought you were *awe'e'*, a babe."

She turned back to him warily, not sure if he was teasing her or not. "It was my first." Then she began to retreat warily as he approached her. Her shoulders came up hard against her horse.

"You would run from me, little one?" he asked. Suddenly, there was a grin in his eyes, a teasing lift to his lips.

Her chin came up defiantly. "You flatter yourself. It is only that I have delivered my message. Now I am leaving."

"Mount that horse and I will shoot him dead," he heard himself answer, and wondered if he had gone mad.

He knew he couldn't keep her there. It was lunacy to believe that he could watch her sleep by his fire and not touch her. Even the thought tightened muscles that should have been sound asleep. Despite her *Kinaalda'*, it was still beneath his dignity to pursue her. It was a squaw's right to choose who she would lie with. It was a warrior's honor to be chosen. She would have to make an overture to him, and he knew in his heart that she would not. Her power had grown, but not her maturity. She still had no comprehension of his wanting her.

He had to send her away again while he still possessed the sanity to do so. Yet he knew in his soul that he couldn't do it.

"I cannot have you traveling alone at night on my behalf."

"I have been traveling alone on your behalf for suns now," she responded defiantly.

"That was not my doing!"

"You were responsible. You put all of us in danger with your thoughtless retaliation!"

His eyes blazed. Frightened, she reeled back. Her reaction made him temper his voice more carefully. "You are no more than a day's ride from the Chuskas if you take a direct route this time. Your band camps in the same place?"

She nodded warily.

"If you leave by morning, you will arrive by nightfall tomorrow."

"Yes."

"Where will you camp if you leave tonight?"

She thought about it. "It is late. I will not leave the canyon."

"Then stay with me, little one. You are still too young and much too soft to go without protection." His smile was grim. "If you should come to harm on your journey, my honor would demand that I find the man who hurt you and kill him. I have enough troubles at the moment, regardless of whether they are of my own making or not."

Slowly, hesitantly, she nodded. She feared him. At moments she even hated him. But the Holy People had sent him to her with a coin and her medicine, and she owed him something for that.

She moved stiffly to the fire. She settled herself before the flames and tossed back a lock of ebony hair.

"I've eaten nothing but *alkaan,* corn cake, for many days," she challenged.

He hesitated, gathering his control. "Then we will eat well tonight."

There was a crevice against the rocks. He moved to it and pulled away stones until he came to the provisions he had hidden there, away from the noses of the animals who called the canyon home. It wasn't long before the aroma of roasting antelope filled the air. He pulled a healthy chunk off the meat and tossed it into the flames; it was considered bad luck to eat without feeding the fire first.

When it had blackened to a crisp, he took another piece and passed it to her silently. "Tell me what you know," he said finally.

Gray Eyes cast a quick, suspicious glance at him. But he didn't look forbidding anymore and she relaxed.

"This man you shot," she answered. "A dark one? You were right. He was a captive belonging to the man Brooks. I think he was a very valued possession."

Hawk made a sound of assent and bit into a piece of meat.

"His death was a great affront to the headman who owned him," she added.

"Good. He must pay."

"They will never pay enough," she answered fiercely, the memory of the pale-eyes still fresh in her mind. "They must be driven out."

Her response surprised him, then he thought he understood. "They harmed you!"

She shook her head quickly, wondering at the anger in his eyes. She didn't understand its cause, but she knew that she didn't want it there.

"No," she assured him. "I ran. But I saw one of them. He was so pale, the color of milk. I fear having men like him living among us. There can be nothing inside them. They are men without souls."

His eyes narrowed as he studied her. "And yet you think I was wrong to kill one of theirs when I had the chance?"

"Like the bobcat, I fear they will be even more dangerous when provoked."

Hawk was surprised anew at her sensitivity. There was some small consolation in knowing that he had been right about her, right in mentioning her to his uncle, even if it had brought her to him in this intimate, isolated place alone. He gave her a thin, pained smile and got to his feet.

She watched him, dismayed. What was he doing? He had demanded that she stay for protection, and now he was leaving her.

"Where do you go?" she demanded.

His voice came back to her out of the night. "I seek sanity. Go to sleep, little one. Morning will come soon and then you can go home."

Gray Eyes stared in the direction of his voice, baffled. Then she made up her mind. She'd moved on instinct, on her medicine, too much in the last few days to do differently now. Clutching her blanket close around her, she moved tentatively after him and lay down halfway between him and the fire.

Somewhere in the darkness, she thought she heard him groan.

Chapter 8

Wildcat's shriek blistered the sultry autumn air, but only two of the eighteen people who lived with Gray Eyes' band seemed to notice. Black Spot dropped the poultice he had been pushing into his pony's hoof and looked around the pole corral questioningly. Black Spot had seen so many summers that both he and his family had stopped counting, and he wasn't sure if he'd actually heard anything or not.

Gray Eyes had no such doubts. She straightened away from the pot of boiling, smoking piñon gum with a sigh.

"I do not know why they get so angry with each other," she muttered, looking off toward the wash as another excited, staccato rhythm of Navajo erupted from that direction.

"You think of your brother and the captive rather than this wool we are trying to dye," Quite Enough scolded. Then she relented. "Perhaps they love each other but are unable to acknowledge it."

Gray Eyes was surprised. "But they act as though they hate each other!"

"Not if you look very closely."

She scowled. It seemed preposterous, but then, what did she know of men? Only enough to know that they confused and troubled her, and she didn't want to think about them.

Nearly a moon had passed since she had slept that night in Canyon de Chelly. Hawk had been gone when she'd awakened in the morning. The only evidence that she hadn't dreamed his presence was the slab of antelope he'd left behind, and a quiver of finely crafted arrows with which to protect herself on her journey home.

It was just as well, she thought now. She hadn't wanted to see him again. All of their meetings seemed to end just like that one had, with his dark eyes forbidding and shuttered as he walked away from her. He didn't like her. She didn't like him. Shaking her head, she turned her thoughts back to the piñon gum.

But she had no sooner resumed her work when Yellow Horse approached. "It is time," he announced. "The other warriors approach. We must go now and meet them." Gray Eyes felt her concentration wash out of her again like a fallen tree being swept along by a strong current.

She had been dreading this moment for suns. The pale-eyes' deadline had passed and Sandoval had returned to Long Earrings' camp to renew Major Brooks' threat. The People would either have to turn Hawk over to the soldiers, or war would be declared against them. Warriors all over *Dinetah* would gather today and go to *Tsehotsohih* to see what Hawk and Manuelito had decided to do.

"The Hawk? Is he with the approaching warriors?" she asked hoarsely.

Yellow Horse shook his head. "We do not know what he has decided. You know that. You eavesdropped on our last council."

There was the slightest edge of disapproval in his voice, but Gray Eyes was too panicked to care. "Could you not see if he rides with his clan?" she demanded.

"They are too far away to tell."

Her heart dropped. She left him and Quite Enough abruptly and ran to the edge of the camp.

The sheep roamed industriously there, nosing for food beneath rocks and boulders. She shoved her way among them then stopped at the ridge, scanning the desert valley below. There were easily two hundred men gathered at the foot of the mountain, their blankets creating a riot of red and blue and gold. As she watched, Jackrabbit, Yellow Horse, Achi'i'h, and Na'acoci rode down to meet them. Vittorio was going as well. This time, the People would match headmen with headmen.

She sat down hard on the edge of the cliff, her heart pounding with fear as she watched them depart. She didn't know Wildcat had slipped up behind her until she spoke.

"I do not like these new white men," the girl muttered. "Each time our men go to speak to them, I fear they will not come home."

Gray Eyes nodded mutely as Wildcat sat down beside her, and together they watched until the warriors had disappeared from view, each set of eyes searching for a certain one.

Hawk was indeed among the men as they approached *Tsehotsohih*.

The sound of a bugle rose thin and strident in the afternoon air as the Indians gathered on the cliff. Shouts came from below, followed by the dull echo of boots hammering down on packed earth. Horses whinnied and rifles were engaged with a steady clicking that sounded throughout the valley. Then the warriors were moving again. Their ponies slid down the incline, all the headmen who were present maneuvering their mounts to form a line at the front.

They waited only a moment before the man Brooks emerged from the center building, talking in urgent undertones to another man who moved beside him.

There was no preamble this time. The second man threw out his challenge immediately.

"I am Lieutenant Colonel Miles. Major Brooks' request for military reinforcements has been honored. I have been ordered here by the adjutant general to lead raids against you should you so choose. Have you come to settle our differences, or do you come to make war?"

"We have nothing to gain by fighting you at this time," Manuelito responded.

Brooks' face settled into satisfied arrogance. There was a murmur from the crowd of soldiers as they relaxed.

Only Miles remained grim. "You're telling me that you've come to make restitution for the murder of the houseboy?" he reiterated.

Brooks' grin vanished. "For God's sake, don't provoke him!" he snapped. "That's what he said."

Miles made a sound of impatience. "Fool! What he said was that they won't fight us. Think, man! Do you trust these thieving savages enough to make assumptions?"

Brooks frowned. "Then talk to the old guy. He's the one I've been negotiating with and he seems honest enough. They call him Long Earrings."

Miles nodded and pointed a finger at the old headman to motion him forward. "You. Long Earrings. We'll negotiate directly with you."

There was a sudden surge of angry voices from the crowd of warriors. Hawk pushed through them suddenly and rode to his uncle's side.

"He points at you and condemns you to death by lightning!" he hissed. "He insults you by calling you by name. Who is this man? The captive belonged to the other one, the man Brooks. This man has no right to speak on the matter."

But Long Earrings only shook his head. "It is the way of these pale-eyes. Now retreat, my nephew, before they recognize you as the killer of their dark one. I will deal with this."

Hawk resisted, but he knew that he was more helpful to his people alive than dead. He finally turned away.

Dixon Miles wasn't at all sure he understood what had just happened, but his instincts told him to move on quickly. "We are demanding restitution," he repeated impatiently. "Your man has indicated that you are willing to give it."

Long Earrings adjusted the colorful blanket draped over his shoulders and nodded with cold dignity. "Yes," he answered. "When we have your word that there will be no war."

Miles hesitated, then nodded. "All right. Give us what we have demanded, and there will be no war."

"So be it."

A warrior broke free of the throng. He rode to Brooks and Miles, then unceremoniously shoved a long bundle off the back of his saddle.

Miles stared down at the brightly wrapped bundle. His sense of smell told him that it contained a dead man even while his mind refused to accept it. "You killed him?" he demanded after a moment.

The *hataali* took the question literally, as was the People's way. "I did not. It was Manuelito, the man you wronged once by killing his stock. Now he has sacrificed twice. First his horses, and now he has deprived himself of his own slave, something of equal value to your captive. An eye for an eye. The matter is settled."

"Damn you savages and your animal justice!" Miles bellowed. "He was to have stood trial!"

"Your trial is no longer necessary," Manuelito answered. "We have given my captive and my horses for the loss of your dark one. It is finished."

Brooks bent to unwrap the blanket, then came to his feet in rage. "They lie! Goddamned lying heathens!" He kicked at the body of the dead man. "This isn't the man who killed my houseboy. This is a Mexican! They've murdered a goddamned Mexican and now they're trying to pass him off as the man who killed my boy!"

Miles looked down at the corpse quickly. "What is the meaning of this?" he demanded of Manuelito.

But the war chief had turned his back on him. He had already answered that question to the best of his ability. Now he motioned for his warriors to go.

Miles gathered his voice and shouted, "Hold it right there! All of you!"

The warriors continued to move up the bluff.

Miles went on anyway. "Sufficient time has been given

you to seek, secure, and deliver up the murderer of Major Brooks' Negro and to atone for the insult to our flag. You have failed to do so. Our duty remains to chastise you into obedience to the observances of our land. After tomorrow morning war is declared against you!''

Chapter 9

K'aalo'gii wasn't at all convinced that war with the pale-eyes was as bad as everyone had made it sound.

True, it had forced the Lone Trees to move again; they were camped high on the icy northeastern slopes of the Chuskas. But they were relatively safe from marauding soldiers, and there was an abundance of game as well, more than K'aalo'gii had ever seen in one place. While the rest of the camp ate their evening meal and fretted over the hostilities, she had forgotten all about them. She was stalking a deer.

She had been tracking it for quite some time now, moving consistently further and further down the mountain. She followed a rustling in the tangled mountain growth that was quite different from the sound the October wind made when it blew through the bright gold aspens. Darkness fell hard before she heard a sound that didn't quite fit the rhythm of delicate hooves and snapping twigs. She stopped and cocked her head, listening intently to the vibration of movement far below her.

Riders, approaching from the south.

She forgot the mule deer instantly. Crashing now through the brush that she had slipped through silently the first time, she sprinted back the way she had come. She was shaking and out of breath when she ducked into her grandmother's shelter.

"We must hide!" she gasped before either Quite Enough or Vittorio could speak. "I hear horses approaching."

Vittorio pushed himself to his feet with a force that was

59

startling considering his girth. He collected the bow that hung near the hogan door, adjusted it quickly over his shoulder, and disappeared to gather the few able-bodied men the Lone Trees had left.

K'aalo'gii stood frozen, staring after him. Never before in her eleven summers had she seen her grandfather arm himself. Never before had she seen his lumbering body move so quickly. He was wise; he was powerful, but he left the raiding to the young.

But this was not merely a raid. It was war, and finally, horribly, it came to her that it involved more than just an adventure in a new and different land. Her heart hurtled into her throat as her grandmother prodded her.

"Warn the others," she commanded, and K'aalo'gii bolted out the door.

Gray Eyes began moving even before K'aalo'gii had fully delivered her message. She doused the cook fire with handfuls of dirt from the floor, then began grabbing sheep-skin bedding.

"We may not be able to return for a while," she said calmly. "We will need these to keep warm."

K'aalo'gii hesitated, feeling suddenly awkward. Gray Eyes was her friend, her cousin; she was the last person in the world she might expect to take charge. A shrill cry in the distance, a war cry, made her forget the disconcerting thought. Grabbing the bedding, K'aalo'gii dashed out the door.

Quiet Woman took her sheepskin less hastily. "We will go up to the grove of aspens," she decided. "From there we can see down into the camp."

"No."

She looked at her daughter, surprised but instinctively trusting her judgment. "Why?"

"There may be . . ." Gray Eyes swallowed carefully. "Perhaps something will happen here that we will not wish to see," she said, remembering the last *Naakai-idine'e'* raid when they had lost her sister. But not even the cold horror of that memory would prevent her from being among the first to see who was attacking their camp this time.

"We should go down the mountain," she finished. "Then we can see who it is as they approach."

She ran off without waiting for a response. When she came to a copse where she could peer out at the trail, she dropped to her belly to conceal herself. She spotted the riders almost immediately and came to her feet again with a joyous cry.

"It is our warriors!"

Then they were there, laughing and shouting as Vittorio and Black Spot brought up the rear. Only Black Spot looked disgruntled. Grumbling to himself, he dismounted near Little Left Hand's hogan and began to stalk off. Gray Eyes, who had run along behind their horses, was close enough to overhear him.

"Foolish boys. They should call out before they approach. They should warn us."

Vittorio moved heavily past him on his way to his wife's hogan. "You are only sour because you had to make your ancient bones move again," he chuckled. Then he thumped his brother-in-law heartily on the shoulder, totally disregarding the bones he had just mentioned. Black Spot gave a long-suffering sigh.

Everyone was in high spirits. Even Yellow Horse, so often grim and thoughtful, took a moment to tease K'aalo'gii about her hunting. Yet the cheerful banter died away all too soon. K'aalo'gii hadn't even finished protesting before Yellow Horse ducked into his mother's hogan. Gray Eyes hurried to catch up with Na'acoci, but she was too late. He too disappeared to hold council with Vittorio. She stood staring after him as a shadowy fear began pushing at the elation inside her.

Something was wrong. Something bad had happened. They had only returned home to apprise Vittorio.

She hesitated long enough to watch Achi'i'h and Jackrabbit move inside as well, then she hurried after them.

"You wish to help serve mutton or are you only here to

eavesdrop?'' Quite Enough asked. Gray Eyes latched on to the excuse. She carried a bowl to her grandfather and was immediately rewarded for her efforts.

"Tell me of this pale-eyes war," Vittorio prompted without observing the usual eating and banalities that preceded a council.

Yellow Horse obliged. "The blue-coats search the more accessible parts of our country in great numbers," he reported. "It it good that you brought our people here."

"You do not believe they will find us?"

Yellow Horse chewed thoughtfully. "No," he said finally. "Not unless they found and deciphered the signs you left for us at our summer camp to tell us where you had gone. But I destroyed them, and unless the Utes have reason to believe that they can count an easy coup here, I do not think they will lead the pale-eyes in."

Vittorio nodded. "Have all of our people hidden?"

"No. The Bitter Waters and their *hataali* stay in their homeland. And Manuelito has gone to *Kinlichi'i.*"

Vittorio's brows shot up. "They have separated?"

"Their band numbered in the hundreds. As they were, they provided a large, accessible target for the pale-eyes. The split was amicable, and in the best interest of their people. Long Earrings does not believe the pale-eyes will attack a man with whom they have no direct quarrel. Those who agree with him have stayed. Those who prefer a more aggressive stance have gone with Manuelito to settle right under the pale-eyes' noses."

"I suspect he will find the war before the war finds him."

Yellow Horse hesitated just a second too long. "I fear that has already happened."

There was a brittle and thin silence. Then Yellow Horse nodded in Na'acoci's direction. "I will let my nephew tell it," he finished. "He was there at the time."

Gray Eyes glanced at her brother, amazed. What had he been doing in Manuelito's camp without the other warriors? He was so young, only fifteen summers. He was untried. Yet even as she looked at him, she knew that that was no longer the case. Last spring, when he had ridden out with the Bitter Waters on his first raid, he had been a cocky, eager boy. Now he was still cocky, but his anger had grown and he seemed harder.

As she watched, he gathered his blanket around himself, taking the moment to collect his thoughts. "It was the new headman we met at the fort. Miles," he explained. "I believe he is after Manuelito more than he is the rest of us."

Vittorio frowned. "What more could these pale-eyes want from him?"

"Manuelito has become too powerful. The pale-eyes wish to break him."

Vittorio absorbed this. "Why were you with him?"

"His people do not hide like cowards. They fight back," Na'acoci answered belligerently. "The pale-eyes cannot attack our people because they cannot find us, so they go after our sheep, our corn fields, instead. When we know that they are coming, our men let themselves be seen. Then we hurry off into the canyons and they follow. The pale-eyes are stupid. Even those with Ute guides get lost. And so we save our corn fields, but we do not win the war."

"But this is our way. It has served us well for centuries," Vittorio said calmly. "You think Manuelito will do differently?"

Na'acoci nodded. "I do. And that is why I was with him when the pale-eyes came. They attacked at dawn there at the new camp at *Kinlichi'i* and burned the village to the ground."

"How many dead?"

"I cannot be sure. Six before I escaped. After that . . ." He trailed off and shrugged.

"What of Manuelito?" Vittorio asked.

"He lives. He killed the only pale-eyes of the raid, then he escaped unharmed."

Gray Eyes could no longer control herself. She stepped

suddenly, jerkily, into the circle of men. "What . . . what of Hawk?" she asked.

Na'acoci stared at her dumbly, surprised by her intrusion. Then he said, "I do not know what became of him."

"He was there? He was in Manuelito's camp when the raid occurred?" But she knew he must have been. He would not be content to herd sheep with Long Earrings while Manuelito fought for the honor of *Dinetah*.

"I cannot be sure," Na'acoci answered. "I did not see him while we were fighting. But that means nothing."

For a long moment, she only stared expressionlessly at the wall. Six dead. She felt as though her blood, the very part of her that kept her alive and warm, was draining out of her.

Hawk frightened her. He made her feel uncomfortable deep inside herself. But she knew that she wouldn't rest until she found out if he was one of those who had died.

Chapter 10

When the conversation had dwindled to personal exploits, and Vittorio's pipe was brought out and passed around, Gray Eyes slipped outside. The frigid air helped to clear her head. She had to speak to Na'acoci, she decided. She hunkered down beside the hogan and waited for him to head out to the ravine as he would inevitably have to do before long.

Jackrabbit and Yellow Horse had already made the trip before her brother finally emerged. "Where is your war chief now?" she demanded. Na'acoci jumped at the sound of her voice and spun back to face her.

"Do not sneak up on me so!" he snapped. "I have been poised for danger for weeks. I expect every voice behind me to be *Naakaiidine'e'*."

Gray Eyes nodded, but she was not to be deterred. "Where is he?" she asked again, getting to her feet.

Na'acoci shrugged. "Manuelito has vanished, but I suspect that he is somewhere near the pale-eyes."

"And you will search until you find him." It wasn't a question. She knew that he would scour each nook and cranny of *Dinetah* until he rejoined Manuelito and his band. Soon he would see Hawk or hear something of him, while she waited for word. The prospect was intolerable. It made something itch deep inside her.

"I wish to travel with you when you and the other warriors leave tomorrow," she announced suddenly.

Na'acoci was clearly shocked. "You wish to fight the pale-eyes?"

"No. K'aalo'gii would like to be a warrior, not I. I wish only to go as far as Long Earrings' camp."

He stared at her and she held her breath, praying that he would agree.

Instead, he shook his head hard. "There is much danger in the lowlands now. You know that. You are safe only here."

"But I cannot stay here."

"Why?"

He was pleading with her. Gray Eyes took a deep breath and closed her eyes. "I must find out what has become of the one who knew my name," she whispered. "His uncle will tell me."

He frowned as he struggled for another tactic. "You act crazy lately. Not like a girl should at all."

"Then perhaps I am not so much the girl any longer," she snapped. "I have had my *Kinaalda's*. I have found my medicine. And now I must know if the man who brought it still lives. Will you deny me this?"

She knew that she wasn't being fair to him. It was a man's duty to protect and care for his sister. But in this case he could not do both.

Finally, grimly, he shook his head. "Even if I wanted to do it for you, I could not do it to our mother. She has already lost a daughter. Would you have me help her lose another?"

Briefly, desperately, she searched his eyes. He would not be swayed. She saw that clearly now.

She felt a brief stab of betrayal. How could he refuse her when this was more important to her than each breath she took? But he didn't know that, couldn't know that, and as she watched him leave, she felt only grim determination.

She would defy him then.

She left three nights later even though fear mushroomed inside her each time she considered what she was

about to do. The valley would be crawling with pale-
eyes, just as Yellow Horse had said. And yet she had to
go.

Since she had spoken to Na'acoci she had had a dream
of blood and flames and fireballs. She knew, in a spot
deep inside herself, that something was terribly wrong.
Her medicine had told her so. Someone was in horrible
danger, and she was convinced that it was Hawk.

Her heart pounding, she felt around beneath her sheepskin until her hand fell on the bundle she had hidden
there. Then she eased clear of her bedding and crawled
toward the door without waking Quiet Woman or One
Whisker. She didn't stand up until she was well clear of
the hogan, then she sprinted up the slope toward the
herd.

The ponies and even the sheep were quiet as she inched
slowly among them. She was well within their midst
before they spotted her, and by then they were able to
recognize her scent. None of them sounded an alarm.

She made her way quietly to One Whisker's least fa-
vorite pony, an ugly piebald even older than she was.
She'd tossed the blanket she carried over his withers
and was digging in her pouch for his bridle when she
heard the bawl of a sheep, indicating that she wasn't
alone.

"Who is there?" she whispered.

There was no response. For a paralyzing instant, she
forgot her determination. She thought of wolf-men and
ghosts and the certain danger of darkness. Then she recognized K'aalo'gii's hushed and urgent voice.

Gray Eyes let out a harsh burst of breath that hung white
in the frigid air. "Over here," she called back quietly.

K'aalo'gii trotted to her side. "What are you doing?"

Gray Eyes hesitated. "I must travel to the camp of Long
Earrings."

"Through the night?" she asked incredulously.

Gray Eyes moved away from her. "Do not try to stop

me. If I would not obey my own brother, then I will not obey you.''

But K'aalo'gii shook her head. "Stop you? I was only thinking to give you my pony.''

Gray Eyes was speechless. K'aalo'gii had won the mare in a race against a warrior whose reputation would probably recover long before his pride. The pony was her most treasured possession.

"She is much faster than that bony old thing,'' K'aalo'gii went on, throwing an offended look at the piebald.

"No.'' Gray Eyes shook her head quickly. "I do not have far to go. The *hataali* still camps straight south of here, near *Tsehotsohih*. Even moving slowly, this pony will get me there before dawn.''

K'aalo'gii snorted. "I am not thinking of the length of your journey. I am thinking of the pale-eyes. Jackrabbit tells me that the soldiers have very large horses. They are fast.'' She moved back into the herd and whistled for her mare. The sleek black pranced up on white socks. "But I do not think even they could be as fast as this one,'' she finished proudly.

Gray Eyes hesitated, torn between reluctance and common sense. Then an image of her mother's face filled her mind, and she heard again Na'acoci's challenge. She had to return safe and unharmed, for both of their sakes.

She nodded. "I thank you, sister. I will honor her well, caring for her before I care for myself.'' She mounted and gathered the reins. "Sister?''

K'aalo'gii looked up at her expectantly.

"How did you know to find me here tonight?''

Her cousin grinned. "You have been acting very strange lately. I could not sleep for wondering what you were up to when I heard you leave the camp.''

Gray Eyes smiled tensely. "You are nosy, but I am glad.''

"I am also. I will tell Quiet Woman what you have done

in the morning. Now, before someone else awakes, you must go.''

Gray Eyes hesitated, then touched her heels to the pony and disappeared into the night.

Chapter 11

The journey to Long Earrings' camp was longer than Gray Eyes remembered. The night faded and still she found no sign of his people. The familiar silence that fell over the desert as the nocturnal animals crept off to their lairs suddenly seemed ominous to her. By the time the sun peaked in the sky, she once again began to feel the crippling, uncertain fear of being on her own.

Then, without warning, the little black mare spooked. Gray Eyes felt her heart leap into her throat. She grabbed her mane to steady herself as the mare veered sharply, going back the way they had come. There was a distant, acrid smell of smoke in the early morning air from which the pony was instinctively running.

Gray Eyes panicked. She reined the mare in and stared about wildly, but all she could see were fragments of her dream and an oily black cloud rising on the horizon. Flames. There had been flames in her nightmare. And she knew then, with sudden and sick certainty, that it was not Hawk for whom her medicine had told her to fear. It was the *hataali*.

She jerked the mare around again and beat her into a gallop.

She crested a low mesa and came suddenly upon the camp. For a moment she only stared, breathless, her blood roaring in her ears. Pale-eyes. They were everywhere. They veered around the hogans on huge horses just as K'aalo'gii had described. There were tall ones, thin ones, fat and squat ones. And one, amazingly, had the face of a sheep. Thick, woolly hair covered his jowls and hid his mouth. He chased a squaw as she raced wildly toward the hills, her long hair streaming.

Gray Eyes' breath came hurtling back to her in one thin scream. She crammed a fist against her mouth to silence herself and sent her pony hurtling down the incline because she could do nothing else. The *hataali* needed her.

A fireball whizzed past her head. It struck the hogan nearest her with an impossible impact, splintering wood and splattering pieces of mud and sod and twigs into her eyes. She ducked her head in pain just as her mare screamed and spun and dumped her on the ground.

She didn't see the white man on the giant horse bear down on her until she felt his hand in her hair. There was a jerk as she scrambled to her feet, then singing pain from her scalp as she was tumbled backward again. She landed hard and felt her breath being pounded free of her. She looked up to find his massive horse moving above her.

She didn't have the breath to scream again. She could only roll instinctively, grunting softly with the effort, as the strange hooves, big and shiny with round metal on their bottoms, rose up over her head. Terrified, she came to her knees to try to claw her way toward the nearby hogan.

The soldier began shouting words she couldn't understand.

"Hey, Hatch! We supposed to take captives?"

An answer rose up from the nightmare of exploding fireballs, crackling flames, and screams. "Miles only wants the chief! Find him and kill him!"

"Yeah, but what about all these squaws and kids?"

"Just grab them, for Christ's sake. We'll figure out what to do with them later."

Gray Eyes glanced wildly over her shoulder. Her gaze met that of the man with the sheep's face just as he leaped from his horse and moved toward her.

She launched herself to her feet with a surge of fury that defied the shortness of her breath. "Where is he?"

she hissed. "Where is the *hataali*? What have you done with him?"

The soldier chuckled and crouched slightly to move closer to her. "Easy there, little lady. I don't know what you're saying, so you might as well just quiet down. Hey!" For the first time he seemed to notice the color of her eyes and he straightened, startled. "Hey, Hatch! I think this one might be half white!" He turned to look for his captain.

Gray Eyes lunged at him with all the strength of her hatred.

She hit him hard at the waist, doubling over to drive her head into his gut. His breath left him in a stunned grunt. He staggered a few feet, but caught himself again all too quickly.

"Jesus! Ain't you the feisty one! White or no, you got plenty of savage in you, don't you?" His powerful hand shot out then, catching her solidly above her ear.

Gray Eyes felt her head snap back. There was a stinging, burning sensation along her scalp, a ringing in her ears.

"Should have used your brain, gal. You was all right until you hurt me." He reached for her again, his hand tangling in the long, unfettered cascade of her hair. Gray Eyes twisted and sunk her teeth into the fleshiest part of it, then lunged toward the pony herd.

K'aalo'gii's black mare stood there rigidly, her nostrils flaring, her eyes wild. Gray Eyes gathered the last of her breath and gave the whistle she had heard her cousin sound.

"Please," she whispered, "Let it work."

It did. The pony trotted toward her, and with the last of her strength, she flung herself up onto her back.

She landed hard on her belly just as the hairy hand closed around her ankle. She hugged the pony's neck and urged her on until it finally fell away.

She pulled herself upright and came to an abrupt stop. Her heart thumped crazily in her chest and her head swam.

All around her, flames leaped wildly from the hogans, filling the air with an acrid, stinging smell that burned her nose and brought tears to her eyes. She wiped at them furiously and squinted into the chaos as she began moving again.

She saw only pale-eyes. Long Earrings was either dead or he had escaped.

She trotted around the last of the smoldering hogans, fighting anguish that would surely debilitate her. Then she saw him. He was far ahead of her on an old roan pony. She started to call out to him when suddenly there was a roar of guns and she saw his body jerk.

A curdling howl ripped from her throat and she beat her pony into a gallop. He slid gently from his horse, landing in a cloud of dust even as she heard the call of a hawk from somewhere deep in her grief. But there was nothing in the heavens this time, only the memory of a fearless creature soaring cleanly, flying high. Suddenly she knew that her talisman would not come to her this time. He had already given her her gift. Now she would have to use it on her own.

Her fingers closed around the gold coin nestled in her gall bag. Taking a deep, ragged breath, she reached Long Earrings and dropped to the ground. There was a bellow from the soldiers as they spotted her. A rifle sounded and she saw a brief burst of fire from the corner of her eye. Air fluffed beside her cheek, but she was scarcely aware of it.

The *hataali*'s eyes were hooded, dark with pain. But he was alive.

"Please," she whispered as she struggled to lift him. "I need your help. You must find the strength. I cannot lift you alone, not quickly enough."

His eyes closed. His voice cracked. "You . . . have help, granddaughter." He paused for breath, and a bubble of blood broke at the corner of his mouth. "Listen. They come."

They come? She looked up in dazed exasperation. The

pale-eyes had nearly reached her. Was that what he was speaking of? Then she saw the dust boiling up from the side of the mesa, and heard the thunder of a pony herd racing across the earth. The Bitter Waters had gathered their mounts and were returning.

The last of the decimated clan rode wildly around them to shield them. Gray Eyes gave a soft cry and, grinding her teeth together, got her shoulder beneath the *hataali*'s armpit to push him onto her mare.

A second later she was behind him and galloping up the mesa. Turning her feverish face into the cold, hard wind, she searched the horizon. Behind her, the camp was ablaze. Ahead of her lay a country at war. There was only one safe place left to them. It was a long ride, a dangerous one, but she had no choice. She would take the *hataali* to Canyon de Chelly.

She swerved abruptly and headed north. Behind her, seventy people broke their circle unquestioningly to follow her.

Chapter 12

When she finally had the fire blazing around the large, flat rocks piled in the center of it, Gray Eyes left the sweat lodge and pushed her way past the layers of skins at the door. The men and women of the *hataali*'s clan moved about their new camp in the early morning sun. But the shouts and camaraderie that usually accompanied their chores were conspicuously absent. It had been only a week since the massacre. They were still in mourning for the four women and two young children who had been defenseless enough to provide a victory for the hapless, frustrated pale-eyes.

"Ta'che'e' ghohie'e'h!" she called, although she didn't truly expect anyone to accept the invitation to join her. The people milling about only ducked their heads as though embarrassed and went back to their chores.

Gray Eyes sighed shakily. As usual, the only people who would share her sweat bath this morning were the holy ones. She turned back to the lodge.

"They fear you, little one."

Her heart gave an odd little jump at the unexpected sound of Hawk's voice, then her pulse began to move like the irregular tattoo of a war drum. She looked around quickly to find him leaning lazily against a nearby cottonwood.

He was safe, alive! Her eyes skimmed over him hungrily. So many questions flew through her brain that she couldn't manage a single word.

"You look as though you are seeing a *chindi* spirit."

Was he laughing at her again? She raised her chin defensively just in case. "You cannot mock me for being startled to see you alive and in one piece. I had thought you might have been with Manuelito when his *Kinlichi'i* camp was attacked."

He looked down at her, disconcertingly touched. "Is that how you came to be with Long Earrings? You went to him to check on my welfare?"

She sidestepped the question. "Why are you here if you no longer live with the Bitter Waters?"

"Ah, but I am of the clan. I visit whenever there is a lull in our fight against these pale-eyes." He paused, watching her carefully. "While I was here, I wanted to seek you out to tell you that my heart thanks you for your bravery."

"Me?" Her eyes flew to his, wide and startled. "I have done nothing brave."

"You saved the life of my uncle, our *hataali.*"

"No! Your people did that. They covered me so that I could carry him to safety. Without them . . ." She trailed off as yet another image of Sheep Face leaped into her mind.

The explanation seemed to affect Hawk not at all. The dark, sun-touched skin around his eyes crinkled as he smiled. "This is why they avoid you, I am told, and why you take a sweat bath alone each morning. They honor your courage. They will not offend you by becoming too familiar. Also, your power frightens them." He paused, studying her more closely now. "It is said that a fireball touched you without harming you. Cornhusk Woman saw it."

She shook her head quickly. "No. It missed me."

He gave her a small, unconvinced smile. She turned away.

"Little one, why do you take so many sweat baths these days? My people tell me that you come here each morning."

A shudder of revulsion worked its way through her. "The *Naakaiidine'e'*," she whispered.

"I cannot hear you."

She whirled back to him. "A *Naakaiidine'e'*! He touched me. A horrid man with the face of a sheep."

"Touched you?" The amused crinkles around his eyes hardened.

"My hair." She touched it unconsciously, convulsively. "He grabbed my hair and he threw me to the ground. His hairy hand closed around my ankle. I must cleanse myself. I must get his poison out of me!"

Shaking, horrified anew by the memory, she turned back toward the sweat lodge, grabbed the hem of her shift, and jerked it over her head. She didn't see his dusky skin go suddenly pale.

Hawk stared at her trembling, naked form without moving. She would disappear soon. She had to. If there were Holy People, and he knew that there were, then they would spare him the sight of her this way. But she didn't disappear as he willed her to. She only struggled helplessly with the flaps over the door, too panicked to make sense of their numbers.

He had nearly managed to forget the torment of wanting her. But now the hunger whipped through him again, as though it had never been conquered. The strong, lithe muscles that did nothing to lessen her femininity . . . her slender darkness and flashing silver eyes. The impressions raged through him and he drew in a hoarse breath that seemed to echo in the camp's unnatural quiet.

Gray Eyes threw a startled look back at him. And he knew, suddenly and without question, that she still had no comprehension of what the sight of her did to him.

"Go!" he snapped, his frustration making his voice hard and cutting. "Take your bath. I have no more time to stand here chatting with a child."

Her eyes went wide with surprise and hurt. She turned again and fled into the sweat lodge, shaking even more than she had before.

* * *

When she finally returned to Long Earrings' hogan, Hawk was nowhere to be seen.

Their new camp was nestled in a half-moon curve of the canyon. The *hataali* sat rigidly against the trunk of one of the many cottonwoods there. His pain was too great for him to recline, but it didn't prevent him from noticing her furtive glances around the clearing.

"My nephew is gone," he volunteered in a hoarse voice that barely resembled his own.

Gray Eyes chose to ignore this confirmation of what she had already guessed. She dropped to her knees by his side. "You are in pain."

"Yes. But our next lesson in healing can wait." He collected his strength and went on. "My nephew told me that he found you taking yet another sweat bath. If you keep this up, granddaughter, your skin will shrivel and fall off."

She looked at him, alarmed, not sure if he was serious or not.

"What do you try to purge yourself of?"

She rocked back on her heels with a wretched sigh. She had come to know the *hataali* well enough by now to know that he would not be satisfied with evasions. "It is the pale-eyes' poison," she whispered. "It is inside me."

"Is it? Or is it only the fear and hatred you feel for them that is eating at you?"

Her heart jumped. She wondered if she would ever become accustomed to the way he could read her mind.

"Do you not have faith in your own medicine?" he persisted.

"I am not sure that it is as strong as everyone seems to think it is," she admitted. "Nor do I understand what it has to do with these pale-eyes."

He chuckled hoarsely. "Look at me, granddaughter. I am alive, speaking to you. While it is true that I have many holes in me, they heal. This is because of the knowledge I have recently passed on to you, and because of your power. Healing knowledge does not work in just anyone's hands. It requires the touch of someone with strong medicine.''

She frowned, but his argument was irrefutable. The pale-eyes' fireballs had caught him in the shoulder, the hip, and the belly. They had left horrid, bloody holes on both sides of him. But he had told her what to do for them, and she had done it. Now he was weak, but the sores were clean and they were healing.

Finally, grudgingly, she nodded.

''You have very strong medicine, granddaughter. What you must know now is that it can do so much more than heal.'' He paused. ''Long ago, when the pale-eyes first came to us, I dreamed of a woman with silver eyes. Silver is the color of the fine metal we have stolen from the *Naakaiidine'e'*, a metal that has stood us in good stead, that is used by both our people and our enemies. In some ways, it is a common bond between us. So shall be this woman with eyes the color of its fire. She will be a peace chief, I think. Like the metal, she will bridge a gap, an invaluable gap between war and peace, our enemies and ourselves. She will struggle to save those whom the pale-eyes allow to survive.''

His eyes pinned her then, in a way that pierced her soul and left her breathless. ''You, granddaughter, are that woman.''

She stiffened in denial. She was a headman's granddaughter. She knew what it was to be chosen, she knew the suffocating responsibility and selflessness it entailed.

''This disturbs you?'' In truth, he would have been alarmed if it hadn't.

''Your medicine tells you this?'' she asked softly, finally.

''No, granddaughter. You told me when you arrived at my camp during the raid.'' Although she looked in his direction incredulously, he smiled calmly. ''Several suns before that, warriors came to tell me of the attack on Manuelito's camp. I knew that word would soon spread to all of our clans. I knew, too, that the woman I dreamed of would not be content to sit by placidly and wait for more news. My dream also told me that, like the moon and the sun, this woman and my nephew are bound.''

Gray Eyes felt something quicken at her very core.

''She would risk death and danger to come to me,'' he went on. ''She would have to ask me if my nephew, if the moon to her sun, was with Manuelito and if he was still alive. Is that why you came to my camp, granddaughter? What did you come to ask me?''

Gray Eyes wanted to deny the words. She wanted desperately to swallow them. An uncharacteristic anger surged through her. ''You say we are bound. You say that he will be chief, and that I am destined to lead our people as well. This frightens me, but I believe you. But I know also that your Hawk hates me. You cannot tell me that it is not so!''

Long Earrings chuckled. ''It is just that the sun and the moon dwell in different skies, granddaughter, and too often they find it frustrating. It is their destiny to chase each other across the heavens. Once, when I was young, I saw them catch each other. They matched up perfectly as they shone down upon Mother Earth. It was a magnificent sight, but such a thing happens rarely. Too often, they are apart.'' Carefully, he adjusted his weight against the tree and smoothed his blanket over his shoulders.

She shook her head, frustrated, wanting to hear more. But his pain was too great for him to go on. ''You remember the prayers I taught you to say before you pluck the plants we use for medicine?'' he asked.

Gray Eyes nodded. ''I remember.''

''Then you must use them to go and bring me some *niits'oosiitsoh,* some prairie clover. I need relief from this hurt.''

Pushing to her feet, she went off to collect the plants. Long Earrings was still by the tree when she returned. She knelt beside him again.

''Grandfather,'' she whispered, and his eyes opened. ''I

have not used this herb before. You must tell me what to do with it."

Behind her, Barren Woman, his first wife, spoke. Her words were harsh, as was her way, but her tone ached with concern and love for this man who had shared her lifetime. "Yes, old man," she urged. "Tell her, and quickly."

Long Earrings nodded. "First you must cut off the roots. Then chop them. Mix them with the leaves and boil them. It should not take long."

She did as she was told. Moments later, she dribbled the concoction into the *hataali*'s mouth.

"This will heal your wounds?" she asked, eager to know. "How?"

But the *hataali* shook his head. "It is for the pain. It is for badness inside one's body. It also works in the Enemy Way ceremony to banish the results of witchcraft." He sighed and closed his eyes again. A placid look began to replace the tight, uncomfortable expression on his face. Gray Eyes glanced down at the brew in her hands, awed.

It had worked. She had created it, she had administered it, and now this man she was coming to love and respect was spared his pain.

"Should I sing now?" she asked, looking back at his calm face.

"Yes. You remembered. That is good."

"Which chant?"

"You tell me, granddaughter."

She thought about it, struggling to recall everything he had taught her in the last week. "I think . . . perhaps the Song of the Earth Spirit?"

He smiled, satisfied. "That would be the perfect chant."

She began softly, reverently. "It is lovely indeed, it is lovely indeed. I, I am the spirit within the earth. The feet of the earth are my feet. The legs of the earth are my legs. The strength of the earth is my strength. The thoughts of the earth are my thoughts. The voice of the earth is my voice. The feather of the earth is my feather. All that belongs to the earth belongs to me. All that surrounds the earth surrounds me. I, I am the sacred words of the earth. It is lovely indeed, it is lovely indeed.''

She repeated the chant three more times, once for each of the sacred mountains. When she finished, she looked down at him. ''Are you well now?''

But he didn't answer. He was smiling beatifically, sound asleep and at peace.

Chapter 13

The snows came early that winter of 1858–59. They arrived in December, *Nichi'tso'*, the moon of the Great Wind. When Gray Eyes left the long, narrow tunnel of Long Earrings' doorway, she had to clutch her blanket closely against the bitter cold. She hurried across a shallow wash to duck into a hogan on the other side, the one she shared with the *hataali*'s youngest wife and their daughter. A fire was burning and she hunkered down beside it to warm herself.

For a long time the only sound was the crackle of the flames and the others' deep breathing. Then soft, satisfied noises began coming from the hogan she had just left, as they had nearly every night of the two moons she had been in the *hataali*'s camp. Gray Eyes tried to ignore them, but each sigh, each moan, made her feel more uncomfortable and edgy.

She knew what Long Earrings and Barren Woman were doing. She wasn't totally ignorant of the ways between men and women. She'd watched through the years as Vittorio had gravitated between Little Left Hand's hogan and that of his first wife. She'd heard the jokes and the gossip when Sleepiness had married the renowned Achi'i'h but she'd never given any of it a second thought.

Until now. Now the thing that Long Earrings did with his wives seemed darkly mystifying. Thoughts of it both titillated and frightened her.

As though to mock her confusion, laughter began drifting from the hogan nearby. Gray Eyes leapt to her feet, grabbed her blanket again, and bolted out the door.

She'd intended to put as much distance between herself and Barren Woman's hogan as possible. Instead, she found herself drawn to it. Firelight flickered behind the hides at the door, and shadows moved there slowly and gently. With a small cry, she pressed her palms to her eyes.

"You do not feel so old and wise now, do you, my husband's granddaughter?"

The voice was coarse but not altogether unkind. Gray Eyes jumped then looked up to find that Barren Woman had stepped out of the hogan.

"It is to be expected," the older woman went on, dropping down onto the bank of the wash to light the pipe she occasionally smoked.

"It is?" Gray Eyes echoed, feeling uncertain and stupid. "Why?"

"You know much. My husband has taught you and you have great medicine." She broke off to puff in silence for a moment. "But I suspect that you are a babe yet in many ways."

A babe? After all she had been through since the last full moon? Indignation rose in Gray Eyes' throat but Barren Woman only chuckled quietly.

"Do not let it trouble you. There are some lessons that even our *hataali* cannot teach you. But someday you will find one who will. Be patient. He will turn up soon and then you will understand."

"But I want to understand now," she complained.

The old woman merely shrugged as she emptied her pipe against the earth. "I cannot help you. You must wait for the man who makes your blood run fast and your breath fall short." She chuckled again, and the sound was deep and private this time. "There is one like that for all of us, child. Whoever he is, you will join with him perfectly and there will be no fear. With all others," she finished thoughtfully, "there is usually pain, if only in the heart."

She shrugged again, then moved stiffly toward her hogan. Gray Eyes opened her mouth to call her back. But the first snow of the season had begun to fall, and soon the old woman was lost in it, disappearing into a cloud of swirling white.

"Blood and breath," she muttered aloud. "This tells me nothing."

Then, suddenly, her heart moved into her throat and she gasped. Because even as she stared into the snow, Hawk's face came to her, a face she sometimes hated, sometimes feared, but one that always affected her. She shook her head in disbelief and raced back to her hogan.

The snow stopped the next day but the canyon remained silver-white and sparkling in the sun. Gray Eyes sat with Long Earrings beneath the cottonwoods, wrapped in her blanket. The *hataali*'s wizened face was creased even more deeply than usual as he concentrated on the body of a gutted dove that he was wrapping tightly in beads and red wool. Gray Eyes watched him out of the corner of her eye as she practiced taking short, accurate shots with the bow he had made for her and the arrows that Hawk had gifted her with.

The quiet morning was suddenly shattered by the sound of hoofbeats. Gray Eyes jumped to her feet, her pulse pounding furiously, even though she knew that it couldn't be soldiers. No white man had ever mastered the intricacies of the canyon's slopes to enter there. The sound of hoofbeats could mean only one thing. "The Bitter Water warriors are returning!"

Then, even as they came along the ice-covered river, looking thin and gaunt yet somehow triumphant, an uncharacteristic shyness gripped her. If Hawk was among them, she didn't want to face him. She had so many questions now about the nature of the bond between them.

"I will go tell your wives so that we can prepare food," she announced quickly and ran off to the safety of Barren Woman's hogan.

At the doorway she stopped, peering past the edge of

the sod to search for a rider in black. But all the men rode in on gaily colored blankets that flapped wildly against their ponies' rumps. Their high-held lances were adorned with decorative tails and birds and silver that whipped in the wind. They drove a noisy herd of horses ahead of them. None of them rode like the dark wolf-man who had once descended upon her out of the night.

Then, just when she was sure he didn't accompany them, there was a wild whoop from around the curve of the massive walls and Hawk's big bay stallion galloped smoothly and surely over the canyon floor. Gray Eyes stared at him, then yelped as Barren Woman poked her in the ribs.

"There is no time now for you to contemplate life's mysteries," she said gruffly. She pushed a large blanket filled with ground cake into her arms. "Take this to the fire pit. There are many of them and they will all be hungry."

Gray Eyes hesitated, but the warriors were still in a far reach of the canyon. She could make it to the pit and back again by the time Hawk arrived.

Clutching the bread to her breasts, she left the hogan. The heavy, woolly aroma of roasting mutton had already begun to fill the air. People rushed around busily. She dodged them until one of the precious sheep they had saved from the raid was dragged by in front of her. Then she had to stop to let it pass and when she looked up, the warriors were upon them.

They drove the horses into a corral on the far side of the stream. The animals were pale-eyes' horses with silver on their hooves, just like Sheep Face's mount.

Gray Eyes forgot Hawk and ran the rest of the way to the fire pit where everyone was gathered.

". . . right from the corral at their fort!" one of the warriors called. "They slept. They awoke this morning to find them gone."

The loud guffaws of laughter tapered off as the *hataali* stepped among his people. "I would speak to the man whose coup this was," he ordered.

The crowd parted and Hawk rode up to Long Earrings. "I stole them, my uncle," he answered, "with the help of some brave men. It is my gift to my mother's people."

Long Earrings' shoulders went rigid. "I wish no such gift," he replied. "It can only bring trouble."

Hawk's eyes narrowed. "Trouble has already found you, my uncle. I wish only to send it on its way again."

Long Earrings sighed and his annoyance seemed to slide out of him with the sound. "I cannot argue that. But I must caution against instigating these pale-eyes further."

"They need no instigation beyond their own craziness," Hawk scoffed. "They raided your home and took your ponies. Many of your people no longer have mounts. I have merely replaced what was stolen. I only wish I could replace the lives we lost as well."

He paused, and for a brief moment, he looked dangerous. His black eyes glittered with tangible hatred for his enemy. Then, without warning, they swiveled away from his uncle and fell on Gray Eyes.

There was a moment when she was sure that every voice in the camp faded. She sensed the crowd milling around her, felt an unseen elbow jostle her as someone tried to push past. But she didn't hear them. *Your blood will run fast and your breath will fall short,* Barren Woman had said. She dropped the bread with a soft cry and shouldered her way blindly through the crowd.

Night fell quickly. Gray Eyes sat close to the fire in Barren Woman's hogan, refusing to move. Shouts of merriment filled the air outside as the Bitter Waters celebrated the return of their horses. Drums pounded and there was singing. She ignored it all until she heard footsteps outside.

"You are not so tense as you were last time you visited, my nephew. You are a warrior indeed if you can gain such satisfaction from one victory," said the *hataali*.

Gray Eyes stiffened as she realized that he was speaking to Hawk. She crept closer to the door.

"It has been a day of many victories," came the reply.

"You speak of the one with the silver eyes?" There was no answer. "She has done much growing this winter and not always easily," the *hataali* went on. "But I would caution you to be certain before you call a coup. Surely you can see that, at the moment, she is nowhere to be found. She is hiding from you."

Hawk laughed, a quiet, satisfied sound. He had noticed. But he had noticed, too, the stunned and very aware look she had given him before she had run away. Her medicine was indeed growing, and her maturity was growing with it. She would come to him soon. He laughed again, confidently.

Long Earrings gave a cluck of disapproval. "If you will have her, then I think you will have to pay her well to become your first wife," he warned. "She is not like your others. She is different, special."

Hawk looked at him, startled. Then he laughed again. "As you once bought Barren Woman? Do not wish that on me, uncle!"

Both men laughed this time.

"The little gray-eyed one is as unmanageable as your first wife and just as stubborn," Hawk went on. "I would have to go out and buy two more wives, just like you, to keep my sheepskins from becoming cold when she is angry or feels that she must follow her own mind. No, my uncle, I cannot afford that. I have no plans to take a wife, not like that one."

There was more laughter, then the *hataali* sobered. "No," he agreed. "Not yet, not now."

Silently, shakily, Gray Eyes moved back to the fire. She didn't hear Hawk's response. She hugged herself and stared at the *at'sii*, the sheep's head, cooking slowly over the flames.

Was Barren Woman the fool, or was it only she who was stupid? She bit her lip. Fool or not, she would not cry. How could she, when she wasn't even surprised? She'd never been under the impression that Hawk liked her. Despite the way he made her feel, he would not be willing to teach her any of a lover's secrets.

They were talking about the war now. She left the fire to crawl stealthily toward the door again, her pride forgotten.

Long Earrings' voice was thoughtful. "Perhaps it is not too much to hope that the pale-eyes will give up soon."

Hawk hesitated before he answered. "It is a hope many of our clans are beginning to share. Our people are hungry. Our warriors cannot fight the pale-eyes and hunt too. Our women are forced to slaughter their sheep to eat. Next year we will have to do extra raiding to replace them."

"And that will bring another outcry from the pale-eyes. It would appear to be an endless circle."

Gray Eyes heard the harsh anger in Hawk's voice. "They are crazy. Manuelito is right. We must defeat them. We must keep fighting at all costs."

"The cost you speak of may be our children. Not all of our clans have many sheep to slaughter, and they cannot exist entirely on corn. Their young may starve before it is time to raid again. Perhaps there is a better way."

Gray Eyes leaned further into the doorway to watch Hawk glance at the *hataali* guardedly. "What do you suggest?"

"That perhaps we should give the pale-eyes an opportunity to give up. I will go to the fort," the *hataali* decided. "I will speak again with this man Miles. I do not believe that they knew they were raiding a peace chief when they attacked my last camp. If I go to them in the name of peace, I think they may take the excuse to give up. Then you and others like you can feed our women and children. There will be no need for raiding next year if we can stop this craziness now."

Hawk considered this, then finally nodded. "There will always be a need for raiding, for the Utes and the *Naakaiidine'e'* will always raid us. But perhaps you are right. We could return to hunting for a while to preserve our flocks and our children."

He got to his feet and moved away from the hogan. He wore dark, fringed leggings and a loincloth, but he was naked above the waist despite the frigid cold. Gray Eyes' stomach tightened at the way the firelight played on the long, bronzed lines of his muscles.

"I will leave with the sun to see if I can find other headmen to back you," he continued. "I do not think Manuelito will do so, but it may work if we have enough others. For now, though, I think I will join in this celebration." He glanced back with a smile. "Believe me, my uncle, it has indeed been a good day."

He was so smug! Anger twitched inside her. Before she knew she was going to, Gray Eyes scrambled out through the door opening.

"Yes," she contributed. "I have learned much."

For a moment, Hawk's smile faltered. Then as her chin came up with all of the defiance he remembered, he threw back his head and laughed.

"Eavesdropping again, little one?" He chuckled. "Perhaps you would have been more comfortable if you had simply joined us."

She rose to the challenge. "And would I have heard anything different if you had been speaking to my face? Would you have called me something besides unmanageable and stubborn?"

His eyes found hers in the darkness and he sobered. "No. I always speak the truth to you, even when it appears to be less gentle than a lie. I do not want a wife, little one. And in any case, you are one I could ill afford." And suddenly, looking at her brilliant eyes, he knew how very true that was. Her power over him would be depthless, more dangerous than any *Naakaiidine'e'* foe. He wanted her ceaselessly, as he had wanted no other before her. If he ever took her, she would burn through him to the very depths of his soul. She would sap his power. She would block his mind. He would be able to think of nothing but possessing her again and again.

Tread carefully, a voice inside him cautioned. Disturbed, he turned away from her rudely.

In spite of herself, Gray Eyes winced. A sharp pain caught her deep in her middle. There would be a man to teach her all the secrets between men and women, but it would not be this one who made her senses react crazily. He had brought her her medicine, and he had made it clear that he would offer her nothing more.

She gathered her dignity around her and turned back to the *hataali.* Her expression was calm, her eyes haughty. The old man watched her, a sad, knowing smile in his eyes.

"Grandfather," she managed in a thin voice. "I think it is time for me to go home."

Chapter 14

When the last sheepskin was firmly secured behind the last kettle, Quiet Woman heaved a sigh and pulled herself up onto the mare as well. All around her in the mountain hideout ponies jostled for space as they, too, were loaded with the clan's possessions. The war was over and Vittorio's people were going home.

As Quiet Woman looked around the mountain clearing for the last time, she saw her daughter lead up the ugly little piebald that would have seen her through the raid on Long Earrings' camp had it not been for K'aalo'gii's generosity. "I think I should take this one," Gray Eyes announced.

Quiet Woman glanced at the pony and lifted a brow. "We will not see you again until long after the *Yebichai* is over." Before going to their old valley home, they would visit at the camp of the Towering Rock people to celebrate a Night Chant. Part of the ceremony would include Gray Eyes' first initiation. It was one of four, and necessary if she were to be respected as a medicine woman. Their warriors would meet up with them there as well.

Gray Eyes gave a fleeting smile. "No, Long Earrings would never forgive me if I did not show up." Still, there was the matter of the gelding. "I am afraid that if no one rides this old man, he will never get there," she explained. "Someone needs to be on his back to spur him along."

Quiet Woman shrugged, knowing it would be useless to

argue with her. "Have your way then," she answered. "I will see you when you get there."

Gray Eyes nodded her agreement, then mounted the old pony to go in search of Wildcat and K'aalo'gii. She would ride with them, she decided. As long as she had company, distressing thoughts and memories would be kept at bay. Two moons had passed since she had left Long Earrings' camp, but the sting of Hawk's parting words stayed as close as her heart.

She shook her head angrily as she looked for her cousin and the captive. What did she care about his opinion of her? Long Earrings had said that they were bound, but even he had not argued that they would get along well together. As for Barren Woman's opinion, if she were all that wise, she, too, would be a *hataali*. The headman had been right; his wife had been wrong. That was all there was to it.

She squared her shoulders as she nudged the piebald down the incline. Wildcat and K'aalo'gii were teasing each other when she caught up with them.

"Is your voice strong enough, sister?" K'aalo'gii asked Wildcat. "You have not had much practice shouting lately, except at the sheep."

Wildcat flushed prettily. "Na'acoci can be so maddening I do not have to practice to shout at him."

"And, of course, you are not looking forward to having him underfoot again," Gray Eyes heard herself join in.

Wildcat's eyes sparkled as she considered this. "No," she lied agreeably. "It has been peaceful without him."

"Peaceful for the rest of us, maybe." K'aalo'gii giggled. "We would never hear the quiet again if the two of you married."

This time the *Moqui* blushed scarlet. "He has never offered me anything to be his wife."

"He will," Gray Eyes mused. She had been watching the horizon, but was suddenly uncomfortably aware that both girls were staring at her expectantly.

"No, I do not say this because of my medicine!" she

snapped irritably. Then her attention drifted to Wildcat. "You do not fear him, sister, or what he might do to you in your sheepskins?"

"I would rather hunt up something for our evening meal than talk about marriage and sheepskins," K'aalo'gii grumbled. Adjusting her quiver over her shoulder, she nudged her mare and they galloped off.

When she was gone, Wildcat looked at Gray Eyes speculatively. "Why do you ask such a question, my sister?"

Gray Eyes shrugged stiffly, wondering why she had ever brought it up.

"Is it because there is someone you wish to lie with?"

The question, so simply put, made every nerve in her body twitch and tighten. But Gray Eyes shook her head vehemently. "No." Then she muttered, "And there is no one who wishes to lie with me."

Wildcat was silent for a moment, then she laughed. "I think I should tell you the answer then, just in case. I do not fear your brother because he cannot hurt me." She hesitated, searching for the Navajo words that were still sometimes difficult for her. "He would not need to cause me pain because I would be willing," she finished thoughtfully, then blushed again. "When he is near, my heart beats so fast, I—"

But Gray Eyes had heard enough. Chagrined, she nudged the arthritic old pony into a canter.

She reached the camp of the Towering Rock people well after dark and, thanks to the plodding piebald, far behind the others. Easily two hundred people had gathered for the chant, and most of them buzzed around the cook fires of the respective clans. She found Quiet Woman, Talks Often, and Wildcat roasting a big pronghorn in a camp near the edge of the village.

Her mother sliced off a piece of the antelope and handed it to her. "Here," she said. "Eat before you wander off. You grow too skinny."

Gray Eyes nodded absently and dropped down beside

her. But she scarcely tasted the antelope. Her gaze skirted the village restlessly as she chewed. There was no sign of Hawk. Would he be here? Of course he would. He was an honored warrior, and this was an important ceremony, both medicinally and socially. She wished she could be sure of his whereabouts. She didn't want to see him, she told herself; she only wanted to know where he was so she could avoid him.

But instead of locating him, she found herself staring straight into the eyes of another warrior.

Startled, she dropped the piece of meat. He was beside her in a moment. He smelled, not unpleasantly, of smoke and sweat as he kneeled to retrieve the antelope for her.

"I apologize," he murmured. "I did not mean to be rude. I meant only to catch your attention."

"No. It was not your error. I was . . . looking for someone." He brushed the food off and handed it back to her. She looked down at it blankly, her appetite gone.

"It does not look as though you need to eat this dirty piece of meat," he observed slyly. "Your man has provided well for you."

"My man?" She glanced up again, confused. He nodded at the roasting antelope. "Oh, no. My cousin made the kill."

"That is good news." He smiled roundly, satisfied. "I am of the Suddenly Crazy clan, born for the Big Deer people."

"And I am of the Lone Trees, born for the Red Goats," she answered automatically. The People always introduced themselves to strangers by identifying both their mother's people and their father's. In the event that they were somehow related by clan, it would help to avoid a dangerous, embarrassing mistake before a romantic overture was made.

Belatedly, Gray Eyes' heart gave a startled little jump. Ducking her head, she looked at the Suddenly Crazy warrior more closely.

His onyx eyes were more rounded and less intimidating

than Hawk's. He appeared neither as tall as the one who
had brought her her medicine, nor as well-muscled. But
he was pleasant enough to look at, she decided dispassionately. She waited for her body to react, for it to tell
her that this was the sort of man Barren Woman had spoken of. But nothing happened.

The warrior straightened and stood over her. "I will go
then, beautiful Lone Tree," he announced. "You can find
me later where my clan camps." She watched as he rejoined a group of warriors at the next fire.

"They call him *Tl'iish A'ni'ni'gi'i*," Quiet Woman volunteered. "Rattlesnake. I have heard of him." She paused,
watching her daughter carefully. "Will you approach him
later?"

Gray Eyes nodded, then shook her head. "Yes. No. I
do not know." Abruptly, she scrambled to her feet. The
cold piece of antelope fell once again into the dirt.

She wandered off into the village. Vittorio, Quite
Enough, and Little Left Hand had apparently exhausted
their social curiosity; she spied them huddled in their blankets near the medicine lodge, waiting for the chanting to
begin. Yellow Horse, Jackrabbit, and Na'acoci stood
nearby. But as she watched, Na'acoci left the group and
moved around to the Lone Trees' fire. There he took a
piece of meat and dropped down onto his haunches next
to Wildcat. The *Moqui* smiled, despite the fact that, for
all appearances, he was ignoring her.

Gray Eyes smiled too, finding it hard to believe that she
had ever misread her brother's behavior. Then she stepped
around the medicine hogan and her breath caught in her
throat. Standing outside, clad only in a loincloth and leggings and grinning at her rakishly in the red-gold light of
the flames, was Hawk.

Before she could react, he pushed away from the lodge
and moved infinitesimally toward her. "You seem to be
enjoying yourself, little one," he observed.

"I was," she allowed deliberately.

Just as he had that night outside Barren Woman's hogan,

he threw his head back and laughed. "You mean before I appeared?" he asked.

"You are not always pleasant to be around."

"Pleasantries can often be boring."

She shrugged carefully.

"Are you trying to tell me you prefer boredom, little one?" His voice dropped suddenly, becoming soft and husky as he watched her. "Do you prefer that tired little gelding I saw you ride in on over your cousin's sleek black mare? He is pleasant, I would guess. He moves slowly, comfortably, with none of the spirit of the other. Is that why you ride him?"

He paused, and she stared down at her toes. She couldn't answer. She was sure that no matter what she said, he would twist it to make it sound foolish.

But he did nothing of the kind. Instead, for the first time since she had met him, he touched her gently, with no mockery at all.

He reached for her the way night closed over the desert at the end of a winter's day, smoothly and without warning. And like the day, she felt as though she would melt completely when his fingers brushed her throat.

"I think not, little one," he murmured, so quietly that no one else could hear. A sense of unreality gripped her as people slid past them without noticing anything out of the ordinary. How could they not see that her pulse was pounding at her temples and that her head felt as light as the air? But they didn't; they only swam around her, jostling and pushing until she was so close to him she could smell the wild, masculine scent of him. She began to tremble.

"No," he went on, "not you. You will not be content until you soar like the hawk, until you ride like the wind. When you are ready, little one, I hope in spite of myself that you have figured out where to find those things."

For a fraction of a second, his fingers remained on her skin. She stood motionless beneath them, every nerve in her body alert, keen, waiting. Then he dropped his hand and turned away.

Her breath returned to her in a sudden, almost painful rush. She stared after him, feeling stunned and disoriented. He didn't like her. He had said as much to the *hataali*. And yet . . .

She moved back into the crowd vacantly, unable to believe that life had really been as simple once as riding a piebald pony.

Chapter 15

The Night Chant didn't begin until well after the moon had left the sky. Then the pounding of drums began to vibrate in the air. Long Earrings' voice rose and fell eerily from within the shadows of the medicine hogan.

Gray Eyes moved closer to it as three masked figures emerged, dressed only in loincloths. They represented *Haschelti,* Talking God, *Haschebaad,* Goddess, and *Haschelapai,* Gray God. As she watched, determined to memorize every movement, they danced around the hogan in the first of the rituals designed to heal the Towering Rocks' sick brother.

Suddenly, something about Haschelti caused Gray Eyes to straighten. Her eyes narrowed, then slid down to the tight, flexing muscles of the dancer's buttocks and thighs. She knew of no other man who could move like that, fluidly but contained, gracefully yet controlled. It had to be Hawk.

She leaned forward unintentionally as the *hataali* emerged from the hogan and began to sing in earnest. But her gaze lingered on Haschelti as he waved his ceremonial sticks over the patient's body. His voice was strong, vibrating with power, as he gave his chant. Gray Eyes felt her skin rise in gooseflesh.

As Haschebaad and Haschelapai gave their own performances, the pounding rhythm of their chants became the very measure of her heartbeat. Then, abruptly, silence fell. Haschelti took a shell filled with medicine and carried it to the patient. He gave him four sips before handing the shell back to Long Earrings. The *hataali* swallowed the little bit that remained. The first night of healing was over.

The people broke the silence with shouts and cheers as two of the dancers began moving back toward the hogan. But Haschelti stopped at Gray Eyes' feet, his fierce mask glaring down on her. Adrenaline coursed through her veins as her eyes met the depthless holes in his mask. Then he pulled it off with a quick jerk, and his lips parted in an arrogant smile.

Suddenly, she was sure he knew she had been staring at him all the while.

She was still acutely aware of him by the ninth and last sacred night of the chant. But by then, his gaze was strangely comforting.

It was time for her initiation. She was shivering when Quite Enough slipped inside the medicine hogan to find her. She was naked beneath the huge blanket she wore, as the holy ones had dictated. But far more than her nakedness had her teeth chattering together.

"Does it hurt?" Her voice cracked on the last word.

"You talk nonsense, granddaughter. How would I know? Am I a medicine woman?" She took her by the elbow and pulled her outside. But although her words were impatient, her touch was gentle. She was bursting with pride. So few girl children were initiated into the order of the *Yeibichai*.

The flames outside threw wild light over Gray Eyes' pale face. To her panicked eyes, it seemed to be the largest, fiercest fire she had ever seen. Quite Enough led her up to it and she knelt as she had been coached to do. Then her grandmother faded off into the background and the drums and singing began, one thumping, one ululant.

With her head bowed, she could see only the moccasined feet of the dancers as Haschelti, Haschebaad, and Haschelapai approached again. She concentrated on the feet of Haschelti and willed her heart to stop beating so hard and fast. She was terrified that she would disgrace herself and faint. The heat from the flames beat at her and the drum rolls seemed to resound in her brain. But Hawk was Haschelti and she clung to that. He teased her; he confused her. But at least he was familiar, a known quantity.

Suddenly, he stopped in front of her. His voice came so softly she almost couldn't hear him.

"Do not look so stricken, little one. It is not as bad as it is for the boys."

Her head jerked. For one perilous moment, she nearly forgot all the *hataali* had taught her and looked up at him, her heart and all her gratitude in her eyes. But she caught herself in time and went rigid.

What had he meant by 'not as bad'? The boys were stripped naked in front of the entire crowd and flogged with yucca leaves. Oh, if only he could have told her more!

But the next thing she heard from him was a soft chuckle coming from behind her. Even as it sounded, she felt something soft tickling the soles of her feet and she twitched so noticeably that she was sure everyone had seen it. Then another dancer appeared in front of her, and he tilted her chin upward to sprinkle her face with the sacred pollen as well.

And then, miraculously, it was over. The people hooted and cheered and Quite Enough came back, helping to pull her to her feet. Gray Eyes looked around dazedly, but the dancers were gone now.

She looked out at the crowd and felt a hot flush of pride. Although young and untried, although she would have to undergo different initiations by the *hataali* and her grandfather, she was a medicine woman now.

The visiting clans began to depart early the next morning. Gray Eyes stood alone on a small sandy knoll just outside the village and watched the processions of ponies stretch away into the distance. Hawk was among them somewhere. She had seen him leave, although he had not said good-bye to her.

Behind her in the camp, a few bands remained, and Gray Eyes suspected that last night's peyote had as much to do with it as the People's inherent dislike of keeping to a schedule. Barboncito, Delgondito, Long Earrings, and Vittorio had all stayed on to share a sweat bath and a smoke with Agua Chiquito, the Towering Rock headman. When the caravans of ponies were so distant that they looked like ants meandering among the sage and mesquite, Gray Eyes left the knoll and went to join them.

For a long time they only talked of the latest treaty.

"Who is this man Bonneville?" Barboncito demanded. "He is not the man who started the war. What right had he to end it?"

It was a rhetorical question. He knew who Bonneville was as well as Gray Eyes did. He was the man the pale-eyes had chosen to be their headman in "new" Mexico after the war had started. He, Miles, and another man named Collins had bickered incessantly among each other when Long Earrings had instigated the peace negotiations. Miles had been ready to end the war. Collins and Bonneville had been infuriated at such cowardice. They had wanted to continue until the People had suffered as much as possible for their transgressions, both real and exaggerated. In the end, they had had their way even though the war was stopped.

"Rights is a pale-eyes word," Delgondito grumbled. "It means that they were justified in stealing the eastern third of *Dinetah* that they have coveted for so long. They will not have to send their sheep in there illegally any longer. It is theirs now."

"And what of the clans living there?" Barboncito demanded.

"They will leave their burial grounds and their grazing lands to go west toward the land of the Dead Ones. But even that offers them little protection. Did you notice there was no stipulation in the treaty that our enemies cannot enter *Dinetah*? It says only that we may not leave our new boundaries."

"I am beginning to think of siding with Manuelito," Barboncito answered. "He is already gathering men for retaliation. He wants to attack Fort Defiance; he wants the pale-eyes gone for good."

But Long Earrings was violently opposed to his plan. "Bonneville will be gone within a moon as all the white leaders are. But the pale-eyes themselves will remain, and I fear that nothing Manuelito can do will change that. If he succeeds in gathering men for this raid on *Tsehotsohih*, nothing will ever be again as it once was. And you will no longer have this *hataali*."

"You will not support us?" Barboncito demanded.

"I will not live, my friend, to make such a decision. When I see this raid, I see my own death, and I see doom for the People as well."

A stunned silence fell over the headmen. Gray Eyes stared at Long Earrings, horrified.

It was Agua Chiquito who finally spoke. "What of your nephew?" he asked. "What does he think?" But Long Earrings only looked pensively toward the distant horizon.

"Hawk," he replied eventually, "has once again joined with Manuelito."

The headmen fell into another disturbed silence. Long Earrings' simple answer spoke volumes. But Gray Eyes scarcely noticed. Icy fingers of foreboding tripped down her spine as she followed the *hataali*'s gaze.

Despite the uncluttered blue of the sky, distant storm clouds were brewing.

Chapter 16

The storm clouds spent themselves long before April came. It was *Da'chil,* the moon of Little Leaves, the time when rabbits had their young and the People prepared their fields for planting. But that spring of 1859 was another sultry, dry one. Just as in the last two years, there was precious little water.

When Sleepiness and K'aalo'gii, Wildcat and Gray Eyes caught a lanky colt in the reconstructed corral of their old spring camp, his abrupt stop created an upheaval of dust that seemed to sift into every pore. Gray Eyes put a hand over her mouth and squeezed her eyes shut against it, but K'aalo'gii had no such opportunity. She was on the opposite end of the long noose they had dropped over the horse's neck. When he stopped fighting she tumbled backward, landing with a hard thud in the thickest part of the cloud.

For a moment, the others lost sight of her. Then, as the breeze caught the dust and eddied it up toward the sky, K'aalo'gii crawled back toward them, holding the rope triumphantly.

"He's improving," she announced. The others looked at the colt doubtfully. "It took us twice as long to catch him yesterday," she pointed out. "And even after he was tied, he kept fighting. Now look at him."

Gray Eyes had to concede that she had a point, albeit a marginal one. The long-legged bay was standing still now, but he trembled with fury and his ears were pinned. She sighed. Trust Na'acoci to claim this one for his own out of the fifty he and the other men had raided.

"He is not that crazy anymore," K'aalo'gii insisted. "Watch." She moved up to him slowly, reeling in the rope as she went. But when she was within a few feet of him, he struck out at her with his teeth, leaving a half moon of red welts on her upper arm.

Gray Eyes fought a smile as, in a fine temper now, her cousin threw her small wiry body upon him. After a few minutes of grunting and muttering, she was the recipient of two more bites and a kick, but the colt's front leg was tied up to his belly.

Gray Eyes automatically ran forward to startle the colt into motion. When he tripped and tumbled to the ground, K'aalo'gii plopped down on his neck. Sleepiness and Wildcat moved cautiously to catch and tie his remaining legs.

The dust coating their skin was streaked with perspiration before Gray Eyes had finished stuffing his wounds with the dried leaves of a bottlebrush and binding it in place with strips of old wool. Then they untied him quickly and scrambled out of his way, pausing only when they reached the poles to make sure he didn't tear the bandages off.

"What do you suppose Na'acoci is going to do with him?" Sleepiness asked.

"Ride him, of course," K'aalo'gii gasped, her breath still short. "He is a fine horse, really. He will make a great war pony once he gets used to people."

"*If* he gets used to people," Sleepiness muttered.

"He will." K'aalo'gii shrugged, then grinned widely as she looked at Wildcat. "Perhaps he will give him to you to buy you for his wife."

For a brief moment, the *Moqui* looked appalled at such a possibility. Then her face crumbled. "It is not something I have to worry about. He does not wish to wed me."

K'aalo'gii's mouth dropped open. Only Gray Eyes had the presence of mind to speak.

"That is silly. His eyes follow you wherever you go. He asks for you every time he returns to camp to find you gone. And soon he will have seen sixteen summers. He is of the age to wed." Especially, she thought, since Vittorio had been pressing him to do so. The band needed children. If Na'acoci married Wildcat, he and their offspring would stay with the Lone Trees. It was the way of the People for a husband to live with his first wife's band.

But Wildcat wasn't convinced.

K'aalo'gii took the bull by the horns as only K'aalo'gii could do. "Have you lain with him?" she asked bluntly.

Wildcat colored fiercely. But she shook her head.

Sleepiness straightened away from the poles. "No? You have not gone to him?"

Wildcat looked at her blankly. "Go to him? How? Why?"

The older girl stared at her. Finally, she waved her hands in the air helplessly. "To let him know that you would welcome him, of course. To invite him into your sheepskins."

"Invite him? But he has never let it be known that he wishes to come. He only yells at me and looks at me with eyes as cold as the snow. Even when he comes to sit by me, he doesn't speak. I am beginning to give up hope."

Sleepiness started to object, but K'aalo'gii interrupted. "You forget," she chided. "Only one spring ago, she was one of the Dead Ones. And she was living with the *Naakaiidine'e'*. She may not know the proper way of doing things."

"Explain, please," Wildcat pleaded. "I do not see what you mean by these ways." But Gray Eyes did, and she felt her heart shift suddenly.

She managed to clear her throat. "He . . . he is a warrior," she explained weakly. But she saw not Na'acoci in her mind's eye, but another face, Hawk's face, one that was also hard and uncompromising and, like Wildcat had said, often had eyes as cold as a winter's snow.

"He honors you by not sneaking into your bedding," she whispered. "It is not the way of the People for a man to approach a woman, at least not one who is respected. He would not insult her by doing so if she did not appreciate his advances. The more honored the woman, the less likely he is to seduce her."

She knew that, had always known it. She closed her eyes briefly, unwilling to confront the stupidity, the naivete, that had kept her from applying that knowledge to herself.

A flicker of hope lit the captive's eyes. "He honors me?" she asked faintly.

K'aalo'gii shrugged matter-of-factly. "He must if he has not come to you. Also, you must remember how puffed up a warrior can get, like the owl when his hoot is not obeyed. Some men with no bravery and no coups might take their chances," she added wisely, then shook her head. "But not a warrior. If he was very accomplished, he would never risk his pride and reputation on a woman's rejection."

"Yes," Sleepiness agreed, nodding. "Everything will be fine now. But *you* must go to *him.*"

Wildcat looked awed by such a challenge, but more hopeful than she had in many suns. Gray Eyes only stared unseeingly at the horizon.

"Cousin?" Sleepiness was looking at her worriedly. "Are you ill?"

"I hope so," K'aalo'gii contributed cheerfully. "The last time she was, we got to celebrate a *Kinaalda'.*"

Wildcat sent her a dark look. "Stop teasing." She reached for Gray Eyes' hand. "She is right. You do not look well. And your skin is very cold."

Gray Eyes gave a tinny laugh. "No," she denied. "I am fine." But she got to her feet unsteadily, her heart pounding so fast she thought she might faint.

Hawk wanted her. Could it be? He was, after all, a

warrior like no other. He had even more pride to protect than Na'acoci.

Yet he had called her unmanageable and stubborn that night in the *hataali*'s camp, and he hadn't retracted the words even when given the chance. And, unlike Rattlesnake, he'd never even made a veiled attempt to let her know what he was thinking. Or had he? What of his behavior at the Night Chant?

She shook her head as a strange excitement tingled inside her. She couldn't be sure. But she knew now that she would have to find out.

Her hands trembling, she stuffed the bottlebrush back into her medicine bag. Then, to the others' astonishment, she moved dazedly toward the camp without saying anything more.

Spring passed in a blaze of color despite the dryness. Gold poppies and blue lupine sprang up from the crevices of the desert floor. The long arms of the yucca plants exploded in a profusion of silky white flowers. *Dinetah* blossomed and faded, but Gray Eyes did not see Hawk. Raiding was fast and furious this season, as he had once predicted it would be, and none of the women saw any of the warriors for very long.

As always, with the exposure to other peoples came sickness, and with sickness came a need for *hataalis*. Gray Eyes received her first summons in June. It was a damp morning, promising rain, when she headed for the arroyo and slipped out of her shift. She had just waded down into the thin trickle of red-brown water to wash when she heard the sound of hoofbeats.

She scrambled back up the bank quickly, clutching her shift to her breasts. Once, she would have been glad for the excitement and gossip of visitors. Now her heart pounded as she wondered if the distant riders spelled trouble. She hesitated, indecisive, until Sleepiness stepped out into the clearing, her infant hanging in a cradle board on her back.

Gray Eyes plopped back down into the water with a relieved sigh. "It is you. I was just beginning to wonder if I would have to bathe alone. Did you leave camp before the rider approached? Did you see who it was?"

But Sleepiness didn't answer. The only sound to break the morning quiet was a gurgling whimper from little Squeak.

Gray Eyes twisted around on the bank again to look at the older girl. "Sister?" Gray Eyes tried again. "Is something wrong?" Then her pulse hitched uncomfortably. She had seen Sleepiness' look before, every day that she had spent in the *hataali*'s camp. It was both wary and awed; she knew the loneliness of its distance and the weight of its respect.

Not you, too, Gray Eyes thought, her throat closing.

But the older girl was already backing off into the trees. "The rider is for you," she answered politely. "You are needed for a curing chant. The *hataali* wishes you to help save a patient."

Gray Eyes watched her go with a low, keening cry.

She approached her grandmother's shelter with a remote dignity she had never shown before.

"Granddaughter," Vittorio greeted her. He looked up from his seat near the shelter door and patted the red earth beside him. "Come. Sit."

Gray Eyes did as she was told, but not before she stole an inconspicuous look at the messenger, a nondescript older man of perhaps fifty summers. She remembered him vaguely from Long Earrings' camp, and searched her brain for his name as her grandfather went on. "Our visitor brings a message from the *hataali*," he informed her.

She nodded absently. "Yes. I have been told." *Hastin Dalin*, she remembered suddenly. They called him He Acts Like an Old Man.

Old Man bobbed his head with birdlike rapidity. "It will be at the Coyote Spring camp, near *Tsodzil*, the sacred mountain, in about five suns. It will take that long for all the necessary people to gather.''

"Necessary people?'' She blinked at him as though waking up and seeing him for the first time. ''What chant is this?''

''We will perform the Enemy Way,'' Old Man answered solemnly. ''The patient has been witched.''

A thrill of excitement scooted down her spine. She forgot her distress over Sleepiness' alienation. The Enemy Way required the participation of the finest warriors. Hawk would almost certainly be there.

This was the chance she had been hoping for. By the end of the Enemy Way she would know the truth behind Hawk's cool and mocking smiles.

Chapter 17

As her brother and chief protector, it fell to Na'acoci to escort Gray Eyes across the untamed vastness of *Dinetah*. They left at sundown. The rest of the clan, with the exception of Winter Star, Black Spot, and Quite Enough, would wait to leave with the next morning's sun. Winter Star and Black Spot were simply too old to travel so far, and Quite Enough would stay behind to tend to them.

Despite Old Man's assurances that time was not of the essence, the Lone Trees would probably arrive too late to enjoy the first of the festivities. But none of them were overly concerned. The best part of the Enemy Way was the last night anyway.

When the singing and healing were finally over and it was time for the Squaw Dance, the people would throw saddles and blankets on the ground to make an enclosure. First, the women would dance there alone. Then each would approach a man of her choosing and draw him into the circle. There they would stay until he bought her favors with jewelry or horses and they left the dancing to move on to other, more interesting pursuits.

Thoughts of that last night kept Gray Eyes fidgeting in her saddle as she rode east. As their ponies splashed through the shallow summer remains of the Chaco River, she once again considered her plan, which was both brilliant and terrifying in its simplicity. If Hawk wanted her, he would have her. He would either buy her, or he would decline to dance. The very thought made her bite down on her lip until she tasted blood, but a hot, writhing excitement coiled within her as well, making the journey seem interminable.

Finally, late on the fifth morning, they crested a low, rolling hill to find the camp of the Coyote Spring people sprawled beneath them. The land was less barren here, the soil a soft, fertile brown rather than rocky sandstone. Lush blue grama and buffalo grass lay like a blanket over the valley floor. Seeing it, Gray Eyes understood why the *Naakaiidine'e'* wanted these eastern lands so badly. She shivered despite the baking heat. In an instinctive way, she knew that someday the pale-eyes would greedily lay claim to this part of *Dinetah* also.

She shook her head to dislodge the vision from her mind as Na'acoci gave a shrill cry and left her to gallop down the slope. Men and women alike called out to him, but as Gray Eyes followed, a quiet settled upon the camp. People stopped what they were doing to stare at her.

Armijo, the Coyote Spring headman, barked an abrupt order to his wives to help her get settled. As his shout died in the air, a girl roughly Sleepiness' age came rushing around the corner of a nearby lean-to.

Her eyes remained carefully downcast as she took the reins of Gray Eyes' pony. "Welcome," she whispered shyly.

Gray Eyes nodded as she dropped down off the pony's back. She felt suddenly awkward and self-conscious under the weight of all the eyes upon her.

"The headmen wish for you to join them," the girl went on, unperturbed by Gray Eyes' silence. "There is food there, mutton and antelope and sweet bread. Please tell me if there is anything else you would like." She turned away, leaving Gray Eyes alone in a sea of strange, distant faces.

"She is *Binadini'*, Hurt Eyes," a deep, lazy voice said from behind her. Gray Eyes spun around. Hawk stood in the morning sun, his broad, muscular chest shining like gold.

"It is her brother who has been witched," he went on.

"She will make your visit very comfortable, I think. Do as she says, little one. My uncle waits for you."

Gray Eyes only nodded.

"You do not look much like you enjoy being *estsa hataali,* a medicine woman," he teased.

Her eyes widened. Somehow he knew that she wanted to be anywhere else but here, with all these expectant eyes upon her. In that moment, she didn't care how they were bound. It only mattered that they were, and that somehow he had seen into her soul.

"I do not wish to be so honored," she admitted quietly, throwing a guilty look at the people who still milled nearby. "It is lonely."

"Honor has its constraints, little one."

It was no comfort. Feeling let down, she only nodded again and turned away. But then words crammed her throat, tumbling over each other in a need to escape, and she whirled back to face him.

"Sleepiness!" she exclaimed, her voice trembling. "The people of your uncle's band! Suddenly, they all act as though they do not know me. Will they all do that? Will they all turn away?" She paused, and her voice came back stronger, full of anguish. "Will they all become like . . ." She trailed off to wave a hand at the subdued camp. ". . . like this?"

He knew that he should leave the woes of this woman-child to those in a position to comfort her. He was a warrior, beyond such things. And yet, as he watched her small, stubborn chin struggle to lift and fail, he recklessly defied that knowledge.

"Little one." His voice was a hoarse yet quiet command. "No!" he snapped harshly when she would have spoken. "Say nothing. Just follow me."

He moved away, cutting cleanly through the crowd and disappearing behind a sweat lodge tucked against a red-black butte that shouldered its way into the village. She stared after him for a moment, confused, then left the cool, respectful camp behind and hurried after him.

She knew his smile might be teasing, but it would never be polite.

He waited for her in a tiny crevice between the rocks which, by some whim of the Holy People, had switched back upon itself, leaving a gap in its walls. The mesa swept above him, taller than a hundred men. He stood there, his black eyes shining almost too brightly, relaxing only when she rounded the curve.

She stopped in front of him, feeling suddenly shy and uncertain. "I do not understand."

He smiled bitterly. "No, little one. I never thought you would."

"Then what—"

He cut her off with a finger against her lips. She felt her heart skip a beat. Where he touched her, a strange, feverish heat burned unlike any she had felt before. When he moved his hand away, she instinctively licked the spot where it had rested.

"You asked if everyone would turn away from you now," he went on. "You are *estsa hataali*. And so you are different and you are alone. But not so very alone, little one. You have only eluded the masses."

She looked at him blankly. Somewhere, deep inside, she knew that he was speaking from his heart, from a loneliness all his own. She both mourned for him and knew hope, but she did not know what to say.

"There are those," he finished, "who share your fate. And they will not turn away."

She nodded uncertainly, then recoiled, stunned, as he leaned closer to her and touched his mouth to hers.

He chuckled at her innocence, enjoying it. "You think I would try to devour you?" he asked. "You wonder what I am doing?"

She nodded, her heart moving like that of a trapped bird. Then she moved closer to him again, despite the fact that she thought this strange touching of his mouth to hers bizarre. She felt the pressure of his teeth behind his lips, and so she opened hers. He pulled her closer and she slid her arms around his waist. His skin was warm, smooth, like sun-baked sand, and she gloried in the feel of it. She clung to him, exploring him and the wild sensations he brought to her.

Why had the other women never spoken of this? Did they know? When he again brushed his mouth over hers like the touch of a feather, she watched him, her eyes enormous.

"It is something I have learned from the *Naakaiidine'e'* women," he explained, his voice husky and low. "Not all of their ways are bad. Come, little one, close your eyes. I will show you that you are not alone."

She did, because suddenly there was a hunger moving deep within her, and his voice carried a promise to fill it. He gave a dark, rough growl and his tongue pushed past her lips. For a moment she wanted to pull back again, but then he touched her tongue with his and a weakness swept over her, too debilitating to fight. It was a sweet weakness, a glorious feeling, one that left her giddy with sensation. She moved closer instinctively, seeking more.

He forgot to fear the power of his desire for her. He tumbled into it, helpless and hungry. It was true. She could weaken him when no warrior, no enemy, could.

His hand came up to her shoulders, to the worn fabric of her buckskin shift. It fell away, and her breasts rose softly against his chest, small but full, her nipples taut and hardened. He swallowed the heady scent of her, a smell of something wild and free, something both gamine and flowery. She sighed throatily and pressed against him, her fingers weaving into the loose flow of his hair.

So young, he thought. *So eager. And mine.* The thought rocked him. It took all of his strength, all of his manliness, to pull away. He had waited for her too long. When he took her, he would do it properly, and she would never begrudge him for it.

She reeled backward, looking stunned, when he disengaged her hands from his hair.

"I have come to you," she whispered, her cheeks flaming scarlet, for it was true. She had done exactly what she had prompted Wildcat to do with Na'acoci. What was wrong?

He gave her a pained smile. "No, little one. I brought you here. There is a difference."

She was silent for a moment, grappling with his words. "Pity?" she guessed, her voice strangled. "You touched me, you did this, because I was lonely?"

"That was part of it." He looked away then, upward toward the towering sweep of rock. His black hair fell midway down his back, sleek and unbound. A strange, almost physical longing gripped her and she had to look away.

"But only part of it," he mused, then turned back to her. "Go, little one. Go back to the obligations that await you. Go knowing that you are not alone. And then, later . . ." He trailed off, because he could not explain everything to her. He needed something for his pride.

She interrupted him anyway. "No," she whispered. She moved back into the sunlight, back out of the crevice of rocks where the seduction of darkness could not reach her. And somehow, she managed to lift her chin and meet his gaze. "I have heard enough of your assurances. You have taught me something, and I will accept that. You have shown me that not everyone respects *estsa hataali* and holds her at a distance. And I thank you for that. Nothing more."

She left quickly, before her control could crumble. Now she knew. She would not have to embarrass herself on the last night of the chant. He didn't want her.

She had offered herself and he had sent her away.

Chapter 18

The three days of the Enemy Way were interminable. With a stubbornness that exceeded even Hawk's estimation, Gray Eyes refused to take part in the socializing. The mere thought of those moments between the rocks made her burn with mortification for her stupidity. Seeing him, speaking to him again would be impossible.

The People were not so relaxed or intent upon visiting this time in any event. Ponies stood tethered just behind the camps instead of being turned loose in the corrals. Possessions were not unpacked, but merely used as needed and replaced. No one strayed far from their clan for fear of being lost in the shuffle when the first night's chanting was over. The Enemy Way was an elaborate war dance, designed to exorcise the ghosts of aliens, and it made much of violence. Although it began at the village of the patient, each subsequent night it was moved to a new location. The men would dance a day's journey away each time, and the visitors would have to be ready to follow them there.

Gray Eyes was more than ready to move on when Long Earrings finally took his brightly wrapped birds and began to chant and dance around the medicine hogan. Watching him, a flickering anxiety touched her heart. She looked down at her hands, surprised to find that they were icy and her palms were damp.

Delgondito caught the gesture from his place among the other headmen at Armijo's fire. He read the surprise in her eyes and chuckled softly.

117

"It is always most fearsome the first time, child," he murmured.

"How do you know?" she blurted with unintentional rudeness. "You are not a *hataali*."

But his smile remained. "No. I am a warrior and a headman, though, and it is much the same. Whether it be the power to lead men in war, or the magic to heal, always you must face the uncertainty of wondering if the Holy People will hear you the first time you call upon them."

Gray Eyes glanced down at her palms again thoughtfully. "They will hear me," she mused. "I have already called upon them once before."

"Ah, that is true. When you healed our *hataali*."

"Yes."

"There, you see? Then this is not the first time, and you have nothing to fear after all."

He had known that all along! He had only been nudging her into seeing it for herself. Gratitude rushed through her. She decided, even if she lived to see a hundred summers, that she would never forget him or the precious gift he had just given her.

She left the shelter then and headed toward the medicine lodge where Long Earrings waited for her. She put her full concentration into the healing. Nothing, no man, could interfere with her communication with the Holy People. If she made a mistake in her chanting, even by a single word, it was entirely possible that the witch's evil could turn itself upon her. At the very least, the ceremony would have to be started over again.

She sifted sand through her fingers as the *hataali* had taught her, creating the sacred dry-paintings of the Holy People that would honor them and inspire their help. She sang and watched with wonder as the patient's convulsions begin to ease. Long Earrings observed with a smile both proud and bittersweet. He had chosen auspiciously, guided by his visions, and now this woman with the silver eyes was ready to fill his moccasins.

It was a satisfying realization, but his smile faded as a

handful of mounted warriors approached the hogan wearing full war regalia. One of them was dressed completely in black, and as Long Earrings watched, Gray Eyes looked up and recognized Hawk.

The reverence in her expression turned to panic. She blanched until she was nearly as white as any pale-eyes.

He reached down from his horse to take the small pouch of wolf-man fur that she held out to him as part of the ceremony. Would he ignore her? He almost certainly had to, she thought. A healing was no time for mockery, for teasing. When he began to lift the tiny bundle from her palm without incident, she let out her breath shakily and turned back toward the hogan. Then, almost as an afterthought, she felt the warm stroke of his fingers against her wrist.

"You recovered quickly, little one." He spoke quietly, but the laughter in his tone seemed to scream in her ears. She whirled around to face him again.

"I take great pleasure in knowing that I was able to help," he finished with a grin.

Fury choked her. But as she struggled for a scathing response, he turned away and rode off into the night, the other warriors following him.

Pleasure? she thought wildly. He had taken pleasure in embarrassing her so? But then, he always had. From the first moment she had laid eyes on him, he had been intent upon teasing her. She hated him for it, oh, how she hated him!

Her heart pounding, she turned away and caught her own pony. She remained carefully behind the others until just before sunrise when the warriors slowed their pace to approach the next village.

More mounted warriors were waiting there to greet them; they engaged in a fierce, mock battle with Hawk and his men. The air reverberated with sharp, cracking sounds as their lances came together. War cries, shrill and ghostly, echoed through the preternatural dawn. The Coyote Springs had no idea who their wolf-man masqueraded as during daylight hours, so they were unable to capture and torment him until he confessed. They could only hope that this Enemy Way worked instead. If a wolf-man's victim was too strong or well-protected, his evil almost always backfired. The warriors proved now that they were strong enough to protect their brother and friend.

Under Long Earrings' watchful eye, Gray Eyes concocted a drink from the bark of the *awe'e'tsa'a'l*, the quinine bush. But he administered it to the patient himself before the dancers gathered again and the singing began at dusk.

Finally, the warriors returned, and they were off to another battle at another camp. Almost before she realized it, Gray Eyes found herself sitting beside the fire pit in the third and final village with Wildcat and K'aalo'gii.

When the women began to deposit saddles and blankets around them to form the circle, she jumped suddenly to her feet. She had no intention of getting caught in there when the dancing started.

"Will you join in, sister?" Wildcat asked.

She shook her head miserably. "No. There is no reason to."

"Perhaps I should," K'aalo'gii mused. "There is a Coyote Spring warrior who has many fine, fat ponies. If he bought me with one of them, it might be worth it." Then she wrinkled her nose and shook her head. "No, I do not think so. What if he only gave me some useless trinkets? I think I will go find Manuelito's people instead. He is still trying to talk everyone into attacking *Tsehotsohih*. I want to hear what happens." Then she tossed her hair back and eyed Gray Eyes. "I do not have to be *estsa hataali* to eavesdrop."

Gray Eyes smiled. K'aalo'gii, at least, would never be so impressed with her medicine that she would turn away from her.

A sudden, undulating wail split the air. She jumped, her mouth going dry. The singing was starting.

The chanter's voice mournfully pounded out, peaking

then falling to a guttural low. Women began filling the circle rapidly. Gray Eyes searched the enclosure for the quickest way out. She spotted the opening she wanted and hurried toward it, only to freeze when Hawk appeared there suddenly, his arms crossed over his broad chest, a knowing smile in his eyes.

For a long moment, she only stared at him. Then her blood began to roar so furiously that her skin felt hot. Did he know that she was trapped, that having already failed with him, she had no intention of dancing? Did he think that she was so devastated by his rejection that she would not go to another? She shook her head, her throat closing. She might well be trapped, but she would die before she allowed him to realize it. She would choose another warrior to dance with, someone who would not refuse her as Hawk had.

Her eyes darted around the circle for a likely prospect. Then, as though he were a gift from the Holy People, she saw the warrior Rattlesnake appear beside Hawk.

She peeked inconspicuously at the other women and picked up their rhythm. Heel, toe, rocking forward then back, she moved closer to the perimeters of the circle. Rattlesnake's eyes widened in surprise as he felt her tug, then his dark head fell back proudly and a grin split his features. He was halfway into the circle with her before a cold little worm of practicality nudged at him and he glanced back at Hawk. He realized suddenly that he was not the only one who had expected the *estsa hataali* to choose Nat'aholel.

There was a warmth, a tenderness, in Hawk's gaze that was fading quickly. Rattlesnake felt the hairs on his nape prickle and rise. But the little Lone Tree was pulling at him stubbornly, trying to move him into the circle. She didn't see the look on the other warrior's face, and Rattlesnake was unable to convince himself that she would care if she had. Hadn't she chose him instead? Recklessly, with a temerity he usually reserved for battle, he allowed her to lead him into the circle.

Hawk's eyes narrowed into dangerous slits as he watched Rattlesnake pull her closer.

"A mare," Rattlesnake insisted, leaning close to talk in her ear.

Gray Eyes looked at him blankly. "A what?"

"She is beautiful, the color of your eyes. She is yours."

Those eyes widened in amazement. "I do not want your mare," she began, then broke off as her heart hurtled painfully into her throat.

Too late, her mind cleared. He had danced with her; now he would buy her. She hadn't planned this far ahead. She had forgotten that it would come to this.

"No," she whispered, trying desperately to regain control of the situation. "That is too much."

"Not for one such as you."

"I am not. I . . ." But then she trailed off. His eyes were determined. Tears sprang to her own.

She fought them off viciously. She was not a whimpering, graceless child. Nor was the mare a small gift. She knew that, and knew too that it descrved all she could give in return. But give she would. She had invited him; she had chosen him, in full view of everyone. He had danced with her, fulfilling his part of the bargain. She would not dishonor him now.

She swallowed hard, lifting her chin. "Yes," she answered grimly. "The mare will do."

A broad, triumphant grin split his features. He took the lead from her and danced her out of the circle.

She watched distractedly as the other women collected their gifts. Some of the tokens were small but many; a squaw hurried by with her arms laden with pots, knives, and trinkets stolen from the *Naakaiidine'e'*. Others received wide-eyed *Naakaiidine'e'* children and thick, rich skins.

When Rattlesnake collected the silver-white pony from his own camp and pressed it upon her, Gray Eyes stared at it dumbly. But she led it to the Lone Tree camp, then allowed him to take her arm.

"Do not be afraid, beautiful Lone Tree." He chuckled at her stoic expression.

She opened her mouth to speak, then changed her mind and followed him silently to a shallow arroyo. He dropped to his knees, pulling her down with him, and she reached for him resolutely.

"You are eager. I am pleased." He laughed again, and his breath felt thick and hot where it tickled her neck.

She nodded mutely, struggling to remain calm as his large, meaty hands slid beneath the edge of her shift. His palms felt damp as they moved over her flesh. She bit down on her lip until it throbbed, the pain helping her to remain impassive even as her body cried out for him to stop. He did not know the ways of the *Naakaiidine'e'*, she found herself observing with absurd superiority. As he pushed her down into the sand, his tongue licked only his own lips. She frowned at it thoughtfully before he came down on top of her, driving her breath out of her in a harsh little burst.

Then, suddenly, her shift was jerked up around her neck. It caught there, tangling with her arms, and he gave a satisfied grunt as the air and the moonlight spilled over her breasts.

His fingers caught her nipple and tugged gleefully at it. She gave a gasp of pain as something recoiled within her and curled in upon itself. She twisted away, yearning so desperately and suddenly for the sight of laughing black eyes that she cried out.

"Stop!" The word ricocheted through her brain, and she was mortified to realize that she had cried it aloud. But she knew, abruptly and miserably, that she couldn't do this thing.

Surprised, he pulled away from her. She sat up and reeled back, clutching and tugging at her shift until it fell into place.

"I . . ." she began. But where she expected to find fury on his face, she saw only satisfaction as he watched her. "You are not angry with me?"

"Angry? No, beautiful Lone Tree. It will get better," he murmured complacently. "You should have told me this was your first time," he went on. "But it is of no consequence. We have many days ahead of us."

"The first time? It was not—" She began to tell him of Hawk, of his heat, his finesse, then intuitively backed off.

Heat stained her cheeks as she moved to her knees and crawled out of the arroyo. "Yes," she whispered. "I should have told you." Instead, she had made a promise and reneged on it. She would not, could not, lie with him. Not now, not ever. But she couldn't find the words to tell him. Shamed, she struggled to her feet and ran.

She headed toward her clan's camp, disoriented and humiliated. Without knowing how she had gotten there, she found herself back at the dancing circle again. She looked around slowly, dazedly. There was a new group of women there now, but the man who made her blood run fast and her breath fall short still stood outside the ring. As she watched, a beautiful squaw approached him, her eyes bright with anticipation and promise. They danced, then he led her to two ponies and they left the fire.

"No . . ." Gray Eyes felt the word tug free of her. She slipped slowly to her knees behind the saddles. Suddenly, from someplace deep in her soul, Barren Woman's words came to her again.

With all others there is usually pain, if only in the heart.

Now she understood. Now she knew. But it was too late. As she watched, Hawk's eyes left the squaw and moved to hers. There was no laughter in them any longer.

Like the lava rock that littered the plains, they were hard and impenetrable.

Chapter 19

Gray Eyes saw the approaching riders as she stepped out of her mother's hogan. She gaped at them, surprised.

An unusually large number of visitors had already descended upon the Lone Tree camp to celebrate Na'acoci's marriage to Wildcat. A handful of the Bitter Waters had come, as well as most of the Towering Rocks and the Suddenly Crazies. Now this new group was arriving. She shook her head, nonplussed by all the extra work they would entail.

Then she shrugged. Raiding had been good this season, and there would be enough food for everyone. And considering how long it had taken Na'acoci to buy her, and how confused Wildcat had been about inviting him to do so, it seemed only fitting that their celebration be a huge one. She turned away to find her mother and tell her that they would have to slaughter yet another sheep. Then, as though a wolf-man had thrown a spell over her, a coldness washed over her, chased quickly by a heat that made her skin prickle.

She looked back at the riders uncertainly. But the same unwelcome impression that had nudged her before hit her again. The man in the center rode a tall, lean stallion. Even at a distance, she knew that there were no two horses like it in *Dinetah*. Nor were there two men like its rider.

Hawk. It was Hawk.

Her first impulse was to run. She had not seen him since the Enemy Way, but images of that horrible night were still with her and raw. Rattlesnake's hands. The cold, blank look in Hawk's eyes. The beautiful, confident squaw. Annoyed with herself, Gray Eyes shook her head to push the memories away. She had accomplished what she had set out to do that night. He would never know that his rejection had hurt her. And if the victory was bitter, then it was only because she had once allowed herself to dream the dreams of a fool.

Her face a mask of stone, she turned her back on the visitors and moved away slowly, stiffly. She would not run. It would only amuse him.

The wedding began at sunset. The entire clan and a few close friends crowded into Quiet Woman's hogan, jostling and elbowing each other for space. Still others pressed against the door and hovered outside.

Gray Eyes kept her eyes stonily averted from all of them as she made her way into the hogan. For once, she was grateful that so many people gave her a wide berth. They wriggled aside and let her pass. She went straight to the south wall and pressed her back into the sod and twigs there, keeping her eyes down. She did not know where Hawk was, nor was she willing to find out.

Just when the heat of the fire and so many bodies began to get stifling, Jackrabbit and Yellow Horse arrived. That meant that they had delivered the ten horses Na'acoci would give Wildcat for the honor of becoming her husband. When they were tethered outside, Na'acoci entered and took his seat on the west side of the fire. Wildcat stepped from the crowd to move shyly to his right.

The people grew quiet. Gray Eyes finally looked up and a hint of warmth touched her heart.

The *Moqui* was beautiful. Dressed in a thick wool shift that Quiet Woman had made for her, and adorned with various belts and trinkets that the clan had gifted her with, she looked gloriously happy. Gray Eyes had coached her on the wedding ritual, and as they began, she found herself holding her breath lest she make a mistake.

But Wildcat proved to be far more calm than her tutor.

She poured water on Na'acoci's hands so that he could wash them ceremonially, and he did the same for her. The wedding basket was brought forward, heaped with fresh cornmeal. Then it was time for the *hataali* to speak. The people looked curiously between Long Earrings and Gray Eyes, wondering which of them would do the honors.

Gray Eyes became aware of their attention with a start. For a brief moment, the old, familiar discomfort churned within her. Then she squared her shoulders and pushed gently against the ribs of the person in front of her so that she could pass.

Hawk turned to gaze at her with an empty smile.

She stiffened. She had been braced for his indifference. She had anticipated his withdrawal. But that impersonal smile hurt, horribly and deeply in a way she hadn't expected at all. She felt her head swim and her throat close.

The hum of curious voices brought her back to herself. She jerked away from him and went quickly to Wildcat and Na'acoci.

It took a conscious effort to keep her hands steady as she drew a cross through the surface of the cornmeal, then surrounded it with a circle. She cleared her throat.

"You must both eat a pinch from the east side of the basket," she instructed. "The east symbolizes the land of the sun, the place of all new beginnings. Now take a piece from the other corners, from the north and west and south. You honor our sacred mountains, the peaks that surround the land we emerged into. The Holy People will be pleased. They will bless you and keep you happy."

When they had done as they were told, she stood again, taking the basket. With much squeezing and sidestepping, she carried it to all of the Lone Tree clan. Winter Star and Black Spot were crushed by the north wall, both of them too old and arthritic to do much about pushing their way forward. Sleepiness held up little Squeak, her gaze predictably and respectfully averted. As relatives, they all had to eat from the basket to show that they gave their blessing to the union.

Finally, it was passed among the visitors until it was empty. Gray Eyes went back to Wildcat and Na'acoci.

"You know well the laws of marriage, my brother," she began. "But your bride is new to many of our ways. And so I will speak to her."

Quiet fell over the hogan and everyone settled back comfortably. This was the part they had been waiting for. Now that the wedding rituals were complete, they would enjoy a long night of smoking and feasting as they listened to their headmen and *hataalis* speak to the newly married couple. This young *estsa hataalis* was especially interesting. She had long been a source of curiosity among them.

"Your husband may choose more than one wife," Gray Eyes told Wildcat. The others noticed that her voice was vaguely husky and pleasing to the ear. Satisfied, they nodded.

"Should you not wish to bear his children, should you no longer desire him or him you, then that is his right," Gray Eyes went on. "But always you will be his first, the closest to his heart, the one he shares his soul and secrets with.

"He should pay you handsomely for the right to take other wives. Accept no less than five horses for each one. But in return, you must be good to him and love him well. Do not let jealousy tear you away from him, for although he may bed another, he will always come back to your hogan. Be strong and do your duties. Give him a warm hogan to come to, with food always over the fire. When he goes off to raid or hunt, sing your songs for him while he is away so that he might know success. You do not always have to obey him, but you should do so as often as possible in order to get along."

There was subdued laughter from the men, but Gray Eyes only glared at them with mock ferocity. Then she sat and Long Earrings took over. In his whispery but compelling voice, he instructed Na'acoci in the finer points of caring for a wife.

Gray Eyes glanced restlessly but inconspicuously around

the hogan as Long Earrings spoke and noticed that Rattle-snake had slipped inside. As she glanced in his direction, he grinned widely.

She closed her eyes. He would always be there, she realized bleakly, waiting for her to acknowledge him, waiting for that which she could not give. Unless she finally put an end to it. She got to her feet abruptly and pushed her way out the door.

He followed her, as she had known he would, but she was unaware of Hawk's sharp gaze following their progression. She waited for Rattlesnake in the wintry night air, shivering after the stuffy, smoky warmth of the hogan.

"You are cold, beautiful Lone Tree?" he asked with a sly smile. "I would enjoy warming you."

She shook her head too quickly, but it was partly from frustration over his persistence. "No," she murmured stiffly. "I am fine."

He nodded, but he looked perplexed at her tone. After a short hesitation, he changed the subject. "How is your mare?"

"I would like to give her back to you." The words came so bluntly that even she was surprised by them. But the warrior looked stunned.

"There is something wrong with her? I trained her myself. She is fast, and very smart."

"Yes. Yes, she is all those things. But I have not earned her."

He relaxed. "You will. It is only that all this is new to you, I think. I honor your shyness, *estsa hataali.* I will wait."

"No!" Gray Eyes shook her head hard. "Take the mare back! Please!" In some small corner of her soul, she wondered if she was crazy. He had bought her well. She should be pleased. Instead, she thought of those few stolen moments with Hawk behind the mesa and knew, somehow, that she would never feel or give that way again.

"You must not wait," she finished stubbornly.

To her amazement, he threw back his head and gave a

trumpeting laugh. "You would rather marry me right away!" he decided.

Her eyes widened and her heart skipped a beat. "Marry you? Right away?" How had this gone so wrong, so quickly?

"You have asked me not to wait, although I am willing to do so," Rattlesnake went on. "I can give you only ten horses now, and that is merely customary. I had planned to wait until after this raiding season so I could pay you more."

"No!" She took a quick step backward, horrified. A glint of anger began to appear in his eyes. He grabbed for her jerkily. She whirled away in panic only to look straight into Hawk's blue-black eyes.

He had come up behind her silently, obviously following her from the hogan. His gaze moved to rake over Rattlesnake briefly, then he looked back at her and gave her a hard smile. It held none of the teasing warmth that she remembered.

"Do not let me interrupt," he said. "I have neither the time nor the curiosity to listen to your lovers' spat."

He stepped around her and moved to the fire pit, his hands on his hips as he scanned the camp. Feeling disoriented and uncertain, Gray Eyes followed his gaze. Then she understood. No, he didn't have time for her. His interest was all for Rain Girl, the beautiful squaw he had bought at the Enemy Way.

The woman emerged from a hastily constructed shelter near Sleepiness' hogan. Her shift was of richly woven wool, her moccasins fine. The jewelry she wore was silver and turquoise and spoke of many successful raids. She waited patiently, confidently, while Hawk's gaze swept the camp. When it fell on her, she looked at Gray Eyes and smiled.

There was contempt in the look, and cool triumph. For the first time in her life, Gray Eyes knew jealousy.

There was no time to analyze it. It rose up in her so violently that her hands began to shake. Suddenly, she knew that she would rather have him angry with her than have him feel nothing for her at all. She watched as he approached the squaw, then touched her gall bag thoughtfully.

"Wait!" she heard herself call out. Rain Girl's eyes narrowed. Hawk turned back to her, startled. Rattlesnake only watched on, confused.

"You have not eaten. You left the hogan too soon." Her voice came out smoothly and guilelessly. She felt a quick rush of shame that she could be so deceitful. Then he gave her a mocking smile and the feeling was gone.

"I am not interested in eating just now, *estsa hataali*," he answered. "I have other things on my mind. You should understand what they are by now."

"I apologize for interrupting those things." She shook her head quickly, humbly. "But you came to celebrate my brother's marriage. Would you snub him by not partaking of the feast? Wait. I will get some stew for you. It will take only a moment, and you can take it with you to enjoy later."

She hurried back to the cook fire outside Quiet Woman's hogan, dipping her fingers inconspicuously into her gall bag. She gathered up the stew and glanced down at her palm briefly. Then she separated the weeds there and dropped a small pile of juniper into his bowl.

Hawk hesitated as she handed one to him, but he took it. Rain Girl looked venomous as she watched their eyes linger. Gray Eyes dragged her gaze away with a private smile.

"As you wish," Hawk answered, turning away abruptly. Then, with a final scowl, he disappeared into Rain Girl's makeshift shelter.

"I wish," Gray Eyes whispered after he was gone. "Oh, yes, I wish." And then she giggled. She couldn't help it. She pushed her knuckles into her mouth, but the sound of laughter still escaped her. She ducked her head and hurried off toward her mother's hogan, leaving Rattlesnake behind, forgotten.

Juniper had many uses. The *hataali* had taught her all of them. It had a part in the Enemy Way, and it helped women after childbirth. It could also make a man vomit up everything inside him.

Hawk would almost certainly try to make love with another woman this night. He would try, but he wouldn't stay with her long.

Chapter 20

After years of ignoring the People's urgent need for water, the gods finally capitulated in 1860. January struck the high desert with a seemingly endless assault of snow and sleet. The ravines and arroyos filled and froze over. The People fell to the thick, spongy layer of white, drinking and washing and cooking with happy abandon.

Manuelito saw in the snow the opportunity he had hungered for for so long. The last war had taught him that the pale-eyes did not like to fight in the cold. He had managed to gather only three hundred men, but now he wasn't concerned. When the drifts began to build, he sent word to the valley clans that the time had come to attack the fort.

Throughout the foothills and niches of the Chuska Valley, the pulse of war drums began to sound. Men smoked and sang to enhance their power. In the Lone Tree camp, the moon was ripe and low, the sky a deep indigo, when Gray Eyes' soft, urgent voice echoed through the night and faded into silence.

The Enemy Way there was finished. There would be no Squaw Dance this time. The Towering Rock and the Suddenly Crazy warriors had not come to celebrate the demise of a wolf-man. They were gathered to drive the white man out.

Gray Eyes maneuvered her way out of their midst and watched them pensively from the shadows cloaking Quite Enough's lodge. Her heart felt so heavy it seemed that the Holy People had turned it to stone. Long Earrings had registered his disapproval of Manuelito's plans by declining.to perform the sing. But she had not been able to send their men off without protection. She had performed on her own, her throat so tight the words would barely come out. It had been her first chant without supervision, but she felt no elation. There was only fear, a horrible, suffocating blackness that filled her lungs and blocked her breath.

I will not live, my friend, to make such a decision, Long Earrings had told Barboncito. *When I see this raid, I see my own death, and I see doom for the People as well.*

But no one had listened to him. They still believed, somehow, incredibly, that the pale-eyes could be conquered. Tonight, they would attack their fort while they slept. Perhaps they would slaughter all of them. But Gray Eyes knew, in a place deep inside her soul, that more would come to take their place. And the ones who came would be angry.

She watched, dull-eyed, as the warriors broke apart and began gathering up their weapons and their mounts. Their loincloths rode low on their hips; their chests were naked despite the cold. There were shouts of encouragement and bellows of scorn for their enemy as they began to ride out.

Gray Eyes picked through the throng fretfully, locating the men who were closest to her heart. Jackrabbit and Achi'i'h, Sleepiness' deceptively quiet and ugly husband. Crazy, lovable Na'acoci. She spotted Yellow Horse, riding back and forth among them on his golden pony. Even One Whisker and Spotted Shirt were there, not warriors but willing to fight and die anyway for that which was theirs.

K'aalo'gii was pouting because she could not go along. Black Spot and Vittorio looked unhappy as they watched on. Nearly every man she knew was there . . . except Hawk.

He would depart from Manuelito's camp, she knew. He had no reason to come here, except, perhaps, to see her, to say good-bye to her before the raid had a chance to go wrong. The thought made her flinch, so she pushed it away. It was ludicrous anyway. He hadn't sought her out at all since she had poisoned him at Na'acoci's wedding.

She turned her attention back to the warriors. They were nearly all gone now. Black Spot shrugged and limped off toward Winter Star's hogan. But Vittorio still stood by the leaping fire, his belly huge and round over his leggings and loincloth.

"It is not necessary for you to go," she heard him say to her father. "Manuelito has enough warriors. Who will care for your sister and her children if you should come to some harm? And your daughter if her uncle and brother should fall also?"

One Whisker looked down at him from the back of a dull brown gelding. "I must do what is right," he answered stubbornly. "Manuelito needs horses and herders for this raid, not cunning and power. He says he does not wish to slaughter the pale-eyes. He wants only to run off the cattle they use for food. Without food, they will go back to the land they came from. If they do not, then we will keep raiding them again and again until they do."

"No." Vittorio was adamant. "You should listen to your daughter. She has had a vision, and that is not what she saw."

As always, One Whisker looked uncomfortable with the thought of Gray Eyes' medicine. He was a man who preferred life to be predictable, unexceptional. That he had produced a daughter who was so different, so powerful, disturbed him.

"She is a girl-child," he finally scoffed.

"She is *estsa hataali*. And I believe her."

One Whisker frowned. But in the distance, Yellow Horse called to him to bring up the rear, and he was not flexible enough to change his mind now. Vittorio saw the decision in his eyes and stepped away from his pony.

"Go with them, then," he barked. "But I pray that your daughter is wrong."

With a hearty belch that was at least partially a grunt of disgust, Vittorio moved back to Quite Enough's hogan.

There in the shadows he found Gray Eyes. He chucked her under the chin, although she was really becoming too old and respected for such a gesture, and lumbered on. "Sleep, granddaughter," he muttered over his shoulder. "It is late. They will all be back soon enough."

But he felt her eyes follow him into the hogan, and he knew that she didn't believe him. He didn't even believe himself.

The warriors arrived at *Tsehotsohih* just before dawn. Manuelito's nephew, a round little man with pudgy cheeks, rode to the front as they gathered on the cliffs. The pale-eyes called him Heuro and he had served as the soldiers' blacksmith for four seasons now. Manuelito had turned command of the raid over to him, in deference to his knowledge of the fort.

"You." Heuro's voice was a thin hiss in the shadows as he motioned toward Hawk. "Choose your men. Take the north end. The pasture is there."

Hawk spun off from the crowd and galloped along the perimeter of the valley. As he left, seventy men broke free and followed him. He had already spoken to each of them.

Most were Manuelito's warriors. They would be the strongest, the most inclined to keep fighting, if things turned bad. But Na'acoci was there as well, and Yellow Horse. Hawk knew that living dangerously sometimes had its merits, and he also knew of no man who was as coldly practical as Vittorio's son.

They regrouped at the north rim of the meadow as the sky began to fade to pink and gray. The pasture was directly below them, the cattle and sheep there making splotchy forms in the semidarkness. Here and there, a lantern marked the fort's presence with a pale yellow glow that illuminated the walls of the buildings and spilled in semicircles over the snow. An occasional sentinel wandered through the light, ignorant of the Indians who gathered around him.

Even as Hawk watched, a soldier below him leaned his

rifle against the crusty, whitewashed adobe of the building he was guarding. He stretched his arms over his head and yawned. Then he disappeared into the shadows, tugging at the front of his strange blue leggings as he went. In the eerie stillness of the day beginning, Hawk heard a faint, splashing sound as the man relieved himself. His guard was down; it was time.

Power, hot and vibrating, moved under Hawk's skin. His stallion felt it too. They hit the bank with a mighty lunge even as a long, piercing war cry split the air. They slid into the pasture, landing in the middle of a churning, bawling mass of cattle.

The war cry was followed by discordant shouts of *"Ahu! Ahu!"* All around him, warriors began spilling down into the valley, their flood of motion fast, sleek, and practiced. Hawk held his lance high and his bow at the ready as he galloped through the surging herd, sending them toward the southern mouth where One Whisker and his friends would drive them into the desert.

Less than half of the cattle had been scattered when Hawk heard the first fireball explode and a bloodcurdling cry of pain. He had thought they would have more time to organize their ranks before the pale-eyes reacted. But as he spun around, he saw a warrior behind him slide slowly and gracefully from his mount.

Pale-eyes began spilling from the buildings even before he hit the ground. Four companies of infantry in various stages of undress tumbled into the parade ground. The air roared with their fireballs now. A man with baggy white leggings jumbled around his ankles fired even as he fell out of the door. His fireball hit another warrior, sending him screaming to the ground. The soldier nodded, satisfied, then dropped his rifle to tug his breeches up.

Hawk grinned coldly, contemptuously. A second later his arrow whistled out of the darkness and struck the man in the chest. He died with his long johns at his knees.

Calmly, although his blood ran hot with fury and hatred now, Hawk jerked another arrow from his quiver. He paused for only a moment when Yellow Horse galloped up beside him.

"These pale-eyes are crazy," the other warrior breathed.

"Yes," Hawk interrupted. "Get their cattle. Quickly."

Yellow Horse hesitated only a moment. He was a realistic man, and he knew that what Hawk asked of him was suicide. There were too many of these pale-eyes, with weapons the warriors could not match. And yet, like Hawk, he couldn't conceive of fleeing without accomplishing what he had come for.

He spun away. His golden pony reared as another fireball sounded close, then came down without a rider.

As he hit the ground, Yellow Horse felt his breath leave him in a harsh gurgling sound that was strange to his ears. He puzzled over it for a moment before he felt the pain, searing and black, swim over his chest, into his brain, through his limbs.

He closed his eyes. He saw K'aalo'gii, his sister's child, wild and indomitable, racing across the desert. And his father, growing fatter and fatter as the years went by but never losing his imperious dignity. The ground vibrated beneath him as hooves churned and men shouted. Finally, his eyes fluttered and opened again.

Hawk's face swam in and out of his vision. His voice sounded faraway. "Go with honor, my friend. We may lose much, but we will have vengeance."

Yellow Horse nodded, a spasmodic movement that was nearly imperceptible. Then darkness pressed in on him for a final time.

Hawk leaned low over his stallion's withers and lifted his body with a violent effort. Na'acoci careened by, his eyes widening as he noticed Yellow Horse in Hawk's arms. Then he let out a scream of rage and pain. Hawk's stallion lunged away, carrying their dead comrade from the battle, leaving Na'acoci to his grief.

The searing, acrid smell of gunpowder filled the air as Hawk raced for the opening in the cliffs. Bawling cattle scattered in front of him; once an arrow sang from his bow and found its mark. Then he was free, speeding out into the desert. Na'acoci, his face mottled with barely checked anguish, came on his heels.

Warriors and men churned frantically beyond the cliffs, their mounts laden with their wounded and dying brothers. Cattle and sheep fanned out wildly into the open canyons and arroyos.

"Beegashii!" Hawk spat, stabbing the air with his lance. The men looked dumbly in that direction, still stunned by their defeat. "The cattle! Will you give them back? Then what have our men died for?"

There was a moment of confusion, then a few of the more seasoned men split off, herding in the stock and driving them north again.

"Go." Hawk's voice was dark and hoarse as he spoke to the men who remained. "To the Lone Trees. Their camp is closest. There is a woman there with medicine. She can help you."

They moved out dully. Only Na'acoci reined in stubbornly. His chin was high and arrogant, but it trembled. "And what of you?" he demanded.

Hawk glanced back at the valley, quieter now but still belching with gunfire and the screams of men dying. "We will not leave our dead."

He lifted Yellow Horse over to him. It took both their efforts, with Na'acoci's eyes darkening dangerously as they worked. Then Hawk charged back toward the valley floor.

Shouts and gunfire dwindled around him as he rode for the first warrior who had died. He focused wholly on the sprawled figure of the corpse. He would not be able to stop. Pale-eyes spewed from the buildings now like snakes from a hole, waiting only for such an opportunity to strike him. He leaned low as his stallion raced for the cliffs and as he passed the fallen warrior, he grabbed him beneath the arm and began hauling him up the bluff.

Another roar of gunfire sounded just as he reached the top. At first he felt nothing. Then pain, sharp and piercing, lanced through his shoulder. His arm tingled and went agonizingly numb. His fingers loosened.

For a brief, incomprehensible moment, it occurred to him that he would lose the warrior. But the little one, the silver-eyed woman-child who still had his gold piece, came to him now as she had once before. With a vision of her in his mind's eye, he straightened with a final, heaving effort and the dead man fell heavily over his thighs.

He felt a jolt of pain in his shoulder, a hot stickiness as blood gushed from his wound. He ignored it and rode hard for the camp where the little one and her medicine waited for him. Only when he saw the mountains in the distance, when the sun had climbed to its zenith and the air had frozen the blood on his skin to a hard crust, did he pull up the head of the man sprawled over his thighs.

It was Rattlesnake.

Chapter 21

▼ ▼ ▼ ▼ ▼ ▼ ▼ ▼ ▼ ▼

There were so many of them.

Gray Eyes looked around the tiny Lone Tree camp, her eyes bright and glassy with shock. It was swarming with warriors. Most of the men had scattered across *Dinetah* after their bruising defeat, as was the People's way. But easily fifty had come here, carrying their wounded so that she might heal them.

Even as she reached fretfully for the reassurance of the coin in her gall bag, the sound of more hoofbeats penetrated her anguish. More, she thought. There were still more men coming. Perhaps Na'acoci, Yellow Horse, and Rattlesnake would be among them this time. They were still unaccounted for, as were Jackrabbit and Achi'i'h. And Hawk.

"He lives," she breathed aloud. In the name of the Holy People, he had to.

She forced herself back into the chaos. Moans of grief and mourning throbbed in the air. The women had begun arriving as soon as word reached them that their warriors were coming here. Now they stumbled around each other, carrying food and blankets, searching faces, removing the dead. Gray Eyes left them to their work and moved dazedly to watch for the approaching riders.

They were a long time in coming, but finally Na'acoci topped a ridge and cantered toward her. Na'acoci! And behind him were Achi'i'h and Jackrabbit, One Whisker and Spotted Shirt. She gave a shrill yelp of relief and raced toward them.

Then she saw Yellow Horse's small, golden stallion running riderless beside them. Her steps slowed until she stumbled. She threw back her head and grieved, a sound so raw that the entire camp quieted.

Na'acoci leaped from his pony and shook her to quiet her. "The others?" she finally managed, her voice jagged.

"Some clans fared worse."

"Our uncle?" She knew, but she needed to hear it aloud.

Na'acoci hesitated. "We lost him, but no one else. I buried him not far from here, but safely away from the camp. There was no need . . ."

He trailed off and she nodded. No matter how kind a man had been during his lifetime, his *chindi*, his spirit, would be evil once he was dead.

"I avenged him," Na'acoci finished, his voice chilling in its hatred. "I found three soldiers as we were leaving. They are dead now."

A faint sense of satisfaction touched her heart, but it wasn't enough. The pale-eyes had triumphed again, and this time they had taken more than she'd ever thought she'd have to give.

Something inside her demanded that she cry. Instead, she turned away and went back to the camp, leaning over man after man, packing their wounds with plants and herbs. Her eyes were so dry and grainy they hurt. She worked without thinking, without feeling, until the sun touched the western horizon.

She never heard the last rider approach. He didn't gallop in. His horse walked with uncharacteristic care, stepping gingerly, moving silently. She simply looked up and he was there.

It was Hawk, her Hawk. Her heart slammed against her ribs and tears finally threatened, trembling on her lashes. She gave a little cry and leaped to her feet.

His horse carried him to Quite Enough's hogan out of habit. Gray Eyes ran after him, dodging people and ponies blindly. She caught the body he pushed from his horse without looking at it. She staggered under its weight for a moment, then someone lifted it from her and she pressed closer to the *Naakaiidine'e'* stallion and his rider.

It didn't matter that he mocked her, that he didn't want her. He was alive.

"Little one," he murmured.

His voice sounded odd. It was weary, and there was a tenderness in his tone that she had never heard before. She looked up at him.

"You have lost much," he whispered, "but you are still stronger than I knew."

She opened her mouth to protest. She wasn't strong. She was frightened in a way that reached all the way to her soul. She needed his comfort, his warmth, his reassurance as he had given it to her once before. Then she saw his wound and realized that he couldn't give it to her. Not this time. This time, he needed her more.

With a soft moan, he slid from his horse and collapsed into the snow.

She was too stunned to scream or cry out. She stared at him dumbly, at the blood and the hole in his shoulder and the snow that was beginning to pinken around him. Terror sapped her mind, her strength. Her legs folded clumsily beneath her.

Someone caught her. But even as they did, a violent protest rose up through the cloudy horror in her mind. Not Hawk! They wouldn't take him too. She shook off the person holding her and dropped down beside him to work on his wound.

"You." She motioned to Sleepiness. "I will need wool for bandages. And peyote," she finished, looking at a gathering of warriors. "It gives the quickest relief from pain."

The men hesitated. "Now!" she snapped. "We must act quickly. Would you see him die?"

Na'acoci dropped a quick look at the fallen warrior who had guided him through his first raid with such wisdom and kindness. Then he reached beneath his loincloth for his gall bag.

"If there is not enough there, sister, I will find more."

For a brief moment, she smiled up at him radiantly, her heart full of love.

The warriors moved Hawk into Quite Enough's hogan. Gray Eyes followed. He was so pale. His lips were the color of a December sky. Her breath clogged in her throat. December was a month of death.

"*Aje'i di'shjool,*" she whispered and dropped to her knees beside him. "My heart."

She got no response.

She forced some of the peyote into his mouth with her thumb, then rubbed at his throat until he swallowed it. Sleepiness came in and deposited a lump of wool beside her, then disappeared again unobtrusively. Gray Eyes stirred a mixture of *dibe' haich'iid,* the leaves of the sophora plant, over the fire, then finally bent over Hawk.

His wound was clean, not unlike Long Earrings' fireball holes. She breathed again then, deeply. It was best when a man's flesh was torn on both sides like this. The fireball had entered him and exited again. There would be no need to go through the painful, potentially dangerous chore of digging it out.

She cleaned the hole with the sharp, tangled leaves of a bottlebrush, then tucked the edges of his flesh back into place. Finally, she used more of the sophora, slightly dampened this time, as a poultice to keep the wound from festering. Then she wrapped both sides with Sleepiness' wool and dropped back on her haunches, exhausted.

It would work. It had to work, she thought simply. The alternative was to lose him.

It was dark, very dark, when Hawk woke. In those first moments, he thought that he was dead. Bits of memory scrambled through his brain and none of them were good. Defeat. Screams. Blood and fireballs. Instinctively, he fought against them and tried to sit up.

Pain slashed across his chest immediately and made him realize that he was still very much alive. He dropped back again, breathing hard.

But he recognized the hogan now. There was a bow and a quiver by the door, and the latter was adorned with brilliant red feathers and a black crow's tail. Vittorio's. Yet the shelter was quiet, not rumbling with the snores he knew the old man could make. There was only gentle breathing, soft and shallow, from the other side of the embers that had once been a cook fire. He fought off the pain this time and forced himself to sit up so that he could look more closely.

It was the silver-eyed one.

Her knees were drawn up tightly against her body for warmth. She had been too exhausted to reach for a sheepskin, he thought. Either that, or she hadn't intended to sleep. Hawk guessed that it would have been the latter. He knew her well enough to know that she never expected her energy to fail her.

Tenderness rose up in him. Tenderness and something stronger, something that he pushed violently away. Rattlesnake was dead. His pride and the memory of her going to another were not.

He dug the heels of his hands into the ground behind him and pushed savagely, intent upon getting to his feet to leave her. But pain enveloped him again, boiling up in his shoulder, streaking across his chest. A groan escaped him and he fell back, looking quickly at Gray Eyes to see if he had awakened her.

He had. She moved restlessly, then her eyelids fluttered and she sat up.

Relief swept over her, a sweet, debilitating relief at the fact that her medicine had worked and he was conscious. Then her eyes narrowed warily. Would he be rude again? she wondered. Would his words sting? What would he say now that he was awake and they were here, alone?

But he only grinned at her expression. "You did not

expect me to recover, little one? Or is it only that you hadn't planned to find yourself alone with me when I did? Are you afraid that I will try to bite you again? Come closer. I would be glad to oblige.'' Then, in spite of himself, he winced. The effort of speaking made pain claw at his chest.

She'd been about to retort, but suddenly his teasing—and even the fact that he *was* teasing her again—was unimportant. She jumped to her feet. ''No!'' she ordered. ''Do not try to talk. Do not move. If you want to sit up, I will help you.''

''You think I am so little of a man that I cannot move myself? I thought I proved differently at the camp of the Coyote Springs.''

''I think,'' she snorted, ''that you have a hole in you. If you are truly a man then you will accept that as well as my help.''

His laughter brought fresh pain. He had forgotten that she could give as good as she got.

In the end he allowed her to move him back against the wall. She dropped a blanket over his shoulders and grabbed one for herself before going back to stoke up the fire.

''Little one,'' he mused. She gave him a cautious look over her shoulder.

''Have you ever wondered why it is that we always end up in these uncomfortable positions together?'' He was thinking of the night in Canyon de Chelly. The hardness between his legs was much the same as it had been that night. His willpower was slightly weaker; he had touched her now, and knew what he was depriving himself of.

But Gray Eyes thought only of Na'acoci's wedding, and she flushed. ''Do not try to talk,'' she warned again. ''As soon as I get this fire started again, I will give you more medicine.''

He gave a wry smile. He wondered if she could possibly have anything in her medicine bag that would cure what ailed him.

But he made no protest when she brought him more peyote and bandaged his wound again with fresh sophora. She hovered by his side, leaning over him, studying him critically. Her scent was sweet, subtle, wild. He reached out to her suddenly.

"You never answered my question, little one. Did you think I would try to devour you again if I got you alone?" His hand caught in the ebony length of her hair and pulled her closer.

She avoided his question. "You are better now? Your pain is gone?"

"I think it is just beginning."

Surprise widened her eyes. They moved over him, searching for some aspect of his discomfort she had failed to address. When they finally came to the loincloth that barely covered him and did nothing to hide his arousal, she colored slightly and tried to jerk away.

She couldn't do it unless she wanted to leave half of her hair behind. Furious, she turned back to him.

"You do not need me for . . . for that," she snapped. "I no longer want your pity. You would do much better with Rain Girl, I think."

"Rain Girl?" For a moment he looked blank, then he remembered. Rain Girl . . . the woman he had bought at the Squaw Dance. The one he had tried to go to at Na'acoci's wedding. But he had done both out of anger, and now Gray Eyes was close enough for him to forget the way she had wounded his pride.

He pulled at her again, not entirely gently, until she fell across his knees. She cried out in protest, her thoughts for his wound now. But when she met his eyes and saw no pain there, her heart moved traitorously. His smile was arrogant as only his smile could be. It quickened every drop of blood she had. A weakness slid through her, gathering at central points of her, between her legs, at the pit of her stomach, in her throat.

"Pity?" he whispered hoarsely. "I told you it was more

than that, little one. If you believe otherwise, then you are a fool.''

A fool? Yes, she was, because she knew better than to lose herself in those onyx eyes, and that was what she was doing. She knew better than to crave the touch of those strong, sensual lips, and yet she wanted it with every fiber of her being. She'd never thought to be this close to him again, and it rocked her. She forgot pride, forgot sanity, and leaned closer to touch her mouth to his.

She had thought only to taste him, to explore her reaction and his. But she was no longer naive enough to mistake his answering groan for one of pain. It exploded in her head. He did want her. In some small way, for this small moment, he did. The knowledge made her feel liquid and greedy. She moved over him, seeking his tongue with hers. They met intimately, darting together then moving away, playing with fierce intent. It had been too long since they had touched; the need that had built was too great. Suddenly, there was no wound, no Rattlesnake, no Rain Girl. There was only this night and desire too long denied. He caught her hips and toppled her beneath him.

The weight of him was hot, heavy, glorious. There was nothing between her breasts and his chest but the thin layer of her shift, and the friction was sweet, bringing her nipples to hard little nubs that were exquisitely tender. She wanted, yes, she wanted, him and only him. And if that made her a fool then she would die as such, this moment, happily.

Instinct drove her. She bit the lobe of his ear hard enough to demand reaction. He caught the hem of her shift and yanked it away. His mouth fell to her breasts, no more gentle than Rattlesnake's hands, no less hungry. But when he took the point of her nipple between his teeth, the cry that escaped her this time was one of frenzy and wanting. She drove her hands into his hair and pushed her hips into his.

"Oh, yes, you will be the end of me, my love," he

growled. "I have only to touch you to feel my strength and pride slip away."

She answered with a mindless moan, not understanding, not caring. There would be time to think about it later. But now she needed, oh, how she needed. Her hands skimmed over him desperately, across the cheekbones that marked his face with pride and arrogance, down the long, hard muscles of his back, over the rounded tightness of his buttocks, clenched now with need. They slid around his waist, up his ribs to his flat nipples and his broad chest. And then she froze.

Her fingers came away sticky and hot with his blood. The bandage had come loose. She scrambled free of him, her heart still pumping but her skin cold now. She stared down at her hands, embarrassed and horrified.

"I will kill you," she breathed.

"Yes." But his chuckle was raspy. He had known long before she discovered the blood that it was there again.

He had fought the pain well, but now he was willing to roll over on his back again with a groan. He was silent as she scrambled to her feet, grabbing her shift again and tugging it over her head as she searched for her medicine. It was best this way, he thought, but bitterly ironic that only a pale-eyes' bullet could keep him from acting the fool.

"How many died?" he asked suddenly, knowing that he would have to pull his thoughts away from her if he were to survive this night.

It took her a moment to focus. "Na'acoci says thirty, maybe more." Then she hesitated. "What of the pale-eyes?"

His expression darkened as she had known it would. "I do not know. I got two. Maybe three. I think that is all."

"Na'acoci got three. He found them as he was leaving."

"Six then. It is not enough."

"It is too much."

She answered impulsively, then looked away, embarrassed. Her fear of the unconquerable pale-eyes was not something she ever spoke of. She knew no one agreed with her, least of all this man.

But when she looked back at him, she found that he had opened both eyes to look at her, and his gaze was curious.

"I fear twelve will come to take their place," she confessed.

He closed his eyes and was quiet for so long that she thought he slept. Then he told her what he would have admitted to no other. "Twelve will try," he mused. "They are getting stronger, little one. Wiser. This frightens me, because I am not sure yet how to fight it." He paused. "You remember once before when I took my uncle's horses back from them?"

She nodded.

"I raided *Tsehotsohih* with only three men that time. We stole thirty horses, and we all came out alive. It was not so much different from this time. But this time we failed. Perhaps the fault lies with Heuro's war cry. He alerted them, while I crept in as they slept. He wanted them to feel our fury. I thought they would realize it when they awoke."

"Enemies are far more dangerous when they are awake," she conceded carefully, not wanting to take anything away from his coup.

"Yes. And they are far stronger when they have had time to prepare. The pale-eyes were ready for us this time."

"You think someone warned them? Sandoval?" Such a traitorous action was not beyond the *Dine'' Ana'i'*.

But Hawk shook his head. "No. Not one man. All of us. We are becoming predictable."

His words shook her down to her soul. He will be chief, she thought, remembering the *hataali*'s words spoken long ago. She saw it happening already. He was beginning to pull away from Manuelito, from Heuro. He was developing strategies, opinions, of his own.

A cold hopelessness washed over her. Such opinions, such responsibilities, would leave no time for her, for any woman. She knew that, had always known it from the time the *hataali* had first told her of their destinies. Yet something ached inside her even as she accepted it.

Chapter 22

Gray Eyes woke just after the sun to find Hawk gone. The blanket she had given him was wadded up, empty, on the ground. She moved to it and clutched it to her breasts, closing her eyes. The scent of him drifted up to her gently.

He had wanted her. There was no mistaking it for pity this time.

She folded the blanket carefully and put it away with her memories of the night. Then she slipped out the door to find him just outside. He sat stiffly against the hogan wall. Vittorio sat beside him, his heavy chest sagging. Together they watched children chase around the camp without truly seeing them.

"It is over, my friend's nephew," Vittorio said quietly, and she saw his chin drop a little lower on his chest with the words.

"No," Hawk argued. "Not yet."

Vittorio shrugged as though it were a fine point that didn't bear discussion. "Soon then. Things have changed. The pale-eyes have changed them. They are not like the Utes, not like the *Naakaiidine'e'* and our other old foes. They refuse to die. And we have no way of surviving them because we have forgotten the old ways of fighting."

Hawk remained stubborn. "So we will conquer them instead, with new ways of fighting."

"No, my friend's nephew. We will not. They will keep coming. They will destroy us. The days of the *Dine'* are gone." He shook his head wearily. "My son and the other men who died yesterday were our future. Without them, we have nothing. Without my son, I have nothing. I can stand no other such loss.''

Hawk latched on to this. "Then fight them. Stop them.''

"You stop them, my friend. You are young. Your heart is whole.''

Life came back to Gray Eyes' limbs slowly. She slipped out of the doorway and came to kneel at Vittorio's feet. "Grandfather,'' she whispered. Her heart was moving too quickly; she had heard too much in his voice. Defeat, surrender. Her hands were cold as she took his in her own. "Tell me what you are saying.''

He focused on her slowly. "If I live too much longer, I will live to see them take it all.''

He lumbered to his feet, tugging his hand from hers. Then he pushed aside the door flap and was gone.

"No,'' Gray Eyes whispered, staring after him. Her eyes flew back to Hawk. "No!''

But her gaze was turned inward, and he couldn't see what she saw. There was untouched land where eagles flew free. There were lizards skidding over rocks and sandstone buttes standing tall and glorious in the sun. The People might lose much, she thought, but those things would remain. They might be wounded, depleted, but surely they and their land would remain.

But Hawk only shrugged in response to her plea. "Yes, if men like your grandfather and my uncle have their way. We can no longer hide from this enemy.''

"Neither can we fight!'' she protested. "Manuelito's raid has proved the futility of that.''

"It proved nothing, and that is the problem. Your grandfather is right. They will take everything unless we drive them out, but Manuelito failed to drive them out.'' Suddenly, he looked at her hard. "Little one, how much more are you willing to lose?''

"More?'' She thought of Yellow Horse, of her grandfather's defeat, and her heart began to bleed. It was enough. It was too much.

"You have lost your uncle, your lover," he went on ruthlessly. "Will you give them more?"

She shook her head in confusion. "My lover?" she echoed uncertainly.

"The one from the Suddenly Crazies." He was free of the peyote now. The memory of Rattlesnake was bitter, especially after the way she had offered herself last night. He had to understand why she had done it.

"Rattlesnake . . . ?" she began. Then horror hit her, cold and nauseating as she understood what he was saying. "He is gone?"

"You did not know?" Something black and dangerous glinted in his eyes.

"No," she whispered, "no." Pain began to pound at her temples. Rattlesnake was gone. He had never taken back the mare, but he was gone. "How?" she asked. She had to know.

For a moment Hawk doubted if he could answer, if the words could get past the bile in his throat. But the man had been a warrior, and he had died well. He could not dishonor him, not now, not to the woman he had loved.

"A pale-eyes' fireball caught him as soon as we began the raid," he answered tightly. "I think he was the first to fall. But he died driving off stock."

"That is good," she whispered.

"But not enough?"

"He was too young. He deserved more."

She swallowed painfully. Surely the tears would fall now. But her eyes, like her voice, were parched.

Hawk pushed to his feet abruptly. A tiny sound of pain whiffled out from between his teeth. She reached for him instinctively.

"Where do you go?" she asked, alarmed. But he shook her hand off.

"I leave you with your grief, little one, and my apologies. I thought you knew, that perhaps he hadn't meant as much to you as I first thought. I thought perhaps that was why you came to me last night. I see now that I was wrong.

Had I understood, I never would have dishonored him by taking what was his, even in death.''

She shook her head in mute protest. Her grief, her regrets, over Rattlesnake had nothing to do with last night. But even as she struggled for the words to argue with him, he walked away.

The moon became thinner and thinner as the winter season lost its strength. The flood of people who had descended upon the Lone Tree camp began to depart. Their shelters bowed to the elements and settled back into the earth. By the next full moon, there was little to mark the camp as the scene of such mourning and defeat, except the sod roof of Yellow Horse's hogan. Under different circumstances, the Lone Trees wouldn't have been there to see it begin to sag. They would have taken their grief and their sheep and moved on with the spring thaw. But Vittorio either would not or could not be dislodged from Quite Enough's hogan.

Both of his wives were waiting outside the door, their shoulders stooped and their blankets wrapped tightly around them, when Gray Eyes emerged. "There is no change," she whispered.

Quite Enough raised her wrinkled chin stubbornly. "Then it is time I talked to him. I have lost my son. I do not intend to lose my husband as well."

Gray Eyes hesitated, then shook her head. "No. I do not think you should go in there just yet."

"But you have said that it is not *naalniih,* a white man's disease."

"I said that I do not think it is a sickness that will jump to us. But I am not sure." And maybe, she prayed fervently, maybe she was wrong. *Naalniih* was greatly feared because it was contagious, but it could also be fought. The People had cures for measles, smallpox, syphilis. But a cold, horrible certainty told Gray Eyes that none of these things were ailing her grandfather. She remembered his words on the day after the raid. She did not believe that his body had fallen to a pale-eyes' germ, nor had any wolf-man witched him. He was willing himself to die. The pale-eyes had taken his son and all the simple things he believed in. Now he was leaving before they could take anything more.

She closed her eyes and rubbed her temples at the pain that was building there. "I think," she whispered, "that this sickness is something new. Like *naalniih*, it is brought by the pale-eyes. But like *tah honeesgai*, my medicine may not cure it."

Quite Enough and Little Left Hand looked at her blankly. Such a thing was beyond the orderly realm of their lives and therefore beyond their comprehension.

"When can I talk to him?" her grandmother wanted to know.

"What do we do for him?" Little Left Hand asked.

She stared at them a moment, her mind blank. Then, finally, she sighed. "We can try a sweat bath, if Na'acoci can get him to the lodge. I will give him some juniper to make him throw up all the badness inside him."

Quite Enough hurried off to find her grandson. Little Left Hand went to heat the sweat lodge. Gray Eyes watched them go, then turned and went back into the hogan.

Vittorio was propped up by the fire, staring sightlessly at his bow and quiver on the wall. "Grandfather?" she whispered. There was no response. She kneeled beside him. "Here. Eat this."

He took the juniper without protest, munching steadily, showing no reaction to its bitter taste. She pushed to her feet and went back outside.

Na'acoci was just approaching. She saw in his face that he was frightened but willing to do what she asked and enter the hogan. She tried to reassure him.

"I am no longer sure that his sickness is catching, brother. But even if I am wrong, you are young and healthy. You should be able to fight it off." She hesitated.

"You must hurry. I gave him some medicine. He will begin vomiting soon, and I think it will be a lot."

He was halfway through the door tunnel when she stopped him again. "Brother? If this does not work, I think you should ride out and find the *hataali* as soon as the sun comes."

He felt something cold and rigid grip his muscles. If Gray Eyes did not think she could save their grandfather on her own . . .

But he couldn't complete the thought. For the first time in his life, Na'acoci knew fear.

He didn't wait for the sun. By the time the moon cleared the sky, Vittorio's breathing was shallow and raspy and a fever had taken him. Jackrabbit helped to move him back to his hogan, and Na'acoci rode out right away.

The dawn was thin and hazy when he arrived at Long Earrings' spring camp. To his shock, nearly forty people were ready and waiting to ride back with him. The *hataali*'s eyes were clouded with the unforgiving burden of his wisdom as he stood with his pony near the head of the group.

"You knew," Na'acoci realized.

"Yes." Long Earrings nodded once, briefly. "I had a dream."

"He will die." For a moment, he felt nine summers old again, frightened, lost, and he was terrified that he would cry.

The *hataali* didn't answer. They moved out instead, heading north, the women and children and their travois churning dust up behind them. They arrived back at the Lone Tree camp at mid-morning.

Gray Eyes slipped out of the hogan as her brother and the *hataali* approached. She was taller than her mentor now, but her face wore the same haggard look as his. Her skin was the color of her eyes.

Na'acoci leaped down off his colt, chilled by her appearance. "We are too late!"

She glanced at him absently. "No. He lives." Then she turned back to Long Earrings. "Grandfather, I need your help. I am not strong enough. My medicine—"

But he interrupted her. "Your medicine is as strong as mine."

Her eyes widened. Such a compliment left her stunned. Then the breath rushed out of her and her posture crumbled. "No. I cannot save him. I have tried."

"What you cannot do is change the course of his soul." Long Earrings dug into his saddle blanket for his birds and his fetishes. "He has strong medicine, too, my granddaughter. And his medicine wishes to die. But we will try to change its mind." He moved off toward the hogan. After a brief hesitation, she followed him.

Moments later, the *hataali*'s voice began to writhe in the air. There was a rattling sound as he shook his birds and danced. The people outside nodded at each other, comforted. Only Long Earrings suspected how useless his efforts were.

It was early afternoon before Vittorio opened his eyes again. They were amazingly clear, a glistening black. Gray Eyes' pulse began to pound and she came to her feet with a cry.

"*Hataali*," she gasped. "Come. Look."

But Long Earrings caught her just before she could bolt out the door to summon the others. "No, granddaughter. Call only the Hopi girl your brother has married. She should be safe from his *chindi* since she is not truly of his clan. Have her dress him and move him out of the hogan so his ghost does not become trapped here." He paused, feeling her pain, but still he pushed on. "We must not stay here. His *chindi* will bleed our medicine dry."

Gray Eyes stared at him, then understood and shook her head violently. "No!" she shouted. "No!"

She wrenched away from him and turned back to Vittorio. Trembling, she sank to her knees.

"Grandfather." Her voice broke. She grabbed his hand.

It was icy. "Grandfather," she pleaded. "For the love of the holy ones, do not go!"

But Vittorio only shook his head slowly, with great care. His beloved round face eased into a smile.

"Do not grieve for me, granddaughter," he rasped. "I have won." And then, finally and forever, he closed his eyes.

Gray Eyes got blindly to her feet and fled.

Chapter 23

By dusk, hundreds of people had pushed aside their fear of the dead to come and honor Vittorio. The tiny village was swollen and pregnant, bulging out into the Chuska Valley like a fat toad. Wails of grief and howls of anger floated above it. The People had lost more than a head-man; they had lost another round to the pale-eyes.

Gray Eyes watched the headmen as they murmured solemnly among themselves near the fire pit. Manuelito's eyes were afire with the rage that burned within him. Barboncito's thin, birdlike face was dangerous; in his anger, his crossed eyes gave him a demented look. Even Delgondito, whose expression was normally so placid, looked grim and uncompromising. They all placed Vittorio's blood on white hands. Vengeance was demanded.

Gray Eyes shuddered and covered her eyes with her hands. *He died because he knew that there was no beating these pale-eyes*, she cried silently. But even had she screamed the words aloud, she knew that none of them would have heard her. She turned away, unable to bear watching them any longer.

Then the crowd around her fell abruptly silent. The burial was starting.

They had not been able to get Vittorio out of the hogan in time; it was a *chindi* place now, despite the fact that the door had been boarded up and the north wall torn down to allow his spirit to escape in the proper direction to the afterworld. *Chindi* spirits were most malevolent toward their immediate family. Gray Eyes kept a careful distance as several captives from other clans moved to gather up Vittorio's body. She watched as they hoisted his massive weight between them and carried him to a lonely grave far removed from any of the camp's traffic. Then she had to close her eyes. But she couldn't block out the wailing that started up again as the Lone Trees followed.

K'aalo'gii herded Vittorio's small band of horses toward the grave, sobbing brokenly. Little Left Hand screeched her grief and pulled at her hair. Then everyone had gathered, and the captives eased Vittorio into the hole. Gray Eyes scarcely felt her heart beat before they threw his silver, his saddle, and his pipe in after him. When everything was in place, Long Earrings stepped forward.

"Good-bye, our brother," he intoned, reciting from the burial rite. "Now you go on your way alone. What you are now, we know not. To what clan you now belong, we know not. From now on, you are not of this earth." Then, gently, he laid the red-feathered quiver with its black crow's tail into the grave. The shooting started.

Squeals of terror and pain reverberated through the air as Vittorio's ponies were killed. Fireballs exploded and arrows whirred and hissed. Gray Eyes clapped her hands over her ears. But she could still see the horses leap convulsively as they met their deaths and plunged into the hole.

It was done. Vittorio's *chindi* spirit would go to the north now, to a place below the earth's surface. Yellow Horse would meet him there to guide him and his horses to the afterworld. He would be gone, at peace, his *chindi* no longer able to harm those who remained behind unless someone spoke his name and called him back.

In the real world, the captives began heaping dirt over his grave. The Lone Trees headed back toward camp. Gray Eyes remained in the darkness, her eyes dry and unfocused, until long after both the hole and her family were gone.

There would be feasting; she could hear and smell it beginning already. There would be sweat baths, too, lasting far into the night until everyone who had come close to the corpse was cleansed. There would be four days of mourning. Then the world would go on.

Somehow, incomprehensibly, it would go on without her grandfather.

She clapped a hand over her mouth to suppress a cry and turned quickly away from the grave. Then she froze as the sound of tears—soft and choked—drifted toward her. Stiffly, unwillingly, she turned back again to look into the darkness.

An obscure, solitary figure sat near the fresh mound of earth. She could just see his bony old shoulders as they bent and shook. He held his head in his spidery hands.

"Good-bye, old friend," Black Spot wept. "Good-bye."

The days eased the worst of the People's grief. The nights fed their anger.

Most of them had gone home after the requisite four days of mourning. But many people had stayed even after that. It was not their way to offer condolences or sympathy to the bereaved. Instead, they remained with the family. They butchered sheep, herded horses, and cooked meals, and they gathered each evening at the fire pit to recount the many injustices they had suffered at the hands of the pale-eyes.

Gray Eyes could rarely summon either the energy or interest to join them. She felt exhausted.

As darkness fell and the others began to congregate by the fire pit on the seventh night, she leaned back against the wall of her mother's hogan and listlessly rolled stones for little Squeak to catch. The boy was nearing two summers now, and the discovery of his legs led him into all manner of trouble. Sleepiness could chase after him for only so long before she needed respite.

Gray Eyes took her eyes off him for just a moment to glance pensively at the fire pit. A crash sounded from

behind her almost immediately. She scrambled to her feet
and ran inside.

He was sitting happily amid Quiet Woman's small col-
lection of *Naakaiidine'e'* cooking pots. Gray Eyes yanked
him to his feet and scolded him in the mild manner of the
People.

"Quiet Woman will be angry with you," she warned
as she bent to retrieve the pots. "Would you like it if she
took that little bow your father made you and broke it?"

"Did not break." His little lip protruded in the beginnings of a pout.

"Not yet," Gray Eyes muttered. She finished hanging
the pots again, but when she looked back at him he was
gone.

She darted outside again and ran squarely into Hawk's
arms. The impact robbed both of them of breath and set
little Squeak to howling. His arms were wrapped around
the warrior's neck and he dangled against his back.

"Is this what you were missing?" Hawk gave a fleeting
smile and reached behind him to pull the little boy free.
He hit the ground with both legs churning and took off.

"Yes. No! Do not—" She broke off and took off in
pursuit of the baby. But K'aalo'gii stepped out from behind a nearby mesquite bush and intercepted him.

"I will care for him, sister," she announced, grinning.

As Gray Eyes watched her cousin walk off with her
excuse to avoid Hawk, her heart skipped a beat. She hadn't
been this close to him since the night of the funeral. But
they hadn't spoken then; he had simply sat with her until
she had given in to her grief and exhaustion and slept.
That left a good many things unsaid.

She turned back to him guardedly. "You wished to
speak to me?"

"No."

Her jaw dropped open at the unexpected response. The
look struck a chord within Hawk and he laughed.

"I was leaving," he explained. "I was on my way out
of camp when the little storm blew out of your hogan. I

thought I had better return him to his mother." He sobered. "Instead I found you."

Belatedly, she noticed his stallion waiting obediently on the path where he had left him. Feeling confused and oddly disappointed, she began inching toward the door again. "Do not let me delay you," she answered tightly. "Although I am surprised that you would leave while Manuelito is speaking."

Hawk looked briefly at the fire pit where the headman held everyone's attention now. "I have already heard everything he has to say."

Gray Eyes looked back at him quickly. For the first time in days she was distracted from the shredded, aching feeling in her own heart.

"He would like to attack *Tsehotsohih* again," she said.

"Yes. And many more will back him this time, I think. They consider the slaughter of their warriors and a headman to be a more personal affront than the theft of land that many of them have never seen."

"And you?"

He hesitated only a moment. "I will back him as well. But I hope to persuade him to use more caution and cunning this time."

Gray Eyes nodded carefully. "Then why do you not stay and try to sway him now?"

To her surprise, he chuckled. "You regret seeing me go, little one?"

She tossed her hair back haughtily. "It means nothing to me one way or the other."

"Perhaps. But I will answer your question anyway. This is not the time to sway anyone. Feelings are too raw, too violent. They are not thinking with clear heads."

She nodded as memories of Rattlesnake and Rain Girl came to her. "Yes," she mused. "We often do crazy things when we are angry."

He was silent for far too long. She looked up at him to find his eyes raking her speculatively.

"Now that you speak of it," he answered finally, "I

realize that many mishaps do seem to befall me when your emotions are running high.''

''*My* emotions?''

His laughter was warm, dark, and intimate. She realized too late that he had been baiting her.

''I had a kind of trouble recently.'' He chuckled. ''At your brother's wedding. It was strange. For many hours, my stomach would hold nothing.''

She blushed to the roots of her hair. But she had known that eventually the connection would come to him, so she held her tongue and looked at him innocently.

''Have you any explanation for this, *estsa hataali?* I confess that it has given me a great deal of food for thought. I have wondered if perhaps a medicine woman wanted to interfere with my plans for that evening.''

''Plans? Ah, you speak of Rain Girl.''

He only grinned.

''I would not think so,'' she answered sweetly. ''Why should I care if you want to plant your seed in her? I have heard that she has been used for that purpose often, but that she bathes much less. If that lures you, my friend, then who am I to interfere?''

His brows shot up and he looked momentarily discomfited. ''Then I still have to wonder what might have caused my attack.''

She shrugged. ''Perhaps your bad temper?''

He stared at her for a moment, then laughed long and hard. But all too soon he remembered what had caused his anger that night, and he sobered abruptly.

''What do you plan to do, little one, now that your band no longer has a headman?''

Her eyes, so attentive, slid away abruptly.

''Will you marry for a husband's protection?'' he asked harshly. It was a consideration that had hounded him ever since he'd heard of Vittorio's death.

''Marry?'' Finally, she looked at him again. Her eyes went wide. How could he think she would marry anyone? She was bound to him. She knew that she might never have him completely, but she knew too that she would never again try to go to another. For the love of the Holy People, hadn't she shown him that? What else could she possibly do?

Nothing, she realized suddenly. Nothing but laugh. The sound bubbled out of her without warning, clear and bright. Hawk scowled, his temper building in his eyes. She bit her lip and swiped at her eyes.

"Do not start snarling at me," she managed. "I am not laughing at you, so you do not have to worry about your great warrior pride."

He studied her for a moment without relenting. "Then perhaps you can tell me what you *are* laughing at."

She started to giggle again, then an image of Rattlesnake came to her. Shame lodged painfully in her throat instead. The sound merged into a strangled little gasp.

"You are thinking that I would have married the one from the Suddenly Crazies had he not died," she whispered. "But that is ludicrous when you consider that I could not even honor the promise of my dance."

"Your dance?" His skin, bright with suppressed anger, went suddenly pale.

"At the Enemy Way a summer ago. I . . ." How could she tell him? How could she tell anyone? But the words kept coming in a cathartic need to be heard. "Please," she begged. "Do not tell the others. It is a source of great dishonor to me, worse now. Now I will never be able to make it up to him. Now I will never be able to get him to take back the mare."

He stepped closer to her so suddenly that she flinched. His fingers dug into her flesh like the talons of his namesake.

"What is wrong with you?" she demanded. His grip hurt.

"I want to see if you speak the truth."

"My honor is not *that* muddied! I gave him something, just . . . just not enough for the mare."

He stared at her, stunned. She stared back at him, her

breasts heaving in anger. Then she twisted away from him to rub the spots where his fingers had bitten into her arms.

He barely noticed. *I gave him something,* she had said. *Not enough.* Rattlesnake hadn't had her. The swell of relief he felt was so intense it left him reeling.

Reeling, and frightened. He'd thought once that if he bedded her, her power over him would sap him and bleed him dry. Now he knew that it was too late. He hadn't had her, but the thought of her with another man had eaten at him anyway, at his body, his mind, his soul. He hadn't realized how much it had taken from him until he had heard her words and become whole again.

He took a sudden step away from her and mounted his pony. "We will talk of this later," he said hoarsely as, off in the distance, Manuelito's voice rose violently. It was the sound of thunder, the sound of war to come again.

There was no room in his life for her now. He ached for her, ached to finally and inevitably give in to the lure of her. And he knew he could not. Not yet. Not now. If he went to her now, he would never be able to forget her long enough to save the men Manuelito would lead to slaughter.

With a last look back, he jerked on his reins and spun away.

Chapter 24

▼▼▼▼▼▼▼▼▼▼

Within suns, Na'acoci and Achi'i'h left to enlist more men for Manuelito's cause. Jackrabbit stayed behind to help Gray Eyes, Wildcat, and K'aalo'gii geld the year's new crop of colts. If they remembered that it had always been strong, agile Yellow Horse who had contained the animals for the painful task, none of them let it show. The crop was smaller this year without the fruits of Vittorio's mares, but no one mentioned that either.

It was Wildcat who inadvertently brought up the subject that they had all been trying to avoid. As Jackrabbit toppled one of the last colts, she grabbed for his legs but simply didn't have the strength to hold on. He struck out, his hoof catching her on the cheek as she bent over him. She gave a little yelp of pain and fell backward into the dust.

"Sister, are you all right?"

Wildcat waved them off. "I will be fine. But I fear that we will never catch that colt again now that he knows what we have in mind."

"I am not sure that I blame him." Jackrabbit chuckled.

"Shall we finish the others and go back to him later?" she asked. But Gray Eyes looked at the burgeoning swell of her pregnancy and shook her head.

"Do not worry yourself about it, sister. Your babe drains you. Go back to the camp and rest."

"But if I go, there is no one to take my place."

They all looked vaguely startled, then uncomfortable. Their little clan was so depleted now that even the simplest

168

chores took great organization. Sleepiness couldn't be counted on for anything; she, too, was carrying a babe and was having a difficult pregnancy. Quiet Woman, Talks Often, and Little Left Hand were off slaughtering a sheep. One Whisker and Spotted Shirt were away hunting, and Winter Star was so old and arthritic she couldn't even be considered. Black Spot spent most of his days wandering through camp mumbling to himself, and Quite Enough rarely came out of her shelter since the death of her beloved husband.

"This is silly," K'aalo'gii snapped suddenly. "How long will we hide from what needs to be done? We should join up with another band."

Silence greeted this announcement of what everyone already knew. But none of them had given it the thought that Gray Eyes had. Even were the Lone Trees to join with another band, they would still number nine women, a toddler, two unborn babes and a senile old man. And they would still have only five able-bodied men to hunt and raid for them.

"It would not solve anything," she answered finally, wearily.

"We could join Manuelito," K'aalo'gii insisted stubbornly. "His whole band is made up of people from other camps."

"No!" Gray Eyes barked the word with such ferocity that they all jumped. "No," she repeated more calmly. "I will not live with Manuelito. I do not approve of what he is doing."

K'aalo'gii's eyes sparked. "I could go live with him," she challenged. "If I chose to, you could not stop me. He might even let me raid."

"Yes," Gray Eyes answered with strained patience. "He does not always care who dies, as long as pale-eyes die also."

"His people die honorably."

"His people die young."

"What of Long Earrings then?" Wildcat stepped in before the argument could escalate further. If she agreed with anything K'aalo'gii had said, it was that they needed to go somewhere. Lately she had begun dreading the *Naakaiidine'e'* again. If they were attacked now with so few men in the camp to defend them, she could easily end up back in the Mexicans' clutches.

But Gray Eyes shook her head at that suggestion also. "And leave your husband?" she asked quietly. "Na'acoci would not come with us, you know. He is a warrior. He would not be content to herd sheep and plant crops with old men."

Suddenly, her shoulders straightened. "I will not see this family divided," she vowed. "Rest, sister. Somehow, some way, we will finish gelding tomorrow."

But Wildcat was no longer listening. She was staring off down the mountain at two approaching riders.

"Na'acoci!" All traces of weariness vanished from her eyes. She ran out of the corral to meet him.

"They will have news," K'aalo'gii breathed and hurried after her.

They rode in with the women at their ponies' heels, and the clan began gathering at Wildcat's shelter. Sleepiness struggled to keep Squeak quiet, but she looked pale and unequal to the chore. Gray Eyes moved automatically to take him off her hands as they moved inside to get out of the sun.

It was early, but Wildcat had already laid a sheepskin, wool side down, on the ground. Steaming bowls of food were set upon it. Na'acoci and Achi'i'h dug in hungrily. Gray Eyes found that she had no appetite.

"Tell me," she prompted when her brother had finished half of his mutton. He needed little encouragement to put the bowl aside.

"It has been decided," he announced. "We will attack the fort again in three nights. We will avenge Vittorio and all the warriors who have died."

"We leave tonight." Achi'i'h's contribution was spoken with a fervent edge. "Everyone will gather at either Manuelito's camp or Barboncito's. We will join together on the third night and ride for *Tsehotsohih*."

Ice spread slowly through Gray Eyes' stomach. "How many will go?"

"A thousand men have committed," Na'acoci answered proudly. "The People will truly stand together this time."

"Yes, but a thousand and one men will ride," came a voice from the door.

All eyes swiveled to One Whisker. His tunic was blood-stained and sweat-marked; he had obviously come to find them as soon as he returned from hunting. But he looked neither tired nor harried. His eyes shone with a fierce inner light that Gray Eyes had never seen before.

Spotted Shirt stepped up behind him. "I will join you as well."

All of them. They would all go. Gray Eyes let the realization sink in, then she pushed to her feet. She swayed gently for a moment as fear rocked her. Then she left Squeak playing happily with his mutton and moved for the door.

Gray Eyes stayed in her hogan until she knew that they would be leaving. Three nights, she thought for the hundredth time. They would attack again in three nights. That gave her so little time to decide.

But when she heard the horses being gathered up, she pushed her panic from her mind and got to her feet. She returned to the fire pit, her stomach knotted, to find that the warriors were mounted and ready.

"There is no time for an Enemy Way," she told them, and they went still, frowning. Few of them looked as though they believed they would need one.

"But I will sing for you while you are gone," she went on. "Please," she implored. "Move with caution. Remember the last time."

Na'acoci's eyes glinted dangerously. "They will pay for the last time." Then he spun his pony away and was gone.

The others followed. For a long time she watched them, cherishing them with her eyes. Then she turned away to collect her birds and rattles and go up the mountain.

She sang through the night, quietly, softly, begging the Holy People to intervene with the course of fate. Only when the sun finally crept over the mountain did she fall silent. She watched as the camp came to life again. Talks Often, Quiet Woman, and Sleepiness moved outside to beat bedding. K'aalo'gii ran off to tend to the horses. Little Left Hand carried bowls of mutton into first Quite Enough's shelter then Winter Star's. Gray Eyes watched it all through red-rimmed eyes and finally gave in to her weariness. Her shoulders sagged.

They needed her, these women and babes struggling to maintain a life that was normal. They needed her to organize their chores, to heal them, to settle their squabbles. But she suspected, in a dark, frightened part of her soul, that the warriors needed her more.

If she had been there at the fort during that first raid, could she have saved more of them? How many would die this time if she didn't take her medicine and follow them? She had no answers, only a sweeping vision of the maimed, the wounded, the dying as they had poured into her camp that day three moons ago. Feeling helpless, she got to her feet and collected her prayer offerings, then started back down the trail toward the camp.

When she stumbled, she looked down at her feet, perplexed. Then her eyes focused and she recognized the hawk.

He had come to her again, but this time he lay broken on the dusty red earth. She gave a small cry and bent to him, her pulse hammering. His eyes were dull now. He thrashed desperately, terrified by her trembling touch. A creature born for the sky, an animal magnificent and proud, humbled by a battle with an enemy larger, fiercer, or perhaps only more lucky than himself.

An enemy like the pale-eyes. She closed her eyes.

"No," she whispered. "Please, please, no." But the

decision had never truly been hers to make. It had been waiting for her since the day she'd been born, and now it was painfully clear.

She had to go to *Tsehotsohih*.

Chapter 25

When the moon came again, she collected her medicines and slipped off to Jackrabbit's empty lodge. She dressed meticulously in his warrior's clothing, binding her hair atop her head in his turban. His tunic fit sufficiently well; she was nearly as tall as he was. But his leggings required extra pieces of yarn to keep them up over her hips, and her fingers trembled as she tried to secure them. Finally she crept into the corral.

She saddled Smoke, the gentle, intelligent mare that Rattlesnake would never be able to take back. Then she bent to scoop up handfuls of dry, red dirt and smear it on her face to hide her features. With her bow and her quiver slung securely over her shoulder, she rode south without looking back.

When the sun finally began to turn the eastern sky to a pearly gray, she made a cold camp at the southernmost foothills of the Chuskas. Three nights, she thought again. Two had already passed. Her pulse throbbed steadily as she waited for the moon to return. Then she repacked her meager possessions and rode again for *Tsehotsohih*.

The meadow was still and quiet when she reached it. The barracks were dark, sleeping. She felt her heart move in panic. Had they already been there? But no, the People would not leave the *hual-te* without also leaving behind some trace of their wrath. She was early, only early. She breathed again and moved Smoke back from the cliffs.

Then she froze as movement shifted in the darkness to

the north. Endless movement, stealthy and sure, running like a wave over the desert floor and up onto the rolling hills beyond. It was the warriors. She gave her mare a little kick and melted off in the opposite direction, her pulse pounding hard.

She watched as they gathered on three sides of the fort. They moved close to the rims of the cliffs with a steady, hushed, thrumming sound as bows and firearms were engaged. There was no war cry. The valley remained nearly silent except for a distant, hollow, popping sound that came from somewhere beyond the far ridges. She listened to it for the full length of several heartbeats before she realized what it was.

Fireballs. They peaked with a man's scream. He howled in Navajo.

Gray Eyes' heart exploded. How had this happened? The men had been so quiet, so sure! The opening shots had come from the southwest corner of the cliffs. The warriors on the north and east rims descended immediately. They had lost the element of surprise yet again. They had to reach the valley before all the pale-eyes awoke.

The air began to rumble with the frenzied hoofbeats of a thousand horses being beaten into a gallop. The night brightened with bursts of orange, loud, belching bursts as more fireballs were discharged. Pale-eyes tumbled from their barracks, fumbling for boots and pants and guns as they had on a night not so long before. But the warriors from the western rim managed to take possession of the garden, the wood piles, and the fences. They feinted from the dubious cover of one to the other, their arrows snapping free, their lances flying.

Then Gray Eyes noticed that although the pale-eyes fired back, their volley of shots raked not the Indians, but the corral gate, shattering and splintering it. It was the only true means of protection in the valley. Without it, the warriors were trapped, caught in the relative open like rabbits in the greedy, hungry eyes of a hawk.

They would either have to retreat up the slopes again, or they would die. But Gray Eyes knew that they wouldn't retreat; they would never give up. She grappled with her reins, gave a thin cry to the Holy People, and dug in her heels.

The little mare slid down the slope with more heart than agility, then darted across the parade ground. They reached the creek unharmed. Gray Eyes slipped from her back, splashing loose-limbed into the water.

She clutched her gall bag briefly, drawing courage from the gold coin nestled there. Then she popped her bow free and centered an arrow in it, poised and ready in case she needed it. Screaming the cry she had once heard Vittorio sound, she ran among the lines of warriors.

She stumbled over the first man almost immediately. She dropped to her knees beside him and his eyes focused on her slowly. She did not know him, and he had no reason to believe that she was not just another warrior.

"Go, my friend," he whispered, his voice cracked and dying. "Kill them. Do not fear for me."

She shook her head. "No. That is not what I am here for."

She slung her bow over her shoulder again and gripped him beneath the arms. Strength flooded into her from a resource she hadn't known she possessed. She dragged him away, back to the creek, stopping only occasionally to hitch his weight into a more manageable burden. Then she deposited him in the water and used her shoulder for leverage to roll him over.

A fireball had ripped through the lower part of his back. She knew with a detached certainty that he would not live. Others would. She left him and raced back into the foray.

She dodged among the horses and the warriors, pausing only long enough to examine those who were hunched or fallen. She dragged off dead and wounded alike. Those she had even a chance of saving, she treated, and her small stock of medicines quickly began to suffer for it. Grimly, she realized that she would have to be more discriminating. Then she had no opportunity to worry about it at all. Suddenly, the night blazed into fire behind her.

She'd reached the wood piles again. Chips of mesquite and juniper and fir began to spin and dance in a riot of death as pale-eyes' fireballs riddled the stacks. There were more screams, howls of outrage from the warriors who surrounded her, hoots of triumph from the white men who pressed in. The Indians divided, thinning their numbers dangerously. Half of them fled in the direction of the sutler's store. The remainder turned to face down the unexpected attack from the rear.

Gray Eyes huddled close to the ground as hooves churned about her, missing her by bare inches. She felt the earth vibrate beneath her, felt the backlash of air from the ponies' motion, and her mind went black with terror. Then a hoof nipped at her thigh and she yelped and leaped to her feet again to dodge away in the opposite direction.

She raced blindly past the fences before she skidded to a stop, dazed. The *hual-te* spread out before her, an inferno of fireballs. Behind her, a man in officer's clothing pointed toward the sutler's store. She notched another arrow in her bow and ran again, leaping over obstacles, until she fell panting and depleted into the shadows of the building.

Eventually, sounds from the window above her head rooted her back to her feet. She pushed to her knees, then stood shakily. A handful of the warriors had made it inside. They were looting the supplies there. She climbed up and onto the ledge with the last of her strength.

"They will come here, I think," she gasped. "Pale-eyes. They saw you." Then she tumbled over onto the floor.

If any of the warriors noticed the soft, breathless quality of her voice, a voice that could not possibly belong to a man, it didn't register. They left her for another fallen warrior who would have to be gathered up later. They surged toward a door at the far end of the room, grabbing whiskey, tumbling barrels of flour, spilling casks of hard, black beans. She pushed to her knees to watch them, then felt her heart lurch yet again.

Na'acoci.

He was among the last of the warriors to reach the door. Gray Eyes scrambled into the shadows and held herself perfectly still, her breath tamped. She couldn't let him see her. He would recognize her and then he would turn his attention toward defending her. He would die for her and never think twice.

Finally, when she thought she would either have to breathe or expire, he gave a grunt and moved off. He got as far as the door before gunfire exploded there.

He leaped away, sprinting toward the window again. The other warriors fell back into the room as well, but not without an answering volley of fire from their bows. The pale-eyes were too shrewd to appear in the doorway; the shafts fell uselessly just behind the opening. It wasn't until the warriors had pushed through the window again that the soldiers finally sprinted into the room.

She was trapped.

Her breath heaved out of her again and she collapsed against the wall behind her. She stared in disbelief at the pale-eyes' boots as they ran past her. Surely they would leave. They would chase the warriors and then she could escape.

But if they chased the warriors, they would almost certainly encounter Na'acoci.

A feral growl began low in her throat, growing louder, more vicious, as she leaned onto her knees and crept forward. No. They would take no more from her. With the desperate snarl of a cornered animal, she sprang free of the shelf and raced toward the last of the pale-eyes gathered at the window. They spun at the sound of her fury, their eyes widening first in fear then amazement.

''He's on a goddamned suicide mission!'' a man shouted

as she bore down on them. Another man laughed, then fell silent as she leveled the bow she had armed a nightmare ago.

After a moment's hesitation, the man closest to her leaped and grabbed for her. She feinted out of his way and whirled, keeping her back to the wall. But she had no chance to fire. His hand caught Jackrabbit's turban, pulling it away, and her hair spilled down her back. He reeled away from her, stunned.

"Jesus Christ! It's a squaw!"

"Grab her!"

Her heart began moving too quickly. Her legs threatened to turn to water. But Na'acoci was safe now. As long as these men were occupied with her, they could not go after the warriors.

She screamed, Vittorio's war cry wrenching from her throat again in shrill fury. The men fell back, startled. She lunged at them and had nearly reached them when one lashed out, his thick fist connecting solidly with her jaw.

She cried out and staggered from the impact. Her bow began to slip from her fingers. Then, just as she began to crumble, an answering war cry came from the window.

Na'acoci leaped through again. He froze, staring at her. She screamed at him, begging him to move before the pale-eyes could shoot, and he stumbled forward suddenly as the other warriors spilled through from the window behind him.

Jackrabbit caught her before she fell. She fought him off, leveling her bow again. The arrow came free with a forceful *twang* and the man closest to her gasped, then fell.

"Johnson's been hit!" a pale-eyes shouted. She didn't wait to hear more. She leaped for the window, diving out of it and landing on the hard ground beyond with a force that knocked her breath from her. The night grew blacker, then faded.

Fresh pain brought her back. Someone was dragging

her, and the crumbled granite and sandstone of the soil bit into her tender flesh. She began to fight again instinctively, with everything she had left.

"Stop!" Na'acoci hissed, bending over her. "Would you see us both killed? I will get you out of here!"

She struggled to her feet. Her eyes flashed with a silver fire so fierce that it made him reel backward and release her. "I would see neither of us killed!" she snapped. "Go! Now! Fight if you will, for I know I cannot stop you. But do not fear for me. I will leave now."

He looked doubtful. "I will take you."

She grabbed for her quiver again and centered another arrow in her bow. "Then you will take death as well. I would rather see you die by my own hand than by that of these pale-eyes."

He stepped away quickly, his eyes a maelstrom of emotion. Fury, hurt, then understanding dawned there. Finally, he nodded. She was *estsa hataali,* and he knew that he could protect her no more, not from herself nor from her future.

"The east rim, little sister," he answered quietly. "Do not try to make it to the mouth. There are too many pale-eyes there."

She nodded, lowered the bow, and replaced the arrow. Then she spun away and was gone.

She raced through the compound, emerging behind the buildings on the east side. She made her way toward the slope as she had promised, but she stopped twice for bodies. By the time she returned for the third, war ponies were racing past her, blowing hard, their eyes wild. There were no more war cries. The raid was over. The warriors fled crazily and without order. No enemy would be able to make sense of their retreat to follow.

But the pale-eyes were trying. Soldiers drove after them, choosing one man to track rather than choosing no man at all. And still massive fireballs exploded from the *hual-te,* bigger than anything she had ever imagined. Gray Eyes turned her eyes to the valley again in horrified wonder. The guns were the size of five men. They crouched on huge wheels and were trundled to the edges of *Tsehotsohih* to be discharged up the slopes. There was a scream as still another warrior fell. Terrified, she huddled back into the shadows of a ledge, dragging the fallen man with her.

Then, miraculously, the big cannons fell silent.

"Christ Almighty!" someone shouted. "We're shooting at our own men! Company C is up there following." A shrill whistle went up. The pale-eyes on the slope faltered, then fell back.

Gray Eyes had no idea what had happened, but she knew it was a reprieve. She clutched the warrior again, absently holding her palm in front of his mouth as she began dragging him up the incline. Breath. He was alive. She couldn't leave him, even if it meant ensuring her own safety.

She dropped down to sit, levering herself backward and upward by pushing with her heels and her free hand. The warrior was heavy, so heavy. But she didn't dare put her full concentration into moving him. She kept her eyes warily on the soldiers below. They moved like sheep shocked out of the placid routine of grazing, but they showed no inclination toward following her. She risked a quick look down at the warrior.

Her breath stopped.

For a moment, darkness began to swim over her again. It was Hawk. And his midsection was very nearly gone.

She threw her head back and wailed. *"Nooooooo!"*

"Yes," came an answer from behind her.

Her howl broke off in her throat. Slowly, dread moving sourly in her stomach, she twisted around to look over her shoulder.

A pale-eyes stood a little further up the ridge. There was a deadly, metallic click as he cocked his rifle and leveled it at her chest. She looked at it dazedly and then up into Rush Michaels' face.

Recognition sparked faintly within her. He had been

one of the men at the sutler's store. She remembered his hair, a blazing red, the color of fire. She remembered his eyes, a pale color much like her own. Now they were filled with hatred, and swimming with the beginnings of tears.

"Goddamn you," he breathed. His voice was mangled with grief. "Johnson was a good man."

She shook her head slowly, uncomprehendingly.

"The one you killed," he went on as though she could understand. "He was . . . he was . . ." His voice dipped and broke. "He was only seventeen." His rifle bobbed, then came up again and centered on Hawk.

She screamed then, savagely, the fear and outrage of all the past seasons crowding up from her heart. She dropped Hawk to leap to her feet and crouch in front of him, protecting him with her body, an animal wild with the need to defend her own.

"Take me," she spat. "Put your fireball through me. But know that even as you do it, you will die. You have no chance to take both of us, white man, so make your choice."

With lightning speed, another arrow appeared in her bow. Michaels jerked backward, suddenly frightened. For the first time, he registered that this was a woman and he saw in her eyes that it was not for herself that she fought.

He darted a look to the warrior behind her. Brother, lover, husband, friend. It didn't matter. He could be a stranger. But she would kill for him or she would die trying.

He stepped away shakily, feeling her hatred as though it were a physical blow. And beneath it, something else. Fear. Yes, he felt fear. And a clear acceptance of death. Neither would deter her.

"Go," he muttered wretchedly. "Go! Or so help me God, I'll do it!" He waved the rifle at her again. She turned her back to him as few men would have done and began dragging her warrior away.

He watched her for a long time, feeling shaken and

small. She was a savage, a thief, uncouth and unclean by the standards of his upbringing. But during that one moment when he had fallen into her eyes, he had learned from her the meaning of courage and pride.

Chapter 26

A damp, gray dawn settled over *Tsehotsohih*. Gray Eyes trudged through the mist, over the rolling hills and rocky buttes. Just when her limbs became so heavy with exhaustion that she doubted if she could climb another, she found her mare.

Smoke had raced out through the southern mouth of the valley and was nibbling on the tufts of scrubby grass there. Gray Eyes stumbled to her side, then dropped to her knees with relief so great she nearly cried. The pony nudged her with her muzzle, rousing her, and she climbed up on her back with the last of her strength.

They reached the eastern rim again just as the sun began to climb behind a woolly screen of clouds. The sounds coming from the *hual-te* were subdued now. The warriors had all gone, but the pale-eyes were still active. There was an occasional shout and voices too far away to be heard clearly, but they were close enough to make her skin crawl.

She had to get Hawk away quickly. There would be no more reprieves like the one granted her by the man with hair like fire.

Smoke stood docilely as she pushed Hawk to his feet. There was no way to do it without hurting him. He groaned and his eyelids fluttered at some of her more forceful efforts. Finally, she draped his arms and upper body across the mare's withers. Then she ran quickly to her other side before he could crumble. She pulled on his hands until tears of frustration stood out brightly in her eyes.

Finally, finally, he began to inch up and over. She

184

scrambled up behind him, eased her thighs beneath him and rode for the mountains.

He was bleeding badly now. She urged the mare faster. She had no more medicines.

Finally, the mountains appeared before her. She stopped for a moment, breathless and bone-weary, and slumped over Hawk's body in an agony of gratitude.

When she opened her eyes again, he looked up at her. She shook her head blankly, scarcely able to credit what she saw. He should be dead. She knew that, in some coldly practical part of her mind. His blood had drenched through her clothing, was smeared on her hands and her arms. There was a gaping hole in his midriff so large that it still showed beneath the edges of the tunic she had stripped from a dead warrior and bound around him. Although he looked at her, his eyes fluttered closed again without recognition. But he lived, and strength seeped into her once more.

She nudged the mare back into a gallop and they went on, recklessly and desperately, leaping boulders and brush. She would save him. She glanced at him again and began to speak, softly at first, then more fervently. She knew it mattered little what she said; he would not hear her. But his heart, his medicine, would.

"Cling to me, my love," she whispered. "We are close now, so close. If you could open your eyes again, you would see the mountains. Take their strength. They are so big, so strong. They will last forever, as will you. Come back. Come back. We need you."

He moaned again. She forged on.

"*I* need you. Ah, do I see you smile? Maybe just a little? If you were well, you would give me that mocking laugh. No one should need a hawk. Like you, he is free and lights to earth only when he is wounded or hungry. Only a fool would try to hold him. I will never hold you, my heart, I know that. But I can love you. Yes, when you are here, when you are hungry for me, I will love you. And when you fly free, I will wait."

She went on senselessly, emptying her soul. When she rode into camp, her voice was cracked and raw. The Lone Trees gathered around to greet her, but she didn't see them. She kept her eyes on the warrior who somehow, miraculously, still breathed. She kept her heart bound to his, this man who was the moon to her sun, the man whose soul was now her own.

The moon came again; the stars reappeared. Sometime during the long day, the clouds had lifted. Now the night was sultry and intimate.

Gray Eyes was unaware of it. She looked up listlessly from her place at Hawk's side as her mother came into the shelter. Her muscles screamed from the strain of too many hours awake and her eyes burned with fatigue.

"There is no change?" Quiet Woman whispered, coming to stand beside her.

Gray Eyes shook her head. "No. And I have done everything I know how to do. Still he remains unconscious, and his skin burns."

Her mother shook her head sadly. "It is no wonder," she answered. She had seen his wound. A shiver flicked down her spine now as she considered how he could suffer such injury and still live. But, of course, she knew. Her daughter was *estsa hataali,* and he was hers.

"Where is Na'acoci?" Gray Eyes asked suddenly. "Does he sleep? Will you rouse him and send him for Long Earrings?"

Quiet Woman hesitated a moment too long.

"What is it?" Gray Eyes demanded. "Surely he has not been hurt, too?"

Her mother only sighed. "He sleeps," she admitted. "But I do not believe he can be awakened. The *Moqui* says not."

"Wildcat does? Why?"

"He took some strange liquid from the *hual-te.* He calls it firewater. It came in jugs. It is like peyote, only different. Wildcat has seen this firewater before, when she was a captive of the old *Naakaiidine'e'*. She says it will make him sick tomorrow.''

Gray Eyes' face hardened in anger. ''Then I hope he does not come to me for a remedy,'' she snapped.

''He had no coups. You had the only one. That is difficult for a man to take. It makes them act stupid.''

Gray Eyes felt her anger rush out of her like a hard wind. She sat back on her heels. ''There are no men who can be awakened?'' she finally asked. ''Did they all drink it?''

''All of them,'' Quiet Woman agreed.

''Then get K'aalo'gii.''

Quiet Woman left. Gray Eyes began once again to sponge the beads of perspiration from Hawk's forehead. She was still there, working tirelessly, when Quiet Woman raced back into the shelter, breathless and alone.

''What is it?'' Panic brought Gray Eyes to her feet; despair and exhaustion nearly dropped her again. No more, she wailed silently. Nothing more could go wrong. Her thoughts were clotted, thick. She couldn't think. She couldn't cope.

But her mother was babbling in a senseless rush. ''Heuro,'' she finally gasped in her first decipherable word. ''Manuelito's nephew. He is here. There is war.''

The shelter spun wildly about her. She felt the ground shift beneath her feet. Slowly, her eyes wide and unfocused, she sank down again to sit.

War.

But then, she had known it would be so. Hadn't she only been waiting all night, waiting for word or for the roar of a gun? She had found the hawk with the broken wing. She had heard the *hataali*'s prophecy all those seasons ago.

''Bring this Heuro to me,'' she whispered hoarsely. ''And somehow you must rouse the men. Ask Wildcat if she knows any way how.''

Quiet Woman left again, her face without hope. Moments later, a squat, round man with tiny eyes entered the shelter.

His expression was intense. But his impatience vanished when he saw her. "You are the one they call *estsa hataali*," he said.

She rose to her feet slowly, clinging to her tattered dignity. "Yes. We have no headman now. You will have to speak to me."

He gave a quick nod of acquiescence. Then his eyes widened again as he recognized Hawk. "He lives? We had thought him captured. His stallion returned without him."

"Good. I would hate to see him lose that horse. He deserves a mount who can fly."

Heuro gave her an odd look. As with anyone with very strong medicine, this young woman was not easily understood. She would require a wide berth, he decided. He shifted his feet uncomfortably.

"I do not have much time. I must still travel to other clans," he muttered.

"You will wait, please, just a moment longer. Our men will come soon." *I hope,* she added silently.

But they did come, looking bleary-eyed, dripping water, wafting an aroma that made her step back and gag. Na'acoci noticed Heuro and became suddenly sober as Jackrabbit, Achi'i'h, Spotted Shirt, and One Whisker tumbled in behind him.

Gray Eyes looked to her mother. "How did you wake them?" she whispered.

"The *Moqui* said water."

"Drinking water makes it go away?"

"No. We stuck their heads in the ravine."

Gray Eyes nodded, then sat down again before the cold cook fire. She was startled to find that they had waited for her. She nodded at Heuro awkwardly.

He spoke quickly. "I come from the *hual-te*. The paleeyes there do not know yet that I have organized these raids against them. They still allow me among them. I heard what they are planning. And so I have come to warn you to go.''

Gray Eyes looked at him blankly, her heart moving so hard and so suddenly that she pressed a hand to her breast. "Go?''

"Out of *Dinetah.* ''

There was a hushed murmur of fear from the clan. Gray Eyes felt her head spin dangerously.

"The pale-eyes follow a man named Fauntleroy now that Bonneville is gone,'' Heuro went on. "He has sent for more soldiers already. He will lead them against us. It will be bad.''

There was a chorus of outrage from the men. "Let them bring more soldiers!'' Na'acoci challenged. "We will kill them all.''

"They want nothing but a new treaty! They will fight us only until they get more land!''

"No! We will give them no more!''

"We did not drive them out,'' Gray Eyes whispered into the chaos. "We have only managed to encounter more.'' She was beyond thought, beyond caution. "Do you still not see?'' she cried. "They are maggots! They are everywhere we turn!''

They only looked at her with tolerant, bemused expressions. Her breath shuddered out of her helplessly. She looked back at Heuro. "So be it then,'' she managed, her chin lifting slowly. "I will send our women to Long Earrings. He has gone to the canyon?''

But Heuro shook his head. "No. He, too, has left *Dinetah.* ''

She gasped raggedly, stunned. "No! This cannot be. His medicine will not work outside of our sacred mountains. The Holy People cannot hear him there.''

Heuro's expression was sympathetic but implacable. "He has no warriors, *estsa hataali,* no strong men to lead the pale-eyes off. They all went with Manuelito. And he thinks there will be more pale-eyes this time than ever before.''

She looked at him emptily, then nodded. Her medicine told her exactly the same thing. There would be more pale-eyes this time. And they would not stop at sweeping the valley as they had before.

She looked to Na'acoci. "You will lead our women away first, before you fight," she told him quietly. "Find out where the *hataali* has gone, and take them there."

Na'acoci stiffened. "Them?" he repeated stupidly.

"I cannot go."

There was a stunned silence. Then, one by one, the men looked at Hawk's unconscious form.

"They call me crazy?" Na'acoci exploded at Gray Eyes. "You are worse! He is a dead man! I honored him in life, but I will not see you—"

"He lives," she interrupted quietly. "And as long as he does, I will stay."

He looked at her in appalled fury, then his face crumbled. Outside the council circle, Quiet Woman began to week brokenly.

Pity and regret churned in Gray Eyes' gut. "Surely you can see that another journey such as the one that brought him here would kill him!" she pleaded. "And even if I could take him with me, I do not believe that I could heal him there, away from the Holy People." She hesitated. "He is my heart. To leave him here to die would be to kill myself."

Na'acoci got to his feet and left without another word. The others followed him. Quiet Woman watched her despairingly. "Daughter . . ."

"Please," Gray Eyes whispered. "You must do this thing. If you stay here now, we will lose more. And we have nothing left to give." She stood and pushed Quiet Woman gently toward the door.

Na'acoci reappeared first. He pressed his carbine into her hands, then his hunting knife. He rested his lance against the wall. "Will you take this much?" he asked, turning back to her. "Will you allow me this bit of protection?"

She hesitated, then nodded. Quiet Woman came next.

"I leave you sheep." She spoke with precarious control. "Only a few. But enough to tide you over."

Again, Gray Eyes nodded. But when One Whisker appeared, she dropped helplessly to the floor again, hugging her knees close to her chest as though to control the pain that grew there.

"And a pony," he said. "Your warrior will need one. I will leave you *Hacke'itaswode'*, He Ran Through Warriors. He is one of my best."

She looked up at him, her eyes bright. "Thank you, *Ataa'*." Then she could say nothing more.

She didn't go outside to watch them depart. She clung to an image of Wildcat holding Na'acoci's head beneath the water of the ravine. She thought of K'aalo'gii laughing and racing after the wind. Her gentle mother, her stubborn father, the brother who knew no fear. Helpless, senile Black Spot.

She would remember them living, not leaving the precious, sacred land that was *Dinetah*.

Chapter 27

Rain and mist came again with the dawn. Gray Eyes lay on her back, staring up at the smoke hole as she listened to it. For the first time in her life she found it to be a chilling sound without any activity in the camp to dull it.

But beside her, Hawk still lived, and she took her comfort from that. Sitting up, she bundled her sheepskin more closely around him, and, for the first time since she had pulled him from the fort, she left him alone.

She hurried to the ravine and dispensed with her ablutions quickly. But her thoughts were heavy with the weight of responsibility. Long Earrings was gone. She was on her own. It was an overwhelming thought, but it made her all the more determined to push her panic and pain aside. She shivered as she pushed at the strands of wet hair that clung to her face, then squared her shoulders and went in search of firewood and some sort of nourishment for Hawk.

She kept her eyes straight ahead as she made her way through the camp. When she stumbled again, she looked down slowly this time, unsurprised.

The hawk blocked her path. The branch she had bound to his damaged wing was still intact, but the wool she had used to secure it was frayed from repeated assaults of his beak. His eyes met hers and he flapped his good wing aggressively.

"All is well," she whispered. He cocked his head. "I have saved him, I think. Him, and many of his men. Go now. Go back to the sky that claims you."

He gave a raucous call, then moved off down the path,

his good wing outstretched, his bad one cutting a swath in the earth. With a forceful lunge, he managed to reach the branch of a nearby juniper, then, with a final scream, he soared off clumsily into a western sky that was still murky and dotted with stars.

Only a single feather remained, bent and broken on the ground. Gray Eyes smoothed it carefully against her thigh and slipped it into her gall bag.

Summer came. The pale-eyes didn't.

Gray Eyes spent her days in near-perfect solitude. She rooted for the first seeds of the season and stalked rabbits and deer. She fed them to Hawk in increasingly solid hunks and watched him grow slowly, infinitesimally strong again. Each night she pressed her body close to his, giving him her warmth, her strength, her power. Each morning he rallied to a point that he hadn't reached before.

It would have been a peaceful time had it not been for the war that raged just outside their world. She stumbled upon it occasionally, and each experience was more frightening than the last. Once she hid in a rotted, hollow juniper trunk while blue-coated soldiers with their strange visors galloped across the desert, raising dust and trampling precious medicinal plants as they passed. She watched them, her pulse throbbing with terror and hatred, then hurried back to the camp to tell Hawk what she'd seen.

He was far more interested in the Ute chief. But then, the Ute appeared on a day when his fever was calm.

She left him that morning to move up the mountain and sing her songs. As she gazed down at the valley, her line of vision was suddenly broken. Startled, she looked up into the assessing eyes of an enemy warrior. His pony was muscled and hard, his war bonnet wild in the way of the Utes. He wore the clothing of a white man.

She screamed, an endless sound of terror that ripped from her against her will. But she had the presence of mind to run up the mountain, away from Hawk and the camp. She dodged into a wash and hid, pushing down into the tangled shield of cottonwood branches until the sun set and she could sneak safely back to camp.

"A scout," Hawk murmured when she told him. "He will bring others back. Pale-eyes probably. He is helping the soldiers like last time." Then he drifted off again without saying anything more.

She stared at him in frustration, shaking him gently to wake him again, but to no avail. Finally, she armed herself with her bow and Na'acoci's carbine. She sat up that night and all of the next. For weeks she remained in camp, afraid to hunt, afraid even to go to the ravine. She killed off Quiet Woman's sheep so that they might eat, and she waited for the Ute and whoever he would bring back to slaughter them.

But he never came. And it was August before she mentioned him to Hawk again.

As the moon of A Little Ripening descended upon them, he began to move outside in the mornings to absorb the healing rays of the sun before it became too scorching. At first he had needed her help. But as his periods of lucidity became longer and clearer, so did his strength. Finally, he was able to move on his own.

As he made his way to a fallen juniper tree one clear, hot morning, she bounced a basket on her knee absently and watched him. She'd been planning to go up the mountain to collect the sourberries and the chokecherries that had just recently ripened, but now she was in no hurry.

For a long time he only rubbed fat from one of the slaughtered sheep into the string of his new bow. Then he glanced up at her with a look that was partially curious but at least half teasing.

"You should go, little one," he prodded after a moment. "Or would you starve me?"

She tossed her hair arrogantly, but she couldn't hide a smile. "You must be feeling better. You are becoming disagreeable again."

"Hunger does that to a man."

Her smile faded abruptly. "Yes, I know. But there is little I can do to remedy the situation."

He looked startled. In truth, he had given little thought to the food that appeared every morning and evening to tempt him—sizzling slabs of antelope, succulent legs of rabbit, and mutton in every form imaginable. Then there were the seeds and the plants and the vegetables. Not once had he truly felt hunger during his recuperation. But looking at her now, he realized for the first time that she was far thinner than usual. His eyes narrowed dangerously.

"And why is that?" he asked, an edge to his voice.

"I have picked this area dry," she admitted absently, scanning it with her eyes. "And I dare not venture too far from camp. For one thing, I have seen much evidence of this war, and it is close. For another, I do not like to leave you alone. The animals know by now that they can run easily out of my reach and I will not follow. And the sheep that *'Ama'* left me . . ." She trailed off and shrugged helplessly. "I have already slaughtered three of them, and I wish to preserve the remainder as long as possible."

"So you do not eat?" he asked sharply. "You give it all to me?"

She looked back at him. "Do not be foolish. If I had not eaten since the day I found you at *Tsehotsohih,* then I would be long dead."

He was too intent upon the topic of their conversation to recognize her reference to the raid. "You are too skinny," he declared, his voice hard.

"And you are not in a position to be so choosy! Rain Girl is not here to entice you with her beauty. You will just have to look at what is available."

"I do not think of Rain Girl," he grated. "I think of your health. I will not have you grow ill because of me."

"You should have thought of that moons ago. My health is closely related to my appetite, and you saw that go the way of the wind when you warned me that that Ute would come back! And then you slept and told me nothing more!"

"The Ute?" Suddenly, he looked blank, confused. He had a vague memory of her telling him of one. But it was foggy, like an image of her bending over him in the heat of battle. He had disregarded both as impossible.

"The one who chased me up the mountain," she clarified, leaning closer to him, unconsciously intent upon provoking him. It was so good to have him back. "I stood watch for him for twenty, maybe thirty suns," she finished, "while you slept like a babe."

"And what would you have had me do? I am wounded!"

"But alive, thanks to me. The least you could have done was offer some guidance toward keeping us that way."

"Thanks to you?"

Her eyes slid guiltily away as he watched her. "Now you sound like Na'acoci," she muttered, "ready to rail at me for that which could not be helped."

"What could not be helped?"

"My going to the raid."

For a moment, he only looked stunned. It was true, then, what he remembered . . . that sinking feeling as his pulse had throbbed in pain, the knowledge that she was there again, that she would always be there whether it was time for her or not. Her eyes, silver and sparking into his soul, demanding that he live. Her back shielding him from a pale-eyes' voice and cannon fire. It was distant, but it came back to him, all of it. And now he looked at her with a sense of inevitability that left a warmth in his heart even while it brought a coldness to his gut.

"You fought the pale-eyes," he murmured. "You were disguised as a warrior."

She didn't answer.

"Why?"

Because the hawk had come to her with a wounded wing, she answered silently, wildly. Because she had known that she was needed to save him and his men. Because she had been born for this man, because she could have no life without him, because the Holy People had given her silver eyes.

"Because it was meant," she said aloud.

He went still, looking into the gaze that sparked with a challenge for him to fight her. And suddenly he knew that he wouldn't, not anymore.

"Yes," he murmured, "perhaps it is."

She blinked, confused at his acquiescence. Then her breath caught at the heat in his eyes. It burned without reservation now. Always before there had been stone there, implacable, holding her at bay. But now there was naked fire as he gave in to the commands of fate. A shiver worked down her spine.

She was only vaguely aware that the birds in the trees had fallen quiet, the wind had stilled. Their argument had pushed at them and then faded, leaving them just inches apart. But although her heart pounded in expectation and her breath hung suspended, moments passed and he made no move to close the distance between them.

"*Estsa hataali*," he murmured instead. "So young, so strong, so powerful. What did you do to that pale-eyes? I remember him, you know. And I remember you. He should have killed us both. But you stopped him. How? Was it the curse of the gods that he saw in your silver eyes? Or was it only the protection of the Holy People who honor you so? My uncle is right. They have chosen you for their own."

She shook her head, frustrated. She didn't want to talk of that now. But then, suddenly, she understood. He would, he could, take only what she gave. She, more so than any other woman, had to go to him in the People's way. Her woman's heart recognized that now, but the child remaining within her was terrified that she was wrong. He had fooled her so many times, pulling back with a teasing smile. But he had teased an innocent child, and that child was dying. After a short struggle, the woman conquered her.

She pushed slowly to her feet. The empty basket on her knee fell to the ground and rolled away, forgotten.

"Perhaps," she answered softly. "But I have chosen you."

His nostrils flared. Confidence, pride, steadied her as her fingers climbed down her shift and found the hem. She brought it up slowly.

Without her, he could not be weakened, he thought. But without her, neither could he live. Hadn't he always known that? He had run from her only to turn to her. He had hidden from her only to seek her out. His heart had fought back from death for her. And now she was calling to him again, in the age-old voice of woman. He watched her shift move up over tawny thighs and slender hips. Her small, firm breasts rose as she lifted her arms and pulled it over her head. An agony of need, of wanting, lanced through him. She dropped the buckskin to the earth and waited.

His hand snaked out suddenly and gripped hers.

"Tell me, little wolf-man," he commanded quietly. "Tell me that you chose me before the beginning of time. That I can believe. That I can accept. It is not that I am so weak that I cannot resist you. It is that you are my strength."

She didn't answer. His eyes searched hers and found the answer he would struggle against for the last time.

He pulled her to her knees, then leaned toward her and covered her mouth with his own. His lips were hot and smooth. They possessed neither the playfulness of the day between the rocks, nor the urgency and anger of the last time she had healed him. Instead he claimed her, drawing her in, finally and irrevocably making her whole.

She made a catlike sound of satisfaction and let her eyes drift closed. He tasted of nighttime, she thought, of dark, haunting pleasures and desires too long denied. She drank in the feel of him, the taste of him, the musky, masculine scent of him. Her yearning for him had always been as elemental as thirst, as consuming as obsession. Now she accepted both as simply as the child who had once acknowledged that the Holy People had sent him into her world.

His tongue moved between her lips and parted them, penetrating her mouth slowly. He caught her around the waist, his hands strong and uncompromising as he brought her beneath him. Then his body covered hers, pushing her down, trapping her between his heat and the unyielding strength of the earth.

His teeth nibbled, his tongue soothed as they moved down her throat, along her collar bone, across her breasts. Suddenly, the quiet fulfillment that had been stretching its wings within her turned to such violent need that she cried out.

"No, little one." He chuckled. "This will not be peaceful or easy. It is as I told you long ago. Together we will soar like the one who bears my name. We will race the wind."

And he was, in that moment, a bird of prey, free and wild, haughty and proud as he swooped to the earth he disdained just long enough to capture a long-awaited prize. She drove her fingers into his hair, trailing it between her fingers, ensnaring it tightly to demand that his mouth come back to hers.

More, she wanted more. She wanted the tumult and the danger he promised. They joined again, tongues twining, tastes mingling, but it wasn't enough. Her fingers began plucking frenziedly at the yarn that held his tunic together until it fell free. Still, she arched her back in a primitive, instinctive search for something unnameable that was just out of her grasp.

A dark sound slid from his throat, the sound of a man who was on the brink of control. Had she been any other woman, he would have taken her then. But she was Baa' Ya'zhi', the little wolf-man who'd once fought him, the woman-child who'd once spurned him, the power that fed his own. She was smoke, the promise of fire, and he had waited too long for her to burn.

Her soft hands stroked him, urging him on. He held

back, even as she touched and searched and demanded. Her hands moved down the length of him, over the long, tight muscles of his back, his buttocks, his thighs. He answered by bending to her breasts again, his tongue the rough-soft texture of sand baking beneath the summer sun. Beneath her palms, his muscles flexed, gave, tightened. Need and pleasure coalesced in her throat into a feral growl.

The sound broke him. His hands left her to slide beneath her back, claiming her, pulling her against him. His manhood found the core of her. Then he drove into her, suddenly and hard.

On the slope of the mountain, a jackrabbit paused in mid-leap, his ears twitching. A dove cocked his head, then stopped cooing. Far away, in the valley, a wounded hawk sank his talons into the earth, tipped back his head, and called to the sky.

Hawk filled her, and as her voice rose in sweet, eager, wild cries, the sky darkened and the moon slid over the sun.

Chapter 28

Gray Eyes had only one warning that the jackrabbit would not provide their evening meal. Just as she hunkered down behind a scraggly mesquite bush, she heard a faint, low, rustling sound from the direction of the ravine.

"I know that your life is as precious as mine," she told the rabbit. "But I must kill you. Come to me, rabbit, and do not worry. I will eat your flesh and your life will continue in mine." The Holy People appeased, she drew her arm back. With a practiced flick of her wrist, Na'acoci's hunting knife sliced through the air.

It caught the rabbit squarely in the chest. With a wordless sound of satisfaction, Gray Eyes stood away from the bush. Then the cottonwoods rustled again and a mangy dog bolted out of the branches. She shouted in outrage, but to no avail. The mutt swooped in on the rabbit and carried him off, hunting knife and all.

"I hope it cuts your mongrel tongue to shreds!" she hollered after him, but the only response she got was a low chuckle that came from behind her.

"I am afraid he is too clever for that, little one," Hawk answered. "But I could always go after him and exact revenge with the carbine." His hands spanned her waist easily as he stepped close to her. Then he bent to touch his mouth to the little hollow next to her collarbone.

As always when he touched her, a coiling warmth started low at the center of her. Gray Eyes smiled and tilted her head to give him better access. "For what purpose?" she murmured. "You are far too spoiled to eat dog, my love. Besides, he means no harm."

Hawk paused in his ministrations long enough to laugh again. "Then why does he steal half of what you kill? You feed him enough of our scraps that he cannot possibly be hungry."

"Instinct, perhaps."

"Ah, a strong motivator."

"And for love of the conquest."

"Stronger still."

She gave a haughty lift of her brow. "You speak from experience?"

"Many seasons' worth."

"So I was nothing more than prey to you." Then she sighed as a softness gathered in her eyes and she turned in his arms. "No, my love, you have it all wrong," she went on. "You are the prey, elusive and free. And I never would have caught you had you not been grounded."

She ran a finger along the scars that marked his belly. They were nearly five moons old now and mending nicely. A discordant flash of pain prodded deep within her. He would leave soon. Sooner or later her hawk would return to the skies. The *Naakaiidine'e'* and pale-eyes would beckon to him.

But not yet, she thought, not now. She turned her face up to his again and sought his lips greedily.

Perhaps he, too, knew that the heavens had not relinquished him but were merely waiting for his return. He pulled her closer so suddenly, with such strength, that her breath escaped her in a tiny puff. She didn't hear the sharp clatter of the hunting knife as the hound shook it free of the rabbit and dropped it against the rocks of the ravine. She didn't feel the cruel September sun as it drained the life from an already parched land. Nor was she aware of the faint thrumming of distant hoofbeats as they battered the earth. They grew louder, then slowed, and eventually faded away again, their retreat camouflaged by the small cry of yearning that escaped her.

"Sweet shaman," Hawk whispered. "Always calling to me. Calling when I did not want to hear, calling when I would have been content to die. You made me listen. You made me live. How special you are, *aje'i' di'shjool*, my heart."

His words and his mouth moved over her until her breath became ragged and her eyes wild. They dropped to the earth, too hungry to spare a thought for the more pleasant shade of the shelter. When his hand met the waiting heat and need of her, any restraint he might have possessed was shattered. He moved over her and filled her, more deeply, more completely, than ever before.

It was a long time before the sounds of the earth returned to them. There was a call from a cactus wren, an irritable, buzzing cicada. The mongrel growled as he finished his feast and slunk back into the shade cast by Talks Often's shelter. Gray Eyes stirred as Hawk sat up.

She watched him from beneath partially lowered lids, then her hand snaked out to capture his. "And now, my love?" she wondered.

A grin took his hard features, making him look young and roguish again. "If you will not let me shoot the dog, then I suppose you must find another rabbit," he answered. "You fill me, little one, but my belly still grumbles." He stood and stretched his arms toward the sun, his loincloth falling back into place, the muscles of his shoulders rippling. She watched him with a small, contented smile.

"It is a warrior's job to hunt," she reminded him.

"You forget, I am wounded."

"Ha! Your belly, perhaps, but your laziness is very healthy."

"Would you starve me for it?"

She grinned. "I should."

"I wish only to recuperate fully without straining myself, little one. What kind of warrior would I be if I were always frail?"

Gray Eyes' smile faded abruptly. What kind of warrior,

indeed? He would not be the hawk who flew so fearlessly and free. He would not be the man to whom she was bound.

She sat up quickly. "Sharpen your bows then," she answered a bit too tightly. "I will see to your hunger."

She stood and shrugged into her shift, then moved off in the direction of Talks Often's shelter with a look of grim determination. Hawk hesitated, then put the bow aside to watch her. There would be time enough for weapons, he thought, time enough for the pale-eyes and the *Naakai-idine'e'* later. They would wait. He knew they would always wait, long after these idyllic days were a memory.

She closed in on the dog cautiously, obviously intending to tie him this time. Her voice was soft and coaxing as she tried to lull him, but the mongrel was having none of it. Just as she lunged for him, he leaped up and darted past her.

She fell hard, landing on her stomach. But she rolled quickly, reflexively, coming up on her haunches before Hawk could laugh. She threw him a dark look of warning.

"One chuckle, my love, and you will have far worse troubles than an empty belly."

He lifted a skeptical brow instead. "I was merely wondering if you are adept enough to rustle up our evening meal without my help."

Her shrug was surprisingly benign. But he knew her too well. When she moved toward their shelter and the kettle of indigo dye that was cooling there, he leaped to his feet.

Still, he wasn't fast enough. The liquid sailed in an inky arc, catching him across the shoulders and down the back. For a moment, he stood frozen, amazed that she had bested him. She took the opportunity to dart past him and head for the ravine.

She had nearly reached it when she heard him closing in on her. She opened up into a loose-limbed run, her breath catching in her throat and tripping over her laughter. When she hit the ravine, she slid down the rocks on her heels, her arms waving wildly for balance. But before she could claw her way up the other side, the mutt shot out of the shadows. He stopped directly in front of her, planting all four paws.

Gray Eyes leaped instinctively, vaulting over the top of him, only to land gracelessly in the thin trickle of water. She sputtered and swiped at her face, but before she could rise again, Hawk tumbled down on top of her.

With a single, swift reflex, he pinned her arms over her head. Gray Eyes threw a scathing look at the dog.

"Skinny, useless spawn of a wolf-man," she gasped. "I should have had you shot when I had the chance."

The dog whined and laid down. Hawk threw back his head and laughed.

"You are no better," she snapped, fighting a smile.

His look faded to one that was at once fierce and tender. "And you," he whispered, "you are the sun that brightens my world." He hesitated a heartbeat. "I love you, little one."

He had never spoken the words before. She had read them in his eyes and had doubted her sight. She had felt them in his touch and had scorned her senses. Now her eyes widened and her breath hitched as wonder and joy brought a hot wetness to her eyes.

"And I you," she whispered. Then, for one shining, precious moment, she dared to look up at the gods and smile.

September faded gently. Gray Eyes gathered the last of the wild nuts that had reached fruition and steadfastly readied the camp for winter. If it occurred to her that neither she nor Hawk would be there when the snows came, she pushed the thought away.

October brought the deer down from the mountain. She took to rising early, before the sun, to stalk them. Sometimes she went alone; more often Hawk went with her. At times they caught nothing as their hunt deteriorated into heated debates over the best way to slay their prey. When they came back empty-handed, they had nuts and berries and each other. Then, one clear and wintry morning, she woke to find him gone.

She knew that she was alone even before she opened her eyes. She had woken abruptly, with a dull sensation of unease. Then she identified the low, chafing sound that drifted to her from just outside the door.

It chilled her nearly as much as her initial foreboding. Though it was barely dawn, Hawk was already sharpening his arrows.

Rising slowly, she bundled herself up in her bedding and peered out the door. "You waste your time, my love," she greeted him. "No matter how many times you work over them, I fear you will still insist upon shooting them into the wrong part of the doe."

He looked up guiltily, startled by the sound of her voice. Then he relaxed, dropping the arrow he held to smile at her.

"It is of no consequence," she went on blithely. "I will go with you to show you how to hunt correctly." She began to move back to the shelter to retrieve her own bow and quiver. Then, suddenly, she went still, no longer able to keep up the charade.

"What is it?" she asked finally. "What has happened?"

He hesitated as a primitive urge to protect her swelled inside him. But she would never forgive him a patronizing lie. He pushed the instinct away. It went unwillingly, clawing at his soul.

"I went out without you this morning," he answered shortly. "I found tracks."

"Hooves? Moccasins?"

"Both."

"How close?"

"The other side of the ravine."

"How fresh?"

"Old. At least fourteen suns." Then his voice softened. "It does not matter, little one. Someone was here, and they will return."

But hope fluttered treacherously at her breast all the same. "Perhaps not," she said, whirling back to him. "If they had intended to, then surely they would have done so by now."

He shook his head. "No."

"You cannot know that!"

Something dark and dangerous glinted in his eyes, something she hadn't seen in a long time. "You doubt me, little one?"

She hesitated.

"They would retreat for only one reason," he went on. "To bring others."

"You said that about the Ute," she reminded him, her voice pleading.

"And I say it again."

He rose to his feet abruptly, replacing his arrows in his quiver. She ran forward to grip his arm.

"If you are planning to follow them, then know that I am going with you."

"No!" This time the instinct to protect her was fierce enough to conquer him. "You are of my soul. If you were near I would worry for you, defend you if there was trouble, perhaps even lose my life in the bargain. Would you have that?"

She wouldn't, and he knew it. She flinched, but didn't answer.

"Go up the mountain," he went on. "They know where our camp is. You cannot wait here alone." Then, finally, he softened. "Most likely I will find nothing. I only wish to see in which direction the tracks go. As slow as you are, I will be back long before you can even bring home a rabbit."

He was trying to goad her into acquiescing. She knew that and wanted to smile, but she couldn't. She only swallowed dryly, painfully, then finally nodded.

He caught One Whisker's pony and, with a quick scissoring of his legs, leaped up and disappeared into the cottonwoods. She stared after him for a long time, anger and frustration and fear churning inside her.

"This time," she whispered. Her Hawk would come back to her this time. But somehow she knew that she was about to lose him again all the same.

Chapter 29

Hawk had been right. The sun passed its zenith before she caught a rabbit.

The day was pleasantly cool, and with the heavy weight of the carcass thumping against her hip, Gray Eyes was almost able to forget the tracks that had lured Hawk away. But as she headed down the mountain again, her eyes scanned the valley and her heart began to beat uneasily. Hawk was nowhere to be seen.

She nudged Smoke to a faster pace, eager to know that he was already back in camp waiting for her. But when she approached the abandoned, collapsing shelters, they appeared deserted. The dog ran on ahead, yapping and wagging his tail anyway. She followed at her own pace, her heart heavy.

Then she heard the voices that came from the direction of the shelter that had once belonged to Wildcat.

Pale-eyes? Utes? She couldn't be sure. Their voices were a murmur, no more than the rumble of distant thunder. Her heart pounding, she freed her hunting knife and tied the rabbit to Smoke's mane. Then she dropped silently to the ground and moved crablike into the shade of her own shelter.

Suddenly, her frantic pulse slowed. Not pale-eyes, she realized. And not *Naakaiidine'e'*. She recognized the voice now. It was Na'acoci.

She peeked around the shelter. There were a few other warriors at the fire as well, including Achi'i'h and Jack-rabbit. But whatever joy that touched her heart at seeing them again died quickly. Their faces were thin, gaunt, hardened. And she knew, in a cold place of her soul, that they had come for her Hawk. He was beside the fire as well, holding council with them.

"It is not enough," she heard Na'acoci say.

"What would you have me do?" Hawk asked. "I cannot change the ways of our people. If they are content to hide from this enemy, then that is their right."

"You can strike out on your own," Na'acoci challenged. "You can lead us."

The suggestion made Gray Eyes flinch. There was a grunt from Hawk, but whether of agreement or dissent, she couldn't tell. "Tell me all you know," was all he said.

"The pale-eyes have brought in more war chiefs," Jackrabbit answered. "The big man Fauntleroy has sent three more to *Tsehotsohih*. Some have already marched out in search of us. There is a man they call Canby. He has a mushy face that always looks as though he found manure in his stew. He has gone to Canyon de Chelly. Then there is a man named Sibley. He is evil-looking. His chin is sharp and sticks out almost as far as his visor. Heuro hears that he has gone to Pueblo Colorado. The other war chief will come here, to the Chuskas, at any sun. When Canby and Sibley converge, he will try to capture those of us who come here to hide from them."

"They do not know yet that we are nearly all gone to the land of the Dead Ones," Na'acoci sneered. "Our men all hid like cowards moons ago."

Hawk ignored his animosity. "What does Manuelito do?"

"As always, the pale-eyes search for him most of all," Jackrabbit answered. "They think that if they destroy Manuelito, we will have no great war chief left and we will crumble. They are largely correct. That is why more of us need to fight."

"We have more than one war chief," Hawk pointed out. "There is Barboncito."

"He and his band have joined with Manuelito, at least for the duration of the war."

"What of Delgondito? He will fight if provoked."

"He is gone."

Gray Eyes' heart slammed against her ribs. Not Delgondito! she thought. Surely they had not killed that kind and sensitive man!

She was a moment away from crying her protest aloud when Jackrabbit explained. "His band was attacked just west of the canyon by the man Sibley. Delgondito escaped, but now he too has gone west to *Moqui* country."

This news was met by considering silence. Gray Eyes leaned back against the shelter helplessly.

Hawk would go. She knew it in her soul. He would lead these die-hard warriors to fight the invincible, just as Manuelito persisted in doing. And there was nothing she could do to stop him.

But she too could fight, in her way.

She jerked away from the shelter suddenly, as though the thought had burned her. Yes, she could fight. The *hataali* had told her so.

She moved out of the shadows to join the council.

"Eavesdropping again, sister?" Na'acoci taunted, but there was no humor in his voice as there had been in the old days.

She bent to embrace him anyway. "*Halah*," she greeted him. "My brother."

She left him and moved to a spot next to Hawk. "You will continue," she said quietly. No one answered. She looked toward Na'acoci again.

"What of our family?" she demanded. "What of the other headman? Long Earrings? Agua Chiquito? Have you heard anything of them?"

Jackrabbit answered quickly so she wouldn't speak the last name again. "The Towering Rock headman is dead."

She paled, remembering him, her initiation at his village, and the way his eyes had smiled. She heard her own voice respond as though from far away. "How?"

"The man Sibley again. Our headman stumbled upon a group of soldiers, and the pale-eyes commander turned on him. Our brother was wounded, so he could not defend himself. The man Sibley ordered his soldiers to put him to death."

Gray Eyes nodded carefully, sure that if she moved too quickly she would break. "And the others?" she asked.

"Our clan is well and alive," Na'acoci finally contributed. "They still wait for you, sister, near the land of the Dead Ones. Your heart can rest."

A sigh of relief escaped her. Then Hawk shifted his weight. In his eyes was a feral glint, a vision of hatred and loathing.

"*My* heart cannot rest," he answered after a moment. "If these pale-eyes wish to kill unarmed men, then so shall we. If they choose to fight without fairness or honor, then so be it. They wish to change us, so we will change. We will meet them on their terms. We will fight rather than hide, but we will do so wisely."

There was a raucous chorus of approval from the men. Na'acoci's eyes glittered with satisfaction. Gray Eyes rose to her feet with care.

"Now that that has been decided," she said quietly, "I must see about preparing our evening meal. We will need our strength to travel."

Her words were reasonable, but her tone was too precise. Hawk watched her silently as she moved off, then he rose as well.

"Did you catch a rabbit?" he demanded.

She paused, but didn't turn back to him. "One."

"It will not be enough to feed all of these men."

"No."

"I will send them to hunt down something more."

She nodded, still not looking at him, and turned into her shelter.

He followed moments later. As he filled the door opening, he looked suddenly alien to her, like the forbidding, mocking warrior who had struck panic in her heart for so long. His broad shoulders blocked out the last of the day's dwindling light as he rested a hand on either side of the door opening. There was power in his posture, intimidation in the ruddy, haughty slant of his cheekbones.

Then he spoke, and his voice was still that of her lover. "They are gone, little one."

She nodded stiffly. "For now. But you were right after all. They will return." Somehow she knew without being told that the tracks Hawk had followed had been theirs. They had arrived at the camp fourteen suns ago, but some glimmer of compassion had kept them from immediately disturbing them.

"Yes," Hawk agreed. "But not tonight."

He stepped into the shelter and dropped down on his haunches beside her. "They will hunt the east slopes and camp there until morning," he explained. Then his mouth quirked with the beginnings of a smile. "Is that not where you said the fattest rabbits were? Far, far north and east of here?"

She almost laughed. He was cunning indeed, her warrior-hawk. But her heart was too fragile, her fear too great. She only ducked her head and nodded again.

"Little one." When she didn't respond, his strong hand caught her chin and pulled her face upward. "I cannot stay here any longer. I do not agree with the way our elders would fight this war. If we run from the pale-eyes again, we will always run from them. We must fight back, but we must do it with far more cunning than Manuelito." He paused. "It is time, little one. Time for me to fight the pale-eyes my way."

She had known that for far too long to argue. "Yes," she whispered. "You must go."

"It is not time for us now. But I will return to you. Between raids, between battles."

"No!" Emotion, held so tightly in check a moment before, shattered within her. "I will travel with you," she went on desperately. "Your men will need my medicine." It was the single thing she was certain of. Hawk would fight. It was his way. And she would work to save what survived.

But Hawk was shaking his head vehemently. "You do not know of what you speak! You have no comprehension of war!"

"Then what, wise warrior, would you call the battle at *Tsehotsohih?*" she demanded, suddenly angry herself.

"A foolish chance taken by an impetuous young woman!"

"That foolish chance saved your arrogant hide!"

They stopped suddenly, chests heaving. Then, from somewhere beneath the pounding of her heart, Gray Eyes felt an unnerving sense of foreboding.

Never, ever, had they fought in this way before.

He stood again and paced the shelter. "Those people who are hiding, those who are without their medicine in the land of the Hopi, they need you far more than I," he tried. He knew he was being selfish, knew he was manipulating her through her love for her people. But he felt no remorse, only a vast relief as she seemed to slump in on herself, her defiance conquered.

His words hit her hard, for she knew that they were true. She belonged with her people, with the ones who hid and waited. She had to soothe their ills and ease their pain. She had her own war, and it was not Hawk's.

She wanted to scream against the injustice of being so chosen. She wanted to claw out the eyes of these pale, greedy men who would not leave her alone. Instead she grasped the kettle suspended over the fire pit and threw it wildly. It bounced against the wall, splintering the dry, fragile boughs there. She watched it, her chest heaving, then buried her face in her hands.

"Must I always wait and wonder?" she cried. "How many times am I to watch you go, knowing that I will not see you again until it is time to heal you?" She jerked her head up and stared at him rudely. "Tell me, my brave warrior!" she demanded. "How often am I to wait for you, only to find you dying when you return?"

He didn't answer, but she hadn't truly expected him to. She jumped to her feet and claimed his mouth suddenly. "So be it," she whispered savagely. "I will let you go if I must. I will be obedient and pliable and do as you ask. But this last night is mine, *mine!*"

She shrugged, letting her shift fall to her waist. Then she wriggled her hips and it dropped to the hard-packed floor. He looked startled, then his eyes softened and he reached out to gather her to him.

His body was as warm as the sun, as hard as the trees that grew at the peak of the mountain. She traced the lines and contours of him with her fingers, breathed in and absorbed the musky masculine scent of him. Then, long before he expected it, she arched her hips upward. She captured his body as she had conquered his soul, holding him in the deepest, warmest part of her.

Her hawk, her warrior. He would go again. But this time he would leave a part of himself behind.

▼▼▼▼▼▼▼▼▼▼▼▼▼▼▼▼▼▼▼

PART TWO

Chapter 30

They left at high noon the next day. The men rode hard, but Gray Eyes lagged behind. As they crossed Chinle Wash, she shuddered once, hard, with emotion so fierce that she could barely contain it. Then she turned her eyes back to *Dinetah* and said good-bye.

They rode on until the moon rose full above them and the country began to change. Near the edges of Hopi, the land became close and cluttered. She found it hard to breathe as she looked up at the barren buttes and hills that pressed in on her, crowding her at every side. She both understood why her people chose to hide here, and despaired of ever finding them.

Finally, on the fifth morning, they heard a faint bawling of sheep. Their journey was over, but she felt no joy. She watched dully as Hawk nodded to Jackrabbit and they turned their mounts in the direction of the sheep.

They passed through a gorge so narrow that the hard rock scraped her knees on both sides. Then a valley spread out before them, a rough, dusty place devoid of grass. There were no shelters, only a dead fire and people huddled around it in blankets. The shape of a thin, spidery man nagged at her with its familiarity. Hastin Dalin. He Acts Like an Old Man.

This was the *hataali*'s camp.

Before Hawk or any of the other warriors could react, she leaped down from Smoke. There were shouts of "*No'o'da'i'*, enemy!" from those who hadn't recognized her or noticed Hawk, but she ignored them all and ran until she reached the fire pit.

She stopped there, breathing hard, feeling alive for the first time since Na'acoci had appeared in the summer camp. She nodded eagerly at Barren Woman, who lumbered slowly to her feet. "Where is he?" she demanded.

Barren Woman hesitated for a brief second, then she led her past the fire pit and around yet another sharp, protruding hulk of rock. Long Earrings was there on the other side.

He moved in semicircles around a small fire. His face was as old, as wizened, as dear as she remembered. His birds and gourds rattled comfortingly; his song was low and compelling as he prayed to the Holy People for food, for relief, for rain.

"It is always like this," Barren Woman muttered. "If we do not return to our homeland soon, I fear he will make himself crazy."

But Gray Eyes barely heard her. She moved closer to the fire and began to sing along with him.

Long Earrings stopped abruptly, cocking his head, then he looked around sharply and spotted her. For a moment, there was confusion in his tired old eyes, then they lit from within. "Granddaughter! You have come."

She hurried to him and embraced him fiercely. Tears stung at her eyes, tears that never fell anymore. She laughed shakily.

"I will no longer ask how you knew I would."

He chuckled softly. "Come and sit with me," he urged. "It is too long since I have seen you. Do you travel alone?" Suddenly, his eyes darkened again. "What of our Hawk?" he asked. "I had heard that he was with you."

"He was. He is here, and he is healthy." But the *hataali* saw the pain in her eyes.

"Yes, it is time. He will fight now. I dreamed that, and dreamed too that you would come."

Her heart fluttered with traitorous hope. "You dreamed here? You still have medicine?"

But the *hataali* only sighed. "No. I dreamed this long ago. I rarely hear the Holy People anymore, although I try night and day to reach them. Sometimes my plants seem to work, although my chants do not. I brought medicines from our homeland, and they can still heal. They will not last much longer, but hopefully neither will this war."

She shivered.

"It is bad, granddaughter," he continued. "For years we have tormented the Dead Ones, raiding them, stealing their crops, their wives, their children. Now they seek revenge. They are a weak and sedentary people, this is true. They live their lives in one place, never moving on to visit the chick wrens when they hatch or the mule deer when they run up the mountain. Still, they hate us, and hate is a formidable enemy. If they find us in their homeland, they will not treat us kindly."

She nodded slowly.

"We move with the changing of the suns now rather than the seasons," Long Earrings mused. "The ponies remain saddled for quick escape. Our children remain in cradle boards. Every moment we have sentinels out watching for our enemies." He hesitated. "It is just no good anymore. Hunger gnaws at our bellies. Our babies cry."

"Can you see no means of soothing them?" she whispered.

"I see everything, but that is not always a gift."

Barren Woman chose that moment to bring them mutton, precious and juicy and rare. Long Earrings tore a piece off of it and tossed it into the fire. He ate for a moment before he finally looked off into the distance and continued.

"I am tired, granddaughter," he admitted. "It goes on and on, this fighting. These pale-eyes will never quit, but I no longer have the strength or stamina to keep telling our young men that their attempts to conquer them are hopeless."

Fear mushroomed suddenly in Gray Eyes' heart. She had seen this dull glint of defeat in a man's eyes before.

Memory whirled within her until she was back with Vittorio, watching him give up, watching him die.

"You must not grow weary!" she protested. "You are needed."

"No, granddaughter. *You* are needed, not I. You are grown now. The seasons have passed and you have stretched your wings. You are strong, full of life. This is your time."

"I am not ready," she whispered.

He only shrugged. "Perhaps. Perhaps not. There is one last thing I must tell you, you with eyes of silver, you with the strength to survive. You must triumph, granddaughter. You must live. In your soul dwell the old ways that our people are willing to forget. In your womb await children who will carry on as we did seasons ago. Someday, the pale-eyes will steal everything from us. But the one thing they cannot take is your soul."

He pushed to his feet. "Keep warm with us tonight," he finished. "Tomorrow we must move on. You will come with us. We will take you to your own."

A low, keening cry started in her throat, but he didn't acknowledge it.

It was a long time before she got to her feet and followed him back around the outcropping of rock. Because she couldn't accept what he had said, because she couldn't bear the finality with which he'd said it, she simply pushed thoughts of it away. She breathed deeply, taking in the disparate and familiar smells of mouth-watering mutton and humanity. She watched Jackrabbit flirt with a squaw and Hawk talk passionately to a gathering of warriors. She smiled fleetingly. Then a child screamed and she could no longer pretend that life was still simple and sweet and good.

She looked sharply around at the fire pit. It was alive now with hissing flames that licked and twisted around the last of the mutton. The people pressed close to it in a way she had never seen before. They lunged greedily for each scrap of meat, slapping and shoving each other out of the way. Two women tugged at a bone, and when one felt its smoothness begin to slide from her fingers, she fell screaming upon the other. Immediately more children began to cry, some lustily, others weakly as they stretched their hands out for more food. Gray Eyes watched, feeling sick.

She had known war often in her fifteen summers. She had suffered with it on the Chuska's northern slopes. She had defied it to drag Hawk free of *Tsehotsohih*. But now it crept even closer to her, its breath foul, its eyes glittering. She saw its inhumanity as it turned mother upon daughter, friend upon friend, and something snapped inside her.

"If you truly wish to destroy us, then go fight with the pale-eyes to rob the heart and soul of our people!" she challenged angrily. "Your squabbling will scatter us like sage in the wind, but it will take much longer!"

She watched, her heart pounding, as the crowd began to part and settle back. Across the fire, Hawk's eyes narrowed as he watched her. Pain showed briefly on his strong features. Yes, she was *estsa hataali*, and he knew, as he had always known, that he had done the right thing in bringing her here. But only the knowledge that she would be safe allowed him to let her go.

He turned abruptly back to the warriors. Gray Eyes moved to the fire pit and patted the ground beside her until children began to crawl cautiously to her side.

"Come now," she murmured to no one in particular. "It is cold and we are hungry, but perhaps we can forget all that if I tell you a story."

A babble of voices rose. "Tell of the Great Coyote who was formed in the water!" someone shouted.

"No, a story about Changing Woman!"

"The one about the hare!"

But Gray Eyes shook her head. "They have all been told as many times as there are stars in the sky," she chided. "Something else." When no one answered, she shrugged. "So be it. I will choose. I will tell you the story of why we have day and night.

"You remember the moccasin game that you play so much when you ought to be gathering crops?" she asked. She almost smiled at the furtive exchange of glances. "Who do you think made it up?"

"My sister!"

"The *hataali?*"

She shook her head. "No. It is a very ancient game, given to the People long ago by a mysterious being named One Walking Giant. Our ancestors used to visit him at the House Made of Banded Rock. He was a very nice giant who liked to laugh and play games. And this house of his was in a cave near the Chuskas."

She paused, gathering their full attention, then went on. "One day very many people visited One Walking Giant. Even the Holy People and the Coyote came. There were so many of them that the Giant realized he would have to make two teams if everyone was going to play this moccasin game. So he said that everyone who had traveled to him by day would play against those who had traveled by night.

"He laid out a hundred and two moccasins, and he told the people that the side that won all of them would win the game. If the day people won, there would always be daylight. If the night people won, there would always be darkness. Who do you suppose won?"

The children frowned. Clearly, no one had.

Gray Eyes laughed softly, enjoying their consternation. "I will tell you. They played all night until finally the sun began creeping over the mountains. Then they did not know what to do. There were still several moccasins left, but if they did not stop playing and go home, all manner of terrible things would happen to them. None of our *hataalis* would be able to reach the Holy People since they were busy playing, so we would be without our medicine. None of our hunters would be able to kill game, because they and the animals were playing too. No crops would be gathered and the sheep would stray. Without the Holy People, the animals, the crops and the sheep, the People would die. And so they finally gave up, with neither side winning. And that is why the world now has half day and half night, a place for the moon and a place for the sun." Her eyes clouded briefly.

Then another child called out. "Were the People happy even if there was no winner?"

She swallowed carefully. "Ah, but there was. Both the day people and the night people were winners, because their sheep and their crops and their children survived."

As will all of you, she thought fiercely, all of you. As her hand went to her belly and the child she prayed was inside, she looked up to meet Hawk's eyes.

Chapter 31

The morning brought unseasonably warm sunshine. It seemed to infuse a bit of life and hope into the Bitter Water band. They moved about energetically as they repacked the few possessions they had removed from their ponies. Only Long Earrings and Hawk remained apart from the crowd. They sat near the dead fire, talking intently.

Na'acoci watched them impatiently from the gorge as his colt stomped and snorted at his side. "The sun will be high by the time we are ready to go," he muttered when Gray Eyes approached him. She reached out to touch his arm lightly.

"We have lost our uncle and our grandfather, brother. I could not bear to lose you as well. Please, have patience. You will be on the warpath soon enough," she answered. Then, suddenly, her voice became fervent. "When you are, I ask that you think before you act. Remember who you are fighting for and be cautious. Chances are those people could not live without you."

He looked startled but thoughtful. Satisfied, Gray Eyes left him and went back to the camp.

There was so little time left now. Long Earrings and Hawk had moved apart, and more and more men were joining Na'acoci at the mouth of the gorge. Her heart began to pound with a dull, sick rhythm. She approached Hawk, her fingers on her gall bag and the gold coin hidden there.

He turned away from One Whisker's pony as soon as he sensed her behind him. "Little one," he murmured, touching a long strand of her hair. "I might return to you sooner than you suspect, with your father's pony. If at all possible, I will go directly to Manuelito's camp, then return here to Hopi. The pony was a gift. You can tell One Whisker that I will return him in good health as soon as I retrieve my own."

"If at all possible," she repeated quietly.

He grinned as though she had said something to humor him. "You expect that I will come to some harm? I think not, little one. You have never allowed me to."

She blinked in surprise at his words. Then her heart swelled and she could restrain herself no longer. She stood on tiptoe and touched her lips to his. Like a butterfly lighting and flying off again, she straightened and stepped away before he could react or anyone else could notice.

"May your horse run fast and your arrows fly true, my love," she whispered, "for I have nothing without you." And, she thought, I will be nothing until you return.

But she did not say the last words aloud, for she knew that even that plea would not keep her hawk from returning to the sky. As she watched, he vaulted onto his pony. He trotted into the crowd of warriors without looking back.

She listened to their receding hoofbeats until she could bear it no longer. Her hands clenched into fists at her side; her throat grew so tight it began to ache. She turned away quickly and went to catch her mare. Nearly everyone had evacuated the valley. She mounted and trotted through woodenly, prodding dawdling children and a few slow-moving women. Then a low, vibrating tattoo sounded against the earth again, the sound of a horse returning.

Fear that they had been located by pale-eyes or *Moquis* gripped her first, then elation took her and she became sure against all reason that Hawk had returned. But when she whirled back to the mouth, she saw Na'acoci. A hint of his old, sheepish smile touched his lips as he approached her.

"A message," he said shortly. "Tell my wife that I will return by *Nlchi'tso'si*, the moon of Slender Winds. Her babe will be here by then, and I would see him.'' He hesitated. ''You see, little sister, that I do indeed know what I am fighting for.''

He was gone before she could answer, pounding down the gorge, a cloud of thin white dust the only evidence that he had returned. For the first and last time that morning, Gray Eyes smiled.

She rode behind Long Earrings and his wives at the front of a long meandering line. They kept carefully to the shade of the concealing buttes and the more calcareous land there. Their ponies' hooves came down on the short tufts of sacaton and Indian rice grass, effectively hiding their tracks. Anyone following them would know that they had been there, but they would not be able to tell their number, or if their mounts were Indian ponies or shod, pale-eyes' horses.

At times they passed areas where the soil was deeper and sagebrush abounded, where there was juniper to burn and icy water to drink. They ignored them and rode on until the children began squalling and their cries would alert pale-eyes as surely as the lure of sweet spring water. Then they stopped and nibbled on piñon nuts they had found along the way. When the sun came again, they moved on, but before it peaked they had lost a ewe. Only the elders seemed distressed. The others watched hungrily as she was tied to Barren Woman's saddle, knowing that they would eat well that night.

On the third day they found a sign from a band that had passed that way before them. Long Earrings slid laboriously from his pony as soon as he spotted it.

''They are east of here,'' he said finally, bending to study the design, a thin line of stones pointing toward the sun, lying beside a juniper branch and a footprint. ''They say there has been no trouble. They only thought it prudent to move on.''

Gray Eyes was down off her mare before he even straightened. ''Who? I would like to see.''

He stepped aside to allow her to study the rocks. "My people," she murmured. "My band." Until that moment, she hadn't fully believed she would find them.

Long Earrings mounted again. "Yes. They would be very close to the Hopi mesas, I think. Near Oraibi Wash."

She only nodded, still staring at the treasured sign. Then something about the tone of his voice alerted her. "You know something," she said, looking up at him. "What is it?"

"It is nothing the rocks have told me, granddaughter. Nor is it my medicine. It is only the harsh weight of responsibility on my shoulders." His eyes were tired and troubled.

"I do not understand."

"We cannot accompany you there. Your clan has chosen that place because they are few and can hide easily right under enemy noses. But we would be many if we joined them, even for the space of our evening meal." As realization dawned in her eyes, pain shone in his. "I cannot risk the lives of your people or my own. I cannot take them there so close to the heart of Hopi."

He was telling her that she would have to go on alone. Fear began to clamor in her belly. But she knew that he was right.

"They will have left more signs," Barren Woman stated gruffly. "You will find them if you are not so foolish that you panic and forget to look." Then her normally brusque manner vanished and her face softened.

"May the wind stay at your back and the Holy People at your shoulder," she finished. "Be well, my husband's granddaughter." Then the long winding caravan began to meander out of sight.

There was no hawk to show her the way this time, no female rain to guide her. Instead, the sun slid abruptly behind a cloud and a cold, spattering male rain began to fall. Still Gray Eyes rode on, heeding Barren Woman's advice. Her gaze swept the land incessantly for another, more mortal sign.

The day passed and she found nothing. Her stomach rumbled with hunger even as the damp and the cold seeped painfully into her bones. Finally, on the fourth morning, she rounded the base of a butte and found the tree. It had been stripped of many of its branches, but one was lying splintered and fragmented on the ground. It had been laid to the south of the trunk, and when she dropped off her mare to study it she found twelve bones scattered around it. Sheep bones, one for each person traveling with the band.

Relief made her weak. She destroyed the pattern quickly and mounted again to ride south into the heart of Hopi.

The moon had scarcely appeared when she heard a yelp of excitement. K'aalo'gii. The girl squatted and slid down from her lookout, a finger of rock as high as five men. Her excitement had her spilling on the hard, dusty ground right at Smoke's feet.

To Gray Eyes, she seemed to come out of nowhere. The mare felt the same way, and she spooked and spun. Gray Eyes gripped her reins and laughed aloud for the first time since she had left the summer camp.

"Still you have not learned to act like a woman!" she teased. She looked down at her cousin's sprawled figure, lanky and boyish and so familiar, and suddenly tears burned at her eyes, tears of relief, of emotional exhaustion that left her shaken. She dismounted clumsily.

Spotted Shirt made his way down the rock with more decorum. His stern visage cracked into a grin as he looked at Gray Eyes. She hugged him suddenly, fiercely, until his face began to color with embarrassment.

"Come," he muttered, pulling away from her awkwardly. "My wife will never stop scolding me if I do not take you to the others right away."

They moved around the rocks as K'aalo'gii chattered excitedly. And then they were there, all of them. Quite Enough and Little Left Hand tended a pot over a tiny fire.

A rotund Sleepiness bounced Squeak on her knee while Talks Often stood at her shoulder, advising her animatedly even as Quiet Woman chided her for her interference. Wildcat, nearly as enormously pregnant as Sleepiness, dozed near the cook fire. One Whisker sharpened his arrows, Black Spot mumbled to his pony, and Winter Star worked piñon gum between her spidery fingers. Gray Eyes stared at them for a moment, then a soft, joyous cry escaped her.

Silence fell and all eyes turned to her. There was a moment of stunned surprise, then their laughter and shouts began to fill the night.

"Hush, everyone!" Quiet Woman scolded. Then she too turned on her daughter, plucking at her shift as though to assure herself that she was really there. "You must be hungry and tired," she murmured, practical even beneath a swell of emotion. But Gray Eyes couldn't answer.

She allowed herself to be led to the cook fire, to the thin and stringy-looking rabbit in the pot there. As the aroma hit her, her mouth began to water and her legs went weak.

Later, she thought. Later, she would tell them about Agua Chiquito and Long Earrings. She would talk of Hawk and the vagaries of war. But now she wanted only to inhale the aroma of stewing rabbit and listen to the chorus of cherished voices she missed far too long.

Chapter 32

There was a warm sense of peace to be gathered from being among her family again. Life was busy as well, too busy to allow time for useless ruminations. Like the other bands in hiding, the Lone Trees didn't dare stay in one place too long. They rode hard all day and, except for the sentinels, slept soundly at night. Then, late one afternoon, Sleepiness changed everything with a single gasp.

Gray Eyes looked back at her sharply as they traveled in the shade of the hills. She had fallen far behind the others. As Gray Eyes watched, her hand clutched involuntarily at her swollen belly. Gray Eyes reined in quickly to ride by her side.

"Are you having pain, sister?" she asked. "Is it your babe?"

But Sleepiness shook her head. "I can travel a bit longer. Go, please. Keep up with the others." But she forced her words through a mouth that was pinched, and her face was as ashen as that of a pale-eyes.

Gray Eyes took a rough breath, unsure of what to do. Then she thought of the noisy infants in Long Earrings' camp, the children who had pressed close to hear her story. A sense of conviction rose inside her. The babes, she thought. They were more important than the pale-eyes or the Dead Ones, more sacred than war. This one would not be born in a saddle.

She spurred her mare decisively and rode to catch up with Quiet Woman. " 'Ama'," she whispered. "Sleepiness would have her babe now."

Quiet Woman stiffened in her saddle and glanced toward the horizon where the sky was still a pale blue, inviting soldiers to roam and raid.

"She is in much pain," Gray Eyes went on. "I do not think she can ride much longer."

Reluctantly, Quiet Woman nodded. She disengaged herself from the others, but returned from Sleepiness' side only a heartbeat later to speak urgently to One Whisker. The next time they came to a trickling wash, the band stopped.

Water. Of course they would need water, Gray Eyes realized. But so would the pale-eyes and *Moquis* if they were nearby. Her blood turned cold.

She kept an eye on the hills as Talks Often and Quite Enough pulled a tight-lipped Sleepiness from her pony. The girl protested, but as soon as her feet touched the ground, she tumbled. They helped her up again and moved her behind a tangle of rocks on the other side of the ravine. They worked quietly, matter-of-factly.

Gray Eyes felt the beginnings of anger twitch inside her. "With the babe so close, why did you venture so far into Hopi?" she demanded.

"The babe is early," Quiet Woman muttered. "Sometimes this happens."

It had been an unconscionable risk but there was nothing to be done about it now. She reached beneath her shift for her near-empty gall bag. A scant handful of fleabane still remained there. The People called it *a'zee' na'oolta'dii*, the untying plant, and it was good for accelerating childbirth.

She pulled a cooking pot from her mother's pack and took it to the stream. When she had filled it, she built a small fire and boiled the water. Then she tossed the fleabane inside. It seemed to take forever before the mixture simmered aromatically, longer still before it cooled enough to drink. But when she went back to where Sleepiness lay, little progress had been made.

Talks Often had taken off her belt and tied her daughter

to one of the rocks. She held her hips while Quiet Woman held her knees. They were ready, but Sleepiness was not. She whimpered with pain, but her babe remained stubbornly inside her.

"Here," Gray Eyes said, dropping down beside them. "This will help."

Quiet Woman held it out to her niece. They watched Sleepiness gulp it, then settled down to wait. But when darkness fell to offer them some measure of protection, Sleepiness was no closer to birthing than before.

She writhed against her rock, panting and moaning. Then, finally, she let out a piercing howl. Gray Eyes cringed; Quiet Woman and Talks Often froze. But the ensuing quiet was filled only with fresh sounds of Sleepiness' pain.

"We are still safe," Quiet Woman breathed again.

"This time," Talks Often muttered. "But she is sure to do it again."

Gray Eyes blanched. She couldn't allow that to happen. She reached jerkily for her gall bag again and took out her hawk's feather.

She stared at it for a moment, her heart beating like thunder. Her hands trembled so that she nearly dropped it. If the feather failed, she would know that her medicine was completely gone and she was truly on her own. Then she looked down at Sleepiness again and knew that she had to risk it. Shuddering lightly, she nudged her mother aside.

There was no chant for the being she called upon now. He was hers, her strongest medicine, the harbinger of her first power. Her heart swelled; her blood pumped harder as she searched for him with her mind. Her hawk, her strength, her magic. He would come; he had to come. For Sleepiness, for the clan, for herself.

But although she paused and listened for him, there was no answering call. A chill passed over her and she stuttered to a stop.

"In a moment, I will try again," she whispered

hoarsely. "Do not fear yet. I have never called upon him deliberately before. Perhaps I am doing something wrong."

Quiet Woman nodded cautiously. Then she gave a start of surprise and broke off.

Beside them, Sleepiness moaned, and this time the sound was followed by one of gushing wetness. Warmth flooded Gray Eyes' moccasins where she sat between her cousin's legs.

"It is her water," Quiet Woman breathed, grinning widely. "Your chant has worked, daughter! The babe will wash out now."

Gray Eyes scarcely heard her. Exhilaration swept her, leaving her overwhelmed and numb. She looked up at the sky. Somewhere, although she couldn't see him, her hawk had come.

"This is the problem," she heard Talks Often mutter. She looked at her distractedly, then noticed the tiny foot that had appeared between Sleepiness' thighs. She shrugged. This, at least, seemed like something she could handle on her own. Acting instinctively, she leaned forward again and gently pushed the diminutive leg back inside. She reached and probed, receiving a little kick for her efforts. Then she drew her arm out again and a moment later, the babe's shiny black head appeared.

"There," she announced, satisfied.

Talks Often stared at her with awe, and once again Gray Eyes began to feel the chill of respect and loneliness. She waited until the girl-child's first weak, fretful cries filled the air, then she clutched her feather to her heart and slipped off into the night.

"Sleepiness and her babe should stay at the rock until their time has passed," someone grumbled later as the clan gathered around the rapidly dying fire.

"No, there is no need to stay here," someone else disagreed. "Achi'i'h is not here."

Gray Eyes listened absently as she looked around at the

vulnerable little camp. The ravine was to her right, barely cloistered by sporadic piñons and cottonwoods. Sleepiness' rock lay beyond that. On her left was one of the widest stretches of open land she had seen since leaving *Dinetah*. The cluttered rocks and mesas she had come to associate with Hopi stood entirely too far in the distance to conceal them. They weren't safe here, she thought, certainly not for four whole suns.

Yet the Holy People decreed that they not move on. It was said that if a babe died without its father or anyone but the birthing helpers having seen it, then it couldn't be a *chindi*. Therefore, it was the custom to seclude both mother and babe for four suns. Gray Eyes sighed, realizing that this was one time when they would have to risk the wrath of a babe's ghost-spirit.

"No," she murmured, almost to herself. "I do not think we can risk it. We must not stay here." Her gaze moved speculatively to Wildcat. "And I think that when we leave, we should also leave this land of the Dead Ones."

A chorus of distressed voices filled the night. "But we are safest here!" Little Left Hand protested.

"We are too few to go anywhere the pale-eyes might search for us!"

Gray Eyes nodded. "Perhaps, but someone else's babe could come soon and then we would have to stop again. That is equally dangerous. And even it if should not happen, I no longer have a good feeling about being here."

They looked at her wide-eyed for a moment, then all eyes turned to Wildcat and they began to murmur fretfully. But they wouldn't argue with her, Gray Eyes realized. They would do as she bid, all of them, whether they were uncomfortable with her decision or not. She waited for the old discomfort to come to her, but felt only achingly weary. She sighed and pushed to her feet.

"Rest now," she interrupted. "We should leave here before the sun if Sleepiness is up to it. I do not want to be here at dawn."

She left them and went to her mare to pull Na'acoci's

carbine free of her saddle. Then she headed toward the
ravine. Blood and dust caked her skin, and just this once
she would risk a bath. Sleepiness couldn't be moved yet
anyway; she was far too weak. The *Moquis* would either
stay away this night, she thought grimly, or they would
find them. But her bathing would not make a difference.

The stream was thin and icy. She pulled off her moccasins and stepped into it, walking until she came to a
thick stand of cottonwoods. Then she stripped off her shift
and hung it from one of the branches. She propped the
carbine against the bank and sank down into the water,
loosening her hair as she moved.

She was still sitting there when Spotted Shirt's voice
suddenly rang out with the word she had dreaded from the
first moment she had seen this ravine.

"No'o'da'i!" he screamed. "Enemy!"

Someone had found them.

Chapter 33

Gray Eyes clawed her way up the bank again and grabbed her shift. Her hands were trembling so wildly that she couldn't make sense of it. She fumbled with it for a moment, then whirled at the sound of crashing brush.

"Nizho'ni', pretty, *sí?"* The words came from the cover of the trees, Navajo peppered by Spanish. *Dine''* *Ana'i* then. Enemy Navajo. She screamed.

She dropped her shift and ran. But she had managed only a few steps before the bushes moved again and a hand grabbed her hair. Her breath bounced out of her as she hit the ground, and she stared up into three pairs of cold, black eyes.

A short, pudgy man with a day-old beard stippling his chin bent quickly to pin her legs. "The soldiers will not want this one, no?" he asked the others. He bent over her, looking at her so closely that his foul breath puffed into her face. Gray Eyes twisted away, her heart thundering so hard and erratically that the stars seemed to fade in and out above her.

"Look," he went on, grabbing her chin and jerking her head back. "See here. Her eyes. She is a white-skin. They do not capture their own."

"She is *Dine'*, fool!" spat another man. His black hair was graying and drawn back from his face severely, revealing a bulbous nose. "Take her back to *el capitán.''*

"No! If she is *Dine'*, he will keep her."

"I say take her now, then give her to the soldiers," the

238

man in the middle agreed. "Then it will not matter what they do with her."

He squatted down beside the man with the stubble. Laughing pleasantly, he ran his free hand over her ribs then tweaked her nipple. "You are hot, eh, pretty one?" he chuckled. "Lots of spirit. I like this. We will have fun."

Only then did she understand what they meant to do with her.

She screamed again, twisting and thrashing in terror. She found a hand holding hers and bit into it hard. The middle man bellowed and dropped back, but the Beard held on to her legs, pushing them painfully apart.

She gathered the saliva in her mouth and spat at him. She missed, and Bulbous Nose moved in quickly to pin her arms again. Then the Beard began touching her, his fingers tugging at the hair between her thighs.

No, not like this! her mind screamed. She swallowed convulsively as bile rose in her throat. Icy sweat broke out on her forehead and she tossed her head to the side and vomited.

"You need her dress, see?" The Beard pointed to it. "There. Stuff it into her mouth. No problem."

Bulbous Nose reached for it. She heard him mutter something in the nasal, pale-eyes' tongue, but from the camp she heard only silence. Where was One Whisker? Spotted Shirt? Dead. They must all be dead or one of them would have come by now. Her heart twisted violently against the realization. Then, blessedly, fury came to numb her.

They would have to kill her too before they would touch her again.

"*Dine*" *Ana'i,*" she purred suddenly. Her words spewed from a place deep inside her. "You are dead men! Dead! You may be wolf-men, but even wolf-men die. A strong *hataali* can kill them. A *hataali* can turn their evil back upon them. I will do that to you, *Dine*" *Ana'i.* I am strong, and I will see you die!"

The Beard only laughed. "And how are you so strong, pretty one?" he jeered. "You look very soft to me." He licked his lips, then reached out to touch her again.

She lunged forward, clawing at him in fury. "I am *estsa hataali!*" she shrieked. "I am apprentice of Long Earrings. Your evil spells cannot touch me, spawn of a wolf-man! I am strong enough to destroy you first!"

It wasn't true. She knew that it wasn't, and suspected that they were *Dine'* enough to know it also. How could she call on her power when her gall bag was tied into her shift? How could she call upon anyone when the Sacred Mountains and the holy ones were so far away? She was bluffing, and could only pray that they wouldn't dare to gamble with their lives.

"Bah! I do not believe her!" the Beard scoffed. "She hopes to scare us. Would we be fools enough to fall for her lies?"

"Tie her up," the middle man agreed. "Then even if she speaks the truth, she cannot harm us."

Bulbous Nose sent him an incredulous look. "And would you tie the holy ones as well?" he asked. "If she has power, she will call to them no matter where her hands are."

His words caused a moment's hesitation. "She has no power," the Beard finally muttered.

"Not here," the middle man agreed.

"Try me, fool! Try me and see!" Gray Eyes hissed. "It will be the last thing you do with your mongrel life! I will cast a spell upon you, a spell of my own. I will make you peaceful, like the juniper, frozen to the earth!"

The Beard decided to take the challenge. "You do this, pretty. Do this spell of yours, and we will see if it works."

She met his eyes silently. For a moment, she yearned for the gold coin, for the feather. Then she threw back her head and gave a bloodcurdling shriek.

"I make you quiet." She spoke so softly that the Beard had to strain forward to hear her. "I cast over you the magic formula to make an enemy peaceful. Put your feet down with pollen, evil ones. Put your hands down with pollen. Put your heads down with pollen. Then your feet are pollen; your hands are pollen; your body is pollen; your mind is pollen; your voice is pollen. The trail is beautiful. Be still.''

They knew the chant. Even the *Dine'' Ana'i* had once lived among the People, had listened to their elders' stories, had watched their shamans heal and sing to their spirit-guides. They knew, too, that the words could be powerful when spoken from certain mouths.

Bulbous Nose turned away abruptly. ''Play with her if you are so desperate,'' he told his comrades. ''I will wait for the *Moqui* women when we go back to the village. They are far more willing.''

Then the middle man began to back off as well. The Beard looked up at them accusingly. Gray Eyes took the opportunity to lunge to her side and grab the carbine.

Her first shot was wild, singing upward into the trees. The second went awry as well, but it hit a mark. Bulbous Nose dropped to the ground abruptly, too stunned by the fireball embedded in his thigh to even cry out. She hadn't intended to hit him, but a fierce sense of triumph pounded through her all the same.

Then the rusty old weapon jammed. She flung it away, jerked to her feet and bolted.

None of them dared to follow her. When she lurched clear of the cottonwoods, she was alone. She raced back the way she had come, stumbling once, hitting the ground with such impact that the stars whirled above her head and she thought she would faint. But before blackness could claim her, she was up again and running. She didn't stop until she reached Sleepiness' rock.

She dropped there, her breath snagged and tortured, and touched a finger to the dampened ground where her cousin had given birth. It was the only sign of her now. A wail of grief wrenched free of her throat before she could stop it.

She bit down on her lip, tasting blood, then pushed up

on her elbows to look out at the tiny camp. Only the dwindling cook fire gave testimony that anyone had ever camped there, that and a few *Naakaiidine'e'* kettles rolling gently in the dust. She cried out again, more softly this time. She was answered almost immediately by a bark of fear.

"There! You see? It is her! Her! The she-cat shaman! She will come back to destroy us!" It was the Beard who spoke, and his words prompted an immediate cacophony of conflicting opinions in the pale-eyes' tongue.

She saw a sea of pale, sickly faces as men swarmed down around the rocks near the ravine. They had Quiet Woman, Quite Enough, and Wildcat.

Rage and hatred and anguish rose in her so violently that they blotted out all logic. She forgot that she had no carbine, no weapon at all. She no longer cared that her medicine was gone. She saw the faces of these men who had hounded her for a lifetime, and knew only that she would kill them before she allowed them to take any more.

Then Quiet Woman turned and, in the last of the light from the cook fire, captured her eyes with her own.

Gray Eyes froze as understanding seeped slowly through the red haze in her brain. It was over. The Lone Trees stood no chance anymore. Had they ever? Once perhaps, seasons ago, before that first devastating *Naakaiidine'e'* raid. But now they were far too few, badgered and depleted until all hope of defense was gone.

She looked at her mother again. Quiet Woman urged her desperately, silently not to fight anymore.

Gray Eyes sank down behind the rock again. *You must triumph*, came the *hataali*'s voice from somewhere cold inside her. *In your soul dwell the old ways . . . the one thing they cannot steal is your soul.*

She cried out in spite of herself, a thin sound of anguish. Then she began to fight for the courage to live rather than die.

* * *

When silence fell over the camp, telling her that the raiders had gone, she stepped away from her hiding place and stumbled. She collapsed on top of Black Spot. A *Dine'' Ana'i* hatchet was buried solidly in his head. His eyes were clear now, free of the cloudy confusion that had shrouded them for as long as she could remember. The inequity of that was more than she could bear. A scream of rage heaved up from her throat, rage at the pale-eyes, at the Holy People for smiling at him only in death.

Then, distantly, she became aware of hands pulling her away. "Please, sister, no," K'aalo'gii sobbed. "Please, you must not. They will hear you and come back for us."

Gray Eyes looked up at her dully. She felt cold, so cold. But something small and hard and determined inside of her gave her the strength to go on.

She pushed to her feet to go back to the ravine. Her shift lay forgotten on the ground. Her gall bag was still there. Gray Eyes retrieved them and wondered if Bulbous Nose was still nearby as well. The thought made her hurry back to K'aalo'gii.

"The others?" she asked her.

"I do not know," the younger girl managed. "We all scattered."

But the answer was too quickly apparent. They returned to the clearing to find the bodies of One Whisker and Spotted Shirt as well. Cold, black grief hit Gray Eyes in the gut and dropped her to her knees. The last of her fear for the pale-eyes slid slowly, irrevocably into white-hot hatred.

It was dawn before they found Winter Star and Squeak. The old woman had left the camp in a tottering, pained run and, in her terror, had simply kept going. Sleepiness had told Squeak to hide and not to reveal himself under any circumstances. At only two summers, he had taken her literally and ignored their frantic calls and pleading. K'aalo'gii finally made sense of the obscure trails left by their moccasins and herded them both back to camp.

The others staggered in over the course of the day like

hungry animals whose instincts led them unerringly to a place where they had once been fed. Little Left Hand, Talks Often, and Sleepiness sat huddled together beside the dead fire, stunned and vacant-eyed. The weak November sun revealed packs scattered and looted and more than half of the ponies slaughtered. Smoke, like much of the stock, was simply gone without a trace.

But only K'aalo'gii could fully appreciate the depth of Gray Eyes' loss. "At least she is not a *chindi*, sister," she comforted her. "She must live, as must the others. If the soldiers had meant to kill them, we would have found their carcasses."

Gray Eyes nodded dully. The realization did little to ease the ache in her throat. Her eyes burned and she ducked her head. The pale-eyes, she thought viciously, always the pale-eyes. She found herself praying that the women and her mare were indeed dead, not trapped in the clutches of those men without souls.

Finally, she gathered control again. Somehow, she realized, they would have to start over. Somehow, these remaining eight lives would have to survive in testimony to the others. She looked at Sleepiness and the tiny babe nestled in her arms. "Do you feel well enough to travel, sister?"

"Where?" someone ventured. "Where would you take us?"

Gray Eyes hesitated, then her eyes glittered with certainty. "Home." She nodded, her conviction growing. "Yes. We will go where we belong."

As they began to pack up their scattered belongings, Gray Eyes mounted a spare gelding and looked back at the jumbled, unforgiving rocks of Hopi. Silently, her heart raw, she said good-bye to all those she had loved, those who would have to stay behind. Spotted Shirt and crazy old Black Spot. One Whisker, who would never learn now to accept the fact that his daughter was a *hataali*. For a wild moment Gray Eyes thought she would cry. Her throat closed, but her eyes remained dry. Finally, as the cool wind teased her long, unfettered hair, her chin came up.

She turned the gelding back toward *Dinetah*. Moments later, the others mounted a handful of ponies and formed a tattered band behind her.

Chapter 34

▼▼▼▼▼▼▼▼▼▼

The deserted spring camp was much as she and Hawk had left it. Seeing it again, Gray Eyes felt a longing rise up within her, so fierce that it left her light-headed. Where was he now? Could he feel her heart bleed? Was he as hungry as she was, as cold, as wounded?

"Where are you, my love," she whispered, "now that the unforgivable has happened and I have come to fear that my own strength is not enough?" But there was no answer, only the howl of a cold wind across the mountain, tugging at the limbs of naked trees. He was alive, she thought, he had to be. And until he came back to her, somehow, some way, she would go on.

Life was busy, their edge on survival thin, but their days managed to settle into a pattern. The rickety old shelters needed constant reinforcement. There were seeds and nuts to be collected, fruits and plants to be dried, all in an attempt to fill their bellies after the game left the mountain for the winter. And Gray Eyes had to replace the medicines she had depleted in Hopi. She searched for them in the last hours of daylight and often skipped the evening meal to cure and dry them. It was all for the best; there was barely enough to feed everyone anyway.

Then, on a bright December morning, even that bitter tranquility was shattered. Gray Eyes woke to wide shafts of early sunlight working their way through the cracked patches of her shelter. She would need to find fresh mud to fill the gaps, she thought. But she was tired, so tired.

With uncharacteristic weariness, she rolled over on her side instead of rising.

Then, in an instant, she was wide awake. Even as she burrowed into her sheepskin, a driving pain lanced through her belly. She jerked upright, stunned. Such a pain had not come to her in nearly eight seasons now, since her first *Kinaalda'*. And she should not be feeling it now, not if Hawk's babe lived inside her.

Panicked, disbelieving, she ran a hand over herself. Even as she did, the pain disappeared. She yanked her shift up to her waist. Nothing. There was no blood, nothing at all to prove that the pain had not been all in her mind.

She had too many real problems to cope with. She did not have the luxury of troubling herself over something she could not explain. Rising, she slipped from the shelter to tackle her chores for the day.

The sounds in the camp were a mockery of the ones she had once cherished. Where once the band had come awake with the sounds of children's laughter, now there were only cautious murmurs and wary, unconscious glances down the mountain. Gray Eyes clutched her blanket closer and went to find Sleepiness.

"I will have to go down the mountain to hunt this morning, sister. I will feel safer if you come with me."

Sleepiness went obediently to collect her bow and her hunting knife. Gray Eyes left to borrow K'aalo'gii's mare. By the time she returned to the edge of the camp, Sleepiness was already waiting for her. They started cautiously down the incline.

Almost immediately, they spotted a small herd of antelope, but it was moving too quickly to pursue. They rode on, trying to keep the camp in sight. They saw no pale-eyes, but no more game, either. Then, at midday, they spotted a javelina.

"She will not taste so good," Sleepiness muttered.

Gray Eyes shrugged. Food was food, and there was a

lot of it on the boar. She slipped from her pony and crept forward on foot.

She lifted the knife and hurled it, but she never saw it hit its mark. Pain crashed through her at the same time, doubling her over. It was the same pain as before, but more fierce, more gripping. A tiny yelp of confusion escaped her as she fell to her knees and rolled over.

From somewhere distant, she heard Sleepiness scream. Then there were hoofbeats as she wheeled her mare around and galloped back toward the camp. Gray Eyes listened helplessly as they faded.

Sleepiness would bring the others back. She knew that, and knew too that she would have to rise before they came. They couldn't find her like this. They would panic, she thought. Then the pale winter sky began to swirl above her and she could think no more.

She awoke just after nightfall with only blurred memories of being in the valley. She was back in her shelter with K'aalo'gii crouched beside her.

The girl's eyes were stark with fear. "Sister?" she whispered.

"You cannot be the sister I know," Gray Eyes mumbled. "You never wake before me."

She spoke lightly but her voice sounded like sand. She realized with some amazement that her throat was parched. Panicked, she fought to sit up and found that she couldn't. Any trace of her usual energy was gone.

"What—" she began, but K'aalo'gii shook her head.

"Do not try to talk, except to tell me what to do. I do not have strong medicine, but perhaps if you tell me the cures, I can help you."

She looked at her blankly. The cures? Then everything came back to her. She remembered the weariness, the pains, the way she had collapsed while hunting. Horror washed over her, then a cold, gnawing fear.

"The babe," she gasped. "Did it—" But she couldn't

bring herself to finish the question, and K'aalo'gii mis-
understood.

"Sleepiness' babe is fine," she answered. "Do you not
remember? You birthed her. Then there was the raid and
we came back from Hopi. We are home now."

"No," Gray Eyes moaned. She shook her head in frustration. Then, to K'aalo'gii's horror, she began to thrash
beneath her sheepskin. She pushed it aside frantically and
jerked up on her shift. No blood. She closed her eyes
again, weak with relief. Her babe was still alive, still inside her.

K'aalo'gii watched her, her eyes filling with tears. "It
is *tah honeesgai*," she whispered. "You have been
witched! You must tell me what to do. Please. You must
tell me how to save you."

Tah honeesgai. Gray Eyes shook her head and tried again
to explain. It wasn't that, couldn't be that. Then, like a
stab in the heart, she knew that it was. Every symptom
was there—the sharp, localized pain coming straight from
her belly, the dull buzzing in her ears, speaking of sickness inside her. Her fever, when she had no obvious
wound.

Suddenly, she saw them all again—the Beard, Bulbous
Nose, and the other—and she knew. No, her babe was not
dead, and they had not been able to witch her. She had
been too strong. But she had been outside her mountains.
She had not been strong enough.

She had saved herself, but their evil had gone straight
through her to damage her child.

She gave a sudden scream of terror. She thought of her
last night with Hawk in this shelter; she saw his skin glistening and hot. She remembered her plea with the holy
ones to give her more from that union than a memory, and
the way it had seemed that they'd smiled upon her. But
the *Dine'' Ana'i* had taken that promise away. Fury edged
up in her, then panting, violent denial.

Perhaps it was not too late. Perhaps there was some way
to save it.

She knew that she could not.

She took a dry, shuddering breath. She was no longer in a position of simply warding evil off. It was inside her now; it had claimed her babe. The despair that struck her was intolerable.

You must live. The *hataali's* voice came back to her and she knew what had to be done. Her heart cringed and writhed away from the truth. But she was Vittorio's granddaughter, she was *estsa hataali,* and she knew, had always known, that no one person was ever as important as her people as a whole. Her child was lost and she was not strong enough to survive with the babe inside her. She must act now, for their sake.

"We will turn this shelter into a sweat lodge," she managed, looking for K'aalo'gii. Her voice was steady, if dull. "Tell the others. They will gather what we need to make it ready."

K'aalo'gii nodded. Gray Eyes watched her go, then emptied her gall bag into neat piles and sorted out the fleabane. She would use the untying plant to cut the babe loose. And then she would sweat the last of its illness out of her.

When K'aalo'gii returned with rocks and wood and water, she chased her away again. Her hands trembled as she boiled the water and mixed it with a strong dose of the fleabane. Her feverish skin blanched as she held it to her lips. Shudders of longing, of desperation racked her.

Her babe. Hawk's babe. If it could live . . .

. . . but it would not . . .

The murmuring voices of the clan rallied her. These people were hers now. She had to live. She had to let the babe go.

Painfully, hope died. She squeezed her eyes shut and gulped the water.

Chapter 35

▼▼▼▼▼▼▼▼▼▼

The clan huddled at the cold fire pit, alternately glancing at Gray Eyes' shelter and each other. It was Talks Often who finally spoke.

"This is not good," she muttered. "It looks to me like she would try to cure herself."

"She is strong enough," Sleepiness protested. "You remember she saved my babe."

Talks Often shook her head. "It takes a very strong *hataali* to drive badness from her own body," she reminded her. "The evil, whether it be *tah honeesgai* or white man's sickness, eats at her power. She must have so much medicine that some can survive the sickness to reach the holy ones for their support."

The women fell silent, considering this. Then Little Left Hand cleared her throat. "We cannot risk it. We need her."

With no further words spoken, it was decided. They would do for this young woman what they would not do for another living soul. They would risk encountering more pale-eyes to save her. They would go for more medicine, strong medicine. They would search out the old *hataali*.

"I will do it," K'aalo'gii burst out suddenly. They looked in her direction, some startled, some appalled. Then they all spoke at once.

"You are but a girl-child."

"Only thirteen summers."

"It is far too dangerous for one such as you."

"Who then?" K'aalo'gii demanded. "I can shoot and

ride better than anyone here. My mare is the fastest. I could be there and back while all of you talk about it.''

Before Talks Often could argue, before she could find the endless stream of words she was renowned for, her daughter was mounted and riding determinedly into the night.

She had only to travel as far as Canyon de Chelly to find the *hataali*. She sought some word of him there, but nearly forgot her mission at the sight of thousands of Navajo crowding the fertile riverbed. She stopped her mare at the edge of the chasm and stared down at them. They had all come back from Hopi. Why? But before she could even formulate a guess, a war cry went up behind her.

Terror prickled her skin. She leaned back, spinning her pony around so quickly that the mare reared and nearly moved on her hocks. By the time all four hooves were planted again, K'aalo'gii had freed her bow and had an arrow poised.

Only the quickest of reflexes made her shoot it high. It arced gracefully, then fell harmlessly to the ground not far from the band of Navajo warriors who sat behind her. She gaped at them, her adrenaline still running too hard for her to make sense of what she saw.

"A girl-child," one of the men muttered in disgust. "Little girl, you wander in dangerous land. You should go back down to your mother's people."

The insult rallied her. Her eyes flashed. "My mother's people are far from here," she snapped. "They have sent me on a mission to find the *hataali*. They sent me because I am the fastest and strongest of them all."

The warriors laughed. But one tilted his head to the side and studied her thoughtfully.

"She is quick," he pointed out. "Any quicker, and you would all be *chindis* right now, my friends."

K'aalo'gii was startled by the compliment. She took a closer look at the warrior who had given it.

Suddenly, an odd fluttering started in her belly. She lost

her train of thought. Weapons and raiding, Long Earrings and Gray Eyes were all suddenly forgotten. He was the most handsome warrior she had ever seen. He was strong and lean. Was he as tall as he looked? She couldn't tell; he was astride a vibrant pinto pony with huge splotches of color that even reached his mane. A fine horse, she thought. She moved closer without realizing it and stroked the pony's muzzle thoughtfully.

"He would be swift. A gelding?" she asked. Then, without waiting for a reply, she leaned to the side and peered up between the pony's back legs. No, a stallion. Suddenly, she grinned widely and looked up at the warrior.

"I am a Lone Tree, born for the Two Rocks Sit people. My band lives in the Chuskas. Now you know where to find me." It came out in a rush, then she broke off abruptly as his eyes found hers and he smiled.

"I would like very much to breed my mare to this horse someday," she finished, feeling suddenly awkward. Then she backed off quickly, intending to escape into the canyon. But the warrior's voice stopped her.

"I am one of the Among Scattered Hills," he said. "I am born for the Deer Water people. I will find you, warrior-girl. Have no doubt of that."

She looked back at him, uncertain. He seemed to be speaking of so much more than the pony.

"You know a good horse when you see one," he went on. "I like that. But for now, you say you have come seeking the *hataali*."

"The Bitter Waters' *hataali*." Had she made that clear? She found that she could no longer remember.

He chuckled. "He is here. Mount and I will take you to him."

She hesitated, then leaped up onto her mare. He rode past her and began sliding down the trail to the canyon. His strong pinto pony carried him easily down the treacherous cliff. The *chindis* would take her soul before she would let him believe that she couldn't handle her mare the same way.

She fumbled with her reins and dug her heels hard into Night's sides. For the first time in her thirteen summers, her movements were erratic. The little black leaped dangerously forward, but she had been trained well during her mistress' saner days. Her hooves dug into the trail and she slid downward gracefully until K'aalo'gii rode by the warrior's side.

He looked over at her and smiled. Her heart jumped about like a jackrabbit. "The *hataali* is here?" she asked, because suddenly it seemed imperative that she say something.

"Nearly all of our people have returned," the warrior responded thoughtfully. "We were losing too many, too much of our hearts and souls, in Hopi. And so we came back, and now Delgondito and some other headmen have gone to the *hual-te* again to appeal to the pale-eyes to end this war."

Her spine snapped straight. "No!"

He cocked a brow at her.

"They will only demand more of us!" she protested. "They will want another treaty!"

"Yes, you are right. All that will happen. But until more of our men agree to fight, there can be no other course."

She sagged in her saddle. "Some days I wish we were more like the Apache," she muttered. "My grandfather said that they live to the south and west of here. Not only do their men fight, but their women do too." Her mouth curled in disgust. "These pale-eyes never harass *them.*"

He surprised her by laughing. She looked at him sharply. Was he making fun of her? But no, he was nodding.

"That is true," he answered. Then he broke off as they trotted onto the floor.

People called to him, greeting him, asking questions. When next he was able to speak to her, it was to direct her toward a place where the cliffs formed a conclave. Long Earrings emerged from a hastily constructed shelter there. The warrior smiled briefly and rode off toward the cliffs. K'aalo'gii couldn't help glancing back at him a final time. Then the *hataali* cleared his throat and she colored fiercely with shame. Gray Eyes needed her and she was dawdling and getting sidetracked.

"It is my cousin," she blurted without preamble.

Long Earrings looked startled. "She is not well?" A depth of pain filled his voice, but something in his eyes sparked, some sense of his inner self that would rally him a final time. "Has she called for me?" he asked.

"No. The others sent me."

"Yes, that is the way it would be."

Would he come then? She watched, unsure, but he only turned back to his shelter. He stooped inside and called to a woman she could not see.

"Wife!" he bellowed, his voice suddenly strong again. "Bring me my pony. Pack me some of that ground cake. I must go now."

A barrel-shaped woman with a stern face emerged from the shelter. She studied his face for a moment in a way that bordered on rudeness. Then she nodded once, shortly.

"It is time, my woman," he finished. "Know that I have loved you."

K'aalo'gii thought it a strange thing to say. But apparently, the woman understood. Her smile softened her countenance until she appeared almost young, almost pretty. She touched his face briefly. Her hand trembled. Then, without another word, she lumbered back into the shelter.

K'aalo'gii watched and wondered why she suddenly felt like crying.

The pains came back with the dusk. At first they were intermittent, then, as night fell, they began to grip her consistently. Gray Eyes embraced them, as dearly as she would have embraced the babe had he lived. They were all she would ever share with this child. They were, for a time, all she had left of Hawk. She shuddered and writhed with them, and when they finally exhausted her, she slept.

When she awoke again it was evening and the bleeding had started. She knew the moment the babe passed from her body. There was a thick clot of blood in a thinner puddle of red, and she stared at it, her heart pounding. But she neither cried not railed against fate this time for the life it had chosen for her. Hollow-eyed, shuddering, she only leaned against the wall to grieve.

The fever passed to chills that rocked her. Her throat swelled and closed until she could scarcely breathe. But somehow, through it all, she heard the clan moving and mumbling outside, keeping their vigil. Then, suddenly, panic struck her.

Suppose it didn't work? Every curing chant, every medicine that the *hataali* had taught her was designed to drive out aliens and evil. But this evil had not been an alien being inside her. It had been her babe, and her babe had been a part of her.

"Grandfather," she whispered wretchedly. "Where are you? If only I could send for you. I do not know these things!"

But the *hataali* didn't answer. Instead, the hides at the door snapped and K'aalo'gii appeared.

"Sister? You spoke? You called for me?"

Gray Eyes turned a sightless gaze on her. "No. I called for the *hataali*. Only he can truly know what is to be done now."

K'aalo'gii's face went white. "Should I go back? Should I try again to bring him?"

Gray Eyes looked at her dully. Then understanding began to seep in on her. For the first time in several suns, she felt something other than lethargy. Shame and anger struck hard as she realized what they had done for her.

"You went for the *hataali?* You risked your life for mine? I did not ask you to! I am only a shaman! You need me, yes, but you need me to keep you alive! What good would my life have done you if you were already a *chindi?*''

K'aalo'gii stared at her, miserably unsure. Then her temper surfaced. "I went alone," she snapped. "I did not endanger anyone else. It was my life, my choice! I have seen thirteen summers now. Someone else besides a strange warrior should give me credit for knowing my own skills!''

A strange warrior? Gray Eyes looked at her, then shook her head. She dared not be diverted.

K'aalo'gii had gone alone, she thought, and she was here now. So the clan was safe. "What of the *hataali?*" she asked, swallowing carefully.

"He said he was coming right behind me," K'aalo'gii answered. "But that was early this sun, and he has not arrived yet."

Something icy poked at Gray Eyes' heart. He should have come by now, she thought. The *hataali* would never forsake her.

The conviction sent strength flooding into her from some unimaginable source. She staggered to her feet, swayed, and groped at the wall for support. "Water," she grated. "I need more water."

K'aalo'gii darted out of the shelter again, glad for something to do. When she returned, she hovered in the shadows, waiting for further instructions.

But Gray Eyes only dampened the rocks again to bring the heat in the shelter to an unbearable pitch. Then she jerked her gall bag free of her shift and emptied juniper into her palm. As K'aalo'gii watched in horror, she shoved the entire fistful into her mouth. Chewing, gagging, she spoke again on a gasp.

"My hunting knife."

K'aalo'gii found it, then handed it to her. Somehow, despite the shivers that trembled through her body, Gray Eyes managed to slice a perfect, tiny incision into the tender section of her wrist.

Blood began to seep. She thrust the wound to her mouth and sucked to pull the last of the evil out of her.

"What are you doing?" K'aalo'gii breathed.

"Everything," she muttered. "Everything I know."

I will not live, my friend, the *hataali* had told Barboncito when they had talked of raiding *Tsehotsohih.* And to her he had said, "I am tired."

Something was very, very wrong. Long Earrings needed her. She had to heal herself quickly and go to him.

Chapter 36

The band of *Naakaiidine'e'* rode hard, just as they had in his dream. Long Earrings was inordinately pleased. It was good to know that his medicine had remained strong right up to the end.

They came around a crusty red butte, not soldiers but pale-eyed ranchers, along with a handful of Indians. Long Earrings squinted into the sun. *Dine'' Ana'i? Moqui?* He couldn't tell. He had not been able to see them clearly in his vision, probably because he couldn't see them now as the drama unfolded. As strong as his power was, it showed him only that which was about to take place. It did not unravel mysteries for him.

The silver-eyed one was different.

He knew that she was able to call upon her medicine, to channel it. She might not be aware of it yet, but he knew. She was stronger than he was. She no longer needed him. Perhaps that was why he rode for her camp now. This journey would kill him; he had known that for some time now.

Fleetingly, looking into Barren Woman's eyes for the last time, he had considered remaining safely in the canyon. But even knowing that Gray Eyes had no true need of him, he could not forsake her. Not for himself. Not for a life he no longer wanted to live.

He was old, too old. He was tired. Perhaps Gray Eyes could stop the endless fighting and warring of their people. He had done all he could and failed.

He looked up again. Ahead of him, the *Naakaiidine'e'*

and the red men galloped closer. One of them—an Indian—began to gesticulate wildly. When Long Earrings ignored him, he stopped his motioning and leaped from his pony. They were close enough now that the *hataali* could hear the white men shout. The red man ignored them and began running up and down, stubbornly giving the Navajo signal for an enemy approach. Long Earrings smiled. One of them was a friend then. That, too, was good to know, that his alliances with men of other tribes had lasted the years and the battles, the raids and the wars.

He nodded to himself, satisfied, and kept riding.

The first musket shot sent a fireball whizzing past his ear, close enough to flutter the ends of his red silk headband. The second musket ball struck his pony. The animal lurched and stumbled but Long Earrings touched his calves to him and he staggered gamely on. Then the third fireball shattered the *hataali*'s kneecap.

He didn't scream, but a thick, gurgling gasp tore free of his throat. The pain was sweet, encompassing. So it was time then. He dropped his reins and groped for his quiver. Four sacred mountains—four arrows. It was all he had brought. He would give himself that much of a chance.

He snapped the first one into his bow. The Indian was shouting still. *"Ak'is!"* he cried. *"Hak'is!"* Friend. Brother. Yes, he was, and so the *hataali* would spare him. He aimed away from the Indian and fired.

The first arrow caught a grizzled *Naakaiidine'e'* in the throat. Blood spewed in an arcing geyser and the man fell hard. The second caught an Indian in the chest. He clutched at it, falling backward until he lay prone on his mount. When the animal leaped a wash, he slipped gently to the ground.

Two more. Long Earrings wiped a brown, gnarled hand over the sweat on his forehead and took aim again. The third arrow struck another *Naakaiidine'e'*. The man's pale eyes bulged in revulsion as it pierced his cheek, driving deep into his throat. He brought his hands to it and tugged on it convulsively, then leaped to the ground of his own accord. While the others came on, the lone pale-eyes thrashed on the ground, gripping the arrow.

One left.

The *hataali* raised his bow in a final effort. The arrow sailed through the air, as straight and as true as in those days when he'd been young and he'd ridden for women and stock. They were all around him now, cool-eyed white men and ruddy-faced Indians. All of them carried a gleam of blood lust in their eyes. The attack had little to do with the war then, Long Earrings realized. These men wanted to kill simply because there was no room in their worlds for that which they did not understand. He was a lone Navajo, a hated Navajo, different, threatening, and so he would die.

He freed his last arrow. It drove deep into a man's ear. That pale-eyes' death was sudden and final as the shaft speared his brain. He slumped over his mount's neck and was carried on as Long Earrings jerked on his reins again and galloped back the way he had come, his pony lunging awkwardly.

The pain was wracking now, driving and rushing up from his knee to destroy that part of him which the pale-eyes could not—his mind. He was only dimly aware of the ranchers following him. Fireballs belched free of muskets; hooves raised a blinding cloud of dust. His pony carried him through it all valiantly, whirling through the melee, spinning and dodging when his way was blocked. Then they were free of the cloud of dust and the pony's hooves pummeled the earth as he turned his nose into the wind and the scent of home.

Blinded by pain, his chest heaving from exertion, the *hataali* never saw the juniper.

His pony dodged again to avoid it, and his legs failed him on the turn. Long Earrings was thrown from his saddle. Air rushed at his face, cooling it. Then he landed hard, near a wash that was so shallow and dry and sandy that only a handful of green clung to its banks.

His bones shuddered at the indignity of such an assault.

But he forced himself to his hands and his one good knee and crawled into the thin copse of cottonwoods.

His arrows were gone. There was nothing to do now but wait. As he did, an image of intense silver eyes floated before him.

Gray Eyes. He was prepared to part with life. He found that he was not quite as willing to part with the living. The ache that filled him as he thought of her hurt nearly as much as his shattered bones. Such a serious child. He saw her head bend to watch his hands create medicines, felt again the urge to chuckle at the way her brow furrowed with concentration too intense for her years. He saw her smiling up at the sun and wanted to smile with her. He had found her, had nurtured her, had loved her in a way that transcended passion and blood ties.

"Be strong, granddaughter." His lips worked, his voice thinned as the first volley of bullets pinged through the sparse greenery. "I can give you no more."

The day was weak and pale, trembling on the edge of iciness. When Gray Eyes finally left the sweat lodge, her perspiration dried quickly to salty flakes on her skin. K'aalo'gii darted over to help as she scrubbed handful after handful of near-frozen dirt over herself to remove it.

"Sister?" she asked hesitantly. But she saw immediately that their *estsa hataali* was better. Her skin, as white as the Hopi desert just days ago, was pink again.

"It has worked," she breathed. "The *hataali* was right. You are strong, stronger even than him."

The color faded abruptly from Gray Eyes' face again. "I must find him." She bit down on her lip, forcing her still-groggy mind to concentrate. "I need food. Has anyone been hunting?"

K'aalo'gii shook her head. "No. We feared to leave you."

"Do we have nuts? Berries?"

"They have frozen."

Gray Eyes looked around at her sharply. "What have you been eating?"

"Only ground cake, from the last of the corn."

She closed her eyes. For a blessed moment, she knew the singular comfort that came from seeing that her convictions had been right. Her babe was lost to her, but her heart ached a little less. One life had ended, but seven remained, milling aimlessly, waiting helplessly for her to guide them.

She opened her eyes. "Bring me some of that then. And I will need a pony."

K'aalo'gii nodded and started to move away. Gray Eyes stopped her. "Sister? You will have to watch over the others while I am gone. I fear that after all that has happened, they do not think so clearly."

"They no longer want to," she murmured with rare wisdom.

The others continued to stand just outside Talks Often's shelter. Gray Eyes moved to them.

"You will have to do without me a while longer," she said carefully. She turned away to take the gelding her cousin had gathered up for her. Then, even as K'aalo'gii handed over the reins, she froze.

Gray Eyes jerked around to follow her gaze. She saw nothing, only endless brown desert and distant mountains capped with white. But then, K'aalo'gii's talents were not her own.

"What is it?" she demanded.

"I hear a rider approaching."

For a brief moment, Gray Eyes' breath caught and she felt something soft and sweet touch her heart, something like joy. The *hataali*. He had arrived safely after all.

Then the pony veered around the edge of the foothills and into sight. She galloped furiously, riderless, her mane and tail whipping behind her in streaks of silver-white. Her velvety muzzle lifted to the wind and twitched as she searched the air for scent. Gray Eyes felt a sudden, near-agonizing maelstrom of hope and pain.

Not the *hataali*, but Smoke, somehow escaped from the pale-eyes and following her heart toward home. A new breath of life, an unexpected gift, a blessing from the holy ones that her journey might be swift and sure.

Despite the dull, tired ache of her limbs, Gray Eyes gave a wild laugh and ran to meet her.

Chapter 37

Snow came almost as soon as they left the camp, small, stinging flakes that chapped Gray Eyes' cheeks and crusted her hair. She tucked her nose down into her blanket and dropped the reins to hug herself for warmth. Even without guidance, Smoke plodded diligently on until they reached a shallow, sandy wash. There she stopped.

Gray Eyes dropped her blanket to her shoulders and groped for the reins with hands that had long since gone numb. "Did they turn you into a pale-eyes weakling after all?" she chided her pony. "You can cross something as small as this. You have done it as many times as I have seen suns."

But the mare only stomped a hoof and snorted.

"What is it?" Gray Eyes felt the first tendrils of alarm shimmy down her spine. Pale-eyes? An ambush? Suddenly, she saw them again in her mind, *Dine'' Ana'i* with shrewd and glittering eyes. Her blood went cold and she jerked backward on the reins. The mare retreated willingly, scrambling.

They stopped ten lengths away. Together they stared into the clumps of white snow and green mesquite. Then Gray Eyes focused on another disparate color, a single flash of red.

Her pulse staggered. She knew. In a far-reaching place of her soul, in a cold, certain spot of her brain, she knew. The red would be silk.

The snow fell, icing Smoke's mane and blotting out that awful, unspeakable spark of color. Darkness fell, and still she sat and stared.

"Grandfather," she whispered once, toward dawn. Then she felt something splinter inside herself, something like dry, dead wood, and she dropped her head and wept the tears she'd thought she could no longer cry.

The canyon was quiet when the warriors came upon it. They galloped up to the precipice and stopped with an upheaval of snow.

"She is here. She must be," Hawk mused.

"It looks to me as though they have all returned." Na'acoci gave a sound of disgust. "They are all as yellow as poppies," he grumbled.

Hawk shrugged with deceptive indifference. "Perhaps, but this is not the time to worry over it. Come, my friend. Our women wait."

Na'acoci's response was hidden beneath the sliding, scraping sound of Hawk's stallion's hooves as he started down the incline. It was the earliest part of the day, with a moon still bright and slivered. The People slept, secure for a time in their canyon stronghold. But as the warriors wove through the scattered camps, an occasional door flap was shoved aside and noses poked out. By the time they reached a fire pit still faintly flickering, a handful of people had gathered.

Delgondito came last, looking disheveled and tugging sleepily at his blanket. "So," he said quietly. "It must truly be over for you to have returned. I had heard you joined the fighting forces."

"No," Hawk corrected. "Not joined. We travel on our own."

Delgondito nodded deferentially. "It is no more or less than what your uncle once saw for you." He hesitated. "What of Manuelito and Barboncito? What do they do now?"

Hawk shrugged and dropped down on his haunches to warm himself by the fire. "They are together and fight still. I think they will do so until the last paper is signed, and even then they will continue, only more circumspectly."

"You do not approve," Delgondito observed.

"Not entirely, but I approve even less of this new treaty."

Delgondito shrugged and looked around at the camps spreading out as far as the eye could see. "What choice do we have? We lost babes, women, even warriors in Hopi. Besides, the pale-eyes have not actually agreed to a new treaty. When I went to the *hual-te* with the others to speak with them, we agreed only to meet again in the moon of Baby Eagles. In the meantime, there is no more fighting. And that, my friend, is to our advantage. We need time to rest and heal. Later, perhaps, we will be strong enough to protest their invasion of our land."

Hawk measured him silently for a moment. Then, without warning, he grinned. "Sometimes, my friend, I like the way you think." He pushed to his feet again. "As you say, it is a time for resting, for healing. So tell me, is the little Lone Tree here?"

Delgondito's eyes slid suddenly sideward. "She is in the Chuskas," he said finally.

Hawk experienced a moment of unease. He had known Delgondito too long, too well. There was something more, something the older man was not saying. "And?" he prompted. "Why is she there when all the others are here?"

"Because the silver-eyed one led her people home before the rest of us. Because she learned first what it took the rest of us longer to know. Hopi is not a good place. *Dinetah*, even ravaged by the *Naakaiidine'e'*, is safer."

The silver-eyed one. He had taken care not to speak her name.

Hawk felt his heart stop. He gripped Delgondito's shoulders suddenly, with such force the man winced.

"Tell me. Who taught her this lesson?"

Delgondito shook his head sadly. "It was the pale-eyes and the *Dine" Ana'i,* or so I have heard. They attacked her people while they hid close to the *Moqui* mesas. The little *estsa hataali* survived, but many others died. All their men are gone."

There was a moment of stunned silence. Then Hawk felt the other men jostling him, pushing forward, shooting questions at the sad-faced headman. None of it penetrated the haze of dread and rage that filled his brain.

"Why?" His mind fastening on the only thing he truly cared about. "You didn't speak her name. Why, if she lives?"

Delgondito answered carefully. "She caught a sickness. Perhaps the *Dine" Ana'i* witched her. Or perhaps it is only a pale-eyes disease from her contact with them. Your uncle has gone to her."

Hawk dropped his hands from Delgondito's shoulders and spun back to his stallion. "Come," he snapped to the others. "We must ride for the Chuskas. We will know more when we find them."

Delgondito watched unhappily as the men obeyed and mounted again. He thought of the little shaman and the oval-eyed Hopi.

"I liked those girls," he muttered, but no one heard him.

As the warriors galloped relentlessly through the night and into the frosty, overcast dawn, Na'acoci's face remained closed and cold. He did not need to ride to the Chuskas to know that his enemy had finally and truly bested him. He had seen it in Delgondito's eyes. He had known it when he'd searched for her all through the moon of Slender Winds. Wildcat was gone.

He fought the rage, the grief, and for a while, he was

successful. During those moments, he remembered. The way she had shrieked and clawed at him when he had first dragged her from the *Naakaiidine'e'* herding shack. The way she had glared at him though the suns that had followed. She had been nothing to him then but a thorn in his side, proof that he had once acted foolishly and rashly. But slowly, somehow, she had become something more. She had crept into his hogan one rainy spring morning, trembling and frightened as she had offered him her body and her soul. She had been wisdom and innocence, love and fire, one of the few truly good things in his world.

Now she was gone.

Na'acoci lost his battle for control. A spasm of emotion crossed his face, contorting it for a heartbeat, making his whole body shudder. With it, the last light of kindness within the young warrior died.

None of the others noticed as they drove on toward the mountains, each grappling with their own thoughts of what they would find there. Hawk stopped first, reining in so suddenly that the others rode ahead several paces without him. Then Achi'i'h slowed to a trot and turned back to him.

"What is it?"

Hawk only stared, his nostrils flaring as though he had scented danger. Far in the distance, an obscure speck showed on the horizon.

How did he know it was her? Was it that her proximity alerted his senses? Or was it only his medicine that prickled the hairs on his nape? Either way, there was a certainty in his heart as he stared at the single stab of darkness, so stark against the surrounding white. Inexplicably, impossibly, he knew it was his little one.

He beat his weary stallion into a gallop again. They raced across the snow-swept desert until the speck turned to indigo and red and black. The storm had whipped her hair out from beneath her blanket, and in the stillness of the new day it fell wildly about her, concealing her face.

But her posture told Hawk what her features could not, hers and the silver-white pony's as she stood, neck low, nose inches from the snow. They were unnaturally still, defeated, exhausted.

Hawk dropped from his stallion and approached her on foot. "Little one?"

Her head came up slowly. Her face was impossibly white except for two feverish spots of color on her cheekbones; her eyes were as blank as death.

"Little one," he said again, then he touched her thigh gently, half expecting her to shatter.

She took a sudden, shuddering breath as she focused on him. There was no surprise in her eyes, only dumb relief.

"It is good you have come," she murmured. "I do not think I can lift him to my pony myself."

"Lift him?" Weariness and fear and confusion made his voice harsh. "What—" Then he broke off at a bellow from the ravine. Jackrabbit and Na'acoci and Achi'i'h began calling for the wrath of the holy ones to fall upon the pale-eyes. He looked around sharply as Na'acoci held up a scrap of red silk tinged with crimson and splotches of dark brown.

"No," Hawk said, his voice flat and contained. Then he roared, "No!"

He left the little one and raced into the copse. He broke through the tangle of cottonwoods and went still, panting, his gorge rising. There was nothing left. The *hataali* had not been allowed a warrior's death. They had robbed him even of that. They had mutilated him.

Hawk dropped to his knees beside what remained of his uncle. Violently, frenziedly, he pushed aside the rocks that had pelted him, crushing his skull, shattering his bones. His scalp had been taken as in the crazed coup of a Comanche, but Hawk knew that no Indian had done this. No Indian would leave even less than an animal predator. Only a white man would reduce his enemy to useless blood and pulp after he was long dead.

Blood and pulp . . . and red silk and silver.

A choking sound wrenched from him. Hawk gathered up what remained of Long Earrings, then the haughty, arrogant warrior cried.

Chapter 38

They took the *hataali*'s body back to the canyon while Jackrabbit rode to the Chuskas to collect the last of the Lone Trees. He brought them to the Bitter Waters' camp on the same morning they buried Long Earrings.

Gray Eyes found the tree beneath which he'd spent so many mornings during that winter she'd healed him. She helped to dig the hole there and she spoke the burial rite. She stayed to mourn long after everyone else hurried off to escape the wrath of his *chindi,* but she was no longer able to cry, not for him, not for herself.

Barren Woman found her there, cloaked in shadows as the day drew to a close. Her pipe jerked spasmodically between her thin lips as she sat down beside her.

"I had thought I would find you here."

Gray Eyes only continued to stare at the pile of tortured, dug-up earth that was her mentor.

"You would not fear his *chindi,*" the older woman went on.

"No."

"I think you are right. I do not think even in death he would hurt you."

Gray Eyes finally looked up at her. "And you? Do you not fear him?"

Barren Woman gave a ragged chuckle. "Oh, yes. He will come after me, if only to see me get angry. My temper always entertained him."

For a wild moment, Gray Eyes felt emotion again. She watched Barren Woman's eyes begin to glisten, and a frantic fear rose within her that the proud, overbearing woman would cry. But Barren Woman only sniffed loudly, dragged an edge of her blanket across her nose, and thrust a doeskin bundle at her.

"His *jish,* his medicine," she muttered. "I did not bury it with him. I thought he would want you to have it."

Gray Eyes stared at it, her throat aching. Yes, she realized, yes, he would have. He had been tired, so tired, and would not have wanted to go on healing in the afterworld. Suddenly, she knew how she could make amends for the death that her babe's *tah honeesgai* had brought about.

She would survive as he had asked her to. She would carry on.

She grabbed the bundle suddenly, her chin trembling. Barren Woman pushed to her feet. "He was planning to go to the treaty talks," she murmured as though it were an afterthought. But Gray Eyes knew it was not.

"I will go in his place. I will speak for him."

Barren Woman nodded, satisfied.

Both clans gravitated toward Hawk's leadership. Though Gray Eyes dwelled in an inviolate place in their hearts, she was revered rather than consulted, honored rather than obeyed. In matters of relocating outside the canyon, of raiding to replenish the sheep, it was Hawk's opinion they sought.

They built separate hogans, his near the Bitter Waters' central fire pit, hers toward the south end of camp where she could look out at night and see the tree that sheltered Long Earrings. But daylight always found Gray Eyes in front of Hawk's lodge, brewing her potions and herbs while he settled squabbles and dispensed advice.

She was there the day Delgondito came from his own camp to discuss the new treaty.

"Manuelito sends word that he will attend the talks," he began without preamble, settling his bulky form against the wall. Hawk's eyes narrowed thoughtfully.

"Why, I wonder? He has never been an advocate of peace."

"Because he signs a treaty does not mean that he will end his war."

"Ah, that is true."

"That brings our number to five. You and I and Armijo, and where Manuelito goes, Barboncito usually follows. Five is enough, I think. It is already the time of Baby Eagles. We should go."

"Six will go." Gray Eyes spoke softly, still stirring a pot over the fire.

"Who else, little one?" Hawk asked with casual interest.

"Me."

Lightning might have burst from the opaque February sky to electrify him. "No!" he protested. "I will not allow you so close to the pale-eyes. It is dangerous."

Her chin rose slowly—not with the defiance of a fiery child this time, but with a remote, haunted dignity that frightened him like no enemy could. "You forget," she answered quietly. "I do not need your permission."

The truth of her statement drove straight through him. He was neither husband, brother, nor uncle to her; he had no right to oppose her stubborn willfulness. And yet his heart, his love and his fear for her, were an animal inside him that would not be chained.

"You have no right," he snapped. "You are not a headman. You speak for no one."

"I am *estsa hataali*. I speak for everyone."

He pushed to his feet and glared down at her, hurt and anger clashing in his eyes. "You will do this thing even though I ask you not to?" he demanded.

She longed to bend to his wishes, to still carry his child and have nothing more to occupy her mind than tending the sheep he brought home to her. But her hand strayed to her gall bag. It carried so much more than a coin and a feather now. It contained responsibility.

She would do this thing because she had to do this thing. She dropped her eyes and nodded.

"You have been ill! Such a long ride could make you sick again!"

"Ill?" she began. "But it was—"

And then she stopped.

She couldn't tell him about the babe. She couldn't tell him about the Beard and Bulbous Nose. Telling him would result in even more bloodshed. She could not be the cause of that.

"No," she whispered. "That was only a little pale-eyes' sickness. I cured myself, and I am fine now."

It was the first lie she had ever told him. She bit her lip hard as a small part of her died. Hawk felt it too, although he couldn't understand it. Somehow, their lives were beginning to run separate courses.

Without warning, without ever having truly had her, he was beginning to lose her.

Chapter 39

The headmen began planning their next raids almost as soon as the treaty meetings were over. They might have been forced to sign the pale-eyes' paper, but to adhere to those promises would have meant watching their people starve.

"The inhabitants of New Mexico are now under the protection of the United States government," the man Canby had told them. "Persecute them, and you are antagonizing us. You will, at once, make war on any and all unruly men of your tribe. All of your raiders must be driven out or destroyed. Furthermore, you shall immediately collect your people and establish them in permanent settlements west of this fort. You may not enter the country east of here. Is that agreed and understood?"

Only Gray Eyes had responded. "This fort is in the middle of our land. Two of our sacred mountains are east of here. Do you tell us that we must give them up?"

"If they are east of here, yes." Canby had dismissed her and looked back toward the headmen. "Will you agree? All of you? I'll tolerate no holdouts."

And so they had signed, one headman after another moving forward to scratch his X on the fragile piece of paper the white man seemed to covet. They had signed, but then they had gone home to plot and plan, to rest and heal, just as Delgondito had suggested.

The moon of Baby Eagles had scarcely waned when Hawk gathered up his blanket and crossed the canyon in search of his friend. As he settled himself beside his fire pit, the older man nodded decisively.

"It is time."

"Not quite."

Startled, Delgondito looked at him.

"This canyon is a good place," Hawk mused, "and it sprawls further than the eye can see. But it is still too small for all of us."

"Not any longer. We lost too much to the war, to Hopi."

"When we bring back sheep and horses to replenish our herds, it will be. First I would like to move my uncle's people out of here, to a place where our stock can graze when I bring them home."

"And the silver-eyed one?" Delgondito asked.

"Yes," Hawk answered. "Her people are mine now. I will take them as well."

"That is not what I meant."

Like everyone else, Delgondito was well aware of the strained link between them. They had both gone to the treaty meetings, but they had given each other a wide berth. Most of the men were giving Hawk one as well, for his moods had become unpredictable and sour. But Delgondito had a soft spot in his heart for the *estsa hataali*, and he had long loved the man who had been Hawk's uncle. He decided now to interfere.

"She is not one into whose hogan you can sneak indefinitely," he went on. "She deserves more. Instead, in your anger, you give her nothing. Think, my friend. She too lost the eastern third of *Dinetah*. She too looked into the white man's greedy eyes at Fort Fauntleroy. But while you and I can raid and replenish and forget, she can only remember. And she is remembering alone."

Hawk's expression hardened. "To give her more is to give her less."

"Bah!"

"I have no time for husbandly duties."

"So you take only husbandly rights when the time and mood are of your chosing."

A growl worked its way up Hawk's throat. But before it could escape, Delgondito gave the quiet chuckle that always diffused tension. "More than our stock needs replenishing, my friend. Our hearts need it, and our families need it as well. We must produce children and begin again. The war is over."

Hawk looked up at the black sky. "You would see me wed her then?" he snapped. "No. Not yet. Not while men with white skin still live on our land." Not for anything would he admit his true reservations. Would the little one still have gone to the treaty if she had been his wife? Could she be his wife when she would always follow her own heart?

Delgondito shrugged. "The pale-eyes will always be there; to wait for them to go is to wait a lifetime, and in the meantime, you may well lose her." He pushed to his feet. "Stay and enjoy my fire if you like. *I* have women waiting."

Hawk stared at the dark flap of his doorway long after Delgondito disappeared. Then he grunted and pushed to his feet. He too had a woman waiting.

He crossed to the south end of his own camp. When he stood outside Gray Eyes' door flap, he stared long and hard at the faint light flickering behind it. Then he pulled the hide roughly aside.

Gray Eyes looked up sharply, but she shivered more from the sight of him than from the cold air that wafted inside. "Yes?" she asked coolly, guardedly.

His temper vanished abruptly. A hollow hurt crept in to replace it, a hurt he had known for too long now, one that ate at him in a way pale-eyes' treachery never could. He could no longer fight her.

"Come back to me, little one," he murmured softly. "It is not worth wasting the time we have together. I do not want you rushing off to tackle pale-eyes, but I can see that my wrath will not hold you back."

He stepped inside. The hide rustled closed behind him. He knelt and pulled her into his arms.

At first she resisted, then something snapped inside her and she clung to the front of his blanket. "I did not want to go," she admitted. "More than anything in the world, I wanted to do as you asked and stay."

"I know." He rubbed his hands briskly over her skin. It was frigid. "I would rather that none of us had gone," he mused, "but I feared for you more. Do not blame me for that. It is something I cannot change."

Love for him swelled inside her suddenly and violently. She lifted her face to his, pleading for the kind of strength and comfort that only he could give. Emotion seared through her again, hot and full to fill the voids that pain had etched.

"So many of them," she moaned against his chest. "I did not know, never suspected, that there would be so many pale-eyes there. And the hatred in their eyes . . ."

"Shhh."

"Make them go away," she pleaded. "Take their faces from my mind."

But even as his hands tunneled through her hair, pulling it free of its knot, they both knew that neither of them possessed that power. She had seen too much death, had suffered too much heartache by pale hands. Even as his mouth ravaged hers, she knew the terrible weight of the secret she was keeping from him, the suffocating wrong the pale-eyes had done her.

He lowered her to the ground, pulling at her shift with one hand while the other buried itself in the cascade of her hair. His mouth did all of the things he'd taught her to crave. He loved her, understanding perhaps better than she did the need for the act of creation after witnessing war's destruction. He understood and so he gave that sweet lapse of memory, that renewing, to her now, even knowing that it would only make her strong enough to slip a little further away from him.

Pain pierced him at the thought, but he bent to her anyway, possessing her mouth. Pinning her beneath him, he touched his knee against her most secret flesh until she forgot about everything but the maelstrom of sensation sucking her downward.

He slid inside her and moved within her, and finally, the emptiness she had carried since Long Earrings' death began to fill.

He left her again three suns later, to raid the same land Na'acoci had been so disappointed with in his fifteenth summer. It was still sparsely tufted, still brown and dry, but now the People could no longer claim it as theirs.

"I would like to be with you when you ride in," the man nearest Hawk said as they clustered on the far side of an arroyo. Hawk glanced up. It was He Acts Like an Old Man.

Hawk's gut squirmed at the edge of hatred in the gentle man's tone. He thought of his uncle and for one aching moment, he considered turning back. The *hataali* would have wept to know what his peaceable followers were doing now. Then he remembered Canby's smug face and Long Earrings' battered body, and his resolve hardened.

"No," he answered shortly. "What you know best is sheep. Wait here," he instructed. "When I send the flock to you, have the men ready to drive them north." He threw back his head and punctuated the command with, *"Ahu!"*

Na'acoci reacted before the shout even died in the air. He was first across the ravine, his colt scrambling and sliding as he jerked his bow free of his shoulder. He did not waste time groping with his saddle blanket this time. He had not come for sheep.

He bypassed the flock and went directly to the herders' shack. Three men scrambled out and two more raced in from the fields to see what the ruckus was about. They were *Naakaiidine'e'* again, the white ones, the ones who had stolen his young, pregnant wife.

He caught the youngest, slowest one by the hair as the boy raced by on foot. With a strength born of hatred he jerked him along beside his galloping pony, then he caught him about the neck and dropped him over his mount.

"You have women here? Where are they?"

The boy shook his head wildly, uncomprehendingly. Na'acoci shoved him off his pony and veered back.

There was another building not far from the shack. He raced toward it just as the door was yanked open and a man stumbled out onto the wide, planked porch. Behind him, a young woman shivered in a cotton wrapper, her long blonde hair spilling, her mouth wide and slack.

Na'acoci saw her and dug his heels viciously into his colt. The animal leaped and together they crashed onto the porch amid splintering wood.

The man bellowed and leveled his rifle. Na'acoci met his eyes, then leaped off his pony and took the man crashing to the deck beneath him.

"No, white man, not yet," he spat. "I will die gladly, but not before I see you in an afterworld worse than mine."

He wrenched the rifle from the man's hands even as its sharp report shattered the night. Coldly, calmly, he tossed it over the rail to be retrieved later. The woman whimpered as both men began to struggle.

The settler's fist came up suddenly and caught Na'acoci squarely in the gut, but he never felt it. Eyes gleaming, he reared up, kicking the man hard in the jaw to send him toppling over the shattered rail. Then he grabbed the woman's hair and jerked her toward him, forcing her into a sprawled, sobbing heap.

"No, not her," the pale-eyes groaned. He had clawed his way back onto the porch, the rifle once again clutched in his grip. "Kill me, you bloodthirsty bastard, but leave her."

Na'acoci measured him with feral eyes. The man put the gun to his own head in a language they could both understand. Na'acoci lunged for him, pulling it clear before its fireball belched out and embedded itself in the porch roof.

"Coward," he crooned, his voice too soft, too deadly. "No, I do not intend for you to die. That would be too easy, white man. I want you to know what it is to live when that which gives life is gone."

With a scream of anguish, he raised the rifle again, his own sobs mingling with those of the woman before him. "For the *Moqui*," he told her. Then, with the explosion, her crying stopped.

Chapter 40

▼ ▼ ▼ ▼ ▼ ▼ ▼ ▼ ▼

Hawk's face was stony as he trotted back across the ravine and turned to survey the devastation behind him. Far in the distance, he could hear the sound of bawling sheep. His war band had not waited for him this time; too many of the herders had escaped to bring help. It was dangerous to dally, yet still he hesitated.

When, he wondered, had it come to this? When had raiding ceased to be a livelihood and settled into pure vengeance? By his own order, no pregnant ewes had been left behind this time. The shack and the cabin burned garishly. Three corpses littered the land, and none of them had died gently; they had died as Long Earrings had died. Suddenly, Hawk realized the answer to his question. The hatred had festered for far too long on both sides, and now it was rancid and vile and unconquerable.

Abruptly, he turned away from the carnage and nudged his stallion into a ground-eating canter toward the wash where his warriors awaited him. Sometime after the moon dipped low to touch the horizon, he spotted his men—all forty, plus a thousand sheep and a handful of wiry horses. Na'acoci trotted up the bank to meet him. Hawk took in his blood-soaked clothing and knew another wave of futility.

"It is time to turn west," he said. "If we hurry we can make it past the new *hual-te* by dawn."

Na'acoci nodded and circled back to urge both the sheep and the men along at a faster pace.

They headed out, churning the desert air into a mael-

283

strom of dust and sound. Hawk rode ahead of them, his posture wary, his eyes scanning the horizon. Near daybreak, the sky lit with a dull glow from the lanterns of the white man's new fort.

The place was a beehive of activity. Hawk froze, wondering what had gone wrong.

"North," he spat in an undertone. "Take the sheep north before one of these white fools hears their noise!"

He didn't truly believe that any of the pale-eyes was cognizant enough of his surroundings to pick out the distant, tell-tale bawls of the flock. But neither could he explain the long line of soldiers heading out from the *hualte*.

"What is it?" Na'acoci asked, moving up beside him. "Where are they going?"

Hawk shook his head silently and continued to watch as mules and ponies trundled carts into the parade ground. Men milled about like restless sheep, but throughout all the disorder some pattern emerged. The soldiers crawled into the carts, mounted horses, and continued to ride out.

"We will go to *Tsehotsohih*," Hawk decided. "Heuro will know." He turned away and urged his mount into a hard gallop.

Na'acoci gaped at his retreating back, then raced off after him. They rode without speaking, taking washes and hillocks with reckless speed. Then, when the sun began to climb, Hawk finally stopped.

The muscles of his chest heaved with each harsh, exhausted breath he took. His eyes narrowed as he stared at the cluster of red cliffs that hid the unsightly fort called Defiance.

"*Hoooo-eeee!*" he called, the sound only subtly different than that an animal would make. In the distance, there was an answering sound.

A moment later, Heuro appeared at the mouth of the gorge, then circled back to meet them behind the rise. Stopping in front of them, he chewed his lip thoughtfully.

"You are foolish men," he said finally. "Pale-eyes are

all over this land now. Unless you seek a coup, I would leave here quickly and go home. Why risk trouble?"

Hawk scowled. "I seek no trouble. I came for information."

"Have you been gone long, brother? Word has already spread. I told Manuelito. There is war again."

For an agonizing moment, Hawk felt his heart stop. His thoughts flew to the dry, scraggly clearing so far north of here, the place where he had left the little one without men or weapons. "What now?" he growled. "What has caused this?"

Heuro shrugged. "They are crazy, these pale-eyes. We have always known that. But you do not need to fear for your women this time. The pale-eyes are all going back to the land that first spit them out."

Na'acoci stared at him blankly. Heuro chuckled.

"They signed the paper to not fight with us anymore, so now they must fight their own kind back in the land they came from." He laughed aloud then at the very lunacy of such a thing. "Headmen against headmen. They tell me that those who live to the north of their country are fighting the ones who live to the south."

Fighting themselves? For a long moment, Hawk's mind refused to accept it. Stags rutted for females; stallions fought to drive off upstart colts. But he had never known an animal or a man to choose sides among his own brothers.

"That is crazy!" Na'acoci erupted.

Heuro nodded. "Yes. But what do we care if it takes them away from here?"

And that, really, was the crux of the matter. Hawk's heart moved suddenly with a surge of emotion. The pale-eyes had been a fact of life since his boyhood. He had grown to manhood learning to fight and outwit them. He had grown rich and then poor over the issue of their sheep. And now, now they were going, with no fanfare, no coups counted. It was oddly anticlimactic and, at the thought of

life without them, satisfaction and confusion clashed inside him.

"The old *Naakaiidine'e'?*" he asked. "What of the dark
ones?"

Heuro cocked his head thoughtfully. "I do not know.
But they are all brothers now. Perhaps they will go too."
He turned away from them. "I must return now. Even
pale-eyes are not so stupid that they will not notice I have
gone. There is much to do to close this fort, and they will
be looking for me to do it."

"Close it?" Na'acoci asked quickly.

Heuro looked back and grunted. "They will keep a few
men at Ojo del Oso, I think, but this *hual-te* will be abandoned." A genuine smile finally spread across his fat face.
"Manuelito will once again possess *Tsehotsohih.*"

He skirted the bluffs and disappeared. In the lukewarm
stillness of the desert, birds called and mesquite rustled.
There was another burst of song from the *hual-te* and a
wagon rolled out of the meadow's mouth. Blue-coated soldiers hung from its slats, and Hawk recognized the bottle
of firewater one of them gripped tightly.

Finally, the wagon vanished into a distant cloud of dust.
Hawk gave a sudden, wild whoop and jerked his bow free
to aim an arrow at the sky. He galloped around Na'acoci
in a tight little circle of triumph, first kneeling, then standing on his stallion's back to hoot and chortle. But Na'acoci
only continued to stare at *Tsehotsohih.*

It was over, he thought. He had not won, but the pale-
eyes were gone. "So what of vengeance, brother?" he
demanded roughly. "Are we to forsake that?"

Hawk slowed his horse gradually, then dropped astride
him again. "Where there is no enemy, there is no vengeance," he answered.

"You are willing to forget so quickly?"

A long moment passed in silence. "I know the emptiness of a hollow victory," he answered quietly. "But I
know too that it would be foolish to give this gift back to
the holy ones. Think of our women, friend. Think of the

old men and the children whose bellies have been so empty they cry. Think of sheep and life as once we knew it. That, I think, is enough.''

He pulled his mount around again and cantered the tired animal toward the north. Na'acoci remained for a moment, struggling with a burning frustration unlike any he had ever known.

''Over?'' he repeated. ''No. No, not yet.''

Chapter 41

There was a haunting familiarity about the sounds in camp that reminded Gray Eyes of a mockingbird's song, so similar to reality, but carrying a note of falseness.

Ponies clopped out of the corral, but there were no sheep to follow. People talked, but Vittorio's voice was not booming out orders. One Whisker was not snoring in his sheepskin on the other side of the hogan. Gray Eyes shuddered and sat up, pushing her own sheepskin and a gnawing depression away.

Then she heard the horses, whoops and hollers.

For a moment she almost smiled. She remembered another morning three full summers ago when she had squirmed beneath her bedding and listened to a victorious war band returning. She got to her feet and crossed her hogan to push up the door flap.

The land here was open and sprawling, and she could see the raiding party clearly. Raiders . . . with more sheep than she had seen since before the war. Her heart pounded and her eyes widened. She tried to think of the white men who must have died for this, tried to remind herself that sooner or later their brothers would retaliate. But her eyes still feasted on the soft, tufted white wool and she licked her lips.

Then she glanced at the warrior in the lead, dressed all in black. A ghost of a smile touched her face. This war party was not merely victorious, she realized. They were jubilant.

Hawk raced into the camp with all of the vigor and

carelessness of the young warrior she had once known. His men followed suit. Was that Old Man? She shook her head in mute denial as he hung low on his pony's neck, cavorting like a boy, his toothless gums spread wide in a grin.

Without meaning to, without wanting to, Gray Eyes took a step forward and let and door flap fall closed behind her.

She knew, bless the Holy People, she knew that they had brought nothing that could set the world right again. Her sister had been stolen four summers ago; instead of having her back, they had lost Quiet Woman and One Whisker as well. And yet her pulse did a happy trot as she watched the *hataali*'s youngest wife drop to her knees and dig her fingers into the soft wool of a lamb. Tears coursed down her cheeks and she looked up at the heavens with such a look of gratitude that Gray Eyes no longer cared what the eventual cost of this coup would be.

She moved into the camp and looked across the fire pit straight into Hawk's eyes.

A slow grin spread over the hard, arrogant face she loved so well. Her breath caught and her palms went damp. She backed up more out of memory than anything else. As he whirled around on his stallion, his clothing dark, his eyes fierce, she remembered again that morning of three summers ago. He beat the horse into a gallop just as he had then and dodged around the fire pit. He caught her with a grip more gentle than it had been that day, but then, she was not fighting him with such ferocity. She gasped when he hauled her up onto his horse, but she did not claw at his throat. She wriggled, but she did not fight to be released. Finally, she dropped her head against his shoulder and clung to him, her breath coming in hiccups as he once again whisked her through camp.

This time he dropped her at his own hogan. This time, he dismounted with her. By the time her feet were solidly planted on the ground again, both clans had gathered and were ogling them curiously.

"Will you women stand around all day after your men

have worked so hard all night?'' Hawk demanded of them, but his eyes were smiling. "These sheep are yours, but I would ask that you slaughter as many of them now as we need for a feast.''

"A feast?'' someone ventured. Everyone turned to look at the flock, now contained in the corral. It had been a good raid, indeed, but it was long overdue. They were grateful, but life had taught them not to waste a morsel.

Then Hawk continued more seriously. "Your men brought the stock home by themselves. My brother-in-law and I left them for a while to go to *Tsehotsohih.* '' The people uttered a collective gasp. "Fear not, my friends," Hawk continued. "I am here to tell you that it is over, truly over. The *hual-te* has been abandoned. We saw it with our own eyes. The pale-eyes are leaving *Dinetah.* ''

For a long while, no one spoke. Even little Squeak was silent, falling abruptly to his bottom to stare at Hawk. Then, gradually, a hushed murmur wound its way through the crowd.

Over? It was over? Gray Eyes shook her head disbelievingly. But the warriors and men were still laughing, actually dancing with each other.

"Why?'' she whispered to Hawk. "What did you do to them?''

He looked out over the crowd, his black eyes more calm than she had ever seen them. "Not I, little one, although I wish it were so. I think the treaty was the right thing to do. When they could fight us no longer, they decided to go east to fight elsewhere.''

"Surely there is more to it than that," she said uncertainly.

"No. I spoke to Heuro.''

Heuro would know. Her heart skipped hard as she began to believe.

"Gone?'' she repeated. "All of them?''

"Except a few at Ojo del Oso.''

"We are far from Ojo del Oso," she mused.

"Yes.''

K'aalo'gii yelped suddenly and grabbed Squeak to lift him high in the air. Little Left Hand and Talks Often clutched at each other. The murmurs of the crowd escalated into shouts. Gray Eyes stared at them, then jumped slightly as Hawk took her elbow.

"Little one."

She looked up at him with the beginnings of a trembling smile. She knew how he would celebrate this extraordinary victory.

He turned her toward the hogan that propriety had always prevented her from entering before. He sneaked to her lodge under cover of darkness; she could not be caught creeping into his. But now her emotions were too tangled, too dazed, to be wasted on what the clans might think. She stepped inside as he dropped the door flap behind her, then shivered when he came to hold her face in his hands.

"Could it be?" he whispered. "Could it be that it is time for us after all?"

It had always been time for them, she thought. But now, for this brief, priceless moment, perhaps he would believe it as well. Gently, slowly, she pushed up on her toes until her lips touched his in the kiss he had taught her.

He scooped her up suddenly and dropped her down upon the sheepskins that cluttered one wall. Slowly and calmly, he brushed thick strands of her hair off her cheek and forehead. He smiled once, almost bemusedly, as he touched wet, gentle kisses to her throat and neck. Gray Eyes shivered. Somehow, when she thought she knew all of him, he gave her something more.

He came back to her mouth, his tongue probing lazily this time. It touched hers, darted away, came back. Her breasts began to feel full and heavy, not only from the physical onslaught, but from the look in his eyes.

"I want to touch you forever, little one," he murmured against her mouth. "Here . . . and here, every night of my life."

Her heart lurched with an almost forbidden hope, then

exploded as the hard warmth of him penetrated her and she could think no longer.

Much later, he rolled away from her and stared up at the smoke hole. Her eyes followed his and for the first time she knew a strange, giddy guilt at the fact that she should be here, in his hogan. All the women of both clans had undoubtedly sneaked into men's hogans at one time or other, and they had been teased mercilessly when they were caught. But she had walked in boldly, and she was their *estsa hataali*. Suddenly, she blushed.

"Sooner or later," Hawk said quietly, "they will accept and forget."

She jumped as much from the way he always seemed to know her mind as from his expression, for when she looked over at him, she saw fear and uncertainty there. In her Hawk?

He sat up to grope through some buckskin bundles pressed against one wall. She recognized the pipe he came up with at once. It was Long Earrings'. Her stomach tightened. Then Hawk lit the pipe and spoke.

"I would use this one last time."

"Last?" she asked, confused.

"I have brought another from the *Naakaiidine'e'* camp we just raided. This one . . ." He trailed off. Pain clouded his eyes briefly. "This one should be set aside. Saved, as I have saved his words for seasons now."

She shook her head uncomprehendingly.

Suddenly, he chuckled. "You know the words I mean, little one. You were inside Barren Woman's hogan, just a wee thing then, eavesdropping on us as you are still sometimes wont to do. If you would have her, he said, you will have to buy her. You remember? It was in the canyon, after you saved him, after I returned with the coup of the white men's horses."

She nodded, embarrassed, and pressed her hands to her cheeks. Oh, yes, she remembered. He laughed at her reaction.

"I wonder if I will ever forget your face when you came

out of there," he went on. "Silver eyes sparking, such haughty indignation. But, little one, what I said then was true. I did not want a wife. I wanted Manuelito to fight sensibly. I wanted my uncle to fight a little bit. I wanted the white man to leave. I could not think of buying you and wives to help you."

"I need none of that." The words were out before she could stop herself. She colored fiercely and ducked her head.

"You will leave again, my love," she explained awkwardly. "I know that. I will not marry another. I will wait, as always, with my medicines, because you will always need healing. I will wait with my heart, because in some strange way, we are bound. I only pray that you, too, will not marry. I do not think I could share you."

"And what if we were to marry each other?"

Her head snapped up. Suddenly, her eyes were like the stars at night, something bright and good in the midst of blackness.

A moment of strange fear gripped him. It seemed that all his life this girl-child, this woman, had waited on the fringes for him. Sometimes her eyes had been snapping and haughty. Sometimes they had been soft and lusty. But always they had commanded him. Was that it? he wondered wildly. Was he still frightened by the wild, incomparable heat of her that would surely consume him if he remained near her too long? Or was it just that he was afraid she would say no? He closed his eyes briefly, and his words came out nonsensically when he opened them again.

"You want no other wives?" he asked.

She scowled at him. "For what?"

"For the millions of sheep I bring home."

She felt almost ill with the sudden exhilaration that swept through her. He was serious then. She had never dared to consider that their love could be any different than it had been these last many moons.

"Would they do nothing more than tend to those sheep?" she asked carefully.

His own heart was beating now, hard and crazily. "That is not the way of things."

Her face shadowed. "No."

"Then I would have no other."

She was upon him then, mouth wet and searching, touching his lips, his face, his brow. He laughed and the tension eased from him. He would buy her. The pale-eyes were gone and he would have her. He wondered now if he had ever really had a choice.

"I got only five ponies on the raid." His words were guttural, smothered, as she trapped them with her mouth.

"Keep them," she answered. "All your horses snort and stomp like a winter wind, and I have no desire to tame them."

"I have five hundred sheep."

"I will take them."

That made his brows shoot all the way up. "Who taught you such greed?"

She sobered abruptly. "The pale-eyes."

"They are gone now, little one," he reminded her gently.

"But hunger is not."

Suddenly, he understood. "I would give my gift to the people then, not to you. Is that what you say you want?"

"Two hundred fifty to the Bitter Waters," she agreed. "One hundred to Little Left Hand; she has no one. Fifty to Talks Often, fifty to K'aalo'gii, and fifty to me."

"K'aalo'gii? Why K'aalo'gii?"

Her eyes began to twinkle. "How else is she to win a husband of her own? Do you think she will get one by taking more coups in a raid? No, I think she needs to be wealthy."

He laughed, deeply and richly, but he was not truly surprised by her wishes. That was the way of his little one, generous and meddlesome. He watched her as she stared at the door flap, at the thin slice of sky at its fringes, and her eyes grew misty and far away.

Maybe, she thought. Perhaps. She poked at the joy in her heart as though it were an animal that just might rear up and strike her.

Then she smiled, and once more she dared to believe.

Chapter 42

▼▼▼▼▼▼▼▼▼

Word of the wedding spread like a desert fire. By daybreak, every clan within a fifty-mile radius had heard the news. Delgondito arrived the following evening.

He pushed his way through the men congregated in Hawk's shelter and dropped down in the spot of honor beside the fire. They clasped hands, but it wasn't enough. Roughly, emotionally, they embraced.

"You have heard then," Hawk said.

"About the pale-eyes, and about the silver-eyed one," Delgondito confirmed. "I am not too late then? I had thought you might need me to do the honors."

Hawk nodded, his face darkening. "My father is dead and my uncle is gone. The little one, too, is without anyone to speak for her. Her father, my uncle, they would have been her choices, but . . ." He trailed off.

Delgondito patted his shoulder. "Fear not. I am here for you, and she has her brother, does she not?"

"He has gone raiding again. He will not believe that this is a time of growth, not strife."

The headman nodded thoughtfully. "Who is closest to her besides him?"

Hawk looked around the fire, thinking of Vittorio, Yellow Horse, Spotted Shirt, and old befuddled Black Spot. "Jackrabbit is her grandmother's sister's son."

Delgondito nodded. "So be it."

He crossed to Jackrabbit and, a moment later, the two men left the shelter. The appropriate signs were waiting for them at Gray Eyes' lodge, all those glorious little subtleties and traditions that had nearly been lost during the war. There was soot around the smoke hole, water and food stacked by the fire pit, all to make the groom's messenger feel welcomed. Gray Eyes saw Jackrabbit approach her and her eyes grew misty.

She knew that Na'acoci was gone again. But here was dear, sweet Jackrabbit, unwilling to see her suffer for it.

He dropped down beside her. "I have been told that you have already agreed to the gifts," he whispered.

She nodded. Circumspectly, she leaned close to him and whispered into his ear the division of sheep that Hawk had promised her.

"What of ponies?" Jackrabbit asked.

Gray Eyes shrugged. "I have Smoke. I need none. But perhaps we could have her bred to his stallion."

Jackrabbit nodded, and the negotiations began.

He and Delgondito bickered amiably as the night wore on. People trundled in and out of the shelter, leaving only grudgingly. They wanted to hear every word. Not so grand a wedding or such a generous marriage gift had been witnessed in some time.

Near dawn, Delgondito and Jackrabbit finally pushed to their feet. "It is settled then," Delgondito announced, fighting the urge to smile. In truth, he would have given any of Hawk's possessions to see these two wed.

Jackrabbit agreed. "We will welcome you back in ten suns."

Ten suns, Gray Eyes thought. She had the eerie sense that life could not stay this good for that long. She wanted to hurry, to gather all this happiness to her breast as quickly as possible. But the wait was traditional, and she knew that their people would have it no other way.

The day of the wedding dawned brilliantly. It was the white man's April and the beginning of Gray Eyes' sixteenth summer. She stayed in her hogan, her cheeks flushed a bright red as Talks Often and Little Left Hand hovered over her. Winter Star came to tuck up her hair with the special furred thong, her arthritic hands trembling, her eyes misting frequently. Then Delgondito arrived with the sheep, a huge procession that knocked down looms and damaged hogans as they were driven directly through camp. Hawk's stallion stood at the central fire pit as a symbol of the agreed-upon breeding. There was shiny glass that she could see herself in and bright silky ribbons, all tokens of Hawk's last raid. The trinkets were more than she wanted or needed, so she shared them with Little Left Hand and K'aalo'gii.

Then, finally, Jackrabbit came for her.

The ceremony was to take place in Hawk's hogan. He sat at the west side of the fire, his gaze unwavering as he watched her slip through the door opening. Her eyes caught the firelight as they met his. She was radiant, he thought, not only with happiness but with the inner strength that he sometimes rejoiced in, sometimes despaired over. But it was his now, she was his, to depend upon and cherish from this day forward. A depth of emotion, a frightening vulnerability, swept over him.

People began to press into the shelter after her, and the moment was over. They reached and wriggled as the basket of pollen was passed among them and out the door. When it was empty, the newly married couple stepped outside. Delgondito and Armijo would talk by the fire pit so that everyone could hear. The people jostled for space, then finally settled in.

Gray Eyes looked around at them all, her heart feeling so soft and tender that it was nearly a physical pain. She glanced up at Hawk and felt her soul get caught in his black eyes.

"Finally, little one," he said just as Delgondito began speaking.

Finally, she thought. The *hataali* had seen the sun and the moon touch only once. But her blood would run fast and her breath would fall short for a lifetime.

* * *

The moon was full and bright, the camp still raucous and reeling with celebrators, when K'aalo'gii dropped down beside Gray Eyes at the central fire pit. For a long time they only sat side by side, breathing in the smell of good, rich life. There was sheep dung and horse manure and the heavy woolly aroma of the mutton that had been roasting for days. There was the bite of burnt mesquite in the air, and the cloying, sweet scent of spring in the desert. Gray Eyes shivered and smiled beatifically. K'aalo'gii sighed.

"Why did you give me sheep instead of those fine ponies?" she asked suddenly, eyeing the herd.

Gray Eyes was surprised and panicked. It was too late to change her gift now.

"Do you think, sister, that if I do not have many sheep, no husband would put up with me?" K'aalo'gii went on. "It is not so, you know. I love you for caring, but it is simply not so." Her voice had taken on a dreamy quality. Startled, Gray Eyes gazed at her profile.

For the first time she realized that at fourteen summers, K'aalo'gii had become a beautiful young woman. Unorthodox, perhaps, but beautiful. "I am sorry," she apologized. "I never thought—"

K'aalo'gii's laughter interrupted her. "Do not be. A man who wants only my sheep would bore me silly. I thank you, sister, from the bottom of my soul. You have staved off hunger even if the pale-eyes should someday return. But you have not lured a husband for me. I would not have him. I know who I want, and he cares more for my skill with an arrow than whether or not I can feed him when the winter winds blow."

Gray Eyes frowned, then, suddenly, she remembered the conversation between them back in the Chuska camp when she had been ill with her babe's *tah honeesgai*. "You mentioned such a warrior once. Who is he?" she asked.

"I do not know his name. But he rides a stallion with glorious painted splotches. And someday I will see him again."

For a moment, the world blurred for Gray Eyes. Yes, life had become good, and again she felt the urge to grab it close before it could slip away. Instead, she reached over to hug her cousin quickly.

"You are still stuck with the sheep," she answered.

Na'acoci returned just as the revelers were beginning to drop into their sheepskins. His tunic was once again streaked with blood. He went immediately to Hawk's shelter.

The handful of people still there fell silent as he entered. After a long moment, someone passed him the pipe.

"I have much to tell you, brother," he said to Hawk.

Hawk looked up distractedly. "Now?" he asked. "Have a smoke, brother. Relax. Change your clothes. There is time enough for talk later."

Na'acoci plowed ahead anyway. "There are still white men in *Dinetah*," he told him. "I have seen them."

For a moment, everyone froze. Gray Eyes, curled wearily against the wall, jerked upright. Then Delgondito spoke casually, and the tension in the air eased.

"It is bothersome," he admitted. "But I have heard that those who remain are not the Something-Sticking-Out-from-the-Foreheads. They are herders, ranchers, and are no threat to us. I, for one, am glad that they remain. They provide a livelihood."

Na'acoci nodded and grinned. "There is more," he went on. "I went to the *hual-te* at Ojo del Oso. There are still soldiers there, but very few. I spoke to them. It is true that they are fighting their brothers in the east. They are so busy fighting them that they have no time for us. We can raid without worry of reprisal. Still, they would try to coax us into not raiding."

"How?" Hawk's voice broke the utter silence. His black eyes narrowed as he considered what new trick the white men could be up to.

"They have devised something they call 'ra-shuns',"

Na'acoci explained. "If we go to their *hual-te* once every moon as it wanes, they will give us food and trinkets."

All around the shelter, jaws dropped. "It is true!" Na'acoci persisted. "They think that if they give us these gifts then we will not steal them from those brothers who have stayed behind."

More than a few men smiled. It was reason enough for them to stay home with their wives.

"And you, brother?" Hawk asked. "What do you think of this?"

Na'acoci's eyes gleamed. "I will take from them any way I can, even when they give vengeance willingly."

Hawk nodded in agreement, but Gray Eyes fought a swell of despair as she realized that her brother was so consumed by vengeance that he hadn't even realized she and Hawk had been married.

Chapter 43

Summer settled easily upon the land. The weather seemed like an act of contrition from the holy ones, as though they were asking forgiveness for all the bad seasons that had gone before. There was rain, enough of it to make the crops flourish. There were songs and feasts and once again there was food enough for everyone.

Gray Eyes accepted the good fortune with quick glances behind her, wondering when the gods would stop smiling.

The first changes began on a crystalline morning when a battalion of children gathered outside her shelter to ask if they could run her sheep out to graze. She heard their voices calling to her from far away and responded by burrowing more deeply into her sheepskin. One hand snaked out groggily for the warm reassurance of Hawk's flesh, only to encounter cool earth instead. Confused, she blinked and sat up.

The branches above her head began to spin immediately. She struggled to her feet. The walls swayed as she made her way to the door opening.

Beyond the sea of expectant faces, the sky was a brilliant blue. The sun was pushing its zenith. She shook her head dazedly. She had overslept.

Suddenly, her eyes focused on the children and widened. To their astonishment, she turned away from them again without speaking. She went back to her sheepskin and sat down hard.

She never overslept. She had done it only once before in her life, and that had been . . . How many moons had

302

it been since she had bled? It was now the time of the Great Seed Ripening, the pale-eyes' July. Nothing had happened during the last moon, the time When Few Seeds Ripen, but the moon before that, she was sure she had gone through her time. Two moons then. Two whole moons.

She was carrying a babe again.

"Ah," she breathed. Then her heart began pounding. She jumped to her feet only to stand there, her hands clutched to her breasts. She made a move toward the door, then stopped again and whirled back to the fire pit. "Ah!" she said again.

Hawk. She would have to tell Hawk. He would know this one. Surely he would. There were no pains this time, and it had been five whole moons since she had been anywhere near a white man. She spun again toward the door.

She had just reached the opening when Hawk entered. She gave a little gasp of surprise and backed up to stare at him. Her husband, finally. Her love, always. He would be so pleased when she told him.

Then her eyes fell to the tunic he wore.

It was black as night, tied together with dark brown yarn. She felt the joy within her wither and blow away like autumn leaves.

"Again?" she whispered. "So soon? You have only just returned."

He turned away from her pleading eyes. Anger struck him, fueled by indignation. He was doing this for her.

"Do not look so aghast," he snapped, moving to take the bow and quiver that hung against one wall. "You know the importance of this."

"Importance?" she wailed. "You are wealthier than any headman. I have enough sheep to feed both our clans. And you have the largest herd of ponies between here and the Chuskas."

"And you," he answered tightly, "have a brother who is no end of a fool."

Her face drained of color. "He would raid again?" she managed.

Hawk nodded.

"You cannot stop him?"

"A thousand blue-coats could not stop him," he muttered, then he turned toward the door.

But one glance at her stricken face stopped him. "Little one," he sighed.

"No." She shook her head before he could say anything more. "Do not apologize. I was not thinking. If I had, I would have known that this was not your idea."

"You know what the others have said about him."

Gray Eyes nodded. Her brother was crazier than ever before. He raided incessantly and took chances no sane man would take, all in the name of vengeance for a wife who was gone.

"Watch over him, my love," she whispered.

"It is why I am going."

She nodded. He leaned toward her and touched her mouth with his. "If we leave now, I should be able to bring him home in two suns, maybe three. Wait for me, little one."

She managed a tremulous smile. "Always." Then she watched him duck through the door and disappear.

"Come back alive," she pleaded aloud. Then she gathered her medicines, put the babe from her mind, and went to tend to Winter Star's arthritis.

Three suns later, Hawk brought Na'acoci home safely, but he was not jubilant. He looked so tired that Gray Eyes' heart clenched. But she had no chance to go to him as the clans clustered about him, shouting excitedly for details of the raid.

Later, she promised herself. In their sheepskins tonight, she would soothe him and tell him of their new babe.

But when the moon rose, he was still at the fire pit, recounting coups with the others. Finally, he got up and came to where she stood outside the circle.

"Do not wait up for me, little one. You look tired."

She nodded. Tomorrow, she thought. Tomorrow they would have some time alone. She turned away, then caught sight of Na'acoci standing by the fire.

"Did he . . . ?" she began, then trailed off.

Hawk sighed. "It was not so bad this time. He killed only one herder."

"And you?" she asked quietly.

He shrugged. "I took the sheep and one pony. There was nothing of consequence in the shack, so I burned it."

She gave a bittersweet smile. Hawk had his own brand of vengeance, she realized, even if it was not as rash as Na'acoci's.

"I am weary," she admitted.

He patted her shoulder before he turned away. "I will join you soon."

But he didn't, and they had no time alone the next sun. Little Left Hand came to their shelter to share their evening meal rather than eat alone, and when they moved outside to the fire pit, Na'acoci joined them.

"The moon is waning," he observed idly as Gray Eyes went through her nightly custom of sorting her medicines. She felt the hairs on her neck rise.

"What is on your mind, brother?"

"The day the blue-coats give the thing they call ra-shuns is coming up soon."

"You wish to go?" Hawk asked absently.

"If they wish to give me food and trinkets, why should I stop them?" Na'acoci asked. "Besides, they say that the soldiers race their horses against our warriors, and everyone puts wagers on the outcome. I would like to join in the betting."

Hawk nodded. It did not seem to be risky. The pale-eyes were many things, but they were not good horsemen. "So go," he suggested.

"You would not wish to come?"

"No." Gray Eyes said the word so quickly she startled even herself. What harm could a ration day prove to be?

she thought wildly. It was safer than a raid. Still, she could not dispel the horrid blackness that gathered in her soul with the idea.

"Little one?" Hawk prompted her curiously. Her face was white in the moonlight. He knew that look. His uncle had always gotten it when he had been visited by his medicine.

"What is it?" he went on. "Is there some reason we should not go?"

Yes! she wanted to say. But she only shook her head feebly. If there was, she didn't know what it might be. She thought of going off by herself to see if it would come to her, then realized that she was afraid to know.

Suddenly, K'aalo'gii appeared out of the shadows. She dropped down beside Gray Eyes. "Well, I think we should do it," she contributed.

Hawk looked at the younger girl with a lifted brow. "Why?"

"To see the other clans, of course."

Hawk shrugged. "So be it, then. We will all go." He saw Gray Eyes' hands clench around her herbs. "Little one," he murmured. "It is, after all, not so different from a raid."

She knew what he was saying. Na'acoci would go, and K'aalo'gii, in her innocence, would go with him. Left to his own devices, he would almost certainly lead the girl into danger.

Slowly, stiffly, she nodded. "So be it," she echoed.

A sniveling boy-child came to Gray Eyes' shelter just as they were about to depart the next morning. His mother was ailing. Could she come right away? She could and she did, gladly, and the August heat kept them from the next Ration Day as well.

Gray Eyes accepted the respite with both despair and relief. She dared not tell Hawk about their babe until she emerged unharmed from this new contact with the pale-eyes. When the September moon waned, she anticipated their imminent departure with tangled emotions.

Only the very old and the very young remained at home when the day finally came. The others formed an endless, winding caravan across the desert, their trail alive with laughter and bursts of song. Gray Eyes rode at the front, near Hawk, and tried hard to join in the revelry. But the sight of Fort Fauntleroy still chilled her when they came upon it.

It subdued the others as well. They congregated on the bluff, frowning and staring, and for a moment Gray Eyes allowed herself the prayer that they would turn back. The *hual-te* was not nearly as oppressive as the first time she had seen it when she had come there for the treaty. There were no throngs of blue-coated soldiers staring up at them with avarice and hatred in their eyes. The Bitter Waters and the Lone Trees saw the clans that were already safely settled there, and proceeded down the bluff without further hesitation.

Only a few of the People had ventured inside the fort's planked wooden fences to collect their food. The vast majority remained outside, visiting acquaintances as they would have at a *Yeibichai* ceremony. Hawk and Gray Eyes tethered their horses near a wagon brought by Delgondito's wives. Her fingers wound like tenacious ivy through his as they wandered the valley. Though they did not venture too close to the fences, an occasional white face popped up out of the crowd to startle them. Each time, Gray Eyes' pulse raced. She concentrated hard on keeping an eye on Na'acoci.

She spotted him coming through the fences, K'aalo'gii on his heels. They carried armfuls of the soldiers' food. Na'acoci tossed his to the ground with a disgusted snarl, but K'aalo'gii kept on until she stopped in front of her.

"Do you see this?" she demanded. "They think to feed thousands of us with it, but I have never seen such things before."

Gray Eyes looked down and frowned. The food was

strange indeed. There was a chunk of meat that looked to be nothing more than fat. Back in her own camp it would have been tossed away to appease the coyotes. She touched a finger to the grainy white stuff that coated it and sniffed suspiciously.

"I would not eat this, sister. It does not burn my finger, but it could be dangerous."

K'aalo'gii quickly dropped the salt pork into the dust. "What of these?" she asked, pulling two burlap bags from where they had been tucked beneath her arms.

Gray Eyes took the first and opened it. Hard black beans spilled out into her palm. She put one between her teeth and found that it was as hard as granite. She shrugged.

"We can boil them and see if they soften. Right now they are not edible." She handed the coffee beans back to K'aalo'gii and took the other bag.

This one contained a white powder. She cringed. "No, sister. Rid yourself of this one quickly. It could be corpse-poison." But the warning was unnecessary. K'aalo'gii reeled away from it as soon as she saw the flour inside.

"Bah!" she snapped and turned back into the crowd again. "I did not come for their stupid white food anyway."

Gray Eyes watched her go, then she saw something that drove K'aalo'gii from her mind. Yet another band had arrived to pick their way down the bluff. They were led by Manuelito.

She hurried over to where Hawk spoke with Delgondito. Amazingly, the older headman chuckled when he looked up to see what the interruption was about.

"So," he mused, "his ego is greater than his hatred. I had thought as much."

"No," Hawk argued. "I think not. It is his hatred that brings him here for another chance to best them."

"I do not understand," Gray Eyes protested.

Hawk glanced down at her. "Our men have been trying to entice Manuelito to a Ration Day for some time now. They know there is none like him on a horse. They want him to race tomorrow so that they might bet on him, for they know that he will win.''

Gray Eyes looked thoughtfully at Manuelito. She agreed with Hawk's opinion. She had met the war chief only briefly at the treaty talks, but she knew that he would do anything to best the pale-eyes.

Oddly, her stomach chose that moment to clench again, and she shivered.

Chapter 44

K'aalo'gii followed on Manuelito's band's heels as they wound their way through the camps. Her face wore an absent look that belied her thrumming heart. She searched each and every fire, each and every knot of warriors until her eyes burned.

Then, suddenly, she found the one she was looking for. She reached unceremoniously for the warrior standing closest to her.

"The Holy People have smiled upon me," he murmured, looking down at her.

K'aalo'gii ignored him and nodded instead toward the warrior who had once admired her skill with an arrow at Canyon de Chelly. "What is his name?" she demanded.

Disgruntled, the man looked up. "I know him only barely," he answered. "His clan lives far north of here. I would not think to see him this far south."

"His name!" K'aalo'gii insisted impatiently.

"*Daago,* I think," he answered. "He Was Born in the Spring."

K'aalo'gii grinned and dropped the man's arm as suddenly as she had gripped it. Born in the spring, she thought, like the coyote, who shared his laughing eyes; like the mountain lion, with his graceful walk. He finally spotted her as well and moved toward her. She forced a cocky smile.

"They tell me you live far from here," she said by way of greeting. "I had not thought to see you."

"I would not miss the chance to see you beat the pale-eyes."

Her jaw dropped. "Me?"

"You will not race them tomorrow?"

Her spine straightened. Why not? She was better than almost anyone except Manuelito. K'aalo'gii grinned again.

"Yes, perhaps I will."

"Does one such as you need practice?"

For a moment, she didn't understand. Then her eyes darted to where the pony herds were tethered away from the barracks, intimate and isolated.

"Perhaps," she said again, suddenly breathless. "My mare is over this way."

The ponies nickered and made room for them as they passed among them. Then she felt his hand, strong and big, on her shoulder. She turned toward him willingly.

"This is something the *Naakaiidine'e'* women have taught me," he began. "I think you will like it." He lowered his mouth to hers, and a wild thrill scooted up her spine.

In that moment, K'aalo'gii could no longer remember why she had never liked being a girl.

Very few people went to bed early the night before the races. When a bugle pierced the morning quiet, the People scrambled awake, bleary-eyed and subdued. But as soon as the first race was announced, the crowd came alive again. The clans pressed close to the makeshift track that ran around the *hual-te,* and when a pale-eyes soldier and a Navajo rider took their places, an expectant hum filled the air.

Gray Eyes looked up absently and spotted the familiar, agile form crouched on her black mare. She promptly dropped the piece of ground cake she was nibbling on. *"K'aalo'gii?"*

Hawk threw back his head and roared with laughter. "That one is much like you."

She gave him a haughty look. "How so?"

"She is headstrong when she gets an idea." He hesitated. "Should I try and stop her?"

Gray Eyes thought a moment, then she began laughing as well. K'aalo'gii's pale-eyes opponent had no idea what he was getting in for. "No," she answered. "Bet something. I, too, would enjoy besting these pale-eyes for once."

He looked down at her incredulously. "And if we lose?"

"When did you last see her ride?"

Hawk cocked a brow at her, then moved off toward the fences. Gray Eyes watched him go and felt her first surge of excitement. Then Hawk returned from the parade ground and, almost instantaneously, a fireball shattered the morning to begin the first race. She whirled back to the track, her heart in her throat.

K'aalo'gii was taken by surprise at the suddenness of the gunshot. The blue-coat shot off to a sizable lead while she spun her mare around and gathered her reins. But before they rounded the first curve, the little black mare was gaining on him. Night's hooves pounded against the earth in a ground-eating stride while K'aalo'gii leaned low over her neck, driving her on. They took the lead around the second curve.

The People jubilantly swarmed the finish line as soon as K'aalo'gii crossed it. The mood was infectious and Gray Eyes allowed herself to be swept along by it. Her cold foreboding over this day had been nothing more than fear of the pale-eyes, she told herself. She began to relax.

The sun was low on the horizon when the last race was called. She looked up with a start as the excitement was regenerated. Women and warriors rushed again to the racetrack. Men abandoned peyote and firewater. Gray Eyes frowned as she saw Na'acoci lurch drunkenly by, then hurried after him.

She knew what the excitement was about before she reached the track. Manuelito had decided to race.

He was waiting at the end of the clearing, his face ex-

pressionless. The massive crowd surged toward the fences
to bet on him. Even as they did, a hard-muscled quarter
horse with a pale-eyes rider trotted up to join Manuelito
on the track. Gray Eyes watched him absently. He looked
so cocky, she thought, so smug and hateful. Then, suddenly, a nerve at her temple twitched and her muscles
went liquid with panic.

Something was wrong. The pale-eyes was too confident.

She spun, searching wildly for Hawk. Only he had any
hope of stopping Manuelito. She ran in the direction of
the *hual-te*, then stopped in an agonizing rush of indeci-
sion. There was a mob in there; she would never find him
in time.

She turned back to the track just as the gunshot sounded.
She clapped her hands to her ears and watched as Manuelito's pony leaped into the lead. Her heart began to thud
slowly with dread. They rounded the first curve, then the
second, neck to neck. Then Manuelito's pony veered suddenly, wildly, off the track.

The people in his path scattered amid shouts of alarm.
Manuelito flew off and landed hard. There were more
shouts as men took off after his white-eyed pony, but Gray
Eyes barely heard them. Her eyes were glassy and unfocused as she watched the quarter horse round the track
alone.

There was a raucous chorus of victory from the soldiers. They hooted and hollered as they shoved their way
inside the fences to collect their bets. Gray Eyes turned
away from them and grabbed the arm of the woman closest
to her.

"What is it?" she demanded. "What has happened?"

The squaw's eyes glittered with hatred. "It is as it has
always been, *estsa hataali*. The pale-eyes never lose."

Gray Eyes looked over to where Manuelito was standing
now, a single rein grasped in his fist as though he would
choke it. She understood before the woman went on.

"Someone slashed it. I think as soon as he put pressure
on it, it fell apart."

Gray Eyes closed her eyes, feeling nauseous. So much, she thought. The People had bet so much. And the pale-eyes had made sure that they'd lost it all.

She knew before the interpreter made the announcement that the soldiers would not rerun the race. A flood of angry objections swelled from the crowd. She began moving then, pushing among them to soothe them. But too many refused to be quieted. Men who had bet their rifles, women who had lost their family's blankets, all began pushing toward the fort to reclaim their belongings.

Gray Eyes was shoved and hauled along with them. She struggled to regain her footing even as a sudden, unearthly stillness gripped the crowd. Confused, she looked up and saw the big wooden doors swing shut.

The pale-eyes had locked them out.

"No!" someone screamed.

"My pony!" a child wailed. "They took my pony! I want my pony!"

Another bellow of protest, barely human, came from behind her. It lifted the hairs on Gray Eyes' nape. She spun, knowing that voice, knowing its agony, knowing too late. Na'acoci, his eyes dull with firewater, lunged free of the crowd and began scaling the fort fence to reclaim his wager.

Another scream rent the air; she didn't recognize it as her own. She began running. She reached the fence and clawed wildly for the ankle that hung just above her. She grasped it, then lost it again as her palms, slick with sweat, slipped away.

"No," she begged. "Brother, come back! It is of no use." But he was out of her reach now and she was shoved violently aside as more men began to climb after him.

A gun roared, so close to her ears that acrid smoke stung at her nostrils and made her eyes tear. The People reacted frenziedly to the sound of fireballs; they flew blindly past her, their wagers forgotten. She staggered, gripped the wall for support, then turned away just as Na'acoci tumbled down from above her.

"No, no, no!" she wailed. "Not you, not you, too!"

She was knocked again, hard, and sprawled on top of him. Then a booted heel came down hard on her hand, shattering bone. She shrieked and jerked it away just before the roar of cannon fire filled the air. The giant guns with wheels that she had seen at *Tsehotsohih* made the earth tremble as they coughed up their deadly missiles. The People continued to race past, their children screaming as they were dragged from the massacre.

Gray Eyes stood again, gripped Na'acoci beneath the arms, and began to drag him away from the fence.

White-hot pain seared up her arm from her useless hand, but she only gripped him harder with her other. Helpless, dry sobs left her gasping for breath as more bodies jostled her, sending her spilling to the ground again. Then the hard leather boot returned to kick into her ribs as she went down.

She gave a gurgling groan. Then the soldier was gone, grabbing another squaw by the hair to hold her still while he drove his bayonet deep into her midriff.

Even as she died, the woman continued clawing for the two little girls who had slowed her down. "We won," she moaned. "You cheated." The soldier laughed and turned his rifle on the children.

Fireballs rang out, sharp and shattering. Gray Eyes rolled over in the dirt and vomited. She never felt the glancing blow to her shoulder as a riderless pony reared wildly and came down upon her. Nor was she aware of the feet pummeling her as people stumbled over her in their flight toward safety. She clutched N'acoci's lifeless form to her breasts as darkness fanned her vision, then stole it completely.

Chapter 45

Gray Eyes woke to the most consuming pain she had ever known. Her eyes opened to slits, then widened in shock and memory. She struggled to move but couldn't; her limbs all seemed to be bound to splints. Then the fire beside her popped with a spark larger than the rest, and she twitched violently away from the sound so similar to that of a gunshot. Agony rushed through her and she cried out.

Hawk appeared by her side immediately. "You are safe now. You are home."

Her eyes moved wildly from him to the walls. Home, yes. But safe? She wondered if she would ever feel safe again.

Her eyes came back to his. She licked her lips dryly. "My brother?"

His gaze darkened. He didn't answer. He didn't have to. She knew Na'acoci was dead, and that her babe was gone as well.

An immediate and intimate sense of loss filled her womb, her limbs, her soul. She groped for his hand, as though his touch could combat the emptiness. But, as before, her arm would not move, nor did he reach out to help her span the distance between them.

Hawk only stared expressionlessly at the wall, seeing her again as he had found her . . . her slight and still body, the stained ground beneath her, the clotted blood, the tiny human being not quite the size of his hand.

Her babe, his babe, still and silent after its violent, untimely birth.

"Why did you not tell me?" he asked harshly.

"You speak of the babe."

"What else?" His voice became cold, mocking.

Gray Eyes shuddered deep inside herself. "Your uncle, my friend, asked me to believe in peace. I went to the pale-eyes' Ration Day in the hope that I was wrong about them. I did not tell you of our babe because I was afraid I was right. If they had witched me, hurt it . . ." She broke off with a raspy, helpless sigh. "I was afraid you would pursue them to the afterworld and back in the name of vengeance."

He got to his feet without looking at her. "You were right."

Winter howled over the camp. The Lone Trees and the Bitter Waters did not move on, not because of the restrictions of Canby's treaty, but because their *estsa hataali* was still too fragile to be moved.

Their men were rarely there to lead them away in any event. Hawk raided relentlessly, leading his war band through snow and sleet and blustering winds each time the moon offered light. Their corrals became even more swollen with sheep and ponies, but the hatred and the coldness in his eyes did not ebb. When he was in camp, he slept alone at the far end of the shelter with his memories of a child barely formed. A boy-child his wife had concealed from him in the name of her people. Each memory, each stab of pain and betrayal, led him further and further away from her.

Sometimes Gray Eyes caught him studying her with a wounded, hurt look that changed to anger as soon as she noticed him. Her eyes burned with unshed tears, but she could not go to him, could not beg forgiveness for that which she would do again in the same situation. She mourned alone in her bedding each night, and when she awoke in the morning, he was invariably gone.

Barren Woman came to her shelter every day in his stead, toting stew and beans and ground cake. She fed her when her own broken hand and arms would have seen her starve. When the time came, she unwrapped the bandages and massaged life back into Gray Eyes' bruised and mangled fingers. And she talked, even when Gray Eyes did not want to hear.

"It is of no use to chastise yourself, you know," she said one day. "What you did was right. The old man would have done the same."

Gray Eyes looked at her. She would have preferred to have feigned sleep, but the mention of the *hataali* was impossible to ignore.

"You should have tried to see what your medicine was telling you," she went on. "You were a coward. That was where you did wrong."

Gray Eyes moaned wretchedly. Na'acoci, her babe, the squaw and her two children. All her fault, all blood on her hands.

But Barren Woman offered no more censure. "No true harm was done to our band in any event. Your brother would have met his end no matter what you did." She stirred the stew and shrugged. "I do not speak of him anyway."

"What then?"

"Your babe."

Gray Eyes turned her eyes back to the wall.

"You acted as your heart told you to," Barren Woman went on. "Your man will come to respect that in time. He is young yet. They are all like that early on, angry and sullen whenever their wives go against them and follow their own hearts. But as they get older, they get wiser, and they stop fighting us." She ladled up the stew. "Give him time."

Gray Eyes did, but nothing changed. Winter eased; her bones healed, but her heart and her bedding remained cold.

There was no chance for either love or passion to mend

the rift between her and Hawk. They went on in stony silence until spring touched the land with the promise of what would be her seventeenth summer. Then a morning came when Hawk rode in victorious from yet another raid, his men whooping, their ponies thundering.

He appeared in her door opening without warning, jerking a white, spindly-legged girl-child behind him. Gray Eyes stared at her.

"No," she breathed. Then she shouted. "No!"

Hawk was at first stunned by the outburst, then an angry flush stained his haughty cheekbones. They spoke at the same time.

"No!" she gasped again. "Get her out!"

"You act crazy!" he charged.

She stared at him, her breasts heaving, her eyes stark with pain. He saw the grief in them then, grief to match his own.

Slowly, shakily, he smoothed her hair off her forehead, touching her reverently, as though he had forgotten the feel of her skin. Somewhere, deep inside herself, Gray Eyes felt heat begin to seep into the great void that hysteria had left.

But the child, her huge eyes so blue, her skin so pale, continued to stare up at them. "Please," she begged again. "Please. Take her away."

Hawk turned his head and chased the child from the shelter with a harsh word. Still, Gray Eyes pulled out of his arms.

"Do you hate me so much?" she asked softly.

"Hate you?" he sighed wearily. "No, little one, never that."

"Why then? Why did you bring her?"

He sighed and jerked his hair roughly from its bow knot. While his long, dark fingers combed through it, he paced. "She was little enough to replace what we had lost," he said finally. "I had thought it was time to begin again, to heal."

"Heal? I look into her eyes and see the man who kicked

me and slaughtered a defenseless squaw! I look at her young, healthy legs and know my babe will never live to walk and run as she can!''

"I never thought . . .'' Hawk began, then trailed off.

No, he realized. He had never thought. He had felt only that panicked sense of sand running through his fingers, of life and fate racing on without him. He had seen her slipping away from him again. He had learned of her secrets, found out that she was holding a part of her heart and soul from him. And he had hated the pale-eyes and cursed her for allowing it to happen.

He had clung to his own pain. He had forgotten that in a world of enemies, his only peace was her.

He turned back to her now, eyes troubled as they searched her face. "Can you forgive me, little one?''

Her eyes moved slowly to his. "I am not sure there is anything to forgive,'' she whispered. "All hearts bleed differently. All souls know their own way of venting pain.''

She made it sound so simple, made his crimes seem so petty and mundane. Once again, she was the innocent child who spoke words of wisdom that sometimes shamed him, sometimes amused him, but always caught him off guard. His lips crooked into a tender smile.

"Come back to me, then,'' he murmured.

She hesitated, then hurled herself into his arms. She met his mouth with her own, clinging desperately to the healing warmth she had lacked for so long. She tasted it, and when he lowered her to their sheepskins, she let it fill her.

Chapter 46

The Bitter Waters and the Lone Trees were settling down for their evening meal when Heuro rode in. Hawk raised a speculative brow and left the fire pit to meet him. Gray Eyes watched him go, her pulse accelerating.

"I do not like this," she mused aloud. The eyes of the others all turned warily to the little blacksmith as Hawk escorted him back to the fire.

"What is it?" she demanded. "What is wrong?"

Heuro dropped down on the other side of Hawk and waved a hand lazily. "Rumor, *estsa hataali*, only rumor," he answered, avoiding her eyes.

She didn't believe it and left the fire pit to squat in the shadows behind him. Eavesdropping had always held her in good stead before; she was not above resorting to it again now.

After a while, the others slipped away as well and Heuro finally spoke. "Something interesting is happening with the pale-eyes," he said. "For some reason, they have instigated an attack on the Mescalero Apache."

Hawk scowled, then shrugged. "The *Naashgali'dine'e'* are bloodthirsty enough to defend themselves. I care little what happens to them," he decided. "They are enemies."

"I agree. But my concern is over what the pale-eyes are doing to them. They are taking them to something they call a res-er-va-shun."

The word had a similar ring to 'ration'. Hawk stiffened. "What is this thing?"

"It is a place. It is near the desert the old *Naakai-*
321

idine'e' call Cubero. The pale-eyes have built a giant fence around it, and they are putting the Mescaleros inside. I have even heard that there are soldiers at the gates who shoot them if they try to escape.''

''Perhaps such games will keep them so busy that they will leave us alone,'' Hawk mused.

''Perhaps,'' Heuro agreed. ''But there is also a man at Cubero who is trying to talk our people into going inside.''

Hawk looked incredulous. ''Why would we want to do such a thing?''

''That is exactly what the People asked him. He had no answer. He said only that his headman, a man named Carleton, would like us to go there.''

''Car-ul-tone,'' Hawk repeated. ''I have not heard of him.''

''Our old foe, Canby, is gone. He went back to the east to fight with the others. After he left, his authority was given to this new man.'' Heuro paused. ''I have great fear that he is evil. I have heard that his eyes are very small and bright. They are as black as ours, but they glow as though he has a fever. I think that must be because he is crazy. I can think of no other explanation for what he is doing to the Mescalero.''

Gray Eyes stood up shakily and went back to her shelter. A reservation. As Hawk had said, it could be a good thing if it kept the pale-eyes occupied. Yet a cold worm of uneasiness began to curl in the pit of her stomach again.

Even as they spoke, James Henry Carleton was ensconced in Canby's old office in Albuquerque, making plans.

''How many?'' he demanded of the young man sitting on the opposite side of his desk.

Rush Michaels scratched a finger through his thick, red hair and scowled down at the notes in his lap. ''Three hundred forty-nine, sir,'' he answered carefully.

"That's all?" Carleton snapped, and Michaels looked up from his reverie, startled.

"It's been four months," the general went on. "There should be more of them in captivity than that."

"Excuse me, sir, but Commander Canby felt that—"

"Commander Canby is gone, Sergeant! It is my opinion that matters now!"

Carleton began to tug frenziedly at his mustache. Michaels' eyes followed his fingers. "That may well be, sir," he ventured. "But both Commander Canby and the Apache Indian agent felt that the whole Mescalero faction numbered only a thousand or so. You've got roughly a third of them. Perhaps you're confusing them with the Navajo. I'm told there're closer to ten thousand of them."

Carleton's fingers went still. "Ten thousand?" His eyes went to the window. "Not too big a project," he mused.

"Sir?" Michaels scowled.

"It would be a glorious challenge, but we should be able to remove them easily enough," he clarified.

"Cubero isn't big enough, sir, not for both tribes."

"Cubero? No, no, Sergeant." Carleton focused on him again. "Cubero is only temporary. I don't intend to keep them there. We need a real reservation. But first we must lay the groundwork." He jerked up and away from his desk and tugged on his mustache again as he began to pace.

"First, send a letter to Washington," he went on. "Address it to the Secretary of the Interior. I want to inform him that there've been a few amendments to Canby's Indian plan. We will continue to work to remove the Apache to a reservation; however, we will include the Navajo in our schemes as well. It is also my opinion that the reservation should be somewhere other than Cubero. It should be a little further removed from their haunts and hiding places. We need a place where we can immerse them in our own culture, where we can teach them to read and write, the arts of peace and the truths of Christianity— quote that directly. Tell him that it is my heartfelt belief that as long as these heathens are permitted to worship their own gods in their own land, they will carry with them all the latent longings for murder and robbery that are inherent in their breeding, and will continue to jeopardize the lives of our fine citizens in New Mexico. Yes, yes, that's good.

"Now," Carleton went on. "I have one more issue to address." He leaned across his desk to whip a thick sheaf of notes off the corner. "Fools!" he spat suddenly, and Michaels jumped.

"I've found the perfect place," the general muttered. "The perfect reservation land. Unfortunately, that team of simpleminded engineers we hired last month can't seem to see beyond their books and their rulers. They have no vision, Sergeant, none at all."

Michaels scowled. The engineers had rejected a location on the Pecos River that Carleton had deemed an ideal Apache reservation. He had assumed that, based on the engineer's report, the general would leave the Indians where they were.

He was wrong. "That land is ideal for both the Apache and the Navajo," Carleton went on. "Of course the water and soil are alkaline! What matter that there are so few trees? That's precisely why our own settlers can't use it, don't you see, Sergeant? But the Indians, they can grow anything anywhere."

"Trees . . . uh, trees take a while to grow, sir," Michaels heard himself say. He immediately questioned his own sanity. Why antagonize the man over a bunch of savages who had killed his best friend? He tried to recapture the pain, the fury, the horror he had felt on that bloody dawn. Instead, an image of proud gray eyes came back to haunt him.

"Ah, yes, the trees," Carleton was saying. Michaels forced himself to listen. "There are enough cottonwoods at the location to allow them to begin building some permanent shelters. After that, we'll get some wagons in there. They can travel for whatever else they need. And meanwhile, Sergeant, the trees they plant will grow."

"On the Staked Plains, sir?"

Something sparked in Carleton's eyes. "There are trees there now, aren't there? Of course there are. Now kindly inform the engineers that I did not ask them to approve the site for my reservation. I merely wish to ascertain the best spot there for an accompanying military fort. Get a new report out of them. If they won't cooperate, then find me some more open-minded men to employ. This sort of response does me no good whatsoever."

He began to shred the papers. "Where is Carson?" he demanded suddenly.

"In Taos, sir, with his wife and children, recovering from the Apache effort. I hear he's got an embolism in his chest from a kick from his horse. He tires easily these days. But I'm sure that as soon as he feels better, he'll make the trip back here if you send for him."

"Send for him now. He's the only cog missing. Once Kit Carson gets back here, we can open this whole country up. We'll make good, God-fearing citizens out of its heathens. They'll thank me." Suddenly, he collapsed into his chair again as though all his energy had rushed out of him.

"They'll thank me, won't they, Sergeant?"

Michaels licked his lips and found them to be inordinately dry. He couldn't bring himself to ask if the general was referring to the settlers or the Indians.

Chapter 47

▼ ▼ ▼ ▼ ▼ ▼ ▼ ▼ ▼ ▼

December came, and with it the Great Winds. As the snow fell and ice formed over the ravines, Gray Eyes lived with a spooky sense of being watched by eyes she could not see. She knew, with the sixth sense that was her medicine, that the pale-eyes were creeping close again.

It was why she agreed to travel to see Manuelito.

"Perhaps I should take you with me the next time I go to *Tsehotsohih*," Hawk mused one night as they huddled close to the fire. Gray Eyes wrapped an extra blanket around her shoulders and fed another branch into the fire before she looked up at him questioningly.

"Delgondito, Barboncito, all the others see the merit in intercepting this Carleton before he sets his sights on us," he explained. "But Manuelito refuses. I think perhaps you could sway him if you went with me to speak to him."

"Me? He will not listen to me!"

But Hawk shook his head. "He will, little one. He is an angry man, but inside his warrior's soul beats a heart that loves his wives and his people very much. He fights for them. There are those who doubt it, but I know him well and I know that it is so."

"And so you would have me appeal to that side of him?"

"I would have you stay safe and warm in this camp," he answered, scowling, "but my uncle is gone and I have little choice."

As she often did these days, Gray Eyes touched the gall bag at her hip. Then she looked up at Hawk again, her eyes shadowed.

"I do not like your Manuelito."

His eyes softened. "I do not ask you to. I would only have you persuade him to come with us to this place they call Albuquerque. I think the pale-eyes know that he is a leader of many. If he accompanies us, perhaps they will believe that we want peace. Like you, little one. I would like to convince the pale-eyes to leave us alone."

She studied him, her heart in her throat. Her Hawk, her wise and compassionate warrior. He was more right than he knew. The pale-eyes would come again; she felt it in her bones. Sooner or later, they would tire of fighting each other in the east and they would come back. And then, with Carleton, the Crazy One, to lead them . . .

"I will go," she whispered. But when he opened his mouth to thank her, she only shook her head and burrowed into his arms.

She was terribly afraid that nothing she could do would make a difference.

Manuelito bowed to the forces of winter as he would have before few men. He left the high plains of his ancestral lands and moved back within the protective walls of *Tsehotsohih*. Hawk and Gray Eyes felt a clamor of emotion as they entered the meadow to meet him. Gray Eyes remembered Na'acoci intercepting her here during the second raid, and she knew a near-shattering longing to see his face again. Hawk remembered Rattlesnake and Yellow Horse and a physical pain so intense that only his little one had kept him from succumbing to it.

"Memories, only memories," she whispered. "There are friends here now." Hawk nodded and they rode in.

Voices throughout the camp were raised in welcome.

The sound lured Manuelito from his shelter, and for the first and only time in her life, Gray Eyes saw him laugh.

"I have always liked you, friend, because you do not give up," he said to Hawk. Then he sobered. "Come inside and speak your piece one more time. I will feed you even if I do not bend to your will."

"Fair enough."

Hawk dropped down from his stallion. Gray Eyes allowed a boy to take her mare, then she followed the men inside. Manuelito's wives scurried to and fro in an effort to make her feel welcome, but the headman himself didn't acknowledge her until they were seated and digging into bowls of hot stew. Then his sharp, dark eyes came around to pierce her.

"So," he murmured to Hawk, "you have brought along a most formidable weapon this time. You think she can succeed where you have failed?"

Hawk shrugged. "You were often swayed by my uncle."

"A wise man."

"She is a wise woman."

Manuelito nodded, his eyes never leaving her. Then his jaw jutted arrogantly. "So what have you to say, little *estsa hataali?*"

Her eyes sparked suddenly in a way Hawk remembered from long ago. "I would tell you only that which is already in your heart," she answered haughtily.

"You think you know my heart?" Manuelito looked back at Hawk. "If so, she has strong medicine indeed."

"This is true," she replied before Hawk could answer for her. "But my medicine has little to do with this. It is my woman's heart that tells me that a man such as you, with so many depending upon him, must have some goodness that endears him to the hearts of so many. Though," she mused, plucking a piece of mutton from her stew, "I cannot imagine where it might hide." Hawk threw back his head and laughed.

Manuelito's jaw hardened again. "So you do not approve of me. I would ask then why you are wed to one
much like me."

Her eyes flicked over Hawk and she smiled softly. "No.
He is not like you. My husband is a man who thinks first
of his women. Were war to come again, they would surely
be the first to starve. He thinks of this, and he asks you
to help him avert such a catastrophe."

Suddenly, Manuelito's eyes flamed. The fury in them
made Gray Eyes want to reel back. "It is for their sake
that we signed this last treaty!" he charged. "And so we
lost our mountains. It was by their wishes that we went to
collect ra-shuns, and so we were slaughtered liked penned
animals."

Gray Eyes trembled but rallied. "I cannot deny that we
were fools to go so close to them that last time."

"Hah! So you would have us do it again?"

"There is no help for it," Hawk interceded. "You must
know in your heart that she is right, my friend. Our people
cannot sustain another war. We may lose by going, but we
will almost certainly lose if we stay away."

Manuelito's wives stopped in their work and waited.
Their eyes were imploring as they turned to him. Manuelito threw his mutton into the fire with such force the
embers flew.

"My answer remains," he snapped. "If the pale-eyes
wish to fight me, then I will fight them with pleasure. But
I will never again go into their camps for any other reason
than to kill them."

Gray Eyes felt a surge of frustration. "And so your
fool's vengeance will see you bury those women who are
dearest to you!"

"It is my thought, *estsa hataali,* that the fool is the one
who invites trouble. Why go to Albuquerque? There are
few pale-eyes there anymore, only one who is crazy and
those with such a lack of honor that they did not go east
to fight their own war. They are the ones who shamed me.

They are the ones you ask me to encounter now. But why? They are busy with the *Naashgali'dine'e'*. Why remind them that we are here?''

''You think your raiding does not remind them?'' she demanded.

''Brother,'' Hawk broke in again. ''I, too, would prefer to fight them, to see them bleed and die. It is the only way we will ever truly be rid of them all. But we can only defeat them through our own methods, by raiding and robbing and killing them until they are gone. We cannot do that as easily when we are embroiled in one of their wars.''

Manuelito looked at him slowly. From somewhere distant, a babe wailed.

''Is my presence truly necessary to placate them?'' he asked.

Hawk shrugged. ''They know you are powerful. If you are among us, they will think we truly mean what we say.''

''How many others will go?''

''Fifteen, not counting myself, Delgondito, and Barboncito.''

Manuelito turned dark, accusing eyes to Gray Eyes. The air in the shelter seemed to crackle as she waited for him to speak. ''So be it, then, *estsa hataali,*'' he said finally. ''I will help to save your women and your babes. But when it is over, when the pale-eyes have still another paper with my name on it, I will ride again.''

Nineteen headmen went to Albuquerque. When Rush Michaels came upon them in front of the military headquarters in Albuquerque seven days later, his eyes bugged at the sight of them. They looked savage and determined as their blankets whipped in the icy wind. He hurried past them and pounded on the door to Carleton's inner office.

''General?'' He poked his head inside.

Carleton was sitting at his desk, quill in hand, but he was staring vacantly at the air.

"Sir, there are a bunch of Indians waiting outside."

"Indians . . . ?" He had been daydreaming about them, but, in truth, they were little more than vague images in his hectic mind. He saw them productive and clean and God-fearing in a beautiful copse of land along a tumbling river. He saw line after line of the neat adobe shelters they would live in. But what was clearest in his vision, what made tiny goose bumps of pride creep along his flesh, was the picture of blue-coated officials from Washington. The brass on their uniforms would shine in the sun as they gathered to inspect the new reservation and commend him for his foresight. Bugles would blow and the Indians would speak perfect English when they greeted them politely. And far away, on the other side of New Mexico, fresh new trails would lead up into the mountains as prospectors brought wealth to the country via its gold.

He saw it all in such startling detail that he had forgotten all about the nineteen headmen waiting right outside the military headquarters. The knock on his door brought him rudely out of his reverie, and he was not pleased by the interruption.

He stared blankly a moment longer, then his eyes focused and sharpened. "Ah, yes. The chiefs. Very well, Sergeant, show them in."

Michaels cleared his throat. "They don't want to come inside. They want you to go out there."

"They *want*—" Carleton snapped, launching himself to his feet. "Well, I'm afraid that what they want and what I want are two quite different things, Sergeant. It's snowing out there!"

"Yes, sir. It's been doing that for quite some time now while they've been waiting for you."

Once again, Michaels doubted his sanity for antagonizing the general. But Carleton surprised him. Though he bit out a few more waspish words, he grabbed his fleece-lined coat and stalked toward the door.

The headmen had been more or less huddled together

for warmth as the icy flakes pelted their blankets. But when Carleton stepped out onto the porch, they broke apart. Michaels had intended to watch from the door where it was relatively warm. But the faces drew him. They were stark and chapped, with wary, wily eyes and an indefinable haughty pride. Suddenly, he wanted very much to see how Carleton would fare at the hands of such men.

Shivering, he followed him out onto the porch, to a spot near the rail.

"You are the one they call Carleton?" Hawk demanded instantly. And while the translators spoke, he decided it had to be so. He had eyes just as Heuro had described.

"Yes," Carleton answered. "You wish to speak to me?"

"I wished to see you," Hawk answered softly, leaving no doubt that he meant it quite literally.

For a moment, Carleton was nonplussed. "Toward what end?" he asked when he recovered.

"We have heard what you have done to the Mescalero. We have waited all through this sun to find out what, if anything, you intend to do with us."

Carleton's eyes narrowed. "You're Navajo, then?"

The headmen exchanged bemused looks. Delgondito rallied first and stepped forward to stand beside Hawk.

"We are of the People, yes," he answered. "And we have come to avert trouble with you, to sign more of your papers if need be, to show you that we want peace. Our women, our children . . ." He trailed off and gestured eloquently. "They cannot withstand another war, so we are here to help you prevent such a thing from happening."

"To prevent a war?" Carleton looked mystified. "My dear men, there is no need to fight over what's happened to the Mescalero. That's a *good* thing. They've been given a home, so that there is no longer any need for them to roam. They're receiving food so that they no longer need to raid. They are being taught our language, our principles, and they are far happier people for it. I'm glad you've come here to ask me about it. I'm prepared to make the same promises to you."

There was a sharp sound of anger from Manuelito. He shook his head disgustedly and stepped away from the crowd. Barboncito hesitated, then followed suit. Hawk moved closer to the porch, his eyes narrowed in fierce concentration as he studied the white chief.

"We have come to ask for peace," he answered slowly, carefully. "We do not wish to go live inside your fences. We are telling you that there is no need. We will abide by the rules of the last treaty, or, if you prefer, sign a new one."

"And I am telling you, sir, that I have absolutely no faith in your promises," Carleton snapped. "Vows of peace are no longer satisfactory. You've always been better at promise than performance; you'd do well to thank me for giving you a chance to perform now. Go home, gather your people, and prepare to move to my Bosque Redondo reservation on the Pecos River. Go there, be peaceful, and there will be no further wars."

He turned away from the headmen abruptly, then his hot eyes focused on Michaels. "Sergeant," he hissed in an undertone. "Can you identify any of these men?"

Michaels looked, but the headmen were already dispersing and all he could see of them were the tight, black knots of hair at their napes. He shrugged helplessly, then focused on the single man remaining. He was stout and round-faced, and he continued to study them with confused, troubled eyes.

"I think they call this one Delgondito. He's attended several treaties."

"No one called Manuelito?"

"I wouldn't know, sir."

Carleton finally nodded. "Okay. Thank you, Sergeant. Make a note of this Delgonado's name for me, won't you?" He started to move through the door.

"Delgondito, sir," Michaels corrected softly.

"What? Oh, yes." He waved a hand, dismissing the

issue. "You might also want to send another missive to Carson while you're about it. Time's wasting. I want to strike while they're still alarmed enough to come to me with their lies."

Chapter 48

Hawk was not so much alarmed by Carleton as he was confused. He returned to camp late at night, his thoughts so deep that he nearly rode right past the little one. She hovered outside her hogan, waiting for him, and she knew immediately that something was amiss.

"There is war again," she breathed and ran to him. Fury and horror clashed within her so violently that she clutched his leg before he could dismount. "Tell me!" she pleaded, her fingers digging, causing pain.

He covered her hand with his own until her trembling eased. "No, little one, not that."

She backed away, bewildered. "What then?"

"I am not sure."

He dropped to the ground and held her as much for himself as for her. She was soft and warm and familiar in his arms. He had known her since before he knew breath; she was someone he understood, even if he didn't always agree with her heart's determinations. But all too soon she pulled away from him and leaned back to study his face.

"Tell me about him," she insisted softly. "Tell me about your Car-ul-tone."

He did, holding her hand tightly in his own as they wandered back to the fire pit. "I think," he mused, "that he is a man who wants very much to fight. Like Manuelito. But Manuelito is angry over injustices. This man, this Carleton, has suffered none to my knowledge. I think he carries a deep hatred, an inexplicable greed, and he will fight simply because they need to be quenched. I do not think he ever planned to negotiate with us. He had his words ready before we came."

Gray Eyes felt fear shudder low inside of her.

"He would see us leave *Dinetah*," Hawk added.

She sat bolt upright, pushing away from the warm hollow of his shoulder where she had been resting. "Why? You said there was no treaty, no war!"

"I think he would see us go of our own accord."

She nearly laughed, it was so preposterous. Instead, she looked up at the black sweep of sky, clear now with stars twinkling since the snow had stopped. The air was sharp, clean, and somewhere nearby a coyote howled. Leave it? "No," she vowed in a whisper. "Not ever again."

He pulled her back into his arms. "You need not fear, little one. Think about it. He spoke of a place called Bosque Redondo. Since I have never heard of it, it must be far away. How could he ever make all of us go there? He is strange, he bears watching, and I will do that. But one crazy man can not make all of the People do something they do not wish to do, especially when his brothers are all fighting a war elsewhere."

His words were sensible. She clung to them and him with fierce determination.

As the suns faded and the moons passed, it seemed that Hawk was right. The People heard little more from Carleton beyond the blustery messages he sent to them periodically. They always came by way of Delgondito. For some reason even the kind, jovial headman could not understand, the Crazy One had singled him out from all the others who had visited Albuquerque. Every five to seven suns, a lone *Naakaiidine'e'* or a white man would ride into his camp, carrying words meant to coerce, bully, or lure him into taking his people to the Bosque.

Delgondito took it all with his usual good spirits; even Gray Eyes had to laugh at the image of his wives chasing the cowardly messengers from camp with their *Naakai-*

idine'e cooking pots. Then one day his demeanor was changed as he rode into their camp for his regular visit.

It was a startlingly clear day, one of those so unique to *Dinetah*. The sky was an unbroken blue, and there was a hint of real heat in the air. At first, she attributed Delgondito's grim, sweaty face to that. But rather than go to the central fire pit as was his custom, he came to her shelter instead.

"The time has come, *estsa hataali,* that I must ask for your medicine," he said. His voice was humble, formal, not like anything she had ever heard from him before. When Hawk stepped up behind him, his eyes were dark with concern. Her skin went cold.

"Someone is sick?" she asked.

"My youngest wife and another young boy of my band. It is not like anything I have ever seen before, but I think it is a white man's disease. The most recent messenger from Albuquerque seemed to recognize it. It frightened him."

"I will go with you," Hawk announced before she had a chance to respond. He moved around her to the door of their shelter. She watched him blankly for a moment, then a single word erupted from her without warning.

"No!"

His eyes narrowed.

"Not until I know what it is," she finished lamely. "If there is to be a curing chant, of course I will send for you then."

He was suddenly aware of all those things that had tormented him before—the distance between them as she grew into her own, the sense of herself that she would not, could not share with him. Angry, he started to turn away.

"Please!" she pleaded. "There is little enough that I can protect you from. I can not stop you from raiding or encountering the white men if they should come. But I can spare you this, their diseases. Please, allow me that much."

"And you?" he whirled back to demand. He saw again

the tiny, bloody babe that had been wrenched from her body at Ojo del Oso.

But she only smiled wearily. "That is a risk I was born to take."

He didn't stop her as she slipped inside to collect her medicines. Frustrated, he took the current batch of arrows he was working on and stalked off toward the fire pit without saying good-bye. She hesitated, wanting to go after him with every fiber of her being. But beside her Delgondito shifted impatiently, and she thought again of the people who needed her. She closed her eyes and turned away to follow the headman.

Delgondito's camp was but half a sun's ride away. They arrived just before dark to a nightmare that was enough to drive Hawk from her mind. Sunrise, Delgondito's first wife, stood outside a shelter, her arms raised to the heavens, her voice lifted in a mournful wail. Gray Eyes hesitated, not willing at first to credit what her eyes saw. Then she knew. This white man's disease was bad. It had already claimed a life in the short time it had taken her to get here.

"Stay here," she murmured to Delgondito. "I will see what I can do."

She slipped from her mare, her legs surprisingly unsteady. But she moved into the camp, the thumping weight of her gall bag driving her on. Sunrise stepped aside as she hesitated in the shelter door, letting her eyes adjust to the murkier darkness inside.

A solitary figure sat at the back, shrouded now by a sheepskin. She moved toward it, feeling dazed and numb and very, very frightened. She forced her hand down to the edge of the cover. She had to see. She could heal only that which she understood. She jerked at the sheepskin, then she reeled back and gagged.

Had she not known *Hasbi'di,* Dove, in life, she would not have recognized her now. Great, pus-filled sores marked her face, her neck, her shoulders. Putrid disease oozed from them. Quickly, Gray Eyes covered her up again, then she clapped a hand over her mouth and hurried outside.

She breathed in great gulps of air, her pulse pounding. Then she went to the others, six of them now, in various stages of the illness. Some merely burned with fever; others already wore the harsh, open sores. She worked by rote, forcing juniper down them to make them vomit the evil out of them. She chopped bottlebrush and rammed it into their sores despite pained pleas to stop. And finally, trembling with exhaustion, she came out of the last shelter to find Hawk waiting for her.

He had defied her wishes after all, but relief and longing swept her anger away. She wanted to run to him, to lose herself in his arms and forget that she was *estsa hataali*. He held his arms out to her. She breathed, a deep, shuddering sigh, and shook her head.

"No," she whispered, her voice strangled. "I cannot."

His face hardened.

"Please!" she called out. "Put away your precious male pride and listen to me! I think I know what this thing is. You could catch it if I come to you. You could die. Would you have me rush to you and kill you? Would you have me live with that all the days of my life?"

Suddenly his own heart was pounding as hard as hers. He looked down at her shift; it was covered with blood and a foul-looking sticky substance. He knew enough to realize that that substance carried the white man's evil, and in that moment, he knew what his love for her had become. Not only the obsession he had feared, but his very life. If what she said was true, then it was quite possible she was going to die as well.

"The *hataali* talked of it happening to other peoples." Her words came fast now, with a dangerous edge of hysteria. "The white men call it a pox. It has come from them, I am sure of it. Delgondito has had so many messengers lately; they must have carried it in."

He steadied himself, forced himself to think. "Can your medicine stop it?"

She shrugged miserably. "I do not know. I know only that it is very contagious. Many more fell to it in the time it took me to get here, still more since then." Her voice broke. She looked up at the heavens, blinking furiously, gathering control. But before she could go on, another wail rose up from the camp. They had lost someone else.

She turned away from him abruptly to face the people, her face stark but determined in the light of the nearby fire. Then she held a hand up to silence the crowd even as she had silenced him.

"You will listen to me," she demanded of them. "We have seventeen ill now. We may lose them all. But we will see to it that it goes no further."

Someone hiccuped; a wail dwindled. The people pressed close to her, eager for salvation.

"We must burn everything," she went on, her eyes glistening with unshed tears, and then the crowd erupted angrily.

"It is the only way!" she pressed on. "I would not ask you for such a sacrifice if I did not think it might save our lives. This is bad pale-eyes' evil, and it is very strong. We need to kill it, kill everything it has had contact with."

Women wept. Men raged. For the first time in her life, Gray Eyes feared not their adoration, but that it would fail to move them now. They had to listen. She knew of no other way.

Finally, a woman lurched free of the crowd. "I will not lose my babes," she sobbed. Determinedly, she thrust a branch into the flames in the fire pit. Her shelter went up quickly. It was spring; the lodges were nothing more than brush.

Gradually, the other shelters began to burn, igniting the corpses within. Clothing and possessions, even saddles and bridles, were deposited in the central fire pit until the bonfire leaped to touch the sky. Orange light flickered over ravaged faces. A child wailed and clutched at a toy arrow; his mother jerked it from him roughly and threw it into the pyre as she wept. When it was done, Gray Eyes sank weakly to her knees, covered her face with her hands, and grieved.

She felt Hawk's hand on her shoulder and looked up into eyes dulled by horror. Once again she fought the urge to fall into his arms. "So," she whispered instead, "there is more to fear than soldiers."

"No, little one, no. You are strong enough to fight everything else." And, he vowed, I will take care of the rest.

Gently, though she protested, he pulled the stained shift from her body. Naked, trembling, she huddled against him as he tossed the wool into the flames and covered her with his own blanket. She allowed him to lead her to the closest ravine, trusting him to guide her steps as she saw again and again the orange light of the flames. He washed the stench of death from her, and cleaned away the last of the pale-eyes' disease.

Then, finally, he held her as he had wanted to do since he had come to her. But while she slept, he remained awake, praying that his efforts had been enough.

Chapter 49

Dawn turned the sky to pink, and still there was the bitter bite of smoke in the air. Embers snapped and sighed as they glowed softly in the first light of the new sun, but for the most part it was quiet. Gray Eyes awakened feeling drained and heartsick, but she had no fever. It did not seem as though she had contracted the smallpox, nor had Hawk or Delgondito.

They burned more bedding and bodies that night, but Delgondito's band was numb now and little grief was spared for those who were already lost. The ones who still lived required too much vigilance and prayer. There were four of them, and Gray Eyes insisted upon an Enemy Way to drive the last of the *naalniih* from them.

"But why?" Delgondito asked. His dark eyes had lost their laughter. "All that was touched by the evil has been burned."

"You care so little for those who still struggle that you would see them die?" she demanded harshly, and that managed to ignite some spark in him. He finally nodded.

She found Hawk by the ravine, smoking and talking quietly with some other warriors. She pulled him aside.

"You must ride. Find Barboncito, Manuelito, Armijo, all of them. Have them bring their people and whatever bedding, clothing and utensils they can spare. We will have an Enemy Way for those still living, and in the process, perhaps we can help Delgondito's band replenish some of what they have lost."

By the time the sun slipped low on the horizon again,

the People began coming. They did not confine their efforts to clothing and bedding. Manuelito brought sheep and ponies to replace those that had been slaughtered in the frenzied battle against the pale-eyes' germ. Armijo's wives brought toys and cradle boards for the babes. There was enough ground cake and mutton for a week, and pollen and herbs for the women who had sacrificed their own. Word spread quickly beyond even those bands that Hawk and his men had contacted. By daybreak the village was swollen with clans from as far away as the San Juan River.

Gray Eyes watched them rally around the survivors with a swell of pride so fierce that it tightened her throat. And she knew suddenly that Hawk had been right. Carleton might try, but he would never destroy the spirit, the oneness that was the People.

The knowledge rallied her and she began the Enemy Way with far more strength and energy than she might otherwise have. By evening's end, the last patients still survived. They loaded them onto travois and went on to the subsequent camps.

By the time the last night's healing was over, the crowd was a thousand strong. Saddles were thrown to the ground in the best Navajo tradition, a new fire was ignited, and the Squaw Dance began. By now, it was a near-feverish celebration of life, of triumph.

K'aalo'gii appeared at Gray Eyes' side just as the singing started. "Who will you dance with this time, sister?" she asked impishly.

Gray Eyes pushed aside her memories of Rattlesnake; there had been enough death as it was. "Why would I dance?" she countered, smiling. "I am happily wed and have no intention of throwing my husband over for another." Then she noticed her cousin's too-bright eyes. "Will you?" she asked curiously.

K'aalo'gii actually blushed. "Yes, I think I will. I only hope that he pays well. There is but one thing I want."

She moved off determinedly into the circle. Gray Eyes watched as she fell into the heel-toe rhythm, then, impossibly, the girl's color heightened even more. She laughed aloud and closed in on an Among Scattered Hills warrior, grabbing him by the arm and whirling him into the circle before he had either the chance or the audacity to protest.

Her blanket snug about her shoulders in the comfortable April chill, Gray Eyes turned away. But she took no more than a step before she froze again, her pulse quickening. As it had been on a night long ago, Hawk stood just outside the circle. His arms were crossed over his chest; his grin was small and cocky. But he was not looking at the dancers. His eyes were fast on her.

She smiled again, tentatively, feeling suddenly, absurdly shy. His grin widened and he began to cut through the throng. He moved as easily, as gracefully, as he had all those seasons ago: his thighs were strong and solid; his hair, loose now, was a thick, black sheet that swung to his waist. Her heart began to thrum with anticipation.

"Be'asdzaa, wife," he murmured when he reached her. "I had thought I had better find you if I am finally to share your dance."

"You have already bought me, my love, many times over," she answered softly.

"Not enough. Not nearly enough to make you mine."

His grin had vanished and his intense gaze heated her skin. She nodded slowly, dreamily. "Then come dance with me, my warrior," she invited, "the dance we should have had long ago."

She drew Hawk inside the circle, oblivious to the other dancers. She danced for Hawk alone, for their past, for their future, as though her energy alone could make it bright. She danced fiercely, before fate could intercede and take the moment from her. She moved forward with him, then back, belly to belly, hip to hip, until the pounding of the drums became the pounding of her heart. And it was as it should have been long ago, with an anticipation driving their movements, making them sudden and sharp as they awaited the time that she would pay her debt to him.

She ignored the heavy mass of her hair that came unwound and tumbled free, though it swung wildly about her hips until he caught it in his fist and drew her close.

"And what is your price, little one?" he breathed in her ear.

"You, my love. Only you."

He wanted to take her there and then. He wanted to plunge deep within her before smallpox or soldiers or her ideals could take her away from him again. Instead, he bent suddenly and scooped her up in his arms as the spectators hooted and cheered.

"So it shall be then," he answered. Ignoring the crowd, he carried her past the revealing light of the fire to a nearby joshua tree. Its spiny needles of seasons before had fallen to the earth to make a bed. He lowered her into them and took a moment to study her face, to touch it as though he was just discovering her, to realize how precious it had become.

"Not ever again," he whispered. "Promise me, little one, that you will never turn your back again and leave me."

But it was a promise she couldn't give and they both knew it. Instead of answering, she wound her arms about his neck fiercely, as though to cling to this moment and every other one spent with him. He had to hold her away to pull her shift from her, then he moved his hand down to her hard, flat belly, devoid now of child.

"It will happen again," he vowed suddenly. "There will be other babes. I do not think that I could ever have so much of you that I would cease wanting to make them."

He felt her suck in her breath at the promise. The muscles beneath his hand hardened even more. Feverishly, with the same energy she had danced with, she began to touch his brow, his cheeks, his hair.

But when she touched his lips and moved as though to follow her fingers with her mouth, he caught her face. "There is more of me to learn, little one," he whispered.

"Life has conspired against us, often keeping us apart. We are only yet beginning."

"Then show me," she prompted him. "Let no more time go by."

He did, drawing her hand slowly down between their bodies, beneath his loincloth. When her palm rested on him and her fingers closed around him, they stopped breathing together, as one. All timidity and hesitancy left her touch; it became a celebration of her love for him, of this time they had together. She stroked and demanded until he expelled his breath in a throaty groan.

Finally his lips covered hers again. Then he pushed up on his knees suddenly to jerk his loincloth away.

"I am thinking that the *Naakaiidine'e'* women may not have taught me all there is to know about using my mouth," he murmured, the dark, teasing light coming back to his eyes. "Perhaps I can improve upon their lessons to give you what you danced for."

His eyes and hands took their fill of her as he spoke, finally coming to rest between her thighs. His fingers buried themselves in the softness of her. Then, amazingly, his tongue began to follow the same trail. When he touched it to her most secret flesh, she writhed against him and cried out.

She had no words to answer. Instead, she clutched his hair between her fingers and knew that whatever happened in the next sun, she could ask no more of life than this.

A light rain began to fall with the dawn, as though to remind the people that the gods tolerated only so much frivolity. The bands repacked their possessions and headed home. By mid-morning, only Hawk's and Delgondito's people remained.

"What will you do now, brother?" Hawk asked him when they were finally gathering to leave. "Where will you go?"

"Since we must truly start over, I think it is best that

we do so immediately. I am thinking I will move my people north toward the San Juan.''

Gray Eyes, watching from atop her mare, felt a sudden pang at the thought of him going so far. "Then we will see you rarely!'' she cried out.

"Unfortunately, this is true. But I think we will see the pale-eyes even less, and I owe that to my people.''

Gray Eyes sighed. Though it saddened her, she understood. "May your trail be beautiful then,'' she answered softly. "I will miss you.''

Hawk nodded a gruff agreement and mounted his stallion. They rode off, Gray Eyes being careful not to look back. She was sure her heart would break at the vision of the plump, jovial headman now brokenly urging his people on to a land she could only consider as alien as Hopi.

She was so wrapped up in her dismal thoughts that it took her nearly the entire ride home to realize that her own band was still healthy and thriving. K'aalo'gii especially seemed to be in high spirits, cavorting on her mare, perching on first one leg, then the other. When she finally flopped down again and rode up beside her, Gray Eyes lifted a brow.

"It would seem that you truly enjoyed the Enemy Way, sister. Yet I see no gifts.'' That fact had been puzzling her all morning. She had seen K'aalo'gii dance, had seen her and her warrior leave the circle. But there was no mare or gelding trailing along behind Night, no *Naakaiidine'e'* trinkets piled high behind her saddle.

K'aalo'gii grinned. "I got what I wanted,'' was all she would answer, then she rode off again to heckle Achi'i'h into racing her.

Gray Eyes' thoughts returned to Delgondito. She wondered how long it would take him to get to the San Juan land and flinched again at his self-imposed exile. Then she wondered if perhaps he wasn't wiser than them all.

Chapter 50

Surprisingly, as the moon of the All-Wise Fly eased into her eighteenth summer, Gray Eyes found that while they saw nothing of Delgondito, they heard of him more often than she might have hoped. Hawk traveled frequently, conferring with the other headmen, keeping tabs on Carleton just as he had promised. Occasionally, he brought back word of their friend.

Then, during one raid, he learned that even the San Juan was not far enough removed from the white man to protect Delgondito's people. Carleton had found him again, and he was once again sending him messages.

"But how?" Gray Eyes demanded when Hawk told her. Hawk only shrugged. He was more concerned with the Crazy One's renewed messages than he was with the soldiers' tenacity. "The *Dine" Ana'i*, I think," he answered. "They are friends with the Utes, and Delgondito is not so far from Ute country. It matters little anyway. His women drove the messengers out again, and this time the warriors helped them." He didn't add that at least one pale-eyes had been wounded in the process, and that the white men were nearly in as much of an uproar about it as they had been over Major Brooks' black slave boy. If she did not yet sense the tension in *Dinetah's* air, then he was reluctant to enlighten her.

But Gray Eyes did sense the tension, enough that she found herself remembering the Squaw Dance at odd times, with an almost fervent longing for the uncomplicated happiness it had brought her. She was deep in reminiscences of it late one afternoon when two strange warriors rode into the camp.

By the time she became aware of the bands' agitation, the two men were in front of her, their horses stomping and sweating beside them. She dropped her bowl of mutton so suddenly it spilled. She scrambled to her feet, feeling as awkward and flustered as she had at fourteen.

One man was tall, old, with a broad forehead and a shock of unruly white hair. The other was young, his skin unblemished by scars.

"I do not know you. Are you *Dine" Ana'i?*" she asked gracelessly, then looked around wildly as K'aalo'gii let out an aghast wail from somewhere nearby.

The older man tilted his head back and laughed heartily. "No, *estsa hataali.* We are of the Among Scattered Hills people and are here on a mission of love, not war. We are here to see the one you call Jackrabbit."

Love? Jackrabbit? She blinked and looked again for K'aalo'gii. The younger girl stood outside Talks Often's shelter, and she was gesturing frantically. Gray Eyes scowled and looked back at the men.

"Jackrabbit is away." She almost added, "Raiding," then thought better of it. Regardless of who they professed to be, she knew of no real reason to trust them.

"I suppose, then, that your headman would do," the older man decided.

Hawk? Her eyes narrowed suspiciously again. "He is visiting Manuelito."

"You then, if you would please, *estsa hataali,*" he requested. "We need someone who can speak for the girl with the black mare. I am told she has no close male relatives."

Then, suddenly, Gray Eyes understood. She looked back at K'aalo'gii for confirmation. "You?" Gray Eyes mouthed the word, stunned.

The girl was relaxed now, looking smug as she leaned against the shelter wall. She grinned happily.

"Please, you will go inside and get comfortable," Gray

Eyes said to the men. "I—" Then she shook her head and looked around for help. For the first time in her life, she wished for a second wife.

Talks Often appeared instead. "I will settle them and bring them food," she volunteered. "It is just like my daughter to do this without warning us."

Gray Eyes stalked over to K'aalo'gii, who seemed inordinately pleased with herself. "I did not think they would come," she bubbled. "He agreed to give me the cost of the dance, but then I heard nothing from him. I—"

Gray Eyes cut her off. "The cost of the dance?" she repeated.

K'aalo'gii nodded impatiently. "Daago. He offered me horses at the Squaw Dance. I told him I would rather have them for a wedding gift."

"You *told* him?"

"And so he agreed, but I did not want to tell anyone for fear that he would change his mind."

"You told a warrior to wed you and then you did not tell us so that we could be prepared if he came?" Gray Eyes' mind was spinning. She wished desperately for Hawk, then realized that if he were there, he would only laugh at her cousin's antics. She let out a burst of pent-up breath.

"So be it. Am I to take it that you wish me to accept his proposal?"

Now K'aalo'gii looked shocked. "Of course!"

Gray Eyes sighed again, and went back to her own shelter.

The men were happily situated by the fire, eating and sharing news with Talks Often, who hovered about them until Gray Eyes waved at her to sit down and be still. "I wish to offer my apologies," she began formally, still embarrassed. "My cousin did not think to tell us of this. Had I known you were coming, I would have arranged for the appropriate signs and had my husband or our grandmother's nephew here to receive you."

The older man was unperturbed. "It was a long trip. I would be upset only if there was no one here to speak for the girl. We consider it an honor, *estsa hataali*, to deal with you."

The young warrior didn't seem quite as sure. "I am not surprised by any of this," he muttered. "This has not been an orthodox relationship from the start." He still remembered the girl shooting an arrow at him at Canyon de Chelly.

His father silenced him with a dark look. He looked back at Gray Eyes. "My son tells me that the girl is as good with an arrow as he is, and that she rides like the wind. Your cousin is different, *estsa hataali*."

Gray Eyes stared at him, torn between laughter and tears. "Yes, yes, she is. But I do not think you should hold your breath waiting for grandchildren. K'aalo'gii would prefer raiding to mothering."

The old man's laughter rang out, and then the negotiations began. Gray Eyes remembered her cousin's reaction to the sheep she had once given her, and this time she worked to procure horses for her. She put together a herd she hoped K'aalo'gii would be proud of—a tall, black *Naakaiidine'e'* stallion, seven foals, and four young mares. In the end, Daago's brother threw in a breeding to the glorious painted stallion that K'aalo'gii coveted.

Talks Often settled them in Jackrabbit's empty lodge for the night, then stopped by Gray Eyes' shelter again on the way to her own. "So," she mused, "despite all the pain and hunger, we have survived to love, procreate, and grow strong, even my crazy daughter."

"Yes," Gray Eyes responded, looking toward the south where Hawk had ridden for more news. "Despite it all."

Hawk rode in the following morning, just after Daago's father and brother departed. The Lone Trees were still in an uproar over K'aalo'gii's impending wedding and only Gray Eyes noticed him. She rushed to the fire pit to meet him, but he went immediately to turn his stallion free. His face wore a thoughtful, preoccupied frown. Gray Eyes forgot about K'aalo'gii as a feeling of edginess began to pluck at her nerves again.

"You have heard something more?" she demanded, hurrying to intercept him at the corral. "Is everyone all right? Delgondito? Armijo?"

"They are all well, little one," he murmured wearily. "I would like food, a bath, a smoke . . ." He trailed off. "Then we can talk."

She scowled at him, then hurried back to her shelter to gather up ground cake.

It was hot, she told herself, unusually hot for June. Of course he would want a bath after his long, tiring ride. But when he returned from the ravine, his hair slick and wet and plastered to his back, his face still looked haggard. Her pulse picked up even more as she crouched across from him.

"The pale-eyes," she breathed. "What have they done now?"

"The Crazy One is angry that we have not knocked at the door to his Bosque Redondo," he answered finally. "And so he has given Delgondito an ultimatum. Either he must go there by the middle of the moon of the Great Seed Ripening, or yet another war will be declared against us."

Gray Eyes rose slowly, her face ashen. The Great Seed Ripening was the very next moon. "And what of you?" she asked carefully. "What will you do about this?"

"Me? I have called for a council of headmen, but I do not think any of us can or should decide for Delgondito."

She nodded, then, her hands clutched to her breasts, she began to pace. "Will you . . ." She paused, once again seeing him as he had been at *Tsehotsohih*, with his belly gaping open. "Will you fight if the pale-eyes come?" she persisted finally.

He wanted to tell her no. They both knew it would be a lie. "If it were me instead of Delgondito, I would not leave *Dinetah*," he told her as kindly as he could. "That is my choice."

For the first time ever, it was hers as well, but that was little consolation.

K'aalo'gii's impending wedding was forgotten by everyone except K'aalo'gii as the headmen began arriving the following morning. They were all there, Manuelito and Barboncito, Armijo and Delgondito, even others Gray Eyes scarcely knew. There were warriors and older men who had abandoned their pony herds for the morning. But of the women, only Gray Eyes and Barren Woman braved the throng at the central fire pit. Gray Eyes felt Hawk stiffen as soon as she sat down beside him.

No, she thought, please, not again. "Had I not been here, I would only have eavesdropped," she reminded him.

She was rewarded with a fleeting smile. "So you would have, *estsa hataali,* so you would have. I should have learned that by now."

Impulsively, she reached out to touch him. She opened her mouth to tell him that she needed him, that her love for her people, her responsibility toward them, might urge her to defy him, but she would never abandon him. But he turned away, presenting her with his shoulder. Her hand fell back to her side like a wounded bird.

"Brothers, I will let the Crazy One's liaison tell you the reason for this council," he began.

Delgondito scowled formidably. "I do not wish to be so honored," he said over soft snickers from the crowd. "Unfortunately, that is the way of things, and now I am here to tell you of my dilemma." He gave the terms of Carleton's ultimatum briefly and succinctly. For a moment, there was only stunned silence. Then the warriors cursed and the headmen all spoke at once.

Hawk's voice roared over the commotion to quiet them again. "There is more!"

Delgondito nodded. "The sound of this last message is that it is only me Carleton wishes to see at the Bosque. But I am not so sure that that is so. He spoke of the difference between enemies and friends, and he claims that his soldiers will not be able to tell one from another when they come here. He has told me that all men found in *Dinetah,* including those who visited him, will be shot on sight after the twentieth day of the pale-eyes' July!''

Delgondito shouted above the angry response. ''The women and children, he says, will be captured and taken to the reservation. It is my understanding that on that day, he will send his soldiers in here unless all of us are where he wants us to be, at his Bosque Redondo.''

''We have done nothing this time!'' Armijo shouted, ''nothing at all to instigate this!''

''This man is crazy indeed,'' Ganado Mucho agreed. ''What sane man can not tell an enemy from a friend?''

''That is not the issue!'' Gray Eyes said, and the crowd quieted again abruptly.

''You remember our *hataali,*'' she went on, ''and the way he became a *chindi*. Surely you must know by now that it is not a matter of the pale-eyes being able to recognize a man who does not want to fight. It is a matter of them being willing to spot one, and they are not. They do not want to leave any of us, peaceful or hostile, man, woman, or child, alive.''

''Do you say that they will kill us at the Bosque?'' someone demanded.

''I say that they will do everything they can to make this land their own.''

The headmen began to vote; why, she didn't understand. Even Manuelito agreed that any of the People could surrender and go to the Bosque if they so chose. But it was quickly apparent that the headmen themselves would prepare for yet another senseless war. They might win; they might lose again. But under no circumstances would they leave their homeland.

Gray Eyes stood shakily as the council began to disband. *War again*. So easily, and with no more warning than one big council.

She went quietly back to her shelter and dropped the

hide over the door despite the broiling heat of the day. Then she pulled a sheepskin around her shoulders as a chill took her, so deep and penetrating that even her blood seemed to shiver with it.

All of the headmen in the circle had voted except one. Delgondito had only stared morosely at the eastern horizon.

Chapter 51

Hawk's expression was grim when he finally came back to their shelter late that night. "So, little one," he said just as she was about to fall into an emotionally exhausted sleep. "Can I expect you to arm yourself with your brother's carbine and follow me into battle?"

Gray Eyes jerked fully awake. "There was a time when you were glad to have me there," she answered painfully.

"I loved you less then."

She gave a hoarse little cry of relief and rolled into his arms.

"I have wanted to protect you since first I saw you," he confessed into the cloud of her hair. "When you came to me as a wee thing in Canyon de Chelly, at the summer camp where you healed me. I was able to fight it then, but now I have so much more to lose. I did not want you to hear the council, because I did not want you to know."

"Hush," she murmured against his mouth. "I need no shielding. I would much rather be a part of you, of everything you and our people do."

"And that is what frightens and unmans me," he answered.

"Unmans you? Oh, no, my love. Not if the Squaw Dance was any indication."

But the storm clouds had been barely discernible on the horizon then. Now thunder boomed close, and it drove them against each other with greedy force. Though other women had touched him, some wanting to claim him, others to lure him, none left him so shaken as his little one did now. Her unfettered hair brushed against his skin and shielded her face as her mouth explored his body. Her cry was wild and exultant when his control finally broke and he toppled her beneath him. Her mind and spirit and body opened to him, telling him all those things that she had wanted to say at the council.

She slept solidly and deeply, long into the next sun. She awoke to find K'aalo'gii beside her, armed with a bowl of mutton and some ground cake.

"You must eat," the girl insisted. "Hawk says he does not think you have done so since the council."

Gray Eyes sat up groggily and accepted the food because she was truly ravenous. It was a while before she realized that K'aalo'gii was unusually subdued and quiet, even considering the outcome of the council.

"Does something trouble you, sister?" she asked.

"Only that it is beginning to look as though I will not have a wedding after all."

Gray Eyes's heart squeezed with pity. She put her bowl aside and vowed, "Sister, we will see you wed. I will not let the pale-eyes rob you of that."

K'aalo'gii shrugged negligently, but it did not belie the hurt in her eyes. "There is little you can do about it, even with all your power. But I will see Daago often enough, whether or not we are wed. And later, after the war . . . " She trailed off, because there was always an 'after the war' when life would resume.

But Gray Eyes' attention was snagged by her first words. "You will see him? How? Surely he will be fighting."

"As will I, sister, as will I." She stood again. "Even the headmen say that they cannot make choices for the rest of us. What we choose to do now is of our own heart's desire. And my desire is to see these pale-eyes dead."

She didn't wait to see the defeat that filled Gray Eyes' eyes. She left the shelter hurriedly to go work over her arrows.

* * *

K'aalo'gii, as always, was unique among the women. The rest of them were grim and fearful as the days of summer wore on.

Gray Eyes sensed their despair as she sensed all things. It was, to her, as thick and suffocating as the June heat. There were times when she looked into a squaw's eyes and the wretchedness she found there enveloped her so completely that she could scarcely breathe. Silently, wordlessly, they begged her to help them, and she turned away again and again because there was nothing she could do.

She banished all thoughts of K'aalo'gii's vow to fight and coveted the peace and normalcy of her days until she could do so no longer. It was a simmering afternoon when Sleepiness came to her in the garden and shattered her forced serenity.

Her fingers were deep in the husks of healthy, ripe corn when she saw her cousin approach. Something in her eyes made her hands go still. Sleepiness stopped beside her, but for a long time she only fingered the stalks idly.

"It was a good year," she murmured at length. "So much rain, everything grew strong and large, including our babes."

"And their parents," Gray Eyes murmured.

"I am not so strong," Sleepiness answered.

Silence fell between them, filled only by the steady buzzing of a fly and the soft rustling of the corn. Both began to fill Gray Eyes' head until her temples pounded. She stopped working and closed her eyes.

"What is it you want from me?" she whispered finally.

Sleepiness hesitated only a moment. "That you spare me this war. I do not have what it takes to withstand another one."

Gray Eyes' laugh was thin, nearly wild. "You have far too much faith in my power."

"No. I have faith in your heart, in your kindness." Suddenly, convulsively, she swallowed. *"Estsa hataali,* I cannot face it all again! Nor can many like me. They are all alike, our proud, fierce warriors. Achi'i'h is so eager to

fight! But we, the women, we are the ones who must remain at home and suffer the worst of the battles.'' She
paused as tears sprang to her eyes. ''You did not save my
babe in the last war only so I could watch her die in this
one! I do not believe that!''

''You ask of me the impossible!'' Gray Eyes protested.

But Sleepiness shook her head. ''No.'' She swallowed
again and gained control. ''I know you can not stop the
pale-eyes from coming or our men from fighting them. I
ask only that you take us away so that we, too, do not
have to fight the war.''

Gray Eyes felt a great rending in her heart. It seemed
as though the very tissue of it was shredding and pulling
apart. Images swirled in on her, too many, too paradoxi-
cal. Bulbous Nose. Hawk, his body hard and gleaming in
the firelight, rising over her, filling her. The sweltering
shelter where she had watched her babe slip dead from her
body. And finally the mountains, blood-red in the shimmering *Dinetah* sun.

''No,'' she managed, her voice strangled. ''No. Do not
ask it of me. I cannot leave *Dinetah.* ''

Sleepiness looked confused, then her words came back
soft and pleading. ''Not *Dinetah.* Only the fighting.''

Suddenly, the pain in Gray Eyes' chest stopped only to
be replaced by a horrible coldness that filled her very soul.
''What are you saying?''

''That I do not want to go to this Bosque. I will not
leave our homeland while I still have breath left in my
body. But I will take my babes and slip into its furthest
reaches. I would like to hide from the pale-eyes when they
come, somewhere where there is food and shelter.'' Her
eyes were eloquent, pleading. ''Please, you can lead me
and others like me there.''

Gray Eyes shook her head instinctively, desperately, and
backed away from the garden. But even as she did, she
heard again the *hataali*'s dry, papery voice from long ago.
*The moon and the sun. A peace chief and a war chief.
You, my granddaughter, will come to lead your own.*

"No!" She nearly shouted the word. "You do not understand. Our power, the strength of the People, comes from being together."

"Are we together during war?" Sleepiness wailed. "Our men leave. We must wait for them. All I ask is that we wait somewhere where it is safe and there is food."

Gray Eyes turned away and raced back to the camp. But Sleepiness' words dogged her footsteps and bit at her heels no matter how fast she ran.

Chapter 52

The twentieth morning of the pale-eyes' July dawned with deceptive brilliance. Gray Eyes opened her eyes to blue-white sunshine streaming through the door opening.

The usual sounds drifted in to her from outside. Men shouting and Hawk's voice so clear among them. Horses whinnying, children laughing, looms creaking, as though nothing had changed, but everything had.

She wondered when the first of them would come, with their blue coats, their pale skin and their icicle eyes. By the sun's end? Were they already marching out of the place called Albuquerque? Or had the Crazy One been bluffing?

It didn't matter. She didn't truly believe she would be there to find out.

She stood, feeling as though she had seen far more than eighteen summers. She folded her sheepskin with inordinate care, but she did not place it on top of Hawk's. She left the shelter quietly and went to the closest ravine to wash. The water was lukewarm, muddy. It couldn't rinse away the stench of defeat that seemed to cling to her.

Back in the camp, she found the women knotted together at the fire pit. Already they were looking toward the eastern horizon, furtive glances followed by flushes of guilty panic. She watched them for a moment, then irrevocably, she gave in.

They would go with or without her and they would flounder as the Lone Trees had once done without a leader. Her Hawk, her glorious warrior, did not truly need her, not the way these defenseless women did.

She crossed to them, her legs feeling wobbly. They fell silent at her approach. Only Sleepiness looked at her. The woman who had wailed and begged was gone now. In her place was a mother who would move earth and the after-world to protect her young. Her eyes flashed defiantly.

"We are going. You cannot stop us."

"No."

"We will go to the canyon."

"Yes, that is a good place."

She couldn't bring herself to tell them that she would lead them, so she only took a step backward.

"Pack lightly—everything we need is there. It is a very long ride and the children will grow cranky and demand all of our attention. Meet me at the edge of camp when the sun reaches its zenith. If we leave early, we stand less chance of encountering any pale-eyes coming in."

She didn't wait for their chorus of gratitude and relief. She wasn't sure she could bear it.

The sun was just beginning to burn away the cool morning mists when K'aalo'gii finally found Hawk. He was in the pony corral, his dark, broad shoulders presented to the sun as he bent over hooves and inspected legs. For a moment she silently observed the sleek lines of both man and beast, then cleared her throat. Hawk's head snapped up.

"Are they ready for the pale-eyes?" she asked.

He shrugged and dropped the hoof he was holding. Long hair swinging, his chest already gleaming with perspiration, he crossed to her.

"If they come."

"Will they?"

"It is difficult to tell. Even the pale-eyes who are not crazy are unpredictable."

"So we will be ready then, just in case."

Hawk nodded. "We will wait, and at the first sign or word of soldiers, I will do what I did last time. I will gather my men and attack first."

"Does Gray Eyes know that?" K'aalo'gii asked

shrewdly, then immediately wished she hadn't. His face, soft and thoughtful a moment before, became closed. But before his eyes became unreadable, she saw the flash of pain in their onyx depths.

"I cannot imagine she would think I would do anything else," he answered sharply. "She knows me. We have loved long and well."

"She knows me as well," K'aalo'gii answered. "I have already told her that I wish to stay with you and help you fight."

Hawk lifted a brow. "And where else would you be? Are you planning to leave our band and strike out on your own, little warrior?"

K'aalo'gii stared at him, her mouth agape. She had chosen her words deliberately, as kindly as she could. But the implication had been there, as loud as gunfire. There were those in the band who didn't intend to stay. Surely he had to know that!

She opened her mouth to respond, then, uncharacteristically, she clamped it shut again. "I . . . just wanted you to know," she finished lamely. "I am with you." Then she turned and hurried back to the camp.

Hawk watched her go with a blank stare, the pain in his soul absolute. So it was true then. He had denied it with every ounce of power in his body, but his band was dividing.

How long had he known that the women could stand no more? He himself had badgered Manuelito into pursuing peace because he had known that if war came again, he would lose his little one. Though she had pledged her heart and her body to him, the holy ones had pledged her soul to her people.

No, the women would not stay and starve through another war. They would look to their *estsa hataali* to save them, and she would bend to their will.

He felt as though a fireball had caught him suddenly in the gut. His breath escaped in a harsh grunt and he half-jogged, half-ran after K'aalo'gii.

He came upon the men first, a quiet, stunned horde of them near the sweat lodge. Spotting Jackrabbit, he jerked him roughly aside.

"Where is she?"

"Her shelter," he answered calmly, and Hawk dropped his arm and ran on.

He passed lodge after lodge with neatly stacked blankets and *Naakaiidine'e'* cooking pots outside. Children wailed, calling for their fathers, struggling against their mothers' breasts as they were held tight. He ignored them.

He found Gray Eyes where Jackrabbit had said she would be, standing at the door of her lodge. Her mare was laden and waiting patiently beside her.

"Little one." The endearment was jerked from him, nearly a groan, but she showed no reaction. A sharp and savage fear clawed at his insides.

"You would truly go to the pale-eyes?" he exploded and gripped her arms hard.

Her eyes raised slowly to his, as bright as the *Naakai-idine'e'* metal, shining with rare tears that refused to spill over. "Does it matter? I must leave you."

She reached a hand up to his face, tracing his brow, his chin, his arrogant cheekbones as though to brand them in her memory for life. He caught her hand in a viselike grip.

"Why?" he demanded unnecessarily.

"You do not need me. Not as they do."

"Need you?" He laughed harshly, raggedly. "You think I am that strong? Then watch this proud warrior beg!"

She jerked away from him. Her throat closed tightly over a massive swelling that she feared would choke her. "You must not," she whispered. "I could not bear it."

"I cannot do anything else! Do not go, little one. You will take with you my heart and my soul."

A single tear rolled down her cheek. She swiped at it violently, suddenly angry. "Then come along!"

"To live among pale-eyes? That would destroy us both as surely as war!"

"No! To *Tse'yi'*, the canyon! Let them come here with

their white faces and their hatred! Perhaps if they find no one they will go on their way again. But they cannot have the canyon. They cannot get in there. That is ours, ours! We can live there forever and the People can go on. If we stay here, they will kill us!

"It is over," she gasped, her control shattered. She clutched at him, her fingers digging into his flesh. The tears she'd long thought she couldn't cry finally spilled over and splashed his chest.

He crushed her to him fiercely.

"I have loved you," she wept, her hands tracing his face frenziedly as though she would memorize it.

"No," he moaned, a final protest.

But she only stood on tiptoe and touched her mouth to his in a last *Naakaiidine'e'* kiss. When he opened his eyes again, she was gone.

Chapter 53

Hawk had always known that loving the little one would destroy him. In the suns after her departure, he found some bitter consolation in knowing that he had been right. He felt like a man without a soul. An arm, a leg, he could have spared. But the silent nights alone in her shelter nearly robbed him of the will to go on. There was no comfort in remembering that he had left her before. This time she had left him, and he alternately hated her and grieved for her loss.

Old Man came to him before the dust had even settled on her trail. "The *estsa hataali,* she is wise," he mumbled.

Hawk turned contemptuous eyes upon him. "You would follow her then? You would give up?"

"No. Not that. I fear that I am far less brave than she is. I do not dare stay in *Dinetah.* What I would like to do is visit Hopi for a while," he admitted. "It was bad when we went there before, but at least many of us lived to return."

"Go then," Hawk muttered and turned back to the empty shelter he had once shared with Gray Eyes.

They did, the next morning, over three hundred of them striking out for the dubious safety of the west. Hawk watched them go, his thoughts and feelings in a turmoil. Were they cowards or survivors, wise or insane? He no longer knew, and he cared even less.

His jaw hardened and he looked around at the faces that

remained. There were forty of them, mostly warriors. One of the women was K'aalo'gii.

"And now?" she asked. "Will we stay here and wait for the soldiers to come?"

It took him several long moments to regain the determination that had guided him through other years, other wars.

"No," he decided. "We will kill every one of their maggot-ridden hides. We will head east to meet them as they arrive."

They found Barboncito long before they found any pale-eyes. His band was camped north of the Chuskas, not hiding but not fighting either.

"So," Barboncito observed, meeting them at the central fire pit. "You would hunt the blue-coats down as you did last time."

Hawk shrugged. "There does not appear to be anything to hunt."

"The white men have returned to *Tsehotsohih.*"

There was a quiet murmur among the Bitter Waters. Hawk's eyes narrowed.

"They must be planning something," he mused. "Perhaps we should raid them right away and put an end to it before it starts."

But Barboncito shook his head. "This war has not started like the others, and I, for one, would prefer to bide my time and see what it is about. All the pale-eyes have done so far is rename their *hual-te* after Canby. I ride down periodically to check on them."

"I would like to ride with you next time you go," Hawk decided.

"Of course," Barboncito agreed. "In the meantime, why not stay here with us?"

Hawk agreed. If war did come, his forty warriors alone would not be enough for the complete and final carnage he had in mind.

* * *

Ten suns later the pale-eyes finally launched an attack. The enemy cry went up at dawn. The soldiers charged in from the valley, creating a storm of hoofbeats and dust and chaos. Men and women alike rolled out of their sheepskins with deadly intent.

It took only a moment for the fierce pumping of K'aalo'gii's heart to sweep away her grogginess. She stumbled out of the shelter she shared with Barboncito's youngest wife, hesitating as her eyes adjusted to the new light. Then, as she blinked, a warrior fell to a fireball. Her own wail joined his and she was ashamed to realize that her limbs were locked and trembling.

A body careened into her and she toppled backward, landing ignominiously onto her backside. Hawk's face snarled in fury as he loomed above her.

"So you would cower, girl-child?" he taunted. "Kill them if you have the courage of your words!"

Anger gripped her. She launched herself to her feet again and charged into the foray.

There were not many pale-eyes, she realized, but they were going for the pony herd. She screamed her grandfather's war cry, the only one she knew, and raced across the hard-packed earth toward the corral.

A single soldier was there already, jerking the staked poles free from the fence. She came up behind him on soundless feet. Growling like a wounded animal, she let an arrow snap free of her bow. The man fell and she pushed the knuckles of her free hand against her lips as she stared down at the first human life she had ever taken. Then someone jerked her hair from behind and she spun around, loading another arrow as she turned.

The second killing was easier. The Ute fell against her toes and she kicked him away viciously.

She whistled for Night. When the black mare leaped from the scattering herd, she hurled herself onto her back and retreated to the sweat lodge. She could see Hawk there, absorbed in pulling his knife from a pale-eyes sprawled at his feet. He was unaware of the Ute warrior who crept soundlessly around the edge of the lodge, a hatchet raised and ready.

"No!" K'aalo'gii screamed and began to gallop toward them. Hawk straightened and whirled even as his finger pumped on the trigger of his gun.

The Ute staggered and collapsed. "You worry needlessly, warrior-girl," Hawk said quietly. "When they are all dead, then I too will die. Until then, I live to destroy them."

He turned to join the others, and K'aalo'gii followed. They found Barboncito, Achi'i'h, and Jackrabbit driving back the line of white men who were pressing in from the south side of camp. K'aalo'gii flew among them, using her knees to cue her mare. She loosed a volley of deadly arrows and slowly, surely, the pale-eyes began to drop back until finally they were running, retreating, tripping over each other as they fled.

"Hooo-eee!" K'aalo'gii screamed in triumph and took off after them. Hawk leaped on his stallion and followed, his hooves sounding a death knell against the dry earth. Then, abruptly, they stopped, frozen in a stunned tableau at the sight that met them at camp.

"I—I do not understand," K'aalo'gii whispered. But she did. Somehow, in that moment, she knew that this final war would be for all the spoils.

The raiding pale-eyes had been defeated soundly. More white bodies littered the camp than red. But the blue-coats had won after all.

The sheep corral was empty. The garden was ablaze.

Chapter 54

Hawk sat stonily, a nerve twitching in his jaw his only visible sign of emotion. "The pale-eyes are fighting differently this time," he mused to the men huddled around his fire pit. "I do not understand it. They are few and weak, and they do not seem to want to engage in battles that they are sure to lose. Instead, they hurt us in other ways. They steal our mounts and take our food."

Achi'i'h nodded. Two full moons had passed since the pale-eyes' August attack on their camp. They had raided hard in retaliation and had immediately restocked their corrals. But then the pale-eyes had come again. They had not engaged the warriors in battle this time, but had crept in in the night and had stolen the sheep again, and, worse, the ponies.

That had been the most severe blow of all. Without ponies, they were unable to raid. Without raiding, they were unable to eat. Hawk and Barboncito had immediately sent a messenger on foot to ask Manuelito for ponies, but until he returned with more mounts, they could only nibble on piñon nuts and soft overripe berries. Winter was harsh on this side of the mountain and winter was close. The game had all gone. Achi'i'h had the unnerving feeling that the pale-eyes knew that.

"They fight like cowards," Jackrabbit charged.

"Those cowards are winning," Barboncito reminded him.

Hawk grinned coldly. "Not if we fight like men."

* * *

They rode out again as soon as the messenger returned with the ponies. K'aalo'gii hovered nervously at the edge of camp, watching them depart.

"Let me come with you," she pleaded as Hawk passed by.

But he shook his head. "No. Stay here. I leave the women and children in your care."

He rode off. K'aalo'gii went back to the camp, to women staring at her with hollow, hungry eyes. She couldn't face them. Turning abruptly, she headed for a game trail that meandered upward through piñon and pine.

She walked for a while, then dropped down beneath a tree to chew on some cedar berries. Her stomach, desperate for something more, very nearly rejected the scant, bitter gift she could give it. She laid down, waiting for the feeling of nausea to pass. Then she closed her eyes and dozed.

She awoke to the sound of a twig snapping, followed by a rustle that was not made by the wind. Soft, subtle, the sounds reached her and lifted the hairs on her nape. She sat up slowly, quietly, her hand on her bow.

The dull sound of hoofbeats followed. They pounded a quiet, treacherous rhythm against the earth. Eight, she counted. Nine. Ten. Ten horses.

Pale-eyes. Who else but this new breed of soldiers would sneak in right after the men had gone? Something snapped inside her at their treachery and she leaped to her feet and screamed.

The brush crackled behind her again, then crashed. She shot arrows wildly in that direction, with no care for skill. Tears blinded her sight and when her ammunition was gone, she turned and ran.

The camp was in chaos. She heard women scream and a babe's cry cut short as his skull was crushed against a rock. She shrieked her fury and her pain even as she threw herself into the fight.

She hurled herself at a white man who had Barboncito's

youngest wife by the hair. The force of her weight knocked him backward, and Fox yelped in pain as her scalp tore in his grip. K'aalo'gii was beyond caring. She clawed at his face, at his eyes. Even as he cuffed her with his fist, she noticed with distant satisfaction that his blood was on her hands. Then she fell, sobbing.

The white man forgot about Fox. He turned to K'aalo'gii, kicking her hard in the ribs until she groaned again and staggered onto her knees to get away from him. Then hard hands caught her from behind and jerked her to her feet again.

"I will take this one." The voice was guttural, low, half English and half Navajo. *Dine'' Ana'i*, she thought, and fought him until she had half-turned in his grasp. She saw her own arrow buried deep in his shoulder, blood gushing around it. He was the one who had followed her down the mountain then.

She collected the saliva in her mouth and spat at him just as she realized that he wasn't truly *Dine'* at all, but at least part Ute.

"I like her spirit," he chuckled and wiped the spit off his cheek. "I think I will take her as my reward, a tribute for my efforts in a war that is not even my own." He poked his knife into her ribs as he bound her wrists behind her.

"We're supposed to take her to the fort," the white man complained.

"I think I would rather have this than a free horse or twenty dollars for turning her in. You would fight now, little cat?" The Ute spoke to her in her own tongue as the knife pressed harder.

But K'aalo'gii never felt it. She was blessedly unaware of the warrior's hand as he roughly, lasciviously, massaged her breast. Daago's face swam in and out of her mind. She would not fight by his side, would not lay with him. It would end like this, all the skills she had honed, all the defiance she had fostered, all for naught because she had been prepared to fight fairly, with honor, against an enemy who had none.

She had lost the only battle that truly mattered. She raised her voice again in an anguished cry, then her world went blessedly dark.

Chapter 55

▼▼▼▼▼▼▼▼▼▼

Hawk and Barboncito came back three suns later, driving twelve motley ponies and seventeen pale-eyes sheep. The camp was quiet, so quiet that the wings of a red-tailed hawk could be heard beating overhead. Hawk's eyes narrowed.

"Something is wrong. Everyone is gone."

"No." Even as Barboncito spoke, a stooped, beaten figure appeared in the door to one of the hogans.

Fox hesitated as though uncertain about something, then disappeared again into the lodge that belonged to She Smiles, Barboncito's first wife. Barboncito roared inarticulately and beat his mount into a sudden gallop. Sheep and ponies scattered away from his path. He rode to Smiles' hogan and leaped to the ground.

Hawk followed more slowly, his eyes assessing the situation. But the bedraggled group he found inside Smiles' lodge still made him lift a brow.

Delgondito was by the fire. Two warriors shifted uncomfortably behind him. Smiles was nowhere to be seen, but Fox wept brokenly as she leaned against the wall. One of her eyes was swollen shut; a bloody hole showed at the side of her head where a large hank of her hair was missing.

"Where are the others?" Hawk growled into the silence.

"Pale-eyes," Fox whimpered. "They . . ." But she was unable to finish.

374

"Only this woman and four others remain," Delgondito contributed. "They ran into the brush when the raiding party arrived. This one was able to fight and escape. The others, I think, have been captured. There is no sign of them."

Hawk looked around the lodge. "Which others?"

"Your wife's young cousin is gone, my friend. I am sorry."

Hawk violently plunged his hand into the hogan wall. The wood and sod at the door opening exploded into the room. He extricated his fist, then roared and punched the wall again. Finally, for the first time since his little one had gone, he felt true emotion, intense fury mixed with pain.

"How do you fit into this, brother?" Barboncito asked, and Hawk focused slowly on Delgondito again. "How is it that you came to be here?"

There was an ominous silence, and Hawk felt another spasm of emotion, something cold, something very close to fear this time.

"I bear another message from General Carleton," Delgondito finally admitted on a shuddering sigh. "I came to beg you to go to the Bosque."

Total silence greeted his words. Then Barboncito repeated, "You say you would like to see us turn ourselves in?"

"I say that it is the safest thing to do. This raid is only the beginning. You will not win this war."

With a bellow, Barboncito jerked his bow from his shoulder and centered an arrow at Delgondito's heart. Hawk brought his fist down on it in a mighty arc. The arrow snapped; the bow splintered and dropped to the floor.

Barboncito turned wild, accusing eyes on him. "You wish to take more advice from our friend?" He sneered over the last word.

"I wish to grant him the respect of being heard out!"

"He is a traitor!"

"Never," Delgondito moaned. "Never that."

Hawk turned wary eyes back to him. "Talk," he challenged. "Explain."

Delgondito began carefully. "It is true that I have gone to live among our enemies. I went to their Bosque because I prayed that it was only me they wanted. It was not. Since then, I have learned what vast measures they will take in order to call our land their own."

"So you would have us go to the Bosque and give it to them without a fight?"

"They will destroy us one way or the other. If we go, we may survive with our souls."

Barboncito snarled in rage again. This time he brought his lance up to Delgondito's chest, its point raising a thin line of blood.

"Then I give you the same deal, white man," he snarled. "Stay and talk to me with your traitor's tongue, or go back to the pale-eyes who spit you out. If you stay, I will destroy you."

Delgondito looked down at the spear unflinchingly. Then he situated his blanket across his shoulders with the last of his dignity. "I will go."

Hawk stared after him, his fists clenched at his sides. What had that cost him? What had been the true measure of pride and soul? He left the shelter suddenly and went after him.

As Delgondito looked back at the camp a final time, he raised a hand in a silent good-bye, then mounted his pony.

"No," Hawk said flatly. "You have risked much to come to me. I scorn your reasons, but I will not betray you by seeing you ride among your enemies alone." His message was clear. Delgondito's own people would not be forgiving of the choice he had made.

"Thank you, friend," Delgondito answered.

Hawk caught up a pony and joined him. They rode far along the mountain before he spoke again. "Where will you go now?"

"I must find Manuelito."

"If you tell him what you told us, he will kill you."

Delgondito sighed heavily. "I know."

"Why then? You have turned against us by leaving. Why risk your life now?"

It was a long time before he answered. The ponies' hooves clopped hollowly into the quiet. "The Crazy One asked me to speak to you, to persuade you to come to his Bosque," he said finally. "I agreed because I felt that you should be warned."

"Warned?" Hawk demanded.

"I have said that I do not think we will win this war. Now I will tell you why. The Rope Thrower, the one they call Kit Carson, is the Crazy One's fiercest warrior. He leads the army at *Tsehotsohih*. I have overheard it said that he is planning to enter Canyon de Chelly."

Hawk's heart jerked as he remembered the little one's words. *They cannot have the canyon. That is ours, ours!* she had said. But he knew of the Rope Thrower. He had fought other tribes successfully before.

"That is impossible!" he snapped, but his voice lacked conviction.

"Perhaps, perhaps not," Delgondito answered. "But if you insist upon staying and fighting, then I ask you to at least fight for your little Lone Tree. Go to her. Do not let your pride interfere." Delgondito reined his pony in suddenly. "I will leave you here. I would not have the others know that you offered me kindness. For your sake, I would prefer that we not be seen together."

Hawk nodded silently. He remembered their days in Canyon de Chelly, remembered his wedding when Delgondito had stepped in to fill Long Earrings' shoes. Because he could not bear to watch him go, he looked away.

He stared up at the mountain, purple and black now in the late-day sun. He stared as though he could see through it, as though the canyon and the little one were right there before him. She had left him. But she was his life, his soul. Still he fought for the land she cherished, still he yearned for her wisdom and warmth.

He closed his eyes, but he couldn't blot out the image of her that he carried in his heart. He knew then that he would go to her. He would heed Delgondito's advice one last time.

Chapter 56

▼ ▼ ▼ ▼ ▼ ▼ ▼ ▼ ▼ ▼

The first morning of December brought bone-chilling winter to Canyon de Chelly. The peach trees were naked and gnarled; their fruit would not have lasted into the winter and so it had been eaten. The sheep had long since been slaughtered as well. Without them, the canyon was a yawning scene of emptiness and death and loss.

Gray Eyes wandered through it pensively, then stopped at the crooked old tree that sheltered Long Earrings' grave. She dropped to her knees there, digging her fingers into the earth.

"Tell me," she whispered, "tell me why my medicine is gone. It has always worked strongest here. Why can I not see the future? What is wrong?"

The wind howled, but there was no answer from the *hataali*. She raised her face to the wintry sun and closed her eyes.

She tried to listen for wisdom, for the cry of a hawk that would tell her that her people were going to be all right, that they would survive this latest war. Instead there was only a dull, muffled scraping sound, and she opened her eyes, irritated.

The canyon's sweeping sandstone walls were still barren except for the ruins of the Anasazi, the ancient ones whose *chindis* claimed some portions of the canyon. She sighed and looked down again. Her fingers had uprooted a delicate shoot of prairie clover.

"So," she mused aloud to the holy ones, "you are listening to me after all. You tell me I will need my medicine soon. That is frightening.'' She brushed the dirt off the roots of the *niits'oosiitsoh* and stood up. Then the sound of chafing rock grew louder.

This time, she looked from side to side in alarm. She spotted a figure on horseback sliding down one of the smooth, steep gorges that led to the canyon floor. Her breath stopped and a long-dead part of her leaped suddenly into life.

Hawk. Her Hawk. Her warrior had come home.

She dropped the prairie clover. She ran, leaping over sage and splashing through the icy stream, her heart thundering. She knew he didn't see her. He hit the floor and rode hard, raising dust. The people following him were mostly warriors, and they hooted and hollered as they brought up the rear. She stopped, panting, then called out with all the force of the barren days she'd spent without him.

The wind caught her voice and whipped it away, but he heard enough to know it was her. He turned sharply and saw her racing toward him. He leaped off his pony before it had stopped completely, dropping to the ground like a mountain cat.

And then she was in his arms. ''Ah,'' she gasped over and over again. ''Ah, yes.'' Her fingers flew hungrily over the sinewy muscles of his shoulders, over his face, through his hair.

He hadn't changed. His features were a little harder, but there were no fresh scars, no wounds other than those she had already healed. His laughter was still deep and vibrant as he caught her wrists in his hands.

''I am not wool to be pummeled into shape before carding,'' he teased.

''No,'' she whispered. ''But you are truly here, all here, and that is what I needed to know.''

He dragged her closer and kissed her. She had not forsaken him. She answered with all the fire and innocence and greed she saved for him, and told him better than words that she had ached through these long moons without him.

Finally, shaken, he pulled away from her. "The others," he managed, and then laughter overtook her. The men had stopped when they'd realized that their leader was no longer among them. Now they waited for him uncomfortably, faces averted.

She slipped lightly out of his grasp. "We will have to join them, but only for a little while. I do not intend to share you, my husband, not yet. They have had you long enough. Come, we will ride with them back to my shelter."

She ran for his pony. The wind no longer seemed icy but sharp and invigorating instead. He caught her around the waist and swung her easily over the animal's withers. Then he was behind her, warm and solid, all the good things in life she had lost. She tilted her head back and rested it on his chest.

"Ah, love," she murmured. "Hurry."

He needed little urging, but the Lone Trees and the Bitter Waters fell upon them as soon as they reached the camp. There was no way to slip away gracefully, and Gray Eyes found suddenly that she didn't care. The anticipation, ah, the anticipation, she thought. It had been gone from her life for so very long; now she was able to savor it. She watched with a brilliant smile as Barren Woman plucked at Hawk, assuring herself he was truly alive. She accepted a warm hug from Jackrabbit and watched Sleepiness embrace Achi'i'h. Their girl-child, now a toddler aptly named Lupine for her striking blue eyes, was squeezed between them until she squealed.

Perhaps this was the future that she hadn't been able to see, Gray Eyes thought. These moments were too rare to sense, but they were enough to make her go on.

"Must we eat?" Hawk asked as the women began falling upon the sheep he had brought, slaughtering them and hauling them to their fires.

Gray Eyes smiled. "Together," she decided. "Alone."

She took a small chunk of the carcass that Barren Woman brought back. She carried it into her shelter and centered it over the cook fire there. But when he would have taken her into his arms again, she kissed him gently and eased out of his grasp.

"I have missed your body," she admitted, "more than you could know. I have slept at night feeling hollow and empty. But also, I have missed this. Your broad shoulders blocking out the last lingering light of the day as you stand in my door. I have missed watching you smoke and stare at the ceiling as you talk to me and tell me what is in your heart. Please, let us have that again as well!"

He reached out to her, gently twining a piece of her hair around his finger. "Yes, little one," he murmured. "For a little while, we can have it all."

They sat close as the mutton sizzled, her elbow braced on his thigh. They fed each other meat and talked of nothing and everything, sometimes chuckling, sometimes serious. Then, finally, he said the words that he knew had to be spoken before they could go any further.

"Little one, your cousin is gone."

Gray Eyes stiffened. "Gone how?" she asked carefully. "To the *chindis?*"

"I do not know. Pale-eyes raided the camp and took her. It is the same as what happened to your mother, your grandmother, and something I pray we will never have to learn."

She understood. Only those who had fallen into the clutches of the pale-eyes could know what came after. To those who remained behind, they were merely gone into some abyss beyond imagination.

"Oh," she breathed. She squeezed her eyes shut, trying to capture K'aalo'gii's face. Funny, brave, indomitable K'aalo'gii. She had not been able to give her her wedding after all.

"Did she . . ." Gray Eyes paused, dragging in a harsh breath. "Did she get to fight with you? Did she ever get to be a warrior?"

Hawk scrubbed his hands over his face roughly. "She fought well and hard," he answered. "Better than many of the men."

"Yes," Gray Eyes whispered as a single tear spilled over. "Yes, she would have."

She burrowed into his arms again, without passion this time. He held her as she swiped at her cheek. He knew her tears were a gift she was able to give to only a precious few.

But soon she straightened again determinedly. "Tell me everything. There is more that troubles you. I can tell from your voice."

"It is the Crazy One," he admitted roughly. "He would like to see the Rope Thrower come here. He thinks to conquer Canyon de Chelly."

She looked at him sharply, her eyes narrowed. "Then he is not so much the crazy one after all. He knows that this is all we have left."

He nodded, mesmerized by the passionate hatred in her voice. "It will be a long time before they come here. I have done my best to discourage them."

"What?" she demanded. "What have you done?"

He hesitated. "I raided both the Bosque and the fort at *Tsehotsohih*. The sheep and the cattle I took from the Bosque. At *Tsehotsohih,* I took horses. Your people will eat, and mine will raid, and the Rope Thrower's will fight on foot."

She gaped at him.

"We will survive a while longer," he went on, his eyes shining at the memory of the impossible coups he had managed.

"Please, let it be so." She moved closer to him. "Now," she said suddenly, fervently. "Enough talk. Now let us be together."

He was ready for her. He responded fiercely as her hands moved over his body again, reveling in each touch, each kiss, that they had stolen from the war. It might be the first of many times they would share again; it might be the last. Neither of them would take either eventuality for granted.

"Little one," he breathed in her ear. And then he loved her as he had been unable to love any woman since the day her heart had led her from his camp.

Chapter 57

▼▼▼▼▼▼▼▼▼▼

Albert Pheiffer was stark naked as he stumbled toward Fort Wingate. He was at the wrong place. He had been ordered to report to Colonel Carson at the site of the old Fort Defiance, but Wingate, just miles from the old Fort Fauntleroy, was closer.

"Hey!" One of the sentinels shouted an alarm. "Arm yourself and look sharp!"

"Ease off, Joe," said the other man, but he cautiously raised his weapon all the same. "Looks to me like he's white."

Pheiffer looked up at them. His eyes were small and feverish in a face that was streaked with mud and blood.

"Don't debate the goddamn issue," he rasped. "Get me inside."

They recognized him and dropped their rifles with a clatter. Together they carried him into the compound, calling for the commanding officer and the medic.

"What do we have here?" Doc Trelawny asked as he bent over Pheiffer.

"They beat him to a bloody pulp," the second sentinel announced. "I know this guy. Served under him up Utah way. I'd heard he was fighting with Carson. Bet those damned savages got him. They were going into the canyon, you know."

"Not yet they weren't." Commander Chaves came in behind them. "Were you raided, man?"

Pheiffer shook his head. His gestures were groggy but

his eyes glittered. "Not at Canby," he managed. "Arizona. Coming from California to report. Escorting my wife. Apache. White Mountain band, I think." He faded, slipping into unconsciousness. Then, suddenly, his eyes flew open again and they were stark with hatred.

"Goddamned Indians," he muttered. "Killed my wife. Killed her servant girl. Damn near got me."

"Jones!" Chaves spun away. "Get a message to Albuquerque. Tell General Carleton that we have Captain Pheiffer here and that he's been injured by a marauding band. I'll volunteer to take over for him and join Carson at Canby. Nothing I'd like better," he added more quietly.

"No!" Pheiffer barked the word with such force that Dr. Trelawny jumped back, clutching his stethoscope to his chest. "To hell with my injuries. Those bastards are mine. Bring me clothes. Food. I need a good night's sleep. But I'm going to Canby. They're going to pay, goddamn it. They're going to pay."

The men stared at him in mute admiration. No one thought to mention that it wasn't the Navajo he had a score to settle with.

James Carleton was dining when two messages reached him, one from Fort Canby, the other from Wingate. He opened the one from Canby first. His face settled into a dangerous scowl.

"Myers!" he bellowed suddenly. A small black manservant appeared in the dining room door.

"Get Michaels. It's falling apart, Myers." He lurched up from the table to pace. "It's all falling apart."

Michaels appeared in the door of the dining room, breathless, his cheeks red. "You called for me, General?"

Carleton sat down again. "A letter," he answered shortly. "Find someone to carry it tonight."

"What's happened, sir?"

"Carson writes that those damned heathen Navajo have

raided two military compounds. It's incomprehensible—
have they no respect for authority? One of their chiefs
sailed into the corral at Fort Canby, bold as you please,
and *then* he stole stock from his own kind at the Bosque!
By God, Michaels, I'll stop him! I'll see him rot on the
reservation or see him dead!

"Carson's gone home for the holidays, but I intend to
see this sweep succeed when he comes back. Tell him
I'll get him more horses and mules to replace the ones
that were stolen. However, if they don't arrive by . . .
say, the sixth of January, he is to proceed with the plan
anyway."

"Proceed? Surely you can't mean to send them in on
foot—"

"Sergeant, you are here to take letters, not to offer advice. This is precisely the time we want to hit, in the dead
of winter when those heathens are at their weakest. If we
wait until spring as Carson suggests, they'll raid us again
and again until their strength is replenished. But if I take
Canyon de Chelly now, I'll have it all, Sergeant. Those
damned Indians will have no strongholds, no crops, no
livestock. They'll come to the Bosque then. They'll
come," he muttered, trailing off.

Michaels wrote as the general opened the second message from Fort Wingate.

"Ah, here's good news," Carleton mused, his sour
mood vanishing abruptly. "Captain Pheiffer has been located and will be reporting to Canby posthaste. It seems
the Apache got his wife." He grinned hugely. "There is
nothing, Sergeant, nothing, like a man with a vendetta.
Thank God for the Apache. We're going to win this
war."

January roared into *Dinetah* like a wounded bear. Carson returned to Fort Canby amid a raging blizzard that left
him sodden and his mount frostbitten. The snow continued through New Year's Day, and when Albert Pheiffer

finally arrived on the fifth, the trails to *Tsehotsohih* had long been obliterated.

He reported directly to Carson's apartment. "We'll go in tomorrow then?" he asked, glancing at his old friend for confirmation. "I'm not too late?"

"No," Carson answered tiredly. "No, you're not."

"It's snowing again," Pheiffer observed.

"I doubt it will make any difference to General Carleton. We've been ordered to march for the canyon no matter what."

"Good," Pheiffer answered.

"I can give you only thirty-three men."

Pheiffer shrugged. "I'd go in single-handedly."

Carson felt a chill. "I'll take four hundred," he went on. "I'm going to survey the west rim for the best place to get in. I've heard that the most passable trenches are there, although I seriously doubt if we'll be able to get in and out without losing a few men, especially under these conditions. For that reason, our initial purpose is strictly surveillance, Al." The other man showed no reaction to the warning. "Take your men and scout the east rim, then come around to meet me. We'll camp and reconnoiter for a day or two while we decide the best place to enter."

Pheiffer nodded cursorily. "Mounts?" he asked.

"With today's arrival, maybe twenty-five."

"Packhorses?"

"Mules. Twelve of them."

"Still, it's possible."

Carson looked at him incredulously. "You're either a brave man or a crazy one. I've learned through the years not to take unnecessary chances, and this, Al, is an unnecessary chance. Surely you know that."

Pheiffer only shrugged.

Carson turned away abruptly to pour them whiskey. "Look at what we've done!" he exploded. "We've destroyed every single crop within a two-hundred-mile radius of this fort. Everything capable of growing back without replanting has been tugged up by the roots. I've had fruit trees hacked down at ground level. Caches of wheat and corn, as fine as this territory has ever produced, have been burned after we've taken our fill. We've stolen so damned many sheep that it's been impossible to butcher them all or drive them back to Albuquerque for the bounty. I've had to slaughter them by the tens and tens of thousands! Their carcasses have been left to rot on the hillsides!''

Pheiffer nodded calmly. "Good show. The Indians should be sufficiently hungry by now. Even they won't eat carrion.''

The fight went out of Carson in a breath. "No," he responded quietly, "they won't. And that takes all the pride and glory out of this destruction. Carleton will win. With or without taking the canyon, we'll get the Indians to his Bosque. And what will we have accomplished? My sleep is haunted by dreams of starving Navajo squaws and children.''

Pheiffer tossed back his drink. "You've always been too soft. They're killers, for Chrissake. Navajo kids? They're nothing more than newborn snakes. They'll grow up to writhe and strike just like the rest of them. Meanwhile, more and more people are coming in from the east to settle, to make something of this land, and what do we get for our trouble?'' He slammed his glass down, cracked it, then pitched it angrily into the fire. "We get dead," he finished. "Juanita is gone, Colonel. I lost my wife to a band of Apache when we were returning from a visit to California.''

Carson looked at the man's swollen, bruised face and his last hope of avoiding the canyon mission died. Perhaps he could circumvent Carleton's passion. But he knew he could not fight both men.

"I'm going into that canyon, Colonel," Pheiffer went on. "And I'm coming out with my share of scalps.''

* * *

The blizzard was still howling three days later when Pheiffer finally stumbled upon the yawning hole in the earth that was Canyon del Muerto.

"Hooo-eee," one of his men whistled softly. "Now ain't that pretty."

The others looked doubtful. "I don't see no Injuns down there, Captain," someone muttered. "You sure this is the right place? Where's Colonel Carson? Wasn't we supposed to meet him someplace around here?"

Pheiffer took a warming swallow from his flask. "On the west side," he answered shortly. "We're on the north rim. Any incompetent would know that."

Disgruntled, the man turned away. "Call me whatever you want, but I still don't see no Injuns."

They moved on, covering the north rim by nightfall, and proceeded along the west in the dark. The sky was paling again when they finally found a smooth, snaking line of white that led down to the canyon floor. Pheiffer reined in abruptly and went still. His men tumbled up behind him, their hoots and cheers feeble now under the weight of their exhaustion.

"Looks like we found a place to get in, huh, Captain?" Despite their weariness, the men were cheerful and optimistic for the first time since setting out from the fort. They started moving off again at a faster clip. It was several moments before they realized that Pheiffer hadn't followed.

"Now, hey, what the hell?" someone began, then he struggled back through the drifts. "I thought we was supposed to find Carson and tell him?"

But Albert Pheiffer had forgotten about Kit Carson. He saw his wife, bleeding, dying, remembered her pulse faltering beneath his touch. Yes, he could look for his superior. Or he could kill the bloody bastards who had taken his woman. As his troops watched in fascinated horror, Pheiffer made his decision. He gouged his mount roughly with his heels and plunged over the side of de Chelly's sister canyon.

There was a shout of triumph, a crashing of brush, then silence. "Well, goddamn!" someone bellowed. The men hurried to the edge and looked down upon the first white man ever to enter the Navajo's treacherous stronghold system and survive.

Chapter 58

▼ ▼ ▼ ▼ ▼ ▼ ▼ ▼ ▼ ▼

Off to the south, in Canyon de Chelly, the sun had finally returned to *Dinetah*, and its shafts caught and played over the frozen snow. Gray Eyes stood just outside her hogan, savoring the crystalline beauty of it all. Then she smiled softly and turned back inside.

She hunkered down to light her dead cook fire, taking pains to work noisily.

"Warriors have very easy lives," she teased when Hawk finally sat up groggily. "You raid once, then you spend weeks sleeping it off."

He grinned. "Is it so late?"

"The sun has passed its zenith," she lied. But he looked so horrified that she had to laugh.

He caught her and tumbled her beneath him. "I should beat you for your lack of respect."

She smiled beatifically. "Ah, but then I would have to cast a spell upon you to make you weak."

"And if I were weak, what would you eat? You would be very hungry, little one, without all the fine, fat sheep I bring you."

"There are other warriors to raid for me."

His face grew serious. "No," he answered and covered her mouth with his own. "Never. I will share you with our people if I must, but I will share you with no man."

She met his passion eagerly, oblivious to the cold and the sound of galloping hoofbeats. Nothing penetrated her shell of happiness until the soft morning noises in the camp changed to shrill voices raised in alarm. Then Hawk stiffened above her. She let him go reluctantly.

"What is it?" she whispered vacantly, her body still tingling, her heart still throbbing.

"A messenger," he answered from the door flap. He turned back into the hogan and snatched up his tunic and leggings, then ducked out the door.

People were beginning to howl with grief. Ice shot through her veins. She stumbled to her feet, and, clutching her sheepskin around her shoulders, rushed out the door.

A young warrior stood in the center of camp. His pony's sides heaved and froth bubbled on its coat despite the bitterness of the day. The man's face wore a deathly, disbelieving expression. Hawk stood beside him in horrible stillness. Gray Eyes ran to them and clutched Hawk's arm.

"Tell me," she gasped.

She waited to hear that he had come for her Hawk, that her husband would leave her again. He had stayed far longer now than she'd ever dared to hope. He'd stayed when she knew he longed to be fighting the men who were destroying them. Now she would have to let him go once more. She'd have to guide her people through this latest calamity while he once again flew to their defense.

She steeled herself for the blow.

"Pale-eyes," the messenger gasped. "In *'Ane'e' Tse'yi'*, the baby canyon, del Muerto. They have come, *estsa hataali*. The pale-eyes are inside!"

Gray Eyes staggered away from the crowd. Within her heart swelled a horror so hideous, so primitive, that she nearly doubled over with the pain of it. It was Hawk who came to her, Hawk who braved her grief to put his strong arms around her, Hawk who murmured soothing words in her ear.

"No, little one, no. It is not over yet. Del Muerto is not de Chelly."

She shook her head blindly. No matter, she thought, no matter. There was a tunnel, a place where they joined.

"You would give up?" he demanded.

She laughed crazily. "And what would I give? There is little left."

"We can lead our people out the other branches! We can go back to Barboncito's band."

But she only moaned in protest and slipped out of his grasp. Suddenly, terror lashed through him with snarling force.

"Give yourself up to them and I will kill you by my own hand," he vowed.

She froze, looking back at him.

"I will not lose you, little one, not like that. I would see you a *chindi* before I would see you disappear into that abyss. We know not what becomes of those the pale-eyes take. But I know what would become of you." He drove his hands into her hair. He looked down at her face, into her shimmering eyes. Oh, yes, he knew. They would use her strength for a slave, her beauty for a whore.

He dragged her close again. "Come with me, little one. We will be long gone before they arrive."

She shook her head before her eyes widened. "Hide with me!" she pleaded.

But he had not done it before, and she knew with a deep pain that he would not do it now. He might lead her to safety, but he would not hide from a fight.

"Ah," she moaned, and closed her eyes in a final surrender to the holy ones who had chosen him. "Go then, my love. Fight for the last breath of *Dinetah*. But know that I would do no less with my life than would you. I will not give myself up to the white men. I will go up the walls and squeeze my people into every cave, every crevice I can find. I will hide them as long as I am able. But if the pale-eyes find us, then know that I will die by my own hand."

She raised her chin defiantly. "I have known for a long time now that I will die here," she finished softly. "Do not fear for me, my love. I will never leave *Dinetah*, not ever again, and leaving is the only true horror."

He knew he could drag her bodily to the farthest reaches

of the high desert, to a place where the white men might not find them for moons to come. But he knew too that such an assault upon her pride and honor was unthinkable, especially now. He struggled for the last time against the chains of responsibility and medicine that bound her.

She was *estsa hataali*. Now he accepted it with pain that was sweet, with pride that was bitter. In the face of the death of a nation, each of them bowed to the destiny that had given them a life together.

"Baa' Ya'zhi'," he called softly, his voice cracking. The moment was desperate; speaking her war name this time stole not her power, but restored her strength. He said it deliberately, invoking the magic and honor bestowed upon her by Vittorio that it might save her from whatever the future held.

She shuddered once, then she reached out for him, something bright and golden shining in her hand.

He recognized it immediately. It was the *Naakaiidine'e'* coin he had given her, the talisman of his first power. It winked in the sun even as more warriors came thundering down the canyon, their lances raised in a warning of war.

"Little one," he protested. "No."

But she pushed it into his hand before he could stop her. "I may well die, my love, but you will live. Take it. I pray that it will protect you as it has always protected me."

His fingers closed around the coin. It was warm from her gall bag, vital from her power, and then, suddenly, it was all he had left.

"Triumph, my love," she said fiercely. "Carry on, for me, for those of our people who would rather die than hide." She hurried back to her hogan and grabbed her brother's ancient carbine. Before he could call out again, before he could touch her a last time, she raced up the slopes.

She dared not think of him as she huddled high up in the cliffs. She would not picture his face, his sharp black eyes, his taut, hard body, for fear that she would begin to scream out her terror and never stop. He had the *Naakai-idine'e'* coin and her soul. She clung to that, praying that they would be enough when the pale-eyes came down the canyon and into *Dinetah*'s heart.

She moaned softly and tilted her head back as far as she could to ease the ache in her throat. But there was no room to move, no room to breathe. The crevice she had found was barely as wide as a child. She had pushed Talks Often in ahead of her. Now they were squeezed together like twin babes in a womb.

"Perhaps we could turn around," Talks Often whispered. "Or go out. A breath, just a single breath of air . . ."

"No," Gray Eyes cut her off. "Not yet. Please, you must hush."

The wind moaned over the rocks above them. It sent lances of ice down into their hiding place, but no air.

"Cold," Talks Often whined after a time, but Gray Eyes ignored her. There was no help for it. They could not risk a fire, even had there been a place to put one.

She breathed deeply and evenly, waiting as the sun passed the sky. Finally, the thin sliver of light at her shoulder darkened to a hazy gray-black. Her heart began to pound painfully and hard. Now, she thought. Somewhere out there was her Hawk. She had to know if he lived, if he was in danger.

She began to inch her way along the wall. One sharp finger of rock scraped her spine, but she bit down on her lip and kept moving, one slow, shuffling step at a time. Finally, she eased her way out onto the ledge.

The wind buffeted her, and she knew immediately that she was feeling the sigh of death. The canyon was barren. There was no sign of Hawk, of any of the warriors. There were only long, black shadows as twilight fell, and a single, flickering stab of light. Gray Eyes stared at it until it sent pinpoints of pain into her brain.

"What?" Talks Often begged from behind her. "What

do you see?'' But there was no comprehensible way to describe the pale-eyes gathered around the fire, laughing, eating, guzzling from jugs. There were white men camping in Canyon de Chelly.

She hugged herself for warmth against a cold that went deeper than her bones. Then, distantly, she became aware of the sounds that burgeoned from behind her.

Talks Often had pushed out onto the ledge after her. She stood staring down at the soldiers with eyes that were glassy with shock. As Gray Eyes looked up, her aunt pushed her fist into her mouth. Her throat convulsed as she struggled for calm, for control. But it was too late, far too late. The last of her will to go on had ruptured somewhere deep inside her.

She dropped her hand from her lips and screamed. The sound rang out through the canyon, jerking the pale-eyes' heads upward, escalating over their bellows of surprise.

''No!'' Gray Eyes wailed, watching with helpless agony as others began pouring from their caves and cubbyholes as well. There was Winter Star, so old, so feeble, frowning slightly as though struggling to understand what she saw. Little Left Hand hurled rocks down upon thc soldiers, spitting curses in every tongue she had ever learned. Barren Woman clutched a repeater and struggled with its senseless machinations until it began to wildly, aimlessly belch out bullets. And sweet, gentle Sleepiness pushed Squeak and Lupine away to claw savagely for rocks of her own.

The *Dine'* women, the backbone of a mighty, fearless society, had finally snapped. And Gray Eyes knew, in that moment, that they weren't so different from their warriors after all. She watched her world fall apart, then she reached numbly for her own rock.

She heaved it downward at the upturned, stunned white faces. Then she struggled back toward the crevice where she had hidden Na'acoci's carbine. An icy smile touched her lips as she aimed it at the men below.

She hit one, two, then three of them before the white

men began to divide frantically into ranks. She was only peripherally aware of a single soldier, more collected than the rest, taking aim at her ledge. Then Talks Often screamed and staggered beside her. A fireball exploded in her chest, then she pitched forward off the ledge.

Albert Pheiffer gave a cold, satisfied smile and lowered his gun again.

"Scum! She hurt no one!" Gray Eyes screamed. She aimed her last bullet toward Pheiffer's heart, her vow to die rather than surrender forgotten in her rage and grief.

Then more soldiers spilled down from the rim above her. One man slipped and slid until he landed precariously on the ledge, and she jerked the gun back, unfired, as she spun around.

Kit Carson lost his last measure of pride in himself as he looked up into her stricken eyes. As Gray Eyes felt the loathed, treacherous hands of his *chindi* soldiers upon her, her chin came up, her eyes flashed, for a final time.

"You are unconquerable," she said softly, and he knew enough Navajo to understand her. "You are strong enough to take things that never should have been yours. But I will show you, too, what true fools you really are. You think you can have it all. No, white man, no. You can take the land, but you cannot have its people. You cannot have me."

She put the carbine to her breast and tugged on the trigger. It jammed uselessly.

She would die; she had to die! But even as she grappled with the weapon, banging it furiously with her fist, the rest of Carson's party spilled down from the rim and into the melee they had unexpectedly stumbled upon. Strong white hands fell on her gun and began to wrestle it from her grasp.

Too late, it went off. Its fireball flew over her head, ricocheting uselessly off rock. She threw her head back, gathered her voice in her throat, and summoned her hawk.

Her song rose eerie and wailing into the night air. She called for her medicine, for the power that would save her this final time. *Save me,* she prayed. *Take from me this gift you blessed and cursed me with. Snuff it out. Let me die.*

And from the rim of the canyon, an answering cry rang out.

Hawk's voice bellowed in fury. The anguish in his heart was absolute. The very fabric of his soul tore. But he raised his gun.

Her eyes flew to him, to the flash of metal in his hands, and she smiled. The final gift, the last and ultimate piece of his heart. "Thank you, my love. Always my love," she whispered. And then she closed her eyes and waited to die.

The fireball rang out. She felt its heat, its burning sparks against her cheek. There was an unearthly ringing in her ears from the percussion. She waited for the pain, wanted the pain. Instead, there was the twanging, nasal sound of another pale-eyes' voice.

"Got him, Colonel!" cried the soldier.

She opened her eyes again. And then she knew the final irony of her life. She had taunted them. She had vowed that they would not take everything. But they had. They had taken her Hawk.

The front of his tunic had darkened to red. Slowly, gracefully, he swayed and fell. She watched life drain from his beloved body, and she screamed.

As the last of the sun died, her inhuman wails of loss pounded against the blood-red canyon walls.

PART THREE

Chapter 59

So this is the abyss, Gray Eyes thought dispassionately. *This is what becomes of the defeated, the victims of pale-eyes' wars.* She sat against the knotty wooden fences of Fort Wingate as she had every day since they had brought her here a week before. Above her head, the sky was a mottled, leaden gray. The garrison spread out before her, flat, low-slung buildings fronting the parade ground; a tattered red, white, and blue flag whipped in the wind. Beneath the flag huddled a mass of moaning, wretched humanity. An odor of feces and offal hung over them.

The People were ill, very ill. Already a hundred of them had died. Proximity to the evil pale-eyes was killing them, but Gray Eyes couldn't bring herself to care. Only one thing mattered to her anymore, and that was her own death.

As she huddled in her blanket contemplating its elusiveness, a squaw scurried crablike in her direction. Her bowels erupted as she collapsed at Gray Eyes' side.

"Please," she begged, *"estsa hataali,* you must heal me."

Gray Eyes spared her a flickering glance. "I cannot," she answered hoarsely. "Find another with medicine."

The woman began to weep. "Yours is strongest. Please, I do not want to die."

"Why? You would be better off."

She began to rise. The woman clutched at her, sinking

her nails into the flesh of her arm. Panicked, Gray Eyes shook her off.

"No!" she snapped. "Leave me alone!" Turning, she shoved her way blindly into the crowd.

Hundreds of terrified eyes followed her. Without their *estsa hataali*, they truly had nothing. But Gray Eyes was unaware of them. She didn't even notice Winter Star tottering along beside her. Off in the distance, near the officers' quarters, was the blue-coats' kitchen and mess hall. Winter Star smelled the food there, and she shuffled off in that direction.

She stopped at the door and frowned up at the strange shelter, then ran a gnarled hand over its thick adobe walls. She bent to peer inside.

"This ain't for Injuns, you old red hag!"

The butt of a rifle cracked out at her, catching her in the forehead. She staggered backward, sprawling in the snow. A thin line of blood dribbled over her eye and down her creased cheek as she stared up at the door in confusion.

Gray Eyes stepped around her.

Suddenly, hard hands tangled in her hair and whirled her around again. Clutching her head, she swayed for a moment, then focused on Barren Woman's snapping black eyes.

"Do something!" the old woman spat. "Help her! Are you a coward? Did my husband choose a *ha'az'isi,* a gopher, to hide below ground when she is needed most?"

"Your husband is a *chindi!*" she hissed. "What would you have me do, old woman? Should I summon him for help? Even he couldn't save that which has already been lost!"

Barren Woman's hand came up suddenly, like a snake, and struck out at her jaw. Gray Eyes reeled backward, stunned.

"You would strike an *estsa hataali?*" she breathed.

"There is no *estsa hataali* here! There is only a little

girl who does not have the honor to go on! You grovel, little girl! You weep and mourn and give up!''

''I give nothing! It has been taken from me.''

But Barren Woman did not relent. ''You think I do not mourn him, your warrior who flew with the sun?'' she asked harshly. ''You think I do not mourn my own man, the wisest and kindest of them all? I thank the holy ones that neither of them are here to see what has become of you. No, little girl, I mourn, but I damn you, too, for not being what they believed you were. I damn you for failing us all.''

She hunched her shoulders into her blanket and stalked off. Gray Eyes stared after her, her chest heaving with anger, with pain, with defeat.

Yes, she had failed the *hataali*. And she had failed her Hawk, the harbinger of her medicine, the man who had given her the freedom to heal even when it had meant forsaking his own heart. But deep inside her, where her medicine had once been, there was only ice—and welcome—cold.

''Forgive me,'' she whispered to Hawk's *chindi*. ''Ah, love, forgive me. But I cannot go on.''

The moon brought more snow. The People burrowed into the makeshift caves they had dug in the earth in lieu of shelters, but Gray Eyes only went back to the fence. Ice crusted her hair; her teeth knocked together uncontrollably. Perhaps, she thought, this will be the end. Perhaps now I will freeze and die.

But dawn came, and although she found her limbs painfully locked and her brain dull and unfocused, she was still alive. She started to struggle to her feet to find a spot where she could relieve herself. Then Barren Woman appeared again with a tiny girl-child in tow.

Her whiskered chin jutted forward in challenge. She pushed the girl into Gray Eyes' lap.

''Hold her to your breast and tell her why she must

die," she taunted. "You in your wisdom have far more answers than I." She turned and was gone.

The girl whimpered and nestled closer to Gray Eyes for warmth. Gray Eyes moaned as she felt the ice begin to break deep inside her.

Suddenly, it all came back to her, the nightmare that the emptiness inside her had blessedly blocked out. She saw Hawk's blood-stained tunic, saw his precious life draining away. She had not been able to heal him this time. She had not been able to patch his ravaged body together in this most final, most devastating war. Her medicine, her gods, had failed her. Now she longed with fierce despair to fail them as well.

She pushed the girl away and cursed the holy ones. "You take my heart from me and tell me I must go on! You protect me from death but not from life! Damn you!" she cried aloud. "I curse this gift of medicine! You give me power then do not let me use it to save the man who was my soul!" She jumped to her feet to pound her fists against her prison walls. "No! I will not do it! I will not heal another! I will not!"

"Estsa hataali, estsa hataali," the girl pleaded, plucking at her shift. "I do not hurt so bad. Please, do not cry."

Gray Eyes collapsed to her knees again and reached for the child blindly. "I am sorry, so sorry, little one," she wept. "Of course you hurt."

She set the child away from her and brushed the hair from her cheek where it clung wetly to her tears. She truly looked at her for the first time. She could be no more than five summers. So young, she thought, such a babe, and her future was so narrow and bleak. But she knew she would heal her; she would use her wretched medicine to give her that future, because, in the end, she could do nothing else.

She stood up and pulled her gall bag free of her hip, then she collected snow and carried it back to Barren

Woman's fire. For a long moment, the eyes of the two women met.

"I need to melt this," Gray Eyes said finally.

"Then I will see it done."

"I will need your help. There are so many of them."

Barren Woman shrugged. "The old man taught me well."

Gray Eyes gave her a handful of *tle'e' yiigaa'hi,* white primrose. Soaked in the cold water, it would ease the debilitating diarrhea and afford her time to figure out how to attack the evil at its root. She began to move among the stricken people while Barren Woman concocted the brew. She made small incisions in their bellies and tried to suck the badness out from inside them. She knew instinctively that juniper would not help them this time. Their lips were cracked and dry, their bodies starved for moisture. Vomiting would only rob them of more.

She worked well into the next dawn. When her efforts failed, she jerked away instinctively before the *chindis* could rob her of the medicine she no longer wanted. When she was successful, she cleaned up feces, wiped away perspiration, and moved on.

She was hovering over a patient when a swell of shocked, pained voices rose around her. Another death, she thought, and looked up only to see more of the People at the gates, their clothing and blankets tattered, their bodies bent and ravaged by hunger and cold. She knew immediately that they had not been captured like the Lone Trees. No, it was worse, much worse. They had surrendered to the Crazy One's famine.

Delgondito stood at the head of them.

"He has turned against us," Barren Woman spoke harshly at her side. "I had heard this, though I could not believe it. They say he has gone all through *Dinetah,* gathering our people, bringing them to *hual-tes* like this one."

Hawk would have known. He hadn't told her. In some small measure he had protected her to the end. Grief swept through Gray Eyes with fresh force. This time she would have let him shield her, but he was gone and she had only the icy wind to comfort her. She turned into it, her hair whipping behind her, as she crossed the vast compound and stopped by Delgondito's side.

"Traitor!" she spat. "Snake! May your *chindi* soul rot in the grass with the carcasses of your brothers! You who I trusted, you who I loved, you . . ." But she could not go on.

She fell into his arms. He held her close against his thick chest, but this time it was not she who cried.

With Delgondito's refugees, the Navajo population at Fort Wingate swelled to nearly eight hundred. The smell grew worse, burgeoning now to include the stench of corpses that couldn't be buried fast enough. The soldiers could scarcely eat for the odor. They could barely walk for stumbling over an Indian. Rations were running low. The blue-coats sent a desperate message to Albuquerque, begging for further orders.

On the third night of the pale-eyes' February, General Carleton sent word that there was little he could do about the rations; the war in the east was bleeding the Union's supplies dry. It was time, he decided, to begin moving the captives to Bosque Redondo where they could learn to fend for themselves.

The soldiers responded by swarming through the People's camps at dawn, jostling them awake. When a boot connected squarely with Gray Eyes' shin, she yelped and reacted instinctively, wrapping herself around the offending leg with all the strength her starved, cold body could muster. The soldier toppled with a bellow of surprise, discharging his gun into the hand of another pale-eyes nearby.

Pandemonium broke loose. Gray Eyes lunged to her feet, her body poised and ready for a fight. "Touch me again, white dog, and you will die this time," she spat.

The soldier met her gaze and slowly backed off.

"An accident! It was an accident," he called out to the crowd of soldiers who were fast approaching. Then he found the man he knew as Delgonado.

"Christ! Who is that little hellcat?" he breathed.

"She is a shaman, a medicine woman," Delgondito answered in gestures and broken English. "She is very powerful. You would do well to avoid her."

"She's just a kid!" But the white man's heart still thrummed from the horrible look in her eyes, and somehow, that damned bullet had ended up in Jenkins. "Who is she?" he asked.

Delgondito sent him a beleaguered, weary look. Would these men never remember that it was rude to ask a person's name? *'Dje' Nazba'*, Her Heart Went to War," he lied. "You killed her husband, white man. Now you will know what it is to be hated. Perhaps, if you are lucky, you will survive."

Spooked, the soldier moved off abruptly. Delgondito watched him go, then went to help his people gather up their pitiful possessions and prepare for their Long Walk.

Gray Eyes found herself prodded along toward the gate while Winter Star, Little Left Hand, Sleepiness, and her children remained behind. Carleton wanted families and bands broken apart. If they remained together, there was an excellent chance that they would use the last of their strength to revolt.

Gray Eyes went without protest because she was quickly learning to hoard her emotions. Hatred and cunning took a great deal of energy, she had found. She had little left over to spare on grief and pain. She did not look back at the Lone Trees a last time. Instead, when a soldier hefted the butt of his rifle to herd her along, she gathered herself to stare him down. Like the man who had dared to kick her, this blue-coat lowered his weapon and backed down.

Then, as quickly as she turned her back on the pale-eyes, her fire vanished. She joined Delgondito near the front of the line.

"So," she asked dully, "are you to go with us into exile, or will you stay to lead others to their extinction?"

Delgondito's shoulders slumped. As a bugle sounded, he began to walk. "I will go," he answered. "What else can I do? They have taken my horses, my weapons. They know there is nothing more I can do here. I have already talked to every headman I know. The decision is theirs now."

She gave a cold laugh. "A decision between dying and dying. Yes, I can see where that would take time."

"Ah, that is where you are wrong. Such a choice would be easy. It is surviving that takes courage, and that is what I have asked them to do."

"You do not need to explain to me," she muttered.

He smiled sadly. "I think I do. You are one of our last great healers. I have told our people that these *hual-tes* are safe places, but I cannot lie to you. This Bosque where we are going is a place for *chindis*. I have been there two seasons and have seen nothing grow. The winds are incessant, the bugs are bad, and the water is sour."

Her eyes narrowed. "Why then? Why lure us there?"

"You know the answer to that, *estsa hataali*, or you would not be healing those who would be far happier in the afterworld. At the *hual-tes*, we die only as individuals. If we remain in *Dinetah*, if we try to fight the pale-eyes, we will die as a tribe."

Suddenly, in the eyes of her dear old friend, a naked pain bloomed. And finally, fully, she knew that it was both over and just beginning. *Dinetah* and life as she had known it were gone. The land, the blood-red mountains, the scraggly grama grass plains filled with sheep, all were past. But in that moment of intolerable understanding, she found her final renewal.

Even if it required the surrender of their land, the People would stay together. They would continue to procreate; somehow, those that remained would grow strong again.

"I forgive you, old friend," she murmured. "And I think our *hataali* would have done so as well. He always said the white man could not be beaten. Now we will see if the same holds true for us."

Chapter 60

▼ ▼ ▼ ▼ ▼ ▼ ▼ ▼ ▼ ▼

They stopped the first night at a place the People knew as *Tohithle'e'n*. There was a creek there and the water was fresh beneath the ice. They fell to it despite the aching cold, swabbing their faces, their necks, beneath their shifts and leggings. They started fires and divided the pale-eyes rations. As always, the squaws frowned over the hard black beans and the white powder that they had first encountered at Ration Day a long nightmare ago.

"Bah! They would poison us." Barren Woman spat into the snow in disgust. She had not been selected to go with this first group to Bosque Redondo. The soldiers had seen her fraternizing with the shaman, and they wanted to keep that wildcat as far away from her followers as possible. But as her husband could have warned them, Barren Woman was not one to be easily dissuaded. She had marched stubbornly along, fists flailing, legs kicking when they had tried to stop her and turn her back to the fort. She was old, fat, and ugly, and the blue-coats had finally decided that she would not make much of a difference in the overall scheme of things. They had let her go, and now she sat beside Delgondito and Gray Eyes on a rotted juniper log.

The water she had boiled her beans in had long since turned black. She fished them out, tossed the water aside, collected more from the ravine, and tried again. But the next time she put one to her teeth, it still wouldn't crack.

"You should try the powder," Delgondito suggested.

412

"That is mostly what my women at the Bosque have been eating."

Barren Woman looked at him accusingly. A man who could turn against his own kind was a mystery to her, and therefore not to be trusted. She looked to Gray Eyes for her opinion instead.

But Gray Eyes only stared across the fire, her eyes thoughtful. On the far side of the camp were a handful of the pale-eyes who had been charged with escorting them to the new *hual-te*. They ate and drank, chugging from flasks and mugs.

Finally, she pushed to her feet and crept closer to them. Like a silent shadow, she hunkered down behind a copse of cottonwoods to eavesdrop on them.

"How many dropped today?" one of the men asked idly as he lit tobacco. Gray Eyes frowned, then silently, carefully mouthed the words after him to learn the feel of them on her tongue.

"Who cares? If we show up with a few less than we started with, I don't reckon Uncle Sam's gonna know the difference." There was coarse laughter.

"Yeah, but what I don't get is how come they're swelling up with the dysentery." A white *Naakaiidine'e'* scout puffed up his belly in a grotesque imitation of the People's distended guts, and Gray Eyes' gaze sharpened. "Ain't it something you get from what you eat?"

"Hell, I seen some of those old biddies eating gopher parts. It's no wonder they got the shits."

"Well, I don't want no dysentery," the man griped and lifted his flask to his lips.

There was more talk and some good-natured ribbing. Gray Eyes straightened and melted back into the night.

"Dissen-teree," she whispered aloud. It wasn't much, but she knew that the blue-coats didn't have the swollen bellies that the white man had imitated. Nor did they eat the strange black beans. She had watched one pale-eyes grind them down into dust.

* * *

She went back to the pale-eyes camp the next night, as soon as the shadows were deep enough to hide her. The cold wind buffeted her; the smell of food from their cook fire made her drool. She licked her lips, squatted down behind a boulder for warmth, and waited. She would learn the secrets of surviving in their world.

She watched, absorbed, as they tossed a slab of their fatty meat into a flat metal pan not much different from the squaws' *Naakaiidine'e'* cooking pots. The People had been using sharp stones to cut away the fat and the grainy white substance that coated it. They were left with scarcely anything to cook, but the coyotes had eaten well off the scraps. Now she saw that the white men cooked the slabs in their entirety. They ate all of it, and they did not have dissen-teree.

Thoughtfully, she settled back again into the lee of her rock. Then, from the corner of her eye, she saw movement. The dubious merits of bacon fled from her mind.

She dropped her blanket with a single twitch of her shoulders and without taking her eyes from her quarry, snaked out a hand and picked up a rock. The baby pronghorn stepped closer to the copse, nose twitching, ears alert. Then a pale-eyes hooted in laughter, and the animal bolted.

It took off toward the other end of the camp, along its outskirts. Gray Eyes leaped from the cottonwoods and hurled herself across the pale-eyes' fire. If she went straight across, she could intercept the tiny buck.

Behind her, men bellowed. She ignored them. Then she heard the first fireball.

It went wide, smashing into the spines of a joshua tree. She hesitated, confused. The buck was hers, hers! But the pale-eyes swarmed down on her, dragging her back toward their camp.

Then, suddenly, she understood. "Fools!" she hissed, and they dropped back. "Would you rather kill all of us with your bowel disease and starvation than see one of us run off? There is food out there, food! Stupid, white-skinned hyenas!"

She whirled away. No one understood her, but no one tried to follow her. The tales circulating about the powers of Her Heart Went to War were eerily confirmed by her wild, streaming hair and the murderous rage in her eyes.

Gray Eyes ran on through the night. Her heart pumped so hard she was sure the pronghorn would hear it. But when she stopped near a ravine, she found him calmly stepping up to the water. She hefted her rock and pitched it at his crown. He swayed gently and fell. Gray Eyes removed her shift quickly, bound it around him in a sling, and dragged him off before he could awake again.

Just shy of the camp, she stopped. She had no sooner settled the thin shift over her shoulders again than the white men returned. One, whiskey-brave, moved up to take her prize. She screamed and swiped at him.

"He will feed all of us, or he will feed none of us!"

The man retreated as far as the trees, nursing the spot on his cheek where she had drawn blood. He looked accusingly at his comrades, but no one seemed about to chastise her for her insubordination. They only watched, chagrined and confused, as she took a belt from a squaw and tied the young buck, alive and unharmed, to a tree.

She stood back. The buck awakened and began bleating. Within moments, a horde of larger, more meaty antelope approached, lured by his cries.

Barren Woman slipped stealthily to Gray Eyes' side. "It is good that you are back with us, my husband's granddaughter," she whispered. "The white men do not fear a dead woman, only one who is powerful enough to harm them." She pulled out the hunting knife she had managed to secrete against her thigh.

In the end, they took four, including the babe. The mouthwatering aroma of roasting meat soon lingered in the air; coffee and bacon and flour were heaped in the dirt, discarded.

It was late and the moon was high when Gray Eyes finally sat back, her stomach so full she felt vaguely nauseous. She wiped the grease off her hands in the grass, then looked up to find the pale-eyes officer's eyes upon her.

Cold hatred replaced the roiling in her gut. She got to her feet and reached for the baby antelope's thin and bony carcass and walked straight into the pale-eyes' camp. She stared the officer rudely, arrogantly, in the eye.

"This is what you would have been satisfied with," she said quietly. "Now I return it to you to pick from it what you can."

He did not understand her words, but he could decipher her gesture as she dropped the carcass at his feet. For the first time since she had lost her Hawk, Gray Eyes smiled. He had been right.

Revenge was good.

They rose early the next day, trekking east in moccasins that were already beginning to wear thin. The pale-eyes had brought five mules. Two carried packs; the other three pulled carts. But only the very old and the very ill rode in them. The rest of the People walked and were more than willing to stop for a brief rest at midday.

They had reached the Laguna River. There, beside the frigid water, the pale-eyes distributed their rations once again. This time, Gray Eyes moved up cautiously to the pack mules with the others. She took her share of the beans and the meat, then went back to her fire.

She had no cooking pot; the pale-eyes had not allowed her to take any of her possessions out of the canyon. She suspended the meat over the flames instead, but it was too fatty to cook that way. The coals began to sizzle and belch up great clouds of smoke. She yanked the meat away again and tried to eat it. But while the outside was charred, the inside was stringy and raw. Gagging, she spit it out, then turned to the beans.

As Barren Woman and Delgondito looked on curiously, she laid them out on a long slab of rock. "I have found out how to eat them," she explained. Picking up a stone, she banged away at them until they were pulverized.

"You thought you had found out about the meat," Barren Woman reminded her darkly.

Gray Eyes ignored her. Gingerly, she reached for a pinch of the coffee and put it in her mouth.

The sharp, bitter taste made her retch. Delgondito frowned; he, too, had put a tiny bit of the coffee to his lips, but while it had tasted unpleasant, he had suffered nowhere near the reaction Gray Eyes had.

He looked at Barren Woman worriedly. "Is she getting the bowel sickness?"

But Barren Woman shook her head. Her eyes began to glitter knowingly. "It is only that she has just now started to eat again. *Estsa hataali, naat'a'anii,* medicine women, headmen, they are the wisest and yet the dumbest of them all," she muttered. She lumbered up to Gray Eyes and squatted down beside her, using a corner of her blanket to wipe the sweat off her face.

"You traitor, bring me water!" she called back to Delgondito. "When he returns, you will drink your own primrose," she scolded Gray Eyes. "It will ease your belly and it will not harm the babe."

Gray Eyes looked blankly between her and the beans. "Babe?" she echoed.

Realization brought a fear so violent, a joy so intense that she swayed and would have toppled if Barren Woman hadn't caught her. A babe. Hawk's babe. He had been with her nearly a whole moon before she had lost him. And not once in the agony that had followed had she bled.

A low, keening sound slipped from her throat. The holy ones had badgered her, had tormented her and used her. For the sake of her people, they had kept her alive. Now, for the sake of her soul, they had given her a reason to keep living.

One small, tenacious piece of her glorious Hawk still survived.

Chapter 61

While Gray Eyes vowed that his babe would survive the pale-eyes this time, the warrior whose seed she so cherished leaned heavily against his stallion's neck. His face was pale and beaded with perspiration despite February's fierce cold, and his right arm hung at a useless, unnatural angle at his side.

His pride warring within him, he looked around at Jackrabbit and spoke the words he was so loathe to say. "Brother, I will need a leg up."

"You need a healer." Jackrabbit scowled, torn between admiration and dismay.

"No, I need *one* healer."

Jackrabbit cursed. He couldn't understand the consuming emotion that drove his friend. He had had women, many of them, and he understood love and lust. Still, he knew that he would not travel wounded into enemy territory for either of them.

"I say we wait," he suggested. "Let this war calm down. We are reasonably safe here so far from the pale-eyes' raiding grounds. In the spring, when you are healthy again, I will go with you to find her."

Hawk didn't answer. With a violent effort, he grasped his stallion's mane and heaved himself up with his left hand.

Jackrabbit's temper snapped. "For the love of the holy ones, look around you!" he shouted. Their Monument Valley camp was scattered with the few women who had survived the canyon raid and the men who had gotten there

418

too late to make a difference. Some had followed Hawk all along. Others had crawled to him with their last hopes of surviving the pale-eyes.

"They have come to you in times of strife and times of peace," Jackrabbit went on. "They depend on your courage and wisdom. Would you abandon them now in the name of one who is most probably gone? I miss her, too. She was beloved of all of us. But we must think twice before we forsake the others!"

"I forsake no one. I leave them to you and Achi'i'h."

"We do not have your medicine!"

"Be glad of that, brother. Mine was so sour it could not protect the one who was my very soul." Hawk gathered up his reins. "Listen well," he went on, his eyes bright with an inner fire. "Through all the seasons I have loved her, I have put my people first. I gave them the best of me, but she gave me the best of myself. Carry on for me, brother. I tell you that I will not rest, I will not fight again, until I find her."

He jerked his stallion around and galloped off. Jackrabbit stared after him, then whistled sharply for his own pony. Mounting, he sought out Achi'i'h.

"I cannot let him go alone," he explained grimly. "We need him. If he needs her, then there is no help for it."

Achi'i'h nodded. "Look for the gentle one who has my babes," he asked.

"I think we will, if it takes until next winter's snows."

They rode hard for three nights. More often than not, Jackrabbit trailed behind, ready to catch Hawk when the terrible extent of his brother's wounds finally caught up with him. He had been the one to find him that night nearly a moon ago. Battling Kit Carson's tardy regiment on the rim of the canyon, he had heard Gray Eyes' unearthly wails. He knew only one woman who would grieve that way—for only one man.

He'd found Hawk's still form sprawled on a narrow ledge. Further down, Pheiffer's soldiers had desecrated the

People's camps. Above him, the battle raged. He'd dragged Hawk onto his pony and charged through it, but he had not been able to save Gray Eyes.

The last he had seen of her she had been lashed over the rump of a pale-eyes' horse. Still she had struggled and screamed until a soldier had knocked her out. Now, as he stared down at the pale murkiness of Fort Wingate from the surrounding cliffs, Jackrabbit wondered if she had made it this far.

Heuro had learned that everyone who had been captured that day had been brought here. But although it was dawn and the People were beginning to mill about, Jackrabbit did not see his cousin. He wondered if she had been given to the Ute or *Naakaiidine'e'* guides, or if she had killed herself rather than be traded as a whore. He looked at his friend to learn what he would do now.

"I am going down," Hawk said. His voice sent a chill down Jackrabbit's spine.

"Think twice," he begged. "If she is here and we wait long enough, we will see her. Then we can gather more men and perhaps launch an attack. If she is not, then the pale-eyes will not tell us where she has gone. We have nothing to gain by going in there."

But Hawk was implacable. "The pale-eyes will tell me nothing," he agreed. "But our people will."

He dropped laboriously off his pony. Before Jackrabbit could respond, he scrambled over the cliff's edge, down into a narrow clearing between the blockade fence and the rocky wall.

The compound was relatively quiet. He guessed that the pale-eyes were still sleeping. He hauled himself up the fence again and paused there, ignoring the vast, gnawing ache in his mangled arm. Then he dropped down onto the garrison floor.

There would be sentinels at the gates, even at this inceptive hour, he thought. As though to prove his point, a bugle sounded reveille somewhere close by. The pale-eyes were awakening, then. It didn't matter. They would not be suspicious of one more maimed and battered warrior.

His head bent defeatedly, his shoulders deliberately hunched, he moved into the People's camps until he came to a squaw who was sitting alone. He crouched beside her.

"I would ask you a question."

"Then speak, warrior, although I doubt there is anything I can tell you."

"Have the pale-eyes taken anyone away from this place?"

She seemed confused that he wouldn't know such a thing, then finally shrugged. "Three times this moon they have stolen our babes and our men."

Hawk's pulse punched hard at his nerves. "Where do they take them?"

"To the Crazy One's Bosque, or so they say." She gave an ugly bark of laughter.

"Do they take women there? Do they go to the same place or are they sold?"

"Women have gone."

"A medicine woman? Has one left here?"

Suddenly, the blank look on the squaw's face sharpened. "A woman with medicine left with the first group," she remembered. "I did not ever seek her services, but I know the pale-eyes feared her and wanted her gone as soon as possible."

A treacherous hope wound through Hawk's limbs. "When?" he demanded harshly. "When did she go?"

The squaw thought about it hard. "The moon, I think, was in its first quarter. Find her," she added fiercely. "And beg her to use her magic to kill them all."

She clamped her mouth shut again as a group of bluecoats came around the corner of the nearest building. Hawk nodded briefly. He was beyond caution now. Adrenaline gave him the strength to battle pain. He made an obscene motion toward the first soldier, then scaled the wall again quickly and fled to safety even as commotion erupted behind him.

Somewhere to the east, his people trudged on toward the Bosque. Somewhere out there he would find his little one.

The moon grew pregnant and swollen then waned. Hawk and Jackrabbit rode recklessly along the endless lines of moccasin tracks. Sometimes they found blood in the snow, limning the outline of stumbling feet. More often they found the shallow graves of the ones who could no longer walk at all.

They spotted a group the following dawn. It was made up predominantly of old men. Once many of them would have been revered for their wisdom, but now they were herded along ignominiously like sheep. Hawk felt rage boil up inside him. His hand went instinctively to the rifle lashed across his back.

"You cannot, brother," Jackrabbit warned. The intensity of his friend's emotions had left him as weary as though he had fought five pale-eyes wars. "Think of your woman." And so they left the hoary group of survivors, never knowing that they had not come from Wingate, but had surrendered themselves to Kit Carson at Fort Canby instead.

No more than three suns passed before they encountered the next band. Like the first, this contained precious few women and all of them were aged, stooped, tired. Little Left Hand was among them.

"They are all so far past their youth that no Ute or pale-eyes would want them," Hawk muttered.

"That is true." Jackrabbit dared not say more.

Hawk's jaw hardened. "We will ride on."

Before night fell, they were alerted to a third group by the sound of babes wailing. Pulses racing, they left their mounts to creep closer. This party was made up largely of young mothers. At the end of the line, Sleepiness clutched Lupine to her breasts.

Squeak was nowhere to be seen. Jackrabbit felt the last

of his hope drain out of him. It would seem that the pale-eyes were indeed selling off some of the better specimens.

"At least she is still alive." Hawk spoke quietly. "If she makes it to this Bosque, perhaps we could come back for her later." But his voice was grim. Sleepiness was young and comely. He did not think she would make it that far.

Jackrabbit nodded, then forced another observation. "This makes three bands. That is all the squaw said the pale-eyes took." He hesitated. "Your woman has not been with any of them."

Hawk greeted his words with stony silence. But behind his chiseled face, Jackrabbit saw the anguish.

"My heart bleeds for you, brother," he went on, "but we must go back. There is nothing more we can do."

"No."

But the word was not an agreement. Before Jackrabbit could respond, Hawk turned and began riding again hard. When they came upon Isleta Pueblo, sprawled along the Rio Grande, Jackrabbit finally reined in.

This was civilization. The Isletas were Indians, but this was a white man's town. The influence of the old *Naakai-idine'e'* was strong, in the vast adobe mission church with its cross reaching up to the sun, in the oval lumps of ovens set beside each pueblo complex. Jackrabbit's blood ran cold. This was not something he had ever wanted to see.

"No more," he grated harshly. "It is over. She is lost. I am going back."

He looked at Hawk. The sun angled down between thick, woolly clouds and shone on his friend's strong features. Defeat was etched there so starkly he felt his own throat ache at the sight of it.

It was a long time before Hawk spoke. "With the next sun. We will camp tonight. Give me that much."

It was as close as he would come to speaking of the pain in his heart. Jackrabbit accepted it. "On the other side of the water," he agreed. "I do not care to be close to this place."

The Rio Grande was low but rising with the runoff of mountain snows. They waded their ponies across, far from intrusive Isleta eyes. There they camped beside a wild array of scrub on the banks. There was firewood, water, and an aching, empty silence as the day faded and the moon rose.

It was near dawn when Hawk left their fire and moved into the darkness he had been taught since birth to fear. But no *chindi,* no wolf-man, could do worse to him than the white man now had. He slipped into the night's inky embrace and remembered his own wolf-man, the wild, defiant girl-child who had become his wife.

He saw her long legs pumping, her black hair streaming as she had tried to outrun his pony on that dawn six years ago. He remembered the way she had writhed in his lap and clawed at his face. How hard he had fought the seductive lure of her innocence! How long before he had known, finally and fully, that he was hers. He remembered telling his uncle that he would not marry her, only to have her storm out of Barren Woman's hogan like an angry hornet. He grimaced, then laughed, until finally the pain became too great.

"Ah, little one," he whispered, "now that I want you more than life itself, I have lost you." Then he dropped his chin against his chest and wept.

It was past daybreak when he got to his feet again. As he walked back toward the camp, he nudged a shiny golden coin from his gall bag. He knelt beside a scraggly bunch of weed he had noticed earlier by the river and carefully, without disturbing its roots, he dug beneath it. He slipped the *Naakaiidine'e'* coin into the earth.

So well did he know his little one. Never would she pass here without noticing and uprooting this precious piece of wild buckwheat. If she somehow lived, if she had not been traded to the Utes or the pale-eyes, she would find his gift if she passed this way.

But in his soul, he did not believe she would. He patted the earth solid above the coin and stood away from it, knowing it would wait for her forever, for he had no need of it anymore. He vowed that he would raid the Ute camps for her and search every pale-eyes settlement. But he needed no protection from those enemies because his fierce warrior's heart had already died.

Chapter 62

▼ ▼ ▼ ▼ ▼ ▼ ▼ ▼ ▼

As Gray Eyes' party trudged along the southern route through New Mexico, the one their commander had arbitrarily taken, she heard a rumbling in the distance that she found impossible to identify. It sounded like thunder, only it was constant, like a war band galloping, but there were no war cries. She slowed her cracked, bleeding feet to walk at Delgondito's side.

"What is it?" She spoke in an undertone. She had learned that the soldiers were especially wary of her when she whispered to her friends, and she enjoyed tormenting them.

"A large body of water," Delgondito explained. "The *Naakaiidine'e'* call it their Rio Grande."

She nodded thoughtfully. "How do you know of it? Have you raided here?"

"Only once. But I have also crossed it returning from the Bosque."

Crossed it. Her heart skipped a beat. The roar of its water sounded ferocious.

"Tell me more about it," she requested tightly.

"This place we are going to, the Isleta Pueblo, is the best place to cross the river. Several trails converge here."

"So it *is* possible to get through it?"

"Sometimes," Delgondito answered laconically.

They moved along together, forcing one foot in front of the other, as the weak sun climbed. At midday, they came upon Isleta. Gray Eyes stopped and stared. Deep within her chest, her heart fluttered like that of a terrified baby bird.

The pueblo was teeming, seething. Indian and *Naakai-idine'e'* faces appeared in doors, in alleys, in windows. They jeered and heckled and shouted what passed for obscenities in any tongue. They hurled rotten vegetables from the protection of their shadows.

"You will drown! You see the fearsome river? It will swallow you!" someone shouted, and then an overripe tomato exploded at Gray Eyes' feet. Globs of its fetid red meat clung to her knees, her shins, the last frayed shreds of her moccasins. A thin, cold smile touched her lips.

"As you will die, cowards," she said reasonably. "Manuelito and Barboncito still roam free. We look conquered. We are not. We will return, and then you will laugh no more. You are right to enjoy yourselves now."

There was a lull as the crowd regarded the venom in her eyes. The People used the moment to take their lead from their *estsa hataali*. They stared back at their enemies haughtily, with all the pride of their free ancestors.

They passed through the village streets as though they owned them. Then they saw the water.

A child squealed and jumped back behind her mother. A woman moaned softly in fright. The river roared along its banks, wild and full, hurling spray upward in a violent dance. Whitecaps whirled along its muddy yellow surface, so different from *Dinetah*'s calm, trickling ravines. None of the People had ever seen such a thing before, and it did what all the Isletas had failed to accomplish. It subdued and terrified them.

Gray Eyes stepped among them, her jaw grim. "You think it cannot be crossed?" she challenged them. "If that is so, then how did these *chindi* scabs come to be in our land? They came from the place of the sun, *the sun!* That means they came to us across this thing! Are we weaker than they are that we cannot do the same?"

There was an agonized murmur as they realized that she

meant them to ford it. People looked at the pale-eyes, then back at the water. Gray Eyes spun toward Delgondito.

"Make the white men go first," she hissed. "You can communicate with them. Make them show us how it is done."

He shook his head, pained. "It cannot be done, not easily, not when it is like this."

"So you would give up?" Chagrined, he looked away from her. "You tell me that if we stay together, we will survive," she charged. "Do you think that if we refuse to cross, they will shrug and let us go back home?" She laughed harshly. "No, my friend, they will make us cross, but they will not care if some of us fail to make it. They will not chase after us if this water sweeps us away. If we go docilely, without understanding how it is done, then we will be dashed like sage on a wind and *Dinetah* will truly be over."

Delgondito hesitated. Then he moved, slope-shouldered, to talk to the pale-eyes.

They began to murmur impatiently among themselves. They are not so stupid after all, Gray Eyes mused. She had already determined that when they were all caught up in the river, she would take her people and hide. But the pale-eyes left two armed men behind, and soon they were prodding women and children with their weapons, pushing them toward the banks. Gray Eyes dug her heels in stubbornly, quelling them with a glance. She held her people back and watched, her eyes narrowed, as the other pale-eyes began to mount their horses again.

First one then another waded hock-deep into the swirling water. Magically, the ponies sank then were buoyed up again. The reaction among the People was slow, scattered. But they all surmised the same thing their *estsa hataali* did. The ponies were obviously blessed by the holy ones who were in charge of rivers. Unfortunately, ponies were few and very much in demand.

Barren Woman settled for the next best thing. She climbed aboard a wagon pulled by one of the mules. Then mothers began to drag their children forward to hang onto the sides. Gray Eyes and Delgondito moved up to the last cart, gripping it tenaciously as it pitched through the tangled cottonwoods and slid down the bank.

The water was icy as it rushed around her burning feet. Then it began climbing higher and higher. There was a lurch and someone gave a short, aborted squeal as the water rose beneath the wagon and lifted it afloat. The current surged, the mule struggled, and the cart wagged like the tail of a lethargic dog.

"We will not die," Gray Eyes whispered fiercely to the fledgling life inside her. "We will not die."

Halfway across, she heard a shrill scream. Digging her fingers into the wood hard enough to draw blood, she craned her neck to see what was happening. One of the wagons ahead of them was floundering. There were too many people in it; the mule pulled too much weight. It was dragging him and his magic down.

"No," she moaned in horror. But it was too late. The mule began to rotate slowly. She saw his nostrils flare, then vanish, and then there were only his hooves, flailing above the churning water. The cart listed, then upended, its passengers spilling out.

The second wagon began to tilt a moment later. Even as Gray Eyes shook her head in mute, helpless denial, a babe plunged wildly past her on the current.

"There is nothing you can do!" Delgondito shouted.

The pale-eyes had fooled them yet again. But she was not as stupid as they thought. She knew that her own wagon was the heaviest of all. It simply hadn't caught a current yet. When it did, that force, that energy, would kill them all.

Unless she left it. If she made it lighter, perhaps the others might survive, she thought. She knew nothing of swimming, but she saw heads and mouths catch the surface and gulp instinctively for breath. She could do that as well. Mindlessly, she let go. She heard Delgondito shout again, heard Barren Woman wail, and then she went under.

She gulped for air too late; great swallows of water choked her instead. The river's force pummeled her and tumbled her until the world became a spinning maelstrom of sky and foam. Her strength began to ebb. Then she was lifted up again, and she saw the babe once more. His blanket was whipping wildly on the froth. She screamed with the breath she had thought never to find again and lunged against the tide.

She caught his leg and drew him fiercely back to her chest even as she saw one of the pale-eyes ponies churning toward her. Its rider was hanging hard on its neck and even so disappeared from view. She threw out her hand a final time and her fingers closed around the thin hairs of the animal's tail. She tangled her fingers into it and held on.

The babe squalled even as the pale-eyes rider felt the drag on his mount. He looked down at them with the dawning knowledge of his own death in his eyes. He leveled his gun on her.

She would die. She knew that, but she felt no fear, only a blessed warmth as she thought of taking her unborn babe and rejoining their Hawk. But she would die as she had lived, and so with a last gurgling effort, she held another woman's babe high.

"Take him, white man, or kill him," she gasped. "I will go, but first I will see what kind of men you really are."

He hesitated for an eternity. She felt her grip on the pony's tail loosen. Then, finally, he reached down and grabbed the child.

The current wrenched her free of his mount at the same time. There was a surge of weight in the water, different from the current. The pony had found purchase on the bank and kicked out to hurl himself onto it. His hoof caught her in the gut, and as the blow doubled her over, she slipped gratefully beneath the water.

* * *

She awoke to pain. Her belly heaved with it; her chest ached from it. The water, she remembered. Then she groaned in protest and instead of the immediate roar of the river, she heard the impossible sound of her own voice.

She opened her eyes. She had been tossed up on the bank. Her body shivered uncontrollably against the biting, sodden wet of her shift, but she was alive. Barren Woman gripped her shoulders, shaking her, and another squaw bent over her, mouthing a jumble of gratitude as she clutched the babe Gray Eyes had saved.

Gray Eyes gagged and vomited. Great streams of yellow-brown water heaved up from her gut.

"Stupid girl," Barren Woman muttered. "If I had not fought the soldiers and come with you, you would be long dead by now! Vomit! Go on, vomit! But do it on your side so that you do not choke on your own life!" She rolled her over, pushing her face into the dirt as her stomach clenched again.

Finally, Gray Eyes managed a thin, watery smile. For all Barren Woman's fierceness, the old woman's voice had trembled.

"I am all right," she assured her. And then, like a cold rush of the water, she thought of her babe. The pale-eyes' pony had kicked it.

She scrambled wildly to her feet, knocking both Barren Woman and the squaw onto their rumps. She defied decorum to yank her shift up to her waist. Her gut still throbbed. A livid red print showed beneath her navel. But there was no blood on the ground, nothing on her legs. Hawk's child had survived.

She closed her eyes and collapsed weakly. Barren Woman's voice penetrated her daze of relief.

"Bah! Do you think I would not have told you if it was gone?"

"I have lost them for less," she muttered wearily.

"Not this time, silly one. You must not, not now."

Grunting, the old woman got to her feet again. The

squaw tucked her babe beneath one arm and helped Gray Eyes to struggle to her feet as well. They were far upstream from the others who had survived. They began to trudge in that direction.

The land was barren, alien, littered with dry, useless grasses. Gray Eyes' gaze skimmed it listlessly as she walked. Then she passed a scraggly tuft of dingy grass.

Her eyes widened and her head whipped back in that direction. A wild, exultant cry slipped from her lips. Buckwheat. Wild buckwheat! Had she not been swept so far down the river, she never would have found it. *Le'aze'*, a gift from the holy ones, growing so far from home . . . medicine, just when her own precious store from *Dinetah* was running low.

She half-stumbled, half-ran toward the deceptively dirty-looking weed and dropped to her knees beside it. She ignored the soft, sturdy moccasin prints around it. Greedily, gratefully, she plucked its leaves and stuffed them into her gall bag. When the stalk was bare, she wrapped her fist around it to tug the roots up. Then, slowly, her hand relaxed again.

Her heart clamored to take the whole thing. She would need it, oh, how she would need it in this alien, frightful land! But hundreds more people would be leaving the *hualte* and coming this way. Their healers would need it as well. If she left it, it would continue to grow, producing more and more medicine before the others came.

With shuddering willpower, she smoothed the strangely unsettled earth beneath it. Then she turned her back on it and walked away.

Chapter 63

▼▼▼▼▼▼▼▼▼▼

The first band of Navajo arrived at Bosque Redondo at dusk. Rush Michaels moved up to the gates to meet them.

Indians were no longer a distressing novelty to him. He'd spent weeks now with the Mescalero who were imprisoned on the far side of the Pecos River. A large group of *Dine'' Ana'i* had already come in as well. They were a shifty, subservient lot who pleased the soldiers because they dressed and behaved as though they were more white than red. To Michaels' surprise, he felt nothing but disdain for them. He was far more sympathetic toward the party that was arriving now. These were the ones who had been captured in the canyon and taken to Fort Wingate. They had neither surrendered nor bowed to the men who coveted their land. Michaels saw their fear, but even in its grip, they managed arrogance.

As they were led past the fences of Fort Sumner, the women pulled their blankets over their heads as though to shut the pale-eyes out. Even the children studied him with an eldritch mixture of curiosity and contempt. The men, most likely the same warriors who had once tried to kill him at Fort Defiance, stared through the commotion as though it were all beneath them.

Michaels found himself nodding with grudging approval.

Perhaps if he'd stayed on the front line, he would have been able to maintain his animosity toward the Indians. Instead, when Carleton's narrow-minded, near-crazed missives had raised doubts about his conceptions of humanity, his country, and his God, he'd denounced the army and rebelled against his commander. In the end, he'd been charged with insubordination and relegated to Fort Sumner.

Now he stood in the midst of the captives. They were all inside now, and it was chaos. The soldiers charged with organizing them were of considerably less intelligence than the sutler's dog.

Muttering an oath, Michaels moved over and snapped the clipboard from the hands of the boy nearest him. "Let's put them in a line, Private. Then we can dispense ration slips, count them, and disperse them, all in neat, orderly fashion."

The boy blinked at the ingenuity of the scheme and set out to put it into motion. But all he got for his efforts were hostile, suspicious glares. The women drew further beneath their blankets when he spoke and gestured at them; the men simply ignored him. Frustrated, he discharged his bayonet from his rifle and used it to poke at them.

There were screams and hisses and weeping, but slowly the Navajo began to form themselves into a line. Michaels counted, making small marks on the clipboard as each Indian ducked past him, swearing again and again as he counted one body, only to find bright black eyes peering out at him from within the folds of a squaw's blanket. He scribbled and scratched and started over again until he finally looked up into a pair of silver eyes and felt his heart stop.

Heat stained his face, but he was unable to drag his eyes away. She was far more beautiful than he remembered. He had known her for only an instant, in the heat of battle where death stripped all but the most intense impressions away. Now he saw other things: the haughty tilt to her chin, the commanding presence of her tall, lithe body. He felt the tangible force of her hatred and it made him step backward instinctively.

Recognition arced its way through Gray Eyes as well. She heard again the pale-eyes' cannons, smelled again their acrid smoke. *Tsehotsohih,* she realized. This fire-headed soldier was the one who had trapped her on the cliffs then let her go.

Her eyes snapped with fury that he was now one of her captors. "We meet again, white man," she said softly. "Perhaps this time you will come to regret your decision."

She turned her back on him so suddenly that her blanket whipped out behind her. Michaels stared after her.

"That's the one," a man at his elbow hissed. Michaels turned to him slowly.

"Who're you?"

"Stanbull. Second Lieutenant. I helped bring them in." He pointed again at Gray Eyes' back. "Watch that one. She's a witch."

As he proceeded to tell of the night she had flown through their fire to chase the antelope, Michaels grinned to himself. Three long years ago, she had shaken him so badly that he'd let her live. Now she had come to terrorize the men who sought to tame her.

It was something he looked forward to watching.

Darkness descended with icy, predatory calm over the People's first night at Bosque Redondo. Frost settled on the fence posts and the spare tufts of grass; the pale-eyes' lanterns threw out a dull, frigid light. Across the river, the Mescalero had retired and the *Dine'' Ana'i,* too, had crept back to their squalid quarters. Muted laughter drifted from the pale-eyes' barracks along with the strident, thin sound of what Gray Eyes had learned to recognize as a harmonica.

She had brought her people to the near side of the river. Now they huddled together for warmth, trapped between armed sentinels and the hated Apache. They had no fires; the cottonwoods had already been depleted and no one had bothered to plant the new ones. Tomorrow, she realized, she would have to persuade the pale-eyes to allow them to go in search of wood.

"That red-haired one will try to witch us with that board," Barren Woman muttered suddenly. "It was part of some wolf-man magic."

Gray Eyes shook her head. "No. I know that one. He is very weak and stupid. He could have killed me once long ago, but he let me live. What kind of wolf-man would do that?"

"He was making marks on his board," she insisted.

"He was counting us," Delgondito contributed.

"Ha!" Barren Woman barked. "Wolf-men count their victims! They keep notches on sticks! And what of the food he gave us?" she demanded. "Can you deny that it was meant to kill us?"

Gray Eyes scowled. She had no answer for that. Those who had accepted Michaels' ration slips had exchanged them for more of the old beans and fatty meat and flour. But the flour had tiny worms in it this time and the meat was rancid. She had no way of knowing that the Crazy One was unable to feed them. They were being given the dregs from other pale-eyes' forts.

"And what of these other things?" Barren Woman went on, sweeping a hand around the bank. The moonlight caught on scissors and picks and axes. It illuminated thread and bolts of cloth. But this, at least, was something Gray Eyes thought she could address.

"We should save them," she decided. "We can trade them with the *Naashgali'dine'e'* for something useful if we can ever make peace with them."

"No." Delgondito spoke quietly, wearily. "No, it will not be that way at all."

All eyes turned to him. He stared dismally across the water, his heart cold. "I have learned much about the white man since I first came here," he murmured. "I do not think he can accept those who are different from him."

"What are you saying?" Gray Eyes demanded.

"He took our home. Now he must make room for us in his. But I think he would make us live in it the way he does."

Suddenly, Gray Eyes understood. "The metal tools they gave us are intended to tear up Mother Earth. They would have us plant things in one place season after season until the land gives out. The cloth is so that we will dress like them as well. They will replace our holy ones with their white gods. They will . . ."

She trailed off at the implications of such a thing. "No," she vowed finally, fervently. "Never."

Deep in her heart, she remembered the *hataali*'s lessons from long ago, and now, for the first time, she fully understood. In her womb nestled the future. In her heart dwelled the old ways. Yes, she would survive, because only death could prevent her from nurturing both.

She tilted her head back and raised her voice in an undulating melody. Softly, then with more force, Delgondito joined in. As the others understood, their voices mingled as well, until they floated out eerily over the plain. Behind them, the pale-eyes fell into disturbed silence.

"Far as a man can see, comes the rain, comes the rain with me. From the Rain Mount, Rain Mount far away, comes the rain, comes the rain with me. O'er the corn, o'er the corn, tall corn, comes the rain, comes the rain with me. 'Mid the lightnings, 'mid the lightnings' zigzag, 'mid the lightnings' flashing, comes the rain, comes the rain with me. 'Mid the swallows, 'mid the swallows blue, chirping glad together, comes the rain, comes the rain with me. Through the pollen, through the pollen blessed, all in pollen hidden, comes the rain, comes the rain with me. Far as a man can see, comes the rain, comes the rain with me."

It was not a medicine song; it was not sacred. They sang for the Holy People, for the ones who gave rain and corn and all good things. They sang for all the memories and traditions that the arrogant white men would never be able to steal.

Gray Eyes closed her eyes and saw Long Earrings smile.

Chapter 64

▼ ▼ ▼ ▼ ▼ ▼ ▼ ▼ ▼ ▼

"Eat," Gray Eyes said aloud, because she had gotten into the habit of practicing her English when she was alone. "Food." A nearby rabbit froze at the sound of her voice, but her hand flashed out before it could leap away. She caught it by the ears and hauled it back between her thighs where she crushed its head with a rock.

A soft whistle of appreciation came from somewhere above her. She looked up to find Rush Michaels standing on the bank on the Navajo side of the river.

"This is what I think of your white food and medicine," she harassed him in Navajo, shaking her catch at him. "I fear that if we take it we will act as you do, stupid and crazy, as dishonorable as though we had no relatives."

She swept past him and went back toward the fort, the rabbit still twitching in her hand. The People's camps tumbled haphazardly through the parade ground, down past the Indian storehouse and along the edges of the corrals. They were proof that despite dysentery, despite incarceration, the Crazy One could not fully destroy them. As soon as they had arrived, they had regrouped their scattered bands and clans. Now, where the Bitter Waters and the last of the Lone Trees had settled near the river, the Towering Rocks took care of their own.

Gray Eyes greeted each family as she passed, as though they were merely settling in to enjoy a Night Way ceremony. But the truth was starkly evident. Their pitiable shelters looked like debris cast aside by the river. The pale-eyes had let them search for wood, but there was little to be found and what they could gather was needed desperately for warmth and cooking. Only an occasional branch was sacrificed for shelters. The People dug caves in the frozen earth instead, as they had at Fort Wingate. They went as deeply as they could without the walls tumbling in on them, then piled old blankets, sheepskins, and scraps of moth-eaten army canvas above the holes to keep the elements out.

Gray Eyes dropped to her knees and crawled beneath her own heap to find Lupine asleep and Squeak staring up at her solemnly. His eyes lit up when he saw the rabbit, but she shook her head.

"I am sorry, little one. It is for *Na'na,* Crawls Like a Snake. Where did he go?" When she had left, the old warrior had been huddled against the side of her shelter.

Squeak dropped his head so that his *estsa hataali* wouldn't see him salivating. "Back to his own camp," he answered. "The bowel sickness struck him again and he did not want to soil our place."

Gray Eyes nodded and began skinning the rabbit with a sharp, chiseled stone. "Here," she said, handing him the pelt. "Clean this. We can add it to the roof to keep out the cold." She looked up and caught him staring longingly at the carcass once more.

A lump as hard as granite wedged itself into her throat. He had suffered so much in his six summers of pale-eyes wars. Now even Sleepiness was gone, vanished somewhere during her own Long Walk. The rest of her party had woken on the trail one morning to find her gone.

Lupine had been left behind in her sheepskins, squalling from fright and the cold. A young mother from the Two Came for Water clan had taken her to her breast and brought her the rest of the way to the Bosque. Squeak had arrived with the last group to leave Wingate. He had been separated from his mother and sister at the start, and when he finally arrived he fell sobbing into Gray Eyes' arms.

Now, seeing his tears threaten again, she severed one

of the rabbit's legs. "Build up the fire," she said quietly. "Just a little. One or two twigs will do. Then you can cook this for you and your sister."

His eyes widened until they seemed to fill his small face. He snatched the leg from her before she could change her mind.

Gray Eyes took the last of the rabbit and went outside again. Crawls Like a Snake had returned. Like many others, he had been renamed since his capture. His body was now so thin and devoid of strength that he could no longer walk. His belly swelled like a snake in the process of digesting an enormous rat.

"Uncle," she said respectfully and dropped down beside him. He was a distant relative of Vittorio's.

"You bring medicine?" he asked.

"I bring food. It will do just as well." Occasionally, she had learned, a change to freshly killed meat helped fight the dissen-teree.

"But you must not share it," she went on wretchedly. His brow furrowed.

"I know that your women and your babes are hungry. But you must eat this all by yourself. As it goes through your body, it will pull the evil out with it. The more meat, the less badness that remains behind."

He nodded, glanced painfully at his own camp, then back at Gray Eyes. She sighed, but there was no help for it. She knew the responsibilities and the honor that drove him.

"Yes," she answered his silent plea. "You may use my shelter so the others will not see you eat."

She got to her feet again and called to Squeak. He crawled out, dragging Lupine. Grease made their lips and cheeks shine. She almost smiled. Instead, she led them away so that they too would be spared the debilitating aroma of food they could not have.

They went to the Towering Rocks' camp. As they settled down in front of the central fire, Gray Eyes looked absently at the soldiers' barracks. Her gaze once again locked with that of Rush Michaels.

Anger made her hands clench into fists. Oh, how she hated this fire-haired man who followed her all the time. Perhaps Barren Woman was right; perhaps he was a wolf-man. Always, always, he was nearby, watching her. Her eyes narrowed and she turned back to the fire abruptly.

"Glad I'm not in your shoes," muttered the overweight medic standing next to Rush.

"How's that?"

"That witch doctor don't like you at all."

Michaels shrugged. "Considering everything we've done to her, I figure she has cause."

"You sound like a goddamn Injun-lover," Doc Collins charged. "Whose side you on?"

Michaels smiled thinly. "My own."

He turned away. But he had taken no more than three steps before commotion broke out behind him. He heard a bellow of anger, then a screech. He spun back to see Collins descend on the Navajo fire.

A woman had sidled up to Gray Eyes to ask for medicine. Her skin was bright red with heat and her chest was congested. Nu-moan-ya, Gray Eyes thought, and was gratified to encounter something she finally understood. She dug immediately into her gall bag for the appropriate cure.

She dropped sage root into a pot of boiling water and laid out the birds and gourds she always carried with her. The holy ones couldn't hear her anymore, but she thought that calling on them might comfort the woman anyway. She positioned her by the fire and began singing.

Collins had had enough.

"Goddamn quack!" he shouted. He caught her hair and pulled her backward so suddenly that she had no chance to balance her weight. She sprawled, humiliated, beside the fire. Her hand struck out and upended the pot filled with the last of her precious herb.

Dazed, she looked up into blue eyes that hated her. But she hated them more.

She screamed Vittorio's war cry. Someone thrust one of the pale-eyes' utensils at her, a flat wooden spoon that had somehow escaped being burned for firewood. Grabbing it, she struggled to her feet again and attacked with the full force of her rage and shame, and when the wood splintered and cracked, she flung it aside and used her nails. The doctor fell back, instinctively shielding his face.

"You go too far, pale-eyes!" she shrieked, knocking him to the ground and straddling him. "I will use my medicine to destroy you!" As she clawed at his face, the sage water, still steaming, inched over the earth toward him. It slid beneath him and he yelped in pain and scrambled away.

The Towering Rocks shouted their glee. Gray Eyes dropped back onto her haunches, her chest heaving. Then she looked up into a field of pale-eyes' guns.

"Shoot her!" Collins bellowed. He lumbered to his feet again. "She attacked me!"

Michaels stepped in front of their weapons before he knew he was going to. But once he had done it, righteous anger filled him. Turning his back on the soldiers, he looked at Collins. "That's not the way I saw it."

Behind him, a rifle engaged. Doc Collins' eyes bugged in disbelief. "You mad, boy? All I did was try to stop her from killing that poor woman! They all run to her with every goddamn sniff and sneeze. You wanna know what she does for them? She takes her dead birds and waves them around and tells them they're cured! She feeds them rabbit ears and grass and Christ only knows what else. Meanwhile, my hospital is deserted!

"Damned heathens are having more done for them than ever before in their filthy lives," he ranted. "And all they wanna do is munch on their crickets and scream to their pagan gods. I'm just trying to give them the benefits of my education, boy."

He waited righteously for a response, puffing his chest out until the buttons on his uniform strained. The soldiers maintained their stance. Slowly, thoughtfully, Michaels stepped aside.

Then he pulled free his own weapon.

Briefly, he entertained glum thoughts of the punishment this was going to entail. Then he looked into the simmering gray eyes that had haunted him since the first time he had seen them.

Well, hell, he thought. I'm in love with her. For a wild moment he almost laughed aloud at the irony of it. Then he leveled his gun on the doctor's heart.

"Tell you what," he suggested reasonably. "As soon as one of these fools shoots, I'll pull the trigger at the same time. Sound fair?"

Collins snarled like a caged dog. "You're gonna hang for this, Sergeant."

"No doubt."

Silence fell, thick and interminable. Then, slowly, the soldiers began to fall back. Michaels carefully replaced his gun to its holster.

"I look at it this way," he explained. "Christ knows why, but these folks seem to hate that bunch who came in first." He nodded toward the *Dine'' Ana'i* shelters. "Their camp is right next to your hospital. That's probably why they won't go there. In the meantime, their medicine saves as many people as yours does, so leave them alone."

He turned away. Neither he nor Collins was prepared for the howl of rage that came from the woman they called Her Heart Went to War.

She caught at the back of Michaels' uniform. He fought her off, but only barely. Finally, he grabbed the long mane of her hair and twisted it until he could hold her at arm's length.

"You ought to give some thought to learning gratitude," he panted. "It's a big item in the white man's world, honey, and like it or not, you're a part of it now."

Her eyes burned. "The only thing worse than your friend's behavior," she snarled in Navajo, "is having my life spared by a *chindi* scab! What is your goal, white man? You follow me, you save me. What do you want? My crotch?'' Her arm came up in a harsh, obscene gesture.

He didn't understand her words, but he knew body language. His temper erupted. ''Talk English, woman. You have a point, tell me.''

She looked at him expressionlessly. Only her eyes spoke, and they were lethal.

''Eat. Food.'' He mimicked the words he had heard her speak earlier. ''You understand a hell of a lot more than you let on, so listen to me now. I don't give a damn about your hide. I didn't do it for you. I did it for them.'' He nodded extravagantly in the direction of the Indians who looked on, then shoved her roughly away. ''I've got a God, too. And for some reason He says that they need you.''

He pushed her away and she sat down hard on the ice-crusted ground. As he turned and stalked off toward the officers' quarters, her eyes narrowed. Silently, desperately, she called to the Holy People who were beyond her reach now that she was out of *Dinetah*. She called for any and all the power she had ever known.

The snake came out of nowhere. It hissed and coiled its way across the narrow path in front of the barracks. Five feet from a soldier who was sitting on the porch honing his knife, it stopped and rattled. The boy jumped up and flicked the knife toward it.

He missed the snake. The blade spun with a life of its own, hurtling past Michaels, narrowly missing him. It buried itself deep in the top of Collins' boot.

The medic screamed, hopping on one foot as he tried to pull it out again. Red began to stain the leather. A rush of cold went up Michaels' spine as he watched.

Neither he nor Gray Eyes were quite sure where the snake had come from or why the knife had missed him.

Chapter 65

Three months later, well into the People's moon When Few Seeds Ripen, Michaels finally decided that the latrine duty he'd drawn for defending her had been worth it. The change in Her Heart Went to War was as subtle and gradual as the deterioration of Carleton's Indian plan. Through March and April, seven hundred Navajo succumbed to dysentery and pneumonia, and her eyes shot daggers at him. In May, another thousand surrendered to drain the ration supply, and Gray Eyes ignored him when he hovered close by. With the arrival of June, cicadas buzzed constantly and the People crawled out of their dank shelters to slowly plant their fields. And when Michaels strolled into her camp one morning at dawn, Gray Eyes stood up from her fire and greeted him by staring him in the eye.

He didn't know it was an insult. He stared back at her appreciatively. Her cheekbones had grown stark and pronounced, and her arms were as thin as sticks. Her stomach was an incongruous mound. Like many of the other women, she had finally given up the tattered buckskin shift she had arrived in and succumbed to the white man's styles. She had taken her ration of fabric and had fashioned a full, swinging skirt that fell to her ankles and offered some protection against the bugs and the elements. It was bright red; the short shift she had managed for a blouse was a contrary blue. But despite her dissipation and her ragtag appearance, Michaels thought she looked beautiful.

He hadn't spoken to her since her altercation with the doctor. Now he did so carefully, measuring his words.

"More of your people have arrived."

Something flared in her eyes. He knew then that he had been right. She understood a good deal of English.

"Many are wounded. They are not . . ." He trailed off to stumble over the words he himself had learned. "They are not *Dine" Ana'i,"* he finished. "They did not come in voluntarily. They were captured."

She didn't move. He waited through one heartbeat, then another. Then he understood. Although she didn't hurl Navajo obscenities at him this time, neither did she trust him. He turned away with a sigh and went back to the parade ground.

The new arrivals had been counted when she finally arrived. Michaels nearly choked when he saw the small pouch in her hand. It was black and bulging, like Doc Collins' medical bag. She carried it at her side proudly, but whether as a taunt or a badge of honor, he didn't know.

She moved frantically among the wounded, working patiently around the bulge of Hawk's babe. But as she moved from squaw to warrior, her long pale-eyes skirt caught at her ankles and tripped up her feet. After she stumbled for the thousandth time, she pulled the voluminous hem up over her knees and tucked it into her belt. Muttering to herself, she reached into her bag again and stooped over the next body. Then, suddenly, her heart stopped.

"Sister?" she asked in a strangled whisper. But the eyes beneath her opened. They filled with the thrill of recognition, then a wealth of sorrow.

"I am not . . . so much the warrior . . . after all," K'aalo'gii breathed and passed out.

Gray Eyes pulled desperately at the shreds of K'aalo'gii's shift to find her wound, then hurtled to her feet and screamed.

Rush Michaels ran to her. Her fear erupted in a torrent of indecipherable Navajo, but he understood, if only because love was the same in any language. The squaw on the ground had a piece of the medicine woman's heart. Gently, carefully, he lifted K'aalo'gii and carried her back toward the hospital.

Gray Eyes grabbed her bag and ran after him without argument. She knew as well as any pale-eyes' doctor that wounds were ripe for infection. The confinement of a nomadic people made their camps filthy. She could not take K'aalo'gii there.

She paused only briefly before stepping into the gathered shadows of the pale-eyes' building. But once inside, she hesitated again and stared. The walls were whitewashed adobe. Cautiously, she touched a palm to one and her eyes widened. Despite the simmering heat of the day, it was cool.

She turned slowly in a circle, taking everything in. Several beds were pushed up against one wall. She would not have known what they were had Michaels not deposited K'aalo'gii on one of them. She followed him, frowning, then used a finger to poke at the mattress.

It was softer, more resilient, than four sheepskins. She ran a hand along the metal bars of the headboard. They, too, were delightfully cool. Nearby sat a large square wooden object. Its front reminded her of the mirror Hawk had given her for a wedding gift. She went and stared into it, but the glass did not return her reflection. It was clear, shielding a myriad of dust-free instruments and jars.

She was so absorbed in their intricacies that she didn't hear Michaels come up behind her. She jumped and gasped when he handed her a pile of clean, white cloth. Gruffly, embarrassed, she took it and went back to K'aalo'gii.

Once she had possessed a small metal spoon that Hawk had stolen on a raid, but she had been forced to leave it behind in the canyon. Now she had no choice but to probe a finger into K'aalo'gii's wound. A fireball was inside. She could feel its hard roundness. Frustrated, she fought tears. She had no way of getting it out.

Michaels flinched as he watched her hand disappear into

the gaping hole. Before Gray Eyes could protest, he grabbed her by the elbow and dragged her into the next room.

He got her inside before she snarled and jerked away from him. She whirled to leave again, then her eyes fell on the basin of water. She gave a soft sound of surprise and went to stare into it. Michaels relaxed and retreated from the room.

When she followed him a moment later, her hands were dripping. He handed her a pair of forceps. She held them up in wonder, working them in her fingers. In the next moment, he was presented with her shoulders as she bent over the squaw.

The pile of cotton bandages by one elbow dwindled, then reappeared at her other elbow, bloody and crumbled. He brought more. The shadows in the room deepened as the sun climbed to its zenith. Sweat began to form a patch of darkness on the fabric between her shoulder blades. Finally, she gave a sound of satisfaction and turned to face him. She had the bullet trapped neatly in the claws of the forceps.

"Hey!" Relief made Michaels grin until he felt like an idiot. "All right," he added, and then, suddenly, she smiled as well.

She was looking at the fireball, not at him. Still, he thought his heart would explode. She turned away again to dig purposefully into her medicine bag. He dared to inch closer to see what would come out, remembering all too well Collins' claims of rabbit ears and dead birds. But she only produced a dried stalk of weed.

He blanched as she crumbled it and sifted it into the wound. But he couldn't deny that the end result was as neat as any surgery he had ever witnessed. Carefully, precisely, she pressed the wound back together and wrapped it tightly with the last of the cloth.

She looked up to find him close and produced a glare as fierce as any she had ever given him. Whatever tolerance she had felt toward him earlier was gone. Willing to quit while he was ahead, Michaels drove his hands into his pockets and moved toward the door.

He had reached it before he heard her voice, so soft he almost didn't hear it at all. *"Ahe'hee',"* she muttered grudgingly. "Thank you." It was a new word for him. None of the Indians had ever had occasion to speak it to a white man before. For all he knew, she was telling him to go to hell.

Still, he was whistling as he stepped outside.

It was late when K'aalo'gii finally slept comfortably. The infirmary had fallen into pitch darkness. Gray Eyes couldn't summon the energy or the patience to figure out the machinations of the lanterns Michaels had left on the porch. Nor did he return to show her how to use them. It was just as well, she thought. She had no idea how she felt about him anymore.

Toward dawn, Squeak and Lupine conquered their fear of the pale-eyes' building and sneaked inside. Smiling wanly, Gray Eyes gathered them close to her. Together, they stood beside the bed, staring down at K'aalo'gii. Then, as though sensing their presence, the girl jerked awake and her eyes opened wide.

"Am I a *chindi?*" she gasped.

"No!" Gray Eyes whispered. "No. I have put you back together and you will live."

K'aalo'gii scanned the children's faces. Finally, inevitably, she became aware of Sleepiness' absence. "My sister?" she asked carefully.

Gray Eyes flinched, but she couldn't lie. "She is gone. Your mother too." There were others, but there would be time enough to tell her about them later. Winter Star had finally laid down inside her shelter one night and had given up. Gray Eyes had held her hand and had built sweeping visions for her in her mind. Red sandstone mesas. Cook fires flickering wildly with an abundance of juniper and cottonwood. Medicine dancers and mutton. Oh, Aunt, she thought, smell the mutton. And Winter Star had smiled as she had died.

Now K'aalo'gii groaned in pain as though the lost images had reached her as well. "It is over," she moaned. "It is all gone." Gray Eyes gripped her hand so hard it hurt.

"No! Look at us. We are together. We are alive." Her fierce silver gaze blazed with conviction.

For the first time, K'aalo'gii noticed her belly, swollen with the promise of her child. After all of the defeat, hope began to surge faintly in her heart again.

She reached up to take Lupine from Gray Eyes' arms. "Perhaps," she answered softly, cuddling the babe close to her good side. "Perhaps, with cunning and care, we can recover and survive."

She told it then, the story of her shame that she had vowed never to tell anyone. She unburdened her heart and found the strength to go on. She told of her capture, and the moons she had spent with the Utes. She had been treated kindly as far as slaves went. She had fared well because she had been their headman's most prized whore.

Gray Eyes checked her bandages and nodded. "They took your body, sister. They did not touch your heart."

To K'aalo'gii, it was still a moot point. "Daago?" she whispered. She could not bear to have him know.

"You need not fear. He is not here. Like Barboncito, like Manuelito, I am sure he still rides with the wind."

K'aalo'gii prayed it was so. Then her mind surged back to the raid on the Chuska Mountain camp. "I failed your Hawk," she whispered. "He left me to defend the women. But I was napping and the pale-eyes caught me unaware."

Gray Eyes' hands went still. She looked fearfully around the room, her ears ringing with the outright mention of her warrior's name. But no *chindi* appeared, and perplexed, she frowned.

"He is gone," she whispered absently.

K'aalo'gii shook her head fiercely enough to elicit a stab of pain from her wound. "No! I do not believe it!

"Look at me," she went on with all the dogged determination she was known for. "I am but a woman. I have no real power, not like you or the one you wed. Yet I live. I killed my captor. I waited until he stuck his mongrel cock into me, and then, when he was least expecting it, I drove my knife into his back. I escaped to return to *Dinetah*. I would be there still but for the cowards of the Folded Arms band," she snarled. "I joined with them long enough to rest, then the pale-eyes came. Their warriors fought like twittering little magpies, and the soldiers captured us all."

A ghost of a smile touched Gray Eyes' lips at her cousin's disgust. Then memory came back to her, thick and black.

"That may well be, sister," she managed. "But I saw my warrior die. He was in the canyon with me when the pale-eyes attacked there."

"Bah!" K'aalo'gii snorted. "They could never destroy one with his strength and his power. They have not destroyed you or this new babe. The holy ones need him, as they need you and your child. Until I see his bones, I will never believe that they let him die."

Although she knew it was impossible, Gray Eyes almost believed her.

Chapter 66

▼ ▼ ▼ ▼ ▼ ▼ ▼ ▼ ▼ ▼

It was nearly a moon before K'aalo'gii was able to escape the infirmary. Her howls of indignation at being cooped up swelled along with the summer heat. Each time she yelled, Gray Eyes paused in her work and smiled. Life was not good. Her people were still dying. But K'aalo'gii was back, and, as always, K'aalo'gii was indomitable.

No hardship or heartache could slow her down. When small, stinging insects called mos-keet-os swarmed up from the river, she discovered that the smoke from the cook fires could keep them at bay. Late at night, under the cover of darkness, she taught boys the finer arts of shooting an arrow and convinced them that someday they would be free again to use their skills. She tormented the soldiers by playing pranks on them until even they laughed along with the People. Then, slowly but surely, the white men began to join the throng of warriors who trailed adoringly at her heels.

One simmering afternoon Gray Eyes looked up from the skirt she was mending to find that K'aalo'gii had finally found her way to the pale-eyes' barracks. She lazed on the porch, one long, brown leg resting comfortably along the rail. She, too, had taken to wearing the long, full skirts of pale-eyes' cotton and velvet. But she had hiked the cumbersome folds up over her thighs.

The arrangement revealed no more than her old buckskin shift would have, but the pale-eyes had gathered anyway like flies on rancid meat. They hovered and grinned stupidly, and suddenly Gray Eyes knew that K'aalo'gii was teasing them deliberately. Despite the broiling heat of the day, her skin went cold.

"What are you up to?" she whispered to herself. "I know you well, sister of my heart, and you have a plan." But K'aalo'gii's behavior offered no clues. She laughed and tossed her hair back until a lone officer strode down the alley to join in the gaiety. Then, abruptly, her smile vanished.

She leaped off the rail, turned her back on the man and stalked away. Colonel Jeremiah Clarke stared after her with hurt and confusion in his small, myopic eyes.

"I was just beginning to think you were indiscriminate," Gray Eyes muttered as she came to plop down beside her.

K'aalo'gii didn't take offense. "No," she answered cynically, "I am only wiser than they are. Men have taught me well. It will be their downfall." She stared across at the soldier she had scorned.

Gray Eyes knew then that the K'aalo'gii she had loved was gone after all. Her captivating spirit was the same, but the Utes had indeed made a whore of her heart.

"What is it?" she demanded suddenly. "What are you planning?"

But K'aalo'gii only shook her head. The light came back to her eyes. The moment was gone.

"Planning?" she repeated and grinned. "I thought I would find someone who is hungry." She unrolled the hem of her skirt. For the first time Gray Eyes realized that she had been carrying something there. It was a solid chunk of beef from the soldier's storehouse.

Gray Eyes' jaw dropped in amazement. "How did you manage such a thing?" But she knew. Of course she knew. K'aalo'gii still smelled of a man's bedding.

"The pale-eyes chief feeds his own people much better than he feeds us," she explained and shrugged. "The quartermaster brought this in last night." Carrying the meat, she crawled into the shelter. "Find Squeak and Lupine. I will start a fire."

Gray Eyes shook her head, dazed. Then her stomach rumbled. It had been nearly a moon since she had had any meat. She pushed K'aalo'gii's methods from her mind and got to her feet.

She found the children playing by the river. Gray Eyes caught Squeak by the arm as he raced past her. "Get your sister and come back to the shelter quickly," she whispered. She envisioned the chunk of meat and made some quick calculations. "Bring three of your closest friends."

She left the ravine and went to find Little Left Hand, then she tracked down a squaw from the Suddenly Crazies who was nursing a babe. Reluctantly, she went back to her shelter. The meat would not stretch any further.

The chosen few gathered inside, shoulder to shoulder, hip to hip. Gray Eyes felt her head swim with the aroma of the sizzling slab. The children drooled openly. Long before the meat was cooked through, K'aalo'gii pulled it out of the fire and divided it. She hesitated over the piece she would normally have thrown back into the fire, then closed her eyes and handed it to Lupine instead.

It was a long time later when Squeak finally leaned back against the dirt wall and burped. One of his friends giggled; Lupine chortled and slapped her thighs happily. But no one spoke until the children had run off again. Then Gray Eyes grinned as she felt her own babe kick her hard.

"You are welcome, little one," she whispered, "very welcome."

"I brought more than food from the soldiers," K'aalo'gii said suddenly. "There is news of the Crazy One as well."

Gray Eyes felt alarm slide coldly down her spine. "What is it?" she demanded. "What has happened?"

"I am told that this will be our last meal until the crops come in, unless the soldiers give me more of their food. The Crazy One is in trouble because our men would not plant his corn. He still does not understand that only women can dig up Mother Earth. His people in Wash-ing-tone are angry because of this. They say that we will have to make do with what little we harvest, since we were so lazy that we did not plant more. That is why the ra-shuns were cut again.'' Lately, they had been getting only a handful of the coffee beans and the flour. "Tomorrow, they will be cut some more."

The Suddenly Crazy squaw muttered a curse.

"There is more," K'aalo'gii finished reluctantly. "The Crazy One has a new plan now, one that will make him look better in his brothers' eyes. To keep his Bosque Redondo from irritating them further, he has decided not to let any more of us come here."

Little Left Hand and the other squaw looked confused. They couldn't imagine why anyone would want to. Only Gray Eyes understood. "No," she whispered in dread, but K'aalo'gii nodded emphatically.

"It is true. He says that it is our bad luck that his war was so successful, that he destroyed all the crops and sheep in *Dinetah.* He cannot feed us in captivity either, so no more of our people can surrender. Those who remain free will starve just as we will."

Rush Michaels wondered why the animosity and loathing had returned to the eyes of Her Heart Went to War. He came personally to get her the following week because he coveted any chance to speak to her, to be close to her. But when he dropped down onto his haunches to call into the shadowy door of her hut, a snarling, furious hellcat lunged out to greet him.

"Do you bring me food, white man?" she spat. "Do you bring me something to feed the women, the warriors, the babes? If not, go away. Stop sniffing around my tail as though I am a dog in her fertile time."

He was stunned. Heat stained his cheeks. After the incident with her cousin, he was sure she tolerated him, if not actually liked him. He lurched to his feet again.

He started to leave, then remembered why he had come.

"Major Wallen wants to see you in the parade ground, pronto," he flung back at her.

When he was gone, Gray Eyes scowled. "Pron-to?" she repeated.

But she understood "parade ground." It was the place where the pale-eyes put the abominable flag they worshipped. Smoothing her skirt, she hurried off in that direction.

The pale-eyes chief she knew as Henry Wallen stood in the center of a throng of Indians. She frowned again as she approached. Why had the man Mi-kills wanted her here? All those present were headmen from other clans. Delgondito looked up from his seat near the flag and gave her a fleeting smile. She stooped beside him.

"What is this?" she whispered.

"A council. I would not mind so much if the fort commander Wallen would share a smoke."

Gray Eyes nodded and looked around again. "Mi-kills made a mistake. I do not belong here."

"Perhaps. But who else can speak for the Lone Trees and the Bitter Waters if you do not?"

He shrugged mildly. And with that simple gesture, he drove the truth home. Gray Eyes' hands clenched. For the first time since her days at Wingate, since she had lost her Hawk, tears pressed at her eyes.

"My husband was their headman," she whispered.

In a rare show of affection, Delgondito took her fist in his two large hands. "Ah, child. I would truly give my soul to have it that way now, but he is gone to us. Leave if you think another among your band can make decisions. But I trust your wisdom. I wish that you would stay."

Slowly, stiffly, she sat.

Major Wallen began to speak. Gray Eyes had to concentrate hard to keep up with him, but she had learned well; long before the *Naakaiidine'e'* translator finished, she had picked up the gist of the post commander's words.

"He says that the Crazy One is upset about the way we are living," she repeated for the others' benefit. "He wants

us to move outside the fences and build neat little lines of
adobe shelters . . .'' Suddenly, she trailed off and her jaw
dropped.

''What?'' Armijo demanded. But all she could do was
laugh. The sound rang clear over the pale-eyes' speech.
Wallen trailed off uncomfortably. His soldiers exchanged
nervous glances. Without thinking, Gray Eyes pushed to
her feet.

She spoke in Navajo, but she spoke carefully, elegantly,
with all the power and passion of her Hawk. ''You will
tell your Car-ul-tone,'' she declared, ''that we will live as
we have always done. If he thinks our shelters are unsightly, then you must bring us wood to build hogans.''
She hesitated, then, because she believed in being fair,
she tried to explain. ''Our people die here every day. We
can not live in places inhabited by their *chindis*. When
their souls pass, we must destroy the hut they lived in and
move on. We would waste your Car-ul-tone's supplies and
our time to build permanent shelters. As long as you continue to kill us, we would have to keep tearing them
down.''

She spun away, then turned back as conviction made
her righteous. ''Our *hataali* was right. You cannot change
our ways.''

Among the crowd of soldiers, Rush Michaels grinned
at the frustration her words caused.

Chapter 67

Gray Eyes' first labor pains came at dawn one moon later. K'aalo'gii knew about them because she had crept into her shelter to say good-bye.

As she bent over Lupine and smoothed her wealth of black hair, she heard Gray Eyes whimper in her sleep. She froze, sure that she had been caught. But when she looked over her shoulder, Gray Eyes only thrashed briefly while pain skittered over her face.

K'aalo'gii was stricken. Could she leave her now? Like little Lupine, this babe was a whole moon early. Would the birth be as dangerous as Sleepiness' had been?

No. It couldn't be. K'aalo'gii knew little enough about birthing, but she truly believed that the holy ones meant this babe and this woman to survive. Determined, she leaned over her cousin and touched her cheek lightly to hers.

"Be strong, sister," she murmured. "I must go. I will escape today, or I will die trying. I can stand this no longer."

The suffocation of captivity was the worst sort of hell for K'aalo'gii. She didn't mind being hungry. She could withstand the proximity of the loathed pale-eyes. But she couldn't tolerate knowing that someone else had control of her life. When the bugle played reveille and made her wake against her own wishes, when the wind raced by and she couldn't chase after it, when the fort gates were closed and she was trapped inside, she knew that she would just as soon die as remain here.

She straightened abruptly and crept back through the door hole, toward freedom. Then she sprinted off into the autumn chill of the new day.

This time when the pale-eyes' horn announced the sun, she was already on the barracks' porch waiting for it. She draped a long, slender leg over the banister, then she carefully loosened the front of her blouse as well.

She knew that Colonel Jeremiah Clarke always checked his pony before breakfast. This morning was no exception. When he stepped out on the porch a moment later, he stopped dead in his tracks and stared at her. K'aalo'gii smiled at him coquettishly.

"Hello, sol-jer," she said in perfect English.

He blushed fiercely. As K'aalo'gii watched, he moved down the steps to the dusty alley. But she knew he would turn back. She had planned this so well. She had distributed her favors to nearly every other pale-eyes at the fort. And she had made sure that Clarke was well aware he was being shunned. She couldn't believe he would be able to walk away from her now that he was finally being given his chance.

She was right. He took only a few steps before he hesitated and looked back at her. His color deepened. "Me?"

She waved a hand expansively around the deserted alley. "No other sol-jer here."

Slowly, surely, he moved back toward her. "Now I would have sworn," he murmured, gaining confidence, "that you would have spit on the ground I walked on."

She shrugged delicately, letting her blouse gape open a little further. "You have nothing I want, sol-jer. Why should I be nice to you?"

His eyes moved to the swell of her breasts. He opened his mouth to answer; no words came. Ah, she thought, good. He had been without a woman as long as she had hoped. He was not an attractive man. His appearance made her gorge rise as she considered what she was about to do. She swallowed deliberately.

"What do you want?" he asked. His breath was coming

short and fast now. "Ration tickets? I can get you extra ration tickets."

She gave a short bark of disgust and slid off the rail. "All men give me ra-shuns. Bah!"

"Wait!" He fairly screamed as her bare feet touched the dust. "What do you want? Tell me!"

She made a great show of thinking about it, inching into the alley enough to let him think she might be leaving. "Beautiful pony," she finally sighed.

"Beautiful pony?" He looked genuinely dazed. He was so stupid! she seethed. But she needed his stallion. Clarke was an honored member of the calvary, and his mount was one of the fastest, sleekest horses K'aalo'gii had ever seen.

If she could only get on his back, no one would ever be able to stop her. But she would need his master to introduce him to her. He was fiery and hot; she would have only one chance to mount him and get away.

She shook her head impatiently and turned away.

"Wait!" Clarke wailed again. "You want to ride my horse? Is that what you're saying?"

She turned back to him and grinned shyly.

"That's it?" he asked incredulously. "No ration tickets? You'll . . . you'll come to me after that?"

She nodded. "Sol-jer come to river tonight, below the bank. I will be there."

He rushed off the porch. Grabbing her elbow, he pulled her toward the corrals. "Quickly," he muttered. "If the others find out, it's my ass."

They reached the corral. He whistled for Old Iron. The horse trotted up.

"I need push," K'aalo'gii whispered in his ear. She let her warm breath tickle his neck. She felt generous. She had thought she would have to bed him first.

He caught her leg beneath the knee. She was agile. She sprang upward, helping him. The horse pranced nervously as her slim legs hugged him. She grinned down at Clarke even as he noticed the solid, lithe muscles of her calves. And then, too late, he knew he was a fool.

"Good-bye, sol-jer," she whispered. "I thank you." This time the warmth in her voice was genuine. She dug her heels into the stallion's ribs and he flew forward. As they raced across the parade ground, the first soldiers stopped and stared at them dumbly.

Pandemonium erupted. More men spilled from the barracks and raced to the corrals. The Indians gathered to hoot and laugh and cheer. Only one woman stood silent, a small boy and a tiny girl clutching each of her hands.

"Go, sister," Gray Eyes whispered as K'aalo'gii galloped wildly, triumphantly, through the just-opened gates of Bosque Redondo. "Fly with the wind so they will never catch you!"

And, better than anyone, she knew K'aalo'gii would.

The day ebbed before Gray Eyes' labor pains peaked. She worked through them, savoring them. Surely nothing could hurt her this badly and not live. Finally, during the evening meal, she doubled over. Barren Woman appeared immediately by her side.

"Foolish girl!" she scolded. "Why did you let it wait this long?"

Gray Eyes only smiled.

At the fire pit, Delgondito began praying to the holy ones who could no longer hear him. He prayed loud and hard for this child of the two most powerful people he had ever known. Then he helped to carry Gray Eyes into her dark, cramped shelter.

Following tradition, he moved back outside immediately. Only Barren Woman remained to kneel over the woman who was her last link to her beloved husband.

"If it is dead, know that I will save you first," she vowed fiercely, for she too had counted the moons that had passed since Hawk went to the afterworld.

But Gray Eyes knew that her babe was alive. She felt it

with every fiber of her being. Life writhed within her, pushing, clamping down, then pushing again. It worked for her even while it pushed her to the very limits of her strength. Power seemed to scream through her limbs with more force than she had ever known.

She felt something hard and sturdy push against deep parts of her body. There was a rending, a tearing, in her innermost places. She gasped and heaved for breath. And finally, she heard the first cry.

It was weak, thready, faint. But her babe lived, as she had known it would.

Barren Woman struggled against her, but she used the last of her reserves to sit up. "Please," she begged. "I must." And so, while the cord still held him to her, she took her babe in her arms.

A boy-child. Hawk's son. She looked down into his tiny face, red and furious with the upheaval to his world. Joy rushed through her so fiercely that she laughed and wept aloud. And somewhere in *Dinetah*, a hawk spread his wings and gave a raucous, welcoming cry.

Chapter 68

Harvest time descended upon the Bosque with a damp, bone-penetrating chill. "Forgive me, tiny boy-child, tiny heart of my man. I did not realize it would get so cold so soon," Gray Eyes crooned as she blew her warm breath into her son. She had neglected to reinforce her shelter. Large holes still gaped in it to let the summer breezes in. But the babe took all her time and attention these days. His nose was Hawk's. There was a slight hook to it even now. It dominated features that seemed arrogant and proud. Yes, he was Hawk's son. Bless the holy ones; her warrior lived on.

As she held him against the cold, she remembered suddenly that there was a rat skin on her roof. If it hadn't already disintegrated from the elements, she could sew it into the babe's threadbare blanket with the pale-eyes thread.

Squeezing through the door opening, she stood up and stumbled blindly into Rush Michaels' arms. She reeled backward as though finding herself in the grip of a *chindi*.

Michaels ignored her reaction. "How's he doing?" he asked. Because he truly cared for the child, he touched a finger to his tiny mouth. The babe latched on and sucked desperately.

Gray Eyes remained stoically calm and quiet as he touched her babe. That in itself gave him the courage to say what he had to say.

"Wallen sent me. There's to be another . . . a council." He had learned her culture well.

"New laws again?" she asked coldly. "Wall-in can talk all he likes. I will live by my own, always."

Michaels made a harsh sound of distress. He pointed to the parade ground.

Gray Eyes struggled with herself. She truly wanted to hate this man. She wanted to look at his pasty skin and loathe the wolf-man who had spawned him. But whenever he touched her son, he did so with kindness. And in his eyes was a compassion so deep that she could not believe it wasn't genuine. She forgot the rat skin and began walking beside him.

Delgondito was already at the council, as was Armijo. She settled herself between them while Major Wallen looked out at the Indians gathered around him.

"We have cutworms," he began flatly. Then his temper surfaced. Goddamn this job, anyway, he thought. He didn't like Indians, but he had been raised a Catholic. Somehow he doubted that the Father, the Son, and the Holy Ghost approved of starving other human beings.

"Listen to me!" he bellowed. "The worms came in sometime during the week. They'll most likely take all of the corn your women planted before we can bring it in."

The men stared at him expressionlessly. Gray Eyes ducked her head and cooed to her son. She could have told him from the start that nothing would grow outside of *Dinetah*.

"Try to understand, please," Wallen went on wearily. "The boys in Washington said you were going to live off those crops. They've made no other arrangements. They can't feed you. Goddamn it!" he swore suddenly. "You don't get it, do you, you stupid savages? You're going to starve."

Gray Eyes had forgotten what it was *not* to starve. For a year, she had lived off the pale-eyes' spare rations, off wild plants and whatever rodents she could find. But now more than her own life was at stake.

Delgondito realized that as well. He came to her with

the season's first snow. She looked up and smiled wanly as he crawled his way inside.

"Hello, old friend," she said quietly. "What brings you?"

"Barren Woman and I have spoken," he answered. "She sent me to talk to you. She says you never listen to her."

"No one listens to her as much as she would like."

"That may be, but this time I agree with her. She thinks we should name your babe now. She thinks it should happen this sun."

Gray Eyes lifted a brow at him. "He is but three moons old!" she protested. "He has done nothing notable yet. There is no hurry."

Delgondito drew in a harsh breath. "Not if you want him to go to the afterworld this winter without an identity or a name."

She recoiled as though he had slapped her. "You talk stupid, friend," she snapped. "Have you been into the pale-eyes' firewater? Nothing will happen to my son. He has my milk to drink and my body to keep him warm."

"Barren Woman does not think you will have milk for much longer." He accepted her anger grimly and kneeled to go. "I have thought of a good name for him, one that will honor him. Please, child, bring him outside to the central fire. If not for your babe, then for the people who follow you. Many will not live through another cold season without food. Let them die knowing that their *naat'a'anii* has an heir, that through him the People will live on."

It was, perhaps, the only thing he could have said to penetrate her fragile determination. She clutched her babe tightly, desperately. A tiny sigh escaped him, but otherwise he was too weak to protest.

"No," she moaned, "no." But she knew Delgondito was right. Her people needed this babe nearly as much as she did. And though she could hardly bear to admit it, the babe needed a name.

She followed him out of her shelter. Her heart felt like stone. The Lone Trees and the Bitter Waters who were still strong enough to stand were gathered at the center of the camp. Their faces were so reverent, so full of hope, she couldn't deny them. Gray Eyes squatted down and laid her boy-child in the headman's lap.

Delgondito sang strongly, first a Blessing Way chant then one from the Night Way. He sang the origin of a people once proud and free, of warriors who bravely, invariably conquered their foes. And before he finished, Gray Eyes knew the kind of name he would choose. He would call her babe for the land they had all loved so fiercely; he would name him for his conception in the very heart of *Dinetah*.

"*Keyaxai*,'' Delgondito pronounced, breathing power into the name with this first time it was uttered. Of the Old Country. Yes, she thought, her heart breaking. He was her last link to a time when life had been passionate and good. He was the last gift her great land could give her, and she would protect his life any way she could.

Late that night, she pulled out the last remaining leg of a rat she had come across while rooting through the pale-eyes' garbage. She held it over the flames until it was just cooked through.

Keyaxai' screwed up his face and tossed his head aside when she held a piece to his mouth. "Please,'' she begged him. "Please. It is the best I can do.'' Barren Woman had been right. Her milk was thin, dwindling from her own starvation.

Furiously, she tore the meat into even smaller pieces. This time he accepted it only to spit it out. He will not die! she swore, and then, suddenly, she knew how she could ensure it. There *was* food to be had; it belonged to the pale-eyes. But K'aalo'gii had gotten some of it.

She could do as her cousin had done. She could invite a soldier into her bedding in exchange for food. Despite the fierce chill in the shelter, her palms went slick with sweat.

"No," she whispered aloud. "No, I cannot." But as she looked down at Keyaxai' again, she knew that she had no choice.

She lurched to her feet, clutching the babe. She took him to Little Left Hand and set off again into the night. Fresh snow had begun to fall. It sprinkled a crust over that which had come earlier in the day. The ice penetrated the pale-eyes' fabric she had wrapped around her feet and made her move quickly. Once at the barracks, she hesitated only briefly, then pounded hard on the planked wooden door.

Nothing happened. Perhaps this was not the way to go about this. Suddenly, she felt as stupid and naive as she had at her first Squaw Dance.

"Ah, sister," she moaned aloud, "if only I had watched closer, if only I had learned how this was done."

She banged again. She dared not wait until morning to figure out another approach. The hard kernel of desperation in her heart might fail her. If she gave herself time, if she thought about it enough, she was afraid she would never be able to do this thing. She moved to peer in a window, hoping, dreading, to find someone up and about. Then, suddenly, the door creaked open.

A tall, fleshy man peered out at her. "Mi-kills," she whispered. Her voice broke. She drew herself up to her full height. "The man Mi-kills," she tried again.

The man jerked backward and slammed the door. Snow began to edge over the rim of the porch. The building remained dark and silent. Finally she shuddered, closed her eyes, and turned away.

Halfway back to her camp, she heard footsteps behind her. They pummeled the frozen earth with frantic haste. She ducked back into the shadows, then she saw Michaels. He stood, breathing heavily, in the light of a lantern hanging from the empty Indian storehouse. His red hair was wild and tousled from sleep. She wondered what it was to rest so well that she wouldn't feel her belly rumbling. For a moment she hated him again with all the force of her despair, but she knew she dared not harbor such an emotion, not now.

She stepped back into the yellow light, forcing her features into softness. Relief flooded Michaels' face, then fear.

At first he had thought that the men were pulling a prank on him, telling him that the Indian medicine squaw was at his door. But suppose something so treacherous, so heinous had happened to her that she would actually approach the pale-eyes' barracks?

Now he knew he was right. She looked distraught and terrified.

"What is it?" he demanded. "What's wrong?"

"I come to you this time, white man," she blurted. Until this moment, she'd had no idea what she was going to say. The message came out in a garbled tangle of Navajo and motions. But somehow he understood and gaped at her.

His disbelief was quickly overcome by frustrated anger. "That's it?" he shouted. "You scare the living hell out of me in the middle of the night just so you can toss your tail over your back like a mare in heat? Why? For Chrissake, why now?" And then knowledge drained the blood from his face.

Her baby. Something was wrong with her baby.

She observed his anger with little emotion. But her silvery eyes were hollow. Something about her, something inside, seemed to crumble. He sensed it even while her shoulders remained rigid, even while her frail, devastated body spoke defiance.

"Oh, God," he moaned, and without thinking, without caring what she would do, he hauled her against his chest.

Gray Eyes froze. A terrible, mewling sound wrenched free of her throat. But she remained stoically in his arms, her heart pounding so violently through the thin padding over her ribs that he could feel it.

"Food, is that it?" He spoke absently, smoothing his hand over her hair. He knew little enough about babies, but he knew that what went into a mother would have to come out again in her milk. For nearly a year now he had watched helplessly while Her Heart Went to War gave her rations to others. Her people were everything to her. But that had been before her baby. Now she was willing to make the ultimate sacrifice.

He swore quietly and held her away from him. "No, honey, no. Not this way. I won't buy you." He'd made sure that K'aalo'gii had gotten good food. He'd even re-arranged ration tickets to ensure that the Bitter Waters and the Lone Trees often received more than their share. But he wouldn't make love to her, he wouldn't take her, not until she came to him because she wanted him.

"We'll think of something else," he began. "I'll—" But it was too late. Shuddering, her shame and her fear pounding at her brain, she jerked away from him and ran.

He had been her only chance. He was the only white man who had seemed to want her. Without his help, Key-axai' was doomed.

Chapter 69

Her shelter was too quiet. Gray Eyes shivered in the silence and listened to sounds that weren't there. She had left all the children with Little Left Hand last night. She couldn't bear to look into their little faces, knowing that she had failed them.

Nor could she face Rush Michaels. At dawn, she slipped outside again and found him waiting for her. Her face flamed.

"Wait! Listen to me!" he called out. But she ducked past him. Humiliation nipped at her heels and she ran in the icy wind as fast as her limbs would carry her. For a long while, she visited people who needed medicine, trying to push her own despair from her mind. Then, finally, she sought out the relative warmth of Little Left Hand's shelter.

She crawled through the door, then stared dumbly at the cook fire. Flames leaped and danced beneath a flat pale-eyes' cooking pot there. Pieces of meat were inside it, simmering. Her eyes darted to Squeak. He was chewing, grinning. Lupine was inspecting a piece of something that looked like ground cake.

"The man Mi-kills was here," Little Left Hand announced. She paused to ladle precious broth into Keyax-ai's mouth. "He brought the pot, the wood, all of it."

The smell hit Gray Eyes, rich and aromatic. A hunger pang speared through her belly like one of Hawk's arrows. "No," she moaned. "No. I gave him nothing for this. I . . ."

A sob caught in her throat and she buried her face in her hands. It shook her terribly to realize that a white man could be kind.

The gifts of food continued throughout the winter. More often than not, Michaels had to give her a share of his own meager rations. But he showed Little Left Hand how to cook the pale-eyes' flour in the pan, making a sort of pancake, and he taught her that the coffee was not to be eaten, but boiled and drank. On icy mornings, it warmed them and made their bellies feel full. And when the spring thaw came, Keyaxai' was still alive.

On a rare, glorious day heralding the beginning of Gray Eyes' twentieth summer, she looked over her shoulder where he wriggled and writhed in a sling on her back.

"Come, little one. Life has too few joys, too many challenges. We should go to the river and play in the sunshine as I did when I was a girl."

She freed him from the sling and set him on the ground. Holding his tiny hands in hers, she allowed him to take his own toddling steps. The walk was interminable but precious. They settled down on the bank and she lay back and smiled as Keyaxai' splashed his hands and feet in the closest puddles.

She closed her eyes, savoring the moment, and when she looked up again, he was gone.

She gasped in fear. But when she staggered to her feet and whirled, she found him crawling safely toward Rush Michaels' lap. The crazy red-haired soldier sat halfway up the bank.

In all the moons that had passed since his first gift, she hadn't spoken to him. She had wanted desperately to go to him and thank him. Yet each time she meant to, her throat closed tight and her hands trembled. She could not understand this pale-eyes soldier who would do so much for so little. Because she couldn't understand him, she feared him.

Now she took a deep breath and gathered up her skirt to move up the bank toward him.

Michaels looked up at her idly. "Beautiful day, isn't it?" he asked. He held a stalk of grass just out of Keyaxai's reach. The little boy lunged and scrambled for it. Gray Eyes fought the urge to snatch up her babe protectively.

"I guess Carleton won't have to worry about forcing you to build shelters again for a while," Michaels went on. "Looks like the weather's going to hold now. Good thing too, because he's got plenty else on his mind."

He flashed a wide, white grin at Keyaxai' and let him catch the grass. The babe chortled and crawled off to play with it. Then, slowly, deliberately, Michaels looked up again at Her Heart Went to War.

His smile faded. "Sit down. I have to talk to you."

Hostility was her only protection against him. Her chin jutted upward; her eyes flashed. "You come for payment now?" she demanded, motioning crudely.

Briefly, his eyes darkened with anger. Then his hand flashed out and he caught her wrist, tumbling her to the ground beside him.

She hissed in fury, but he waited through her stream of invectives, taking substantial satisfaction in the fact that she didn't get up again and run away. "When you're through, I'll tell you what I came to say."

Slowly, the anger began to fade from her face to be replaced by curiosity.

"You know, each pale-eyes seems to have his own idea of what's right and what's wrong," he began. "As a general rule, those ideas are based upon a need to protect what he has and get more of what he wants. That's the way it is with the men who have backed Carleton. The *rancheros* were pleased that he removed the Navajo, but now the Navajo are stinking up their backyard. And the ones that remain free are still raiding."

Her nostrils flared suddenly, and for a brief moment he

found himself wondering what life had been like for her out in her beloved mountains and mesas.

"Needless to say, the good citizens of New Mexico are in an uproar," he went on. "They're beginning to turn against Carleton. His Bosque Redondo is a squalid, heinous embarrassment, and they're still losing sheep and horses."

She gave a thin, secretive smile.

"Look, I'm just trying to warn you that it's going to get worse around here. Much worse. Carleton claims he's done his 'half' of the job. He doesn't think feeding you, clothing you, governing you should be the military's problem anymore. He's trying to turn the whole mess over to the State Department. Christ, he's washed his hands of you, and nobody's stepping in to pick up the reins!"

Michaels was genuinely distressed by the latest gossip. But Gray Eyes only stood carefully. Her face was pale but calm.

"*Ahe'hee'*. Thank you for telling me so."

She turned away, then went still. Michaels watched her curiously; she seemed to be struggling with herself. Then she whirled back to him.

"You are maybe not so bad for a pale-eyes, Mi-kills. Thank you for the food."

Then she grabbed up her son and ran as fast as her legs would carry her.

Chapter 70

▼▼▼▼▼▼▼▼▼▼

Gray Eyes was tending yet another malady when a tall, mustachioed soldier came to her several suns later. She knew him to be General Crocker, the new pale-eyes commander. Wallen had finally given up and gone home.

"I need to talk to all of you." Crocker scowled as he spoke. He found it hard to believe that this slight girl was a chief. Then Crocker looked into her eyes and saw pride there and arrogance, sorrow and infinite wisdom, and he knew that he had been wrong about her.

"You come to tell me there is no more food?" She spoke carefully, half in English, half in Navajo.

"We've known that for a while now, haven't we?"

Something softened within her for his honesty. "You have solution?"

"General Carleton does. I'm to pass it along."

She followed him to the parade ground and settled in among the other headmen. His talk was brief and to the point. "General Carleton has chosen to award all men over the age of sixteen years a pass off the reservation. Your women and children will remain behind, under guard, in case you should entertain thoughts of not coming back." He paused, and then he had the grace to look abashed. "You've been instructed to raid the nearby Comanche tribe for whatever foodstuffs you can get from them."

The headmen were stunned. Weren't they being punished and confined here for dong the same thing the Crazy One was now condoning? Even Rush Michaels gave a short bark of bemused laughter.

475

Gray Eyes waited until the others had wandered off again, then moved cautiously up to his side. "This is funny?" she asked.

"This is typical." His voice was harsh. "Carleton's a desperate man, but he's determined to go out in a blaze of glory. He'll either find a way to feed you, or he'll have you exterminate each other."

"No." He seemed so genuinely upset that she did something she had never done before. She reached out for him instinctively, touching his arm.

"You're not concerned?" He looked down at her incredulously.

"Our men will not raid Comanches," she replied evasively. And she knew that they would not. They would return to *Dinetah*. They would laugh at the stupid pale-eyes who had released them and then they would raid the settlements until they were strong enough or desperate enough to try to free the wives and children they had been forced to leave behind.

"Go with them," Michaels said suddenly. "You can dress as a warrior and go along."

At first she was stricken that he had somehow read her thoughts. Then she laughed aloud, a soft, husky sound.

"And what kind of warrior would take a babe along?" she asked. Still smiling at the crazy white man, she turned away.

"Wait! There's an alternative."

She looked back at him, her smile fading. "You are *diigis nishli'*. You talk crazy sometimes."

"No. No, listen to me." He licked his lips. Suddenly, he seemed nervous. "My commission is up in less than six months, in November," he went on.

"Com-ish-un? What is this?"

"It means I can leave here." He swallowed hard. "I want to take you with me."

"Why?"

He almost laughed. She wouldn't ask where, she

wouldn't ask how. She only cared why he would want to help her.

And he didn't dare tell her. He couldn't say that she was so fierce and proud she made his blood hot, or that her strange silver eyes drew him in until he had no will of his own. So he only shrugged.

"Because when I'm gone," he answered bluntly, "you'll starve."

The color drained from her cheeks.

"Your warriors aren't going to come back with food," he rushed on. "And the corn and beans your women planted are gone again as well. I'm telling you, there'll be even less food this winter than last. Please. Think of your boy."

She flinched. He had gotten through to her. "Marry me," he pleaded.

She went strangely still. Shock flew over her features, then a sorrow so ageless that he knew it was going to break his heart.

"Ah, white man," she said softly, "there is so much you do not understand."

"What? Tell me."

"I believe your heart is true." And she did, though it dazed her. "I . . . I thank you for all your kindnesses. But for me there is only one man." Suddenly, her eyes felt hot; something hard lodged in her throat as she looked out at the western horizon. "I never abandoned my people for him," she whispered. "I cannot do it now. You see, it is for him, for his memory and his son, that I go on. If not in *Dinetah*, then where my people are, where they need me to be."

She turned away. Both of them knew that her gift of honesty was the most precious thing she'd ever give him.

As the summer moons passed, their relationship eased gently into guarded friendship. Gray Eyes did not profess to understand the funny red-haired soldier who would risk punishment and scorn to help her, but she knew that whatever emotion drove him was good and genuine. Rush Michaels couldn't comprehend a devotion so fierce that a woman would die for it. He accepted that she would never marry him. But he found it harder to give up the hope that she would allow him to get her and her son out of the Bosque.

He dared to broach the subject again on an August day so hot that it prohibited movement. The pale-eyes played whist in the shade of the barracks. Michaels left them to meander over to Gray Eyes' shelter, where she swatted flies from her face and tended the long line of people at her door. When the last patient thanked her for her medicine and left, Keyaxai' trundled up to her and plopped down into her lap for an uncharacteristic nap.

"I think his throat is sore," she mused, stroking it, making him swallow. His skin was hot as well, she noticed.

"Don't do it, Heart," Michaels said suddenly. "Don't stay here another winter. Come with me."

She looked up sharply at the sound of the name she knew the soldiers called her by. "Leave me. My son is sick. I have no time for talk."

"He'll get sicker, goddamn it!" Michaels exploded.

"You are doc-ter?" she demanded with some trace of her old contempt, then she crawled back into her shelter.

Michaels watched her go and let his breath out on a frustrated sigh. Somehow, someway, he had to get her to leave here with him. But he only had two months left to persuade her unless he reenlisted, and that wasn't something he felt sure he could face.

Early the next morning, she came searching for him again. Her bony little fist pounded desperately enough on the barracks' door to wake nearly everyone inside. Michaels somehow knew it was her. He answered the summons himself.

He immediately noticed the blue smudges that rimmed her striking, silver eyes. She had not slept. Her face was splotched, as though she might have been crying. The air was humid, clinging, but she shivered in her blanket as though the winter winds had returned.

"You are angry with me, Mi-kills?" she asked.

"Angry?" He looked at her blankly.

"I need your help. Come quickly, please. It is my boy."

She turned away and faded off into the hazy dawn. He stared after her for a moment, then bolted back to his room to dress.

By the time he caught up with her, she was crawling into her shelter. He dropped to his knees and followed her inside for the first time. Appalled, he stared around and suddenly understood her fascination with the infirmary. Her walls and floor were musty-smelling dirt. Two children slept huddled in yards of the rationed material he had seen Her Heart accept from the pale-eyes but never use. The hut was so tiny, so cramped, that he couldn't help bumping them as he crawled toward her son.

"What's happened?" he asked, but as soon as he looked, he guessed. Keyaxai' lay on the few woolen blankets Her Heart still owned. His cheeks were a brilliant, dry red. His breath wheezed treacherously in and out of his tiny throat.

"Fee-ver," Gray Eyes muttered. But she had no more sage. "His throat," she added. But whatever was stealing his breath was beyond her powers. She had never seen such a thing before. She smoothed brackish river water over his forehead, then she shuddered and looked up at Michaels with stark, desperate eyes.

"Once, many seasons ago, the pale-eyes stopped me from saving someone I loved," she whispered. "This time I come to you for help. Please," she begged. "Do not let him die."

I come to you. Dear God, he thought. He looked down at the baby again as his heart constricted. It was diphtheria. He was almost certain of it. He thought of the wheezing, choking soldier who had come in from Iowa, the one this very woman had helped to treat at his insistence. The soldier had recovered, but Her Heart had carried the germ home.

"I don't know . . ." he began, but he did. He knew perfectly well how to treat it. He simply didn't know if he was capable of it.

He leaned over the boy again. Gently, he slid his fingers into his mouth. He spread his jaws wide and peered inside. And he saw what he knew he would see, a thick, gray membrane at the base of his throat.

Gray Eyes watched anxiously, her eyes darting between Michaels and her son. Without even fully realizing she did it, she began to weep. Keyaxai' stopped breathing again. His face grew red, then turned to a mottled purple. Abruptly, Michaels scooped him up in his arms.

He could go for Collins. But he knew that if he lay this child down again, by the time he returned with the doctor, he would have died.

"Get me something small and sharp!" he shouted, and Gray Eyes crawled frantically around the shelter to do his bidding.

She came up with a tiny pale-eyes' awl, part of her rationed equipment. Carefully, his hand trembling, he rammed the metal down the boy's throat. Keyaxai' gagged and retched. Gray Eyes screamed.

She fell upon Michaels instinctively, her fingers raking his back, terror in her eyes. He knew then that she would never completely trust him. It was beyond her heart, beyond her experience, to do so. He felt a piece of his heart die at the knowledge, then he reached out and shoved her away with all of his strength.

She staggered, then rocked hard up against the wall. He swerved away, shielding the babe from her, and tried to hook the awl onto the membrane in his throat.

It caught. He thanked his god and hers. By the time Gray Eyes got to her knees again, by the time she stumbled up against his back to fight some more, he was able to jerk it free and hold it out to her.

She froze. "What?" she breathed.

"Pale-eyes' disease."

A horrible hatred replaced the confusion on her face.

"I fixed it for now," he went on. "I'll bring you some pale-eyes' medicine as soon as Doc Collins wakes up." Then, stonily, he handed the baby to her and bent to pass through the door.

"Mi-kills?" she whispered.

He looked back over his shoulder at her.

"This pale-eyes' disease, it will kill him?"

His own hurt eased at the terror in her eyes. "No," he sighed. "See? He's breathing now. He'll be fine as long as I bring pale-eyes' medicine."

She closed her eyes in silent gratitude. Her heart moved sluggishly and hard. *Pale-eyes' disease. Pale-eyes' medicine.* No more, she thought on a silent moan. Oh, please, no more. Like the white men who had crawled into *Dinetah,* their store of assaults on her, on those she loved, seemed never to end.

Her hands began to tremble so hard she almost dropped Keyaxai'. If he would die, she thought fiercely, he would do it where *naalniih* and *tah honeesgai* were things she understood. Her people were vanishing from this place, more and more every day. She would find them in *Dinetah* waiting for her; she would find people there who needed her as much as those here did. But she would not be impotent there. She would have her medicines; she would have her holy ones.

Slowly, she opened her eyes again. "I think you are right, Mi-kills," she whispered. "I think it is time for me to leave this place."

Chapter 71

Michaels was too stunned to push her for more. He didn't ask her when or how. He left her to find Collins, to make sure that Keyaxai' lived long enough to see it happen.

The August moon had waned before he came to regret the decision. She never mentioned leaving again. Then, on a day so hot the air seemed to shimmer, understanding hit him like a thunderbolt.

He stood at the edge of the garrison, watching her calico-clad shoulders dip and straighten in the fields. Never, in the nearly two years since they had been here, had he seen her plant or harvest. Her talents were too valuable; her services were needed elsewhere. Until now, until these last few weeks. His heart moved hard. When she headed back toward the gates, he hurried to intercept her.

"What are you up to?" He spoke without preamble, and her absent smile of greeting faded.

"Have you been into the crazy water, white man?"

She ducked past him; he followed. Ingeniously, he plucked her baby from the sling on her back and deposited him on the ground.

Gray Eyes turned back to him with a thoughtful scowl. At a year old, Keyaxai' had mastered the use of his legs, but walking was still a slow, tedious chore for him. As Michaels had intended, he slowed her down.

"You win, Mi-kills. Say what you came to say."

"How come you're harvesting the corn the squaws replanted after the cutworms?"

"It needs to be done."

"You never did it before."

"There were no crops before."

"There are hardly any now."

Feeling cornered, Gray Eyes planted her hands angrily on her hips. "If you are so smart, sol-jer, then why do you ask so many questions?"

"I'm concerned for your welfare!" he answered indignantly. "If you've got something stupid up your sleeve, I want to know about it."

"My sleeve?" She looked down at her arms deliberately. Michaels refused to smile.

"I'll ask you again. Why are you harvesting corn when you don't have to?"

"You would see me sit around and be lazy?" Satisfied that she had evaded him, at least for the moment, she hurried to catch up Keyaxai'. She never realized that she had unwittingly verified what he had already begun to guess. She was harvesting the corn because she had nothing else to do. She wasn't healing anyone anymore. Gradually but deliberately, she was weaning her people, sending them to other shamans.

Cold drenched him as he watched her go. He didn't know whether to laugh or to cry. "Heart," he murmured. "For God's sake, Heart. Why not tell me?"

Maybe she had learned that any Navajo or Apache caught escaping, or any white man found to be aiding and abetting them, would be shot without a trial. Perhaps she thought she was protecting him.

Michaels didn't know. But he was sure that Her Heart and Keyaxai' were going to run away. She was going home, and he was going to lose her.

In the days that followed, he took to hovering close to her again, despite her glowers and sighs of impatience. Each night she devoured one of the flat, flour pancakes he'd taught Little Left Hand to make, and whatever meat he could occasionally bring her. Each morning he found her outside her shelter, sipping her coffee, while she fed Keyaxai' the remnants of a rabbit or squirrel she'd caught the day before. Last winter she had horded every scrap of food she could get her hands on. Now, as summer faded into autumn, she and her son ate relentlessly, whenever and whatever they could.

To build their strength? Nothing else made sense.

He began watching her shelter until well past midnight, shivering as the nights turned cool. He returned before dawn, waiting for her to make a move.

Then, on the first morning of October, he dozed off against the storehouse wall in the last of the darkness. When he awoke again with a start, it was to find that the Lone Trees and the Bitter Waters were already rising. Michaels sat up straighter to watch. As long as the weather held, the People seemed to prefer having breakfast outside together. Her Heart was always among the first to arrive. But there was no sight of her or Keyaxai' this morning, and as the sky paled to a pearly gray, he knew.

She was gone. She'd watched him as he'd watched her, and when he had dozed off, she'd taken the opportunity to creep away.

He scrambled to his feet and forced himself to walk quietly and calmly to the corral. Nonchalantly, he moved to the tack room and took a saddle. He saddled the first gelding he came to and swung up onto his back. Yawning deliberately, he trotted through the compound.

The guards stationed at the gate looked up at him questioningly when he reached them.

"Got a pass, Sergeant?" the youngest one asked.

"Since when have you gotten into the habit of questioning your superiors?"

The kid flushed. "All right, all right." He moved to the gate and leaned on it to push.

They all saw her at the same time. Michaels felt his very blood rush from him.

"What the . . . " the first man muttered.

"Goddamn it! One of 'em is finally going to try to run!" the boy squealed and grappled for his gun.

Michaels drove his heels into the gelding and charged.

Gray Eyes had not tried to scale the fence. She hadn't been sure she could manage it quickly enough with Keyaxai' in tow. Instead, she had waited until Mi-kills had dozed, then she had slipped away toward a ravine off the river the Lone Trees used to relieve themselves. It was outside the fence and there was a guard stationed there, but he recognized her from previous visits and politely moved back into the compound to give her privacy.

She hesitated there briefly, battling a fierce conflict of emotions. She thought of fireballs and Barren Woman and Little Left Hand, of Lupine and Squeak, and knew that she could not possibly risk their lives by taking them along. She thought of Mi-kills again. She had not said good-bye to him. To confide in him, to enlist his help, was to endanger his life. She loathed pale-eyes, but she could not willingly bring about the death of a crazy, kindhearted soldier who had done nothing but try to help her.

"Find a pale-eyes girl, Mi-kills," she whispered aloud. "Take her back to your pale-eyes land and be happy." Keyaxai' whimpered and pressed closer to her side. Slowly, her resolve returned. She hugged her babe close and slogged out into the knee-deep ravine.

She followed it to the river, then dropped and slid clumsily down the bank, out of sight. She did not dare put Keyaxai' in his sling. If a pale-eyes shot at her, he could catch the fireball meant for her. Instead, she reached the end of the fence line and hesitated again. Placing a palm warningly over his mouth, she left him in the water and crawled up the bank to peer over.

Her skirt was soaked and heavy with mud, but she gathered it up until she could peer over the edge. The gates of the fort were still closed. She shut her eyes as adrenaline and a heady rush of exhilaration swept through her. Home. She was going home.

She scrambled back down the bank and retrieved her babe. Then she began forging through the water again, leaving the fence behind. She looked back once, but couldn't tell how far she had come from the fort. The sky was beginning to lighten. She thought she had been walking for a very long time.

When Keyaxai' began shivering from the wet and the cold, she stopped. " *'Ama'*, " he whimpered. She hugged him close.

"Just a little longer, my babe," she whispered. "Soon the sun will come up and it will warm a bit." Then she looked down at him and saw that his little lips were blue. She swallowed dryly. There was no help for it. They would have to move up the bank and get out of the water.

She stopped again at the top and looked back. The fort was still visible in the distance, but its gates remained closed. They could make better time on the prairie, she decided. Soon, the pale-eyes would open the fences. But if she ran for as long as she could, if she dropped low when they finally did it and kept out of sight . . .

She switched Keyaxai' to her left hip, gathered up her skirt, and fled.

Her heart was pounding hard, her limbs were growing wobbly from exertion, when she heard the first shout. She dropped immediately to her belly, falling so hard she knocked the wind from her lungs. But it was too late; she knew it with a dread certainty that turned her heart to ice. *No!* she screamed silently. *No! She had been so close!*

The earth vibrated beneath her. A pony was approaching. She pushed halfway to her knees again and crawled wildly. Then she heard Michaels' voice.

"Heart! Stop!"

She hesitated an interminable moment. Terror and desperation mingled with an overpowering instinct to trust him. She knew, in her heart, that he would not stop her if he thought that both she and Keyaxai' could get away alive.

She bit down on her lip hard enough to draw blood. Then she pushed up a little further and looked back for him.

He was racing wildly toward her. The sentinels raised their rifles to take aim at her and fire blazed from their barrels. Michaels veered sharply at the report, throwing himself and his pony between her and the soldiers. Her heart stopped.

Everything seemed to happen so slowly. It was all so clear, like in one of the dreams she had when she knew the holy ones were trying to tell her something. *That is it,* she thought, *another vision, telling me that I must not try to go.* But the holy ones didn't talk to her here; she no longer had visions. She knew that what she was seeing was real.

Slowly, gracefully, Michaels fell. Energy blazed back into her limbs. She lurched to her feet. "Noooo!" she screamed.

Behind her, Keyaxai' started to wail. She pushed him down into the grass and raced to the spot where Michaels lay.

She found him on his back, staring up at her through eyes that were dull and glassy. "Stupid, stupid, pale-eyes," she gasped. The fireball had gone through his chest. She had been through too many battles, had seen too many wounds to think she could save him.

"Why . . ." he rasped. "Why . . . not tell me? Don't . . . trust me?"

She threw back her head and stared up at the heavens. Her chin trembled as she struggled with a pain she had never expected to feel for a white man. Slowly, gathering strength, she looked back down at him.

"Crazy Mi-kills," she whispered. "I trust you, always. I did not wish to hurt you."

He nodded once. A thin smile touched his lips, as radiant as any sun coming over the Chuska Mountains. Then he closed his eyes and died.

The soldiers stumbled up to stare at them dumbly. Squalling, Keyaxai' half-crawled, half-toddled to her side.

She clutched him as her keening sounds of grief echoed out over the prairie.

Mi-kills was just a foolish, crazy pale-eyes. But she realized, too late, that he had been as kind, as brave, as strong, as any warrior she had ever known.

Chapter 72

The men crowded into Carleton's office were a disparate lot. Michael Steck wore a natty blue suit and a smug expression. Kit Carson sported a stained, tattered military uniform and his mouth was pinched tight in chagrin and pain. He pounded a fist against his chest once, hard, then settled into a chair to watch the others.

Carleton's face was a flaming red as he sat behind his desk and tugged at his mustache. The other men, two high-ranking officials from Washington, milled about the office, pacing.

"Mr. Steck has in his possession a letter of yours stating that the land you wrested from the Navajo is filled with gold," Colonel Tappan said to Carleton. "Pray tell, General, where is this mineral wealth? We've been in possession of that land for three years now. Not a trace has been found."

"It's there," Carleton maintained stubbornly.

"That's hardly the point," General Sherman interrupted. "All I want to know is why another war has been going on out here without my knowledge while I was fighting in the South." He pointed a finger at Carson. "You! You orchestrated the whole damned thing, Colonel!"

Carson only shrugged. "I was under orders."

"From General Carleton," Steck supplied.

Sherman turned on him. "How do you fit into this?"

Steck smiled ingratiatingly. "I'm with the State Department, sir. After General Carleton settled his Indians into

Bosque Redondo, he asked me to take over. I, however, am quite unable to fathom how one would go about maintaining several thousand people on a lot of land that is totally devoid of trees and any potential for growing anything.'' He paused to consult his notes. ''The Indians lost their crops in the fall of 1864 due to cutworms,'' he reported. ''In the spring of '65, they lost them again to a flash flood. They replanted and were able to eke out a small amount of corn and beans that fall. At last count, nearly three thousand Navajo were unaccountably absent from the reservation. While I'm sure many of them escaped, it is also documented that a grand portion of those died from starvation, disease, and general squalor. It has cost the United States government an average of one and a half million dollars a year to maintain the remainder on this unsuitable land.'' He sighed. ''I'm afraid, sir, that it is not within my power to remedy such a debacle. Nor do I consider it my duty, especially considering that General Carleton knew full well what he was getting into. I respectfully submit that it is not my responsibility to dig him out again.''

Sherman's eyes narrowed. ''He knew? Knew what?''

Steck handed over a copy of the original engineer's report of the Bosque Redondo land. Sherman skimmed it, then turned back to Carleton.

''General, you're going to be lucky if you come out of this with your title, much less your job. Damn it!'' He threw the papers onto Carleton's desk. ''Do you have any idea of the embarrassment this can cause the government? What the hell are we going to do with over eight thousand Indians?''

''If I may suggest something, sir?''

All eyes turned back to Steck.

''I believe that if we could arrange for some temporary funding for food and shelter, we could ultimately remove them once again to a place that would sustain crops. I'd like to recommend the land set aside for the Cherokee and the Seminole near Arkansas Territory. I think the Navajo would do well there, and there's certainly room enough for them. In the meantime, perhaps we can reach a treaty with those who remain free in New Mexico. There must be a couple thousand of them—''

"Probably closer to ten thousand," Carson muttered. No one paid him any mind.

"As you know," Steck went on smoothly, "they are still doing some substantial raiding. If we can remove them as well . . ." He shrugged eloquently, his point made.

Sherman moved back to the door and jerked it open. "We'll send some men who can be trusted to this Bosque Redondo to find out exactly what's going on out there," he snapped. "Then, Mr. Steck, I will decide if your suggestions have any merit." He looked back at Carleton. "Good day, General. It may well be the last good one you have."

The men filtered out, Steck on their heels. Carson pushed wearily to his feet.

Carleton was very still. His eyes glittered madly.

"One man," he muttered darkly. "But for one man, it would have worked. I promise you, Colonel, I will get him."

Carson studied him warily. "Which man do you speak of?"

"Manuelito. He's still out there. He's raiding just to spite me."

Carson gave a short burst of laughter. "I sincerely doubt that, General. He's doing it to eat, plain and simple."

Carleton waved a hand impatiently. "What difference does it make? If it weren't for him and his damnable friends striking the ranches, I'd have time! I'd be able to battle off Steck's pompous attacks! I'd be able to get a good haul of crops harvested out there at the Bosque. But if we can bring him in, we can salvage it all. The *rancheros* will be happy. By this time next year, the Bosque could flourish."

For the first time in his life, Carson was beyond speech.

"I want you to go back to Fort Canby," Carleton went

on. "Get some men and sweep that land until you find him. Is that understood?"

Carson shook his head slowly. Carleton's eyes bugged. "Are you disobeying me, Colonel?"

Carson breathed harshly, dragging air into his battered chest. Then, finally, he nodded.

"Yes, sir. I'm going home to Taos and my wife and children so that I might die among them. That, at least, is something I should be able to do on my own terms."

Chapter 73

▼ ▼ ▼ ▼ ▼ ▼ ▼ ▼ ▼ ▼

"No! It is bad water! It will gobble you up!"

Keyaxai' hesitated at his mother's warning. He stood poised with one foot over a thin trickle at the edge of the river, then, disgruntled, he turned to face her.

He was so very much his father's son, Gray Eyes thought. His little shoulders squared with the urge to fight and defy her. As a fierce scowl settled over his features, a swell of love filled her heart so completely that she thought it might break. Always, still, Keyaxai' was her sustenance, her strength, her reason for being.

"I would not let it get me!" he declared. "I would push it and slap it and make it sorry!"

"I am sure that that is what Many Sons thought to do. Did I ever tell you that I knew him back in the old country, when we were free? He was an accomplished warrior then."

Keyaxai' scowled. That was troublesome news indeed. He clearly remembered how Many Sons had gone into the river to bathe. He had taken a single step and had promptly disappeared. If some other man on the bank hadn't fished him out, he would have drowned.

If a man who had fought pale-eyes had nearly succumbed to the water, then perhaps his mother was right. Perhaps it was no place for a boy who was not quite yet four summers old.

Grumbling, he crawled back up the bank again, then meandered along it, looking for treasures the river might have tossed aside during the latest flood. The guard watched him disinterestedly; Michaels' death had not been in vain. Soldiers who had never been completely comfortable with Carleton's shoot-to-kill order had ceased to shoot at all. The People were free now to wander on and off the reservation at will. Some came back, those who were too battered, too defeated to run. But most did not; most left and kept going. If Michaels had not been able to aid in her own escape, at least he had freed others in her stead.

Gray Eyes alone was the exception to the *hual-te*'s new unspoken laws. The soldiers blamed her for Michaels' death. She knew that if she tried to escape again, they would kill her. Thankfully, they were far more lenient toward her son.

When he reached the fence, Keyaxai' practiced his climbing by scaling it to the top. Suddenly, his eyes bugged as he looked at the compound inside.

"Soldiers, *'Ama'!*" he shouted.

Gray Eyes gave him a fleeting smile. "There are always soldiers, little one."

"Pony soldiers!" he insisted.

It was what he called the visiting brass who had been descending upon the reservation more and more often of late. They rode in on hot, sweating horses to pompously and piously observe the blight of the Indian shelters. They inspected the river, the fields. They conferred with the post commander. Then they rode off again.

Delgondito was convinced that someday soon one of the parties would arrange for their release from this hell. But Gray Eyes was far less optimistic. She had been at the Bosque for four years now. She and her son had survived each one of its atrocities. And she had learned more about white men than she had ever wanted to know. They were too proud to admit mistakes. And, as her Hawk had always said, they never gave up what they had taken.

"Go see?" Keyaxai' pleaded, dropping to the ground again, racing back to her.

She sighed, but she knew she would get no rest until

she humored him. "All right. But just for a little while. Then we must come back and take care of the garden."

They set off for the parade ground. Almost immediately she understood her son's excitement. These pony soldiers had so much metal on their uniforms they seemed to flash in the sun.

"Wolf-men?" Keyaxai' asked. "Magic?"

"No, little one. Just more important than the others, I think. Come on." She took him by the hand and they went to find Delgondito.

He was watching from the shadows cast by the soldiers' storehouse. Even as she joined him, the pale-eyes began to spill out of their buildings and mill excitedly. A bugle began trumpeting and more and more Indians approached warily from their scattered shelters.

"What is this?" she asked. "Another in-speck-shun?"

Delgondito was smiling bemusedly. "Perhaps the last."

"You say that every time."

"These are important men. I talked to Post Commander Crocker. He says they are here because Car-ul-tone has been fired."

"Fired?" She had learned, oh, how well she had learned, that hope was an elusive substance. She knew that to reach for it was to see it vanish. And yet it curled insidiously through her now.

She pushed it roughly away. "Bah!" she snapped. "You can watch them stomp around and scowl if you like. My energies, I think, are better used elsewhere. Another winter will come while they talk and mutter among themselves. I would like to see a few of us survive it."

She turned away. Keyaxai' gave a howl of protest as she pulled him along. Then she came face-to-face with a throng of squaws who had pressed in from their shelters. Their eyes were guarded but anxious as they watched her.

"It is not true, then?" asked Barren Woman. "The Crazy One still reigns?"

Gray Eyes sighed wearily. "Delgondito says not."

The old woman thought about this. "Delgondito would not lie," she decided.

"You have called him a traitor! You say you trust nothing he says or does!"

Amazingly, a blush began to touch the old woman's pudgy, wrinkled cheeks. "I have decided he has a good heart and some wisdom," she answered defensively, then she trundled off to join him.

The fight drained out of Gray Eyes. Keyaxai' felt it and stopped whimpering. "We will stay just long enough to find out what comes of this," she told him. "When the pony soldiers leave once again without promising us anything, then there will be broken hearts to mend."

He didn't understand, but he was happy that they were going to stay. He ran off to jump up and down behind Little Left Hand, who was among the women dogging the officials to Crocker's office.

Gray Eyes went back to the storehouse. Delgondito had settled down there to sit against the wall with his pipe.

By the time Crocker and the two pony soldiers stepped out of his office again, it was nearly time for the evening meal. Gray Eyes watched as they convened beneath their cherished flag, then the post commander cleared his throat and spoke.

Gray Eyes translated as best as she could for the people standing nearby. "Crocker says that the visitors are General William Sherman and his friend, Colonel Tappan," she whispered. Then the man Sherman stepped forward, and the official interpreter took over.

"Our fathers in Washington have decided that it would be best if we abandoned this fort. There is some issue as to where we should send you now.

"For many years we have been collecting Indians on the Indian Territory south of the Arkansas River, and they are now doing well. We would like to invite some of your leaders to go and see this Cherokee country. If they like it, we can give you a reservation there. We do not want you to take our word for it, but send some of your wisest men to see it for themselves.''

A troubled silence fell over the parade ground as the official interpreter finished. Only Gray Eyes and Delgondito truly understood. They would not be freed. They would be forced to walk again, even further this time, toward the land of the sun. There would be more rivers to cross, more sickness to battle, and then they would still be captives in the white man's world.

An aching, horrible cold filled Gray Eyes' soul. Then Delgondito pushed abruptly to his feet.

His round face was mottled with anger held rigidly in check. ''When the Navajo were first created, four mountains and four rivers were pointed out to us by our Holy People, inside of which we should live,'' he intoned. ''This was told to us by our forefathers, that we were never to move east of the Rio Grande or west of the San Juan River. I think the fact that you made us do this has been the cause of so much death among our people. This ground was never intended for us. Your Cherokee land is not meant for us either. We can flourish only in our own land.

''My mouth is dry and my head hangs in sorrow to see those around me who were at one time well off so poor now, when we had a way of living on our own. We lived happily in *Dinetah,* we had plenty of stock, nothing to do but look at our stock, and when we wanted meat, nothing to do but kill it.

''I thought at one time that the whole world was the same as my own country. I was fooled; it is not. It seems that whatever we do here causes death. The cries of the women cause tears to roll down my own cheeks. I then think of my own country.

''It appears to me that the general commands this whole thing as a god. If that is true, then I pray to God that you will not ask me to go to any country except my own.''

Quietly at first, then with more force, the People began shouting. Delgondito sat again with great dignity. Tappan, Crocker, and Sherman exchanged thoughtful looks. Gray

Eyes waited, her breath still, as Sherman rose to speak again.

"If we allow you to do this, you must make another treaty. We will make a boundary line outside of which you must not go. You must live in peace and must not fight with other Indians. If they trouble you, you must go to the nearest military post and report to the commanding officer there. It will be his job to punish them. If you want to go back to your own country, you will be sent, but you will be subject to the laws of our country, not your own. And you will be sent not to the whole of it, only a portion, which, as I said, must be defined."

Delgondito nodded stonily. It was, he knew, the best he could hope for from an enemy that would never deal fairly with him.

"I am very well pleased with what you have said," he answered. "We choose to go back to our own country. We are willing to abide by whatever orders are issued to us in order to do this."

Tappan glanced at Sherman again and shrugged. "What the hell?" he murmured. "Carleton was wrong. There's no gold out there." He rubbed an old wound at his shoulder. "And I, for one, am a bit tired of fighting."

"Me too, Colonel, me too." Sherman nodded.

Though Gray Eyes was sitting nearby, she never heard them. Her blood was roaring in her ears, echoing with only a few of Sherman's words. They were the only words that mattered. They told her she was going home.

Chapter 74

The gates of Fort Sumner were thrown open for the last time on a June morning in 1868. Squaws pressed and crowded against the beleaguered soldiers there who had been charged with holding them back while the headmen filed into the parade ground to sign the treaty. Gray Eyes turned her face into the summer breeze as she waited. Her cheeks were hot. Her heart thrummed expectantly.

The sun had nearly reached its zenith before Sherman and Tappan finally arrived with their paper. She watched as the headmen moved to sign it, then turned and found Keyaxai', Squeak, and Lupine with her eyes.

For you, she thought. *For the babes and the children, that they might never know starvation and death again. I will do this for them and for Long Earrings, who was both right and wrong. The pale-eyes cannot be conquered, but they can indeed be fought.*

She turned back to Tappan as he held the treaty paper out to her. "No," she said aloud, succinctly, in English.

"What the hell?" Sherman muttered in disbelief.

"Do we need her?" Tappan asked Crocker. The post commander gave a thin, thoughtful smile.

"No, we have enough signatures. But I think she's going to make sure we remember her all the same."

The other headmen had fallen back, quiet. Tappan watched nervously as the tall, striking squaw with the strange eyes stepped close to him.

She spoke carefully, slowly, in the pale-eyes' tongue.

They would understand her. They would not be able to feign ignorance. She would not trust a translator.

"You ask me to sign your paper," she began. "But my people did not start this war. If we fought you, we fought for honor, for our land, for our way of life. If we sought revenge, it was for your treachery. We did not starve you and kill you and wrench you from your homeland. We did not steal your freedom in the name of our own. You did that. You killed in the name of your god. You ravaged in the name of your country. Now you have decided that this was perhaps not a convenient thing to do.

"To make amends, you have devised another treaty. To apologize, you will send us home to an area which is only one third of the size of that which we left, only one quarter of that which you promised to us in your papers ten years ago. You give back to us a tiny slice of land near the *Moqui* mesas, and you tell us that we should rejoice.

"But I do not rejoice. I wonder what gives you the right to cage me, to confine me to this land and give me boundaries. Are your gods superior to mine? Are you wiser than I? I have two legs, not four; I am not a pony to be tethered and tended by a more intelligent species. I think that I should give you a treaty to sign, one that returns to my people our original land, one that restricts you to the country outside it. We were wronged. Only we have the right to say what we will or will not accept by way of restitution. Our headmen may waive that right. I will not. Your paper does not make sufficient restitution for the lives you have taken, for the despair you have inflicted, for all you have done to me. I will not sign it."

The arrogance and contempt in her eyes made William Sherman quiver. He waited, but only one other headman turned away from the treaty paper as well.

It was Delgondito.

They left the *hual-te* together. No one attempted to stop them. No one counted them.

Keyaxai' paused long enough to scowl back at the fort,

then his short legs began pumping to catch up with his mother and her headman friend. But no sooner did he reach them than Gray Eyes stopped. He looked up at her, confused.

A smile that was neither sad nor happy touched her lips. As he watched in wonder, she left him to race to the river. Her hair slipped free of its knot and fanned out wildly behind her, then she bent and plucked a single flower from the bank. When she turned back, Delgondito's vision blurred. He thought, for just a moment, that she was a child again, sometimes defiant, sometimes frightened, but so brightly and vitally alive. Then she came close and he saw the ageless sorrow in her eyes. He knew then that the child was gone forever, but in her stead was a woman Long Earrings would have been proud to call a friend.

She went to the spot where she had kneeled and wept over Rush Michaels' body three long years before. She kneeled again now and placed the flower reverently upon a spot where the grass was trodden and bent by thousands of departing feet.

" '*Ama*'?" Keyaxai' demanded. "What are you doing?"

She answered without looking at him, speaking as she gently fluffed the grass again. "A man died here once."

"A warrior?" His eyes sharpened with interest.

"No. No, he was a white man."

Confusion and anger made his little face crumble. He had learned well and fully to hate the pale-eyes. He could not understand why his mother would want to pay tribute to one of them.

She looked up and caught his scowl. "He was . . . he was like this flower. A rare spot of beauty in a land of hatred." Keyaxai's scowl deepened. "Ah, little one," she murmured, drawing him close. "Most white men are evil. They are never, ever to be trusted. But we must always remember to judge them as individuals. He was . . . this man was good, different from the rest. I learned that too late, far too late," she finished. But somehow she knew that Mi-kills' *chindi* knew she regretted it.

She stood up again abruptly. Without another word, they left Bosque Redondo behind.

Night fell before they overtook the first procession of people heading back to their homeland. The party had stopped for the night. Gray Eyes lifted Keyaxai' onto her hip and kept walking. She would not stop until she couldn't take another step, until she could no longer carry her son.

Behind them, several hundred people detached themselves from the others to follow her. She didn't hesitate, but continued to lead them westward.

Toward dawn they slept, but they moved out again with the first light. When the third sun rose after their departure, they reached the Rio Grande and the Isleta Pueblo.

"Here," she decided. "We will rest here for a day." Her throat was dry, her lips cracked from the sun. Her feet bled. She dropped down onto the bank, far enough away from the pueblo to feel comfortable. The water was slow and sluggish now, but it was still cold. She closed her eyes as it cooled her soles. Delgondito settled down beside her.

"You were right," she whispered without looking at him.

He chuckled. "I have always known that I am wise. But perhaps now the others will begin to believe it again as well."

"They will," she answered passionately. "Have no fear of that, my friend. Your words proved true. We stayed together. We battled together as a people, for our traditions and our children. And so we have done more than survive. We have triumphed."

"That is true. But I think it will take some time for the others to see that." He hesitated. "In the meantime, I think I will buy Barren Woman for my wife."

Gray Eyes' eyes flew open again. She turned to stare at him rudely.

Delgondito shrugged. "She is much respected. It will

help to repair my reputation if she agrees. I think she will. She is lonely, and she has always liked challenges."

Gray Eyes' laughter rang out over the river. "I wish you luck, my friend," she answered, and pushed to her feet. "I think you will need it."

She wandered among her people, cherishing the sight of them, savoring their freedom. Just enough of the Lone Trees had survived to procreate, and they would, she vowed, they would. The clan would grow again. The children would become older, stronger. They would marry and produce more children, and *Dinetah* would thrive under their influence and guidance.

She reached Keyaxai' and Lupine and reached down to take the boy by the hand. "Play with the other children," she told Lupine. The girl scrambled willingly to her feet. "I will watch this little one for a while."

They meandered down the bank. He stopped to thoughtfully inspect an ant crawling on a blade of grass, then chased off after a lizard. Gray Eyes laughed again, then, suddenly, her smile faded.

Behind his left shoulder, not far from where she was standing, was a lush, hardy bunch of wild buckwheat. Her heart skipped a beat. It had been the last gift her holy ones had ever given her; now they had led her back to it to welcome her home.

She moved to it quickly. Dropping down beside it, she dug carefully around its roots. This time, she would take it. This time, the People behind her would have no need of it.

She was gently dusting the dirt from its roots when the glimpse of gold caught her eye. Curious, she dropped the plant and dug deeper. Then her fingers closed around it and she knew.

Shock ran through her body. She hurtled to her feet again with a strangled sound that was half laughter, half sob. Keyaxai' clutched at her skirt, frightened. Grabbing him to her, she danced him across the wild, untamed country as she looked down again at the shiny *Naakai-idine'e'* coin her Hawk had given her ten years before.

She was not surprised to hear the shrill, coarse cry ring out above her. She looked up slowly to find the hawk's wings silhouetted against the sun. He drove them hard against his body then soared upward as her tears finally spilled over.

"He is talking to you, Mother," Keyaxai' announced.

"Yes," she wept. "Oh, yes, little one, he is."

"What is he saying?"

"That my proud, fierce warrior is alive."

Somewhere in *Dinetah* her Hawk waited for her. And she and Keyaxai' would find him.

The WONDER of WOODIWISS

continues with the October 1990 publication of
her newest novel in rack-size paperback—

SO WORTHY MY LOVE
☐ #76148-3
$5.95 U.S. ($6.95 Canada)